by Michael Malone

FICTION

NONFICTION

first lady

a novel

first lady

a novel

Michael Malone

SOURCEBOOKS LANDMARK™
AN IMPRINT OF SOURCEBOOKS, INC.®
NAPERVILLE, ILLINOIS

Published by Sourcebooks, Inc.
P.O. Box 4410, Naperville, Illinois 60567-4410
(630) 961-3900
FAX: (630) 961-2168
www.sourcebooks.com

Library of Congress Cataloging-in-Publication Data
Malone, Michael
    First Lady / by Michael Malone.
      p. cm.
    ISBN 1-57071-743-5 (alk. paper)
      Police—North Carolina—Fiction. 2. North Carolina—
    Fiction. 3. Serial murders—Fiction. I. Title

    PS3563.A43244 F57 2001
    813'.54

                                                    2001031327

              Printed and bound in the United States of America
                  LB 10 9 8 7 6 5 4

For Josh Griffith

Acknowledgments

My thanks to
Maureen Quilligan, first and best reader always.
To Peter Matson and Pat Kavanagh for their long faith.
To Hillel Black, for gifted editing.
To Maggie Malone for wise counsel.
To Pat Tuite for legal advice.
To Walter Stock for language lessons.

To the ardent and talented people who made this book with me:
Amy Baxter, Brooke Bahnline, Molly Benefield, Megan Casper,
Michele Chancellor, John Cominos, Megan Dempster, Lynn
Dilger, Dianne Wheeler, Vanessa Domoleczny, Sarah Donald-
son, Katie Fries, Jennifer Fusco, Vicki Frye, Brea Grischkat, Deb-
bie Hansen, Beth Hayslett, Brad Hentz, Judith Kelly, Lisa
Kanellos, Heidi Kent, Christine Knaak, Anna Kosse, Rich
Krasin, Alex Lubertozzi, Peter Lynch, Jon Malysiak, Linda Mid-
dleton, Tressa Minervini, Sean Murray, Bob Olson, Taylor Poole,
Maricel Quianzon, Susan Raasch, Suzanne Reed, Michael Ritter,
Todd Stockc, Pat Soderberg, Jeff Tegge, Kelley Thornton, Maggy
Tinucci, Tom Todd, Norma Underwood, Dawn Weinfurtner,
Deb Werksman, Micah Taupule, Paul Weber, and Shelly Weal.

And most of all my thanks to Raleigh Hayes for introducing me
to the remarkable Dominique Raccah, first lady of publishing.

first lady

a novel

Prologue

I go riding in the mornings on a horse named Manassas. I ride the old bridle path that runs behind the summerhouses at Pine Hills Lake. The lake is just outside Hillston, North Carolina, where my family has always lived. A hundred years ago, they drove their pony carts along North Cove Road and tipped their straw hats to one another. My family's circle is wide. My circle is this narrow red clay track around the lake.

At dawn the past is still peaceful at Pine Hills Lake, so I begin my ride just as the sky brightens to pink, while a mist still floats above the cove, curling in slow drifts toward shore, as if restless beneath the dark water the Lady of the Lake were waiting to rise through the mists with her sword. This early in the day, before the Southern sun makes everything too clear, even the Piedmont can be Camelot and that's how I prefer it.

It's rare on my rides to come across anyone out on the old bridle path. Certainly I never expected someone like her.

She was standing, motionless, mist swirling around her, at the far end of the gray wooden dock. In the fog the dock looked like a road floating out into the water that she could walk on to the other side of the lake. I saw her without warning, when Manassas cantered past a clearing in the pines that opened onto a small pebbled beach. It was owned by a luxury resort called The Fifth Season, built a year ago to look like one built in the twenties. The sight of the woman stopped me as if I were racing toward a wall I couldn't clear and I twisted Manassas sideways, his long black neck wrenching at the reins, his wild eye surprised.

Slender, luminous, with hair the color of lions, she was so perfectly beautiful that her appearance startled me the way a great bright tropical bird would have shocked me, flying all of a sudden out of the pines. Maybe it was because of the intense way she was staring across the lake that I thought of the heroine of *The French Lieutenant's Woman*, but the two were nothing alike. This young woman wore a thin short red silk robe instead of a hooded black cloak. No whitecaps beat against a causeway and I didn't call out to her to take care and she didn't turn around to stare at me. She did something more unanticipated.

Just at the moment when the first gold of the sun rose above the trees behind her, she shrugged the red robe off her shoulders and let it fall to the worn wood of the dock. She stood there for a moment entirely naked. Then she raised her white arms, arched her back and sang out a long lovely phrase of notes that came toward me through the woods like a magic message in a fairy tale. As the phrase ended, in a sparkle of slanted sunlight, she dived far out into the misty water and disappeared.

The bright red silk lay like a pool of blood on the gray dock, and fearful that her leap was an act of despair, I kicked Manassas into a gallop. A homicide detective, I am trained after all to respond to matters of life and death and I worried that even if the woman weren't suicidal, she might not have anticipated the hidden rocks into which she'd dived, or how cold the deep North Cove water could be even in late June.

But as I reached the edge of the beach, she burst flying up out of the lake in a spray of shaken gold hair. She looked around, saw me on Manassas, and laughed with pleasure. Then she raised an arm, waved, and as I waved back, she blew me a kiss with her arm extravagantly outflung. As long as I could see her, I watched her swim strongly away, her feet kicking a path of diamonds behind her.

I knew that there was something extraordinary about her. But I didn't know that she was going to change my life.

part one

Light at Midnight

Wednesday, June 20–Thursday, June 21

Chapter 1
Cuddy

The morning mist burned to haze. Even a thunderstorm tossing tree branches onto sidewalks could do nothing to cool the sun, and by noon drizzle steamed from the steps of the building that housed police headquarters. Climbing them, I was thinking about the woman I'd watched diving from the dock at the lake, how unlikely it was that I would ever know her name.

Here in Hillston, we still call ourselves Southerners but it doesn't mean as much. The South has not only forgotten the past, it has forgotten the whole idea of the past. Our old passports have all expired because in the New South they're useless—not because we already know each other so well, but because we have no expectations of ever being more than strangers to one another. In the past, a Hillston homicide came out of the Piedmont particularities of our town, its tobacco and textiles, its red clay farms and magnolia shaded university, its local people tied to town or college or family, it came out of something distinctive and therefore traceable. But that world is as distant as my grandparents' straw hats and pony carts, and in the Hillston we live in today, there are no landmarks to guide me to the murderous.

"Watch where you're going," someone snarled, and I was jostled by the crowd pushing out into the soft rain, hurrying for lunch before the Norris murder trial resumed in Hillston's Superior Court. It was the county sheriff Homer Louge who'd knocked into me while reading a magazine with a rock star on the cover. I turned to watch him shoving his way down to the street. At the intersection his path was blocked by two small foreign women, but he shouldered between them, kicked at a garbage bag piled on the sidewalk, and turned the corner.

They were middle-aged women in cheap black clothes, with thick black straight hair and skin the red color of clay earth. I had no idea whether they were Mexican or Peruvian or Native American—or what odd circumstances might have brought them to Hillston. Each carried a large shopping bag from Southern Depot, an upscale market in the old train station not far from the courthouse. These women did not look like typical shoppers for the good Brie or nice Merlots or chrome cappuccino makers sold there. Silent, they stood by the curb in the rain, just waiting. It was the third day I'd seen them on the corner. They noticed that I was staring at them and hurried away.

In the South it's not polite to stare at strangers, yet staring at strangers has turned out to be my life's work. Since I'm the head of a homicide division, usually the strangers are dead when I first see them, and usually they don't stay strangers for long. Certainly not as long as the murder victim we were still calling G.I. Jane. In mid-March we had found this young woman in the woods near a Hillston subdivision. It was now the twentieth of June and we still didn't know who she was. No identification had been left on her body, no file matched her prints, no one claimed her, no one seemed to miss her. According to the local newspapers, the fact that after three months Hillston's police department still didn't even know the victim's name meant that I wasn't doing my job very well—which meant that our police chief Cuddy Mangum wasn't doing his.

• • •

Cuddy had his old suede loafers up on the cluttered desk of his corner office on the top floor of the Hillston municipal complex known now as the Cadmean Building. His was the biggest office in the place, bigger than the mayor's office downstairs, and the air conditioning was on so high that frost dripped down the two walls of windows. He was eating Kentucky Fried Chicken from a cardboard bucket when I dropped my damp hat on the coffee table. I said, "We lost the South when we lost the past, and what we got in its place was junk food."

Hillston's youngest police chief winked a bright blue eye at me. "Justin B. Savile the Five, it's a small price to pay. Want a Pepsi?"

"I want a blanket."

"How about some Extra-Crispy?"

I showed him my sushi take-out. "No thanks," I grumbled. "Hail the new millennium. The whole country can watch and eat the same trash at the same time."

Cuddy gave me an ironic snort. "I never knew a man so incensed by junk food." He spun his hands in a tumbling circle. "Well, I say roll out the polyester carpet for the new millennium. Let it roll, let it rock'n'roll, right on over the past. The Old South's got a lot worse to answer for than Colonel Sanders' family-pack."

I opened my chopsticks. "Everybody knows the same trash and that's all they know. One story at a time, one new hot story every week."

"What story's that?" Cuddy pulled a KFC wing from the bucket. "I sure hope it's the story of how you just found out who murdered G.I. Jane and you came in here to tell me. Because I am under the tree with a noose around my neck, and the press has an electric prod aimed at my horse's behind."

"I can't find out who killed her 'til I find out who she is."

"Justin, we're talking about a human being. *Somebody* knows her."

I shook my head. "Not in Hillston they don't. Not anymore."

Two teenagers had come across the slender fair-haired woman lying in a rain-flooded incline under wet dead leaves and rotted branches deep in scrub forest on the north edge of town. Her killer had cut her throat open to her spinal cord. He'd apparently used the same serrated knife to saw off her hair close to her scalp and to slice off the skin attaching a small pierced ring to her eyebrow. Then he'd roughly shaved her head. That's why we called her G.I. Jane. She was unclothed except for a new gray Guess T-shirt.

It was the hair and this Guess T-shirt that had brought the press running. For back in November in Neville, North Carolina, a town less than fifty miles from Hillston, the body of another young woman had been found with her throat cut, her head shaved and she was also naked except for a gray Guess T-shirt. There were red roses strewn on this young woman's breast. But her body, lying in a drainage culvert, had been discovered within twenty-four hours of her death. The Neville police had no trouble identifying her as one Cathy Oakes: her fingerprints were on file because they'd arrested her often for prostitution. The fact that her head was shaved and she had worn nothing but a Guess T-shirt had been, at the time, of no particular interest. But when four months later the same kind of shirt was found on our victim in Hillston, an affluent Southern college town, the press jumped. A forensic pathologist thought it was "possible" that the same knife had cut the throats of both women. He wasn't sure about it, but the press was. Patterns suggest a killer with a habit, a killer who likes to call attention to his habit by repeating it. A serial killer.

In the case of G.I. Jane, there was no doubt that the killer had wanted the police to take notice. He had cut off her tongue at its root. There were small burn marks on her arms and torso, inflicted after her death, and there were burnt sulfur kitchen matches arranged in a circle around her head. The small earring that had been sliced from her eyebrow, with her skin still attached, was threaded through a dirty white shoelace and tied around her neck. And just to make things clear, there was a label on a string tied around her toe, and on this label was printed in red marker:

LT. JUSTIN SAVILE V,
PLEASE DELIVER YOUR FRIEND TO:
CAPTAIN C. R. MANGUM, HILLSTON POLICE

The fact that the head of homicide was being asked to pass along a dead "friend" to the police chief gave the G.I. Jane case both urgency and (after somebody leaked to the press what was written on the tag) media pizzazz. Without asking me, the press announced that I knew the victim. I didn't, but it would have been hard to tell if I had. Our medical examiner calculated that her corpse had lain there in the woods unnoticed for about eight weeks before we'd found her. Her blood had drained deep into the earth; her bones had settled. Finally, some animal dragged out from under the leaves enough of a human arm for the teenage couple to see it. By then it was too late. The killer had left his sig-nature behind but no easy way to trace him, or his victim.

Impressions of the girl's beautiful teeth matched none of the missing young women whose dental records were on file in national computer banks. Of as little help were the red painted tattoos of coiled snakes around her ankles and possibly around her wrists as well—but since her hands had been gnawed off by the wild creatures that had presumably also eaten her tongue, we could only guess. She might have been pretty.

As I kept telling Cuddy, I didn't know who the dead girl was because nothing about her was particular enough to tell me. Today, in Hillston, a girl from anywhere could paint on snake tattoos with a Magic Marker, could wear a new Guess T-shirt, Nike shoelaces, Kenneth Cole sunglasses. A girl with expensively cared for teeth could now be murdered without being missed, even in Hillston. But the media was impatient for G.I.'s Jane's killer to do something else, like kill a third woman, or kill me or Cuddy, or kill himself, or at least get caught trying, and when he didn't do any of these as spring turned to summer, they took it out on the Hillston police.

I finished my sushi roll. "Cuddy, these days it's not just big cities where homicides can go dead cold. Three, ten, thirty years or more. Then all of a sudden, you stumble onto a clue and kazaam, the door opens."

He rubbed his paper napkin between his large bony hands. "Tell me that's not a prediction. I want kazaam tomorrow. I'm with Mavis Mahar. I'm living for tomorrow."

"Oh god, even you. Nobody in town's even talking about G.I. Jane anymore. Nobody cares about the Norris murder trial right downstairs either. This week everything's all about this idiotic Mavis." I held up the *Hillston Star* where the front page had a huge headline, "MAVIS COMES TO TOWN." Mavis Mahar, the Irish rock star, had just arrived in Hillston for two sold-out concerts at the Haver University football stadium. "Livin' for Tomorrow" was one of her big hits.

Cuddy stood up, pounded on an invisible piano and started singing:

So I'm givin' you your sorrow
Hug it home without delay.
While I'm livin' for tomorrow,
Stay the king of yesterday.

Then he rolled the newspaper and tapped me with it on each shoulder. "That's you, Justin, the king of yesterday, the Gallant Last of the Moronic Byronics. No wonder your wife headed for the mountains. Years of listening to you yapping on about how the world's turned to trash finally drove her off. Alice has been gone a damn month. When's she coming back?"

I told him the truth. "I don't know."

He tilted his head, looked at me until I turned away. "Go bring that sweet lady home."

"I'm not sure Alice wants to come home." I picked up two old magazines from his coffee table, pretended to flip through them.

He shook his head. "Why don't you ask her?" I ignored him. There was a long silence then he said, "Justin, I know you've been in a bad way. Do you want me to turn G.I. Jane over to—"

"No. No, I don't." I changed the subject. "So, you going to check out this Mavis concert?" There'd been a near riot last night before the rock star had finally made her appearance at her first concert and Cuddy had already predicted security problems tonight as well.

He gave up and walked back to his desk. "The university asked the sheriff and the sheriff doesn't want my help. You going?"

"I don't like rock'n'roll."

He shook his head. "Just 'cause Mavis isn't one of those old dead jazz singers of yours doesn't mean she's no good. Ever listen to her?"

"It's hard to avoid it." I showed him that both magazines on his coffee table had Mavis Mahar with a buzz cut on their covers. As I glanced at them, there was an odd familiarity to her smile. But I suppose that's what stardom means. Everybody thinks they know you. "Look at this. Same cover, same star, same scandal..." I pointed at Cuddy's greasy bucket of chicken. "KFC in Hong Kong tastes no different from KFC in Hillston. That's my point. Same Mexican burritos, same Greek gyros sold in the same plastic wrap coast to coast."

He nodded cheerfully. "You think they were selling sushi in Hillston back in your glorious good old days? Hey, Thai take-out is a nice change from growing up on canned sausages and black-eyed peas. I don't like the way the past treated me." He stroked his air conditioner. "Now I can freeze in June. I'm not squeezed up naked in a tin wash tub in a red-dirt yard, trying to cool off in six inches of water you could boil eggs in. I like tomorrow. And I like Mavis Mahar."

I shrugged. "You and everybody else."

All over town there were Mavis posters in store windows and Mavis CDs by checkout counters, there were bins of her music videos and cases of her trademark bottled stout in stores near the Haver University campus. Even here in Hillston, everyone called her Mavis as if they were her friends, and, after all, they probably knew more about her than they did about their neighbors. Her latest stunt had been so repeatedly covered by CNN that even I knew she had seduced a right-wing politician into meeting her at five A.M. on the steps of Nashville's replica of the Parthenon. Handcuffing herself to this intoxicated national figure (who'd clearly thought he'd been invited to a romantic tryst), she'd sung him a song about hypocrisy while paparazzi (whom she'd previously called) snapped photos that they then sold for vast sums to the tabloids. After the politician resigned, the new Mavis Mahar album went triple-platinum, her new single "Coming Home to You" (the theme song of a popular new movie) sold even more records than "Livin' for Tomorrow." By the time of her arrival in Hillston, millions of teenage girls could sing "Coming Home to You"—a pulsing ballad full of defiant sorrow and mournful Celtic moans—and thousands of them had apparently pierced their left nipples just as their idol had apparently done.

Cuddy went on singing "Livin' for Tomorrow" until Detective Sergeant John Emory poked his shaved coal-black head in the door and handed him an opened newspaper. "Too cold in here," he said, leaving. "Justin's blue."

Cuddy called out after him. "Old blood's always blue, Sergeant, don't you know that? New blood's nothing but fast food, fast cars, and rock'n'roll."

Throwing my sushi box in his trashcan, I stood up to leave too. "I'm not talking against progress, Cuddy."

"No, you're talking against fried chicken."

"I'm talking about how everybody's been swept into one big flood of momentary homogeneity."

"You don't say?" He quickly scanned today's editorial in the *Hillston Star*. "Well, hey, does momentary homogeneity have anything to do with this?" He read out, "'Chief Mangum to Murder Victim: Who Cares?'" and handed the paper back to me. As I read the editorial aloud, Cuddy opened his window to sprinkle fat crumbs from his KFC biscuit to the dingy pigeons waiting on his window ledge. When he finished, he grabbed the newspaper from me, balled it up, and lobbed it off his poster of Elvis Presley into the trash—his one trick shot. The police chief didn't like the *Star's* asking why Hillston should have doubled the size of its police department and yet still be unable even to identify the bodies of homicide victims. He didn't like being asked why in a national survey the Hillston Police Department should be ranked No. 1 in small cities in the Southeast when, instead of catching maniacs who sawed open young women's throats, it spent its time arresting innocent leading citizens of the community for murder—a reference to the Norris trial now going on downstairs in Superior Court where a Haver University professor had been charged with killing his wife. And most of all, Cuddy didn't like the paper's calling for his resignation.

He slammed the window shut against the heat that raced into the room, scaring the pigeons into jumping half-an-inch. "Instead of blaming your troubles on how something fundamental's broken down since your great granddaddy's day, Justin—"

"It has broken down," I interrupted.

The police chief held his drug-store watch to my face and tapped it. "What's broken down is you finding out who killed Jane. Time, my friend, time is doing a fast dance all over your handsome head. I figured while Alice was gone, you'd be on this case twenty-four—"

"I am—"

"Really? Looks like you're up alone nights writing the sequel to *The Mind of the South* and brooding over the collapse of civilization."

I looked at Cuddy's wall hung with civic plaques and framed tributes. "A year ago, you said I had the 'best instincts for homicide investigation of any detective you'd ever met.'"

He said, "That was a year ago. Besides, you're not supposed to see those evaluation reports."

"All the more reason to assume you meant what you said." I picked up a painted wooden queen on the folk art chess set from his Peace Corps days in Costa Rica. The board was laid out for one of the classic games he was always playing by himself. I moved the queen.

He shook his head. "Do that and you're checkmated in eight moves. If it can happen to Boris Spassky, it can happen to you."

I put down the queen and started feeling in my pockets for my car keys. "Cuddy, why do you like to play games you already know the outcome of?"

He tossed me my hat. "To know how the outcome came about."

"That's all I'm saying. There's no more history in America. We used to have fifteen minutes of fame. Now we've got fifteen minutes of memory."

I walked Cuddy downstairs to his meeting with his friend Mayor Carl Yarborough. They were dealing with a sanitation workers' strike that was filling the streets of Hillston with levees of black garbage bags, as if we expected an imminent flood. But the Mayor's secretary told Cuddy that they would have to postpone. Sheriff Homer Louge was in there with Yarborough on an emergency matter and they couldn't be disturbed. Sheriff Louge despised Cuddy and the feeling was reciprocated. They'd had a blowout over how the sheriff's deputies had contaminated the Norris homicide scene—as a result of which, the defendant's attorney had already managed to have most of the state's evidence disallowed during the ongoing trial.

Back in the corridor, Cuddy gestured at the closed door. "See? Sheriff Stooge is in there trashing me to Carl again. Homer's wet dream is me packing up my office bijoux in an old cardboard box, sayonara and hari kari." (Unlike the sheriff, who was elected, the police chief in Hillston was appointed by the Mayor and the City Council and he could be fired by them. Nothing would have pleased Sheriff Louge more.)

I shrugged. "Carl's not going to listen to Homer Louge."

"Carl's going to listen to the people, which these days means the polls, which these days means the press. Close this G.I. Jane thing, Justin."

"Close it or solve it?"

"Solve it and close it. That horse I'm sitting on with a noose around my neck? That horse is dancing."

• • •

It was odd that my car keys weren't in my jacket pocket, and odder that when I went back to look for them in my office, its door was locked. The desk sergeant who let me in with the master key agreed sympathetically that I was not usually so absent-minded. But for the past months I had been dealing with personal problems and so everyone was treating me tenderly, as if—as Cuddy had just said—I wasn't myself. After a frustrating search I decided to walk home for the extra set of keys I kept in a silver bowl on a George IV gaming table in my front hall. I collect what Cuddy refers to as "old stuff" and I live in an "old house" not far from the Cadmean Building.

A decade ago everyone thought I was a lunatic to buy a large 1887 Queen Anne house in downtown Hillston and convert it from the dilapidated dormitory for Frances Bush College for Women it had been since 1936. But today, when Hillston's abandoned tobacco warehouses are sleek apartments and our derelict textiles mills are boutique malls, my folly looks like such foresight that to my wife Alice's amusement, the *Hillston Star* called us "visionary pioneers of urban revitalization." The wedding-band quilt made by Alice's Appalachian grandmother was featured in their photo spread and Alice was shown cheerfully pruning her blue-ribbon antique roses in our garden. Now there are dozens of Range Rovers in our neighborhood, but I'm still one of the few people who actually walks the gentrified streets of urban Hillston; everybody drives if they can, and those who can't take the bus.

My walk home takes me along Jupiter Street toward the crumbling bowed-out facade of the Piedmont Hotel where they recently added a bright yellow awning over the grimy doors, like a cheap blonde wig on an old wino. Because of the strike, the hotel looked even worse, with garbage bags piled beside an overflowing dumpster in its causeway. Flies and bees swarmed at rotted food. In the heat, the stench made a strong argument for settling with the local sanitation workers as soon as possible. I noticed the two small dark foreign women in black whom I'd seen earlier at the street corner looking through the garbage.

They ran away when they saw me.

I found myself stopping in front of a scruffy bar called the Tucson that had opened back in the *Urban Cowboy* eighties as a western lounge, sporting a mural of longhorn cattle stampeding through Texas. A decade later, the rawhide fringe on the cowgirl vests worn by the waitresses had frayed to greasy nubs, the garage bands who sped through Garth Brooks tunes on Saturday night didn't know a two-step from a tarantella, and the red neon in the cactus had mostly spluttered out. Still, with its gargantuan pitchers of beer and its free spicy buffalo wings and its Reba McIntire look-a-like contests, the Tucson had kept its dance floor floating in sawdust for a decade after fashion had passed it by, so we were all surprised when two years ago the owner had finally given up on the Wild West and turned the lounge into something he called The Tin-Whistle Pub.

Cheapness however took him only part way down the trendy road to the Old Country; the "pub" sported Guinness on tap, a Riverdance poster on the wall, U2 hits on the jukebox, a dartboard, and a snooker table, but it still looked like the old Tucson, and the Tucson is what everyone still called it. It had its broken mechanical bull in the corner, and its neon sign over the bar still spelled out "TUCSON" above a spluttering red cactus. Drawn not by ambiance but large cheap drinks, the regular customers may never have noticed any change at all.

Those customers were not the sort to leave a long black limousine parked outside with its driver patiently leaning against the hood reading a magazine while they took advantage of the two-for-one Happy Hour at the bar, so when I saw such a car waiting there, I stopped to look at it. Then I went to the bar door. Standing in the doorway, even before my eyes had time to adjust to the shadowy light, I recognized the woman. It wasn't just the sound of her voice, although it was a memorable voice, singing *a cappella* the old country-western ballad "I Can't Stop Loving You" in a strong, clean soprano that came soaring out from the little black-carpeted band platform across the empty tables toward me. It was the shock of her beauty.

There were only a few other patrons in the place (the Tucson catered largely to a late-night just-lost-my-job and looking-for-love crowd), and they stood off to the side with the waitresses and the kitchen staff, all of them bunched together like a chorus listening to the woman as intently as if they waited on their cue to join in.

There was no mistaking the slender singer with the tangled mass of lion-colored hair. She was the woman I'd seen from a distance this morning standing on the dock at Pine Hills Lake. She was the woman who'd suddenly thrown off her red silk robe and dived, a shimmer of perfect flesh, into the misty lake water. And Cuddy's magazine covers had looked familiar because, as I now realized, the woman I'd seen at the lake, her hair now a tawny swirl of color much longer than the buzz cut she'd worn in those photographs, was the Irish rock star Mavis Mahar.

Chapter 2
Mavis

Watching the singer as she stood alone on the black platform in a tight black top and black jeans, a bottle of Guinness in one hand, half a dozen blood-red tulips in the other, I thought again that she was the loveliest woman I'd ever seen. Photographs just flattened and dulled her. She was resplendent.

She was drunk too, and the famous Celtic lilt was slurred when she called over to me, "Hey you, boyo there in the door! Hello again. Is your big black horse tied up outside?"

I raised a hand, saluted her, shook my head.

She gestured me to her with the beer bottle. "Come in now, won't you, and have a pint with Mavis and her mates? I'm here at the pub having a bit of the past back. I'm rem...in...is...ci...." She had trouble with the word, gave it up, and turned to her small knot of awestruck fans with her arms outstretched. "Isn't it a sad thing?" she asked them, and they all nodded that it was. "I was a wild gaarl, a gaarl from the west country, singing out my heart every blessed night in Dublin pubs the sorry like of this pub here, and I met a man, you know, a man that had that sort of a look to him—" She pointed the Guinness bottle at me accusatively and the crowd turned with a hostile glare in my direction. "That man kept sad Mavis locked away like a song bird in a cage of gold...." And without a pause her voice lifted into the opening line of "Pleeease release me/ Let me go...."

I'd read in the effusive magazine I'd taken from Cuddy's office that Mavis Mahar had close to a four-octave range and that the musical world considered her "one of the phenomenal talents of her time." Her time was undoubtedly now, for according to this article she had "broad crossover appeal, drawing fans from teens, Gen-Xers, boomers, and even Ike-ers" (that ancient crew who'd reached their adolescence in the Eisenhower fifties). The article said she could play three or four instruments and that she loved singing all types of songs—rock, blues, pop, and folk. Listening to her version of this old country tune now, I heard what the critics were talking about. Finishing the song to the fervid applause of her small audience, Mavis accepted another Guinness someone offered her. As she reached out for the bottle with her slim lean-muscled bare white arm, I noticed that she had a tiny dark red birthmark with points like a star just where her neck joined her shoulders—as if, pleased with His Creation, God had stamped her with the star as a sign of her destiny and then sent her out into the world to claim it. On both her hands she wore silver and gold rings (sometimes two or three) on all her fingers, including her thumbs. The fingers were strong and restless. The nails short, purple as hyacinths.

A very pretty waitress had pulled away from the young man next to her and pressed to the front of the crowd where she listened in an ecstasy of infatuation. The waitress obviously believed imitation was at least the most manifest form of flattery for she had the exact same hair cut, hair color, nail color, multitude of rings and black wedge open-heeled sandals as Mavis Mahar. All she didn't have was the talent and that inimitable luminous glow. Holding up a throwaway camera, she was breathlessly asking if Mavis would mind if someone took their picture together. Mavis didn't mind at all, and asked the girl her name.

"Lucy," the waitress said as she jumped effortlessly up on the platform and impulsively hugged the singer. When she did, I noticed the young man move sullenly back to the shadows, staring angrily at the waitress. Handsome, with sideburns and a pouty mouth, in a black leather jacket and tight black jeans, he looked as if he'd styled himself on motorcycle movies made before he was born. I recognized him as someone I'd seen being booked at HPD, although I couldn't remember for what.

The flash of the camera flared as the two young women smiled, looking almost like twins in a play. "We're exactly the same size!" Lucy shouted at her coworkers, thrilled. Then she asked the star if she'd sing "Coming Home to You," and Mavis looked at her with an extraordinarily seductive sigh of a smile. "Ah, daarlin', can't we feckin' forget that feckin' bloody song!?" But with a shrug she handed the red tulips to the ardent girl, walked to the piano, and played the opening chords, known to much of the world, of her No. 1 hit.

The shabby drunks, worn-out barmaids, and skinny dishwashers cheered and stomped their tired feet on the sawdust floor. They knew—even before what was to happen later that night—that they were in the midst of a memory they would keep until they were old. They knew they were standing close to magic that was no part of their own lives and never would be, so close to the light of fame that it made them radiant too.

"Are you leaving again then, beautiful boyo?" Mavis called over to me as I walked to the door. "Is there no song would make you stay this time?"

I turned in the doorway. Everyone was watching her look at me.

She ran both hands from her throat down to her stomach. "I'm all filled up with music."

"I know," I said. "You have rings on your fingers. Do you have bells on your toes?"

She smiled. "Stay and find out."

But I waved and left the bar because I knew I'd order a drink if I stayed. Outside it was raining again; the black limousine sat patiently by the curb, wipers slowly moving over the windows. I assumed the driver was waiting behind the wheel, but with the dark tinted glass, I couldn't tell for sure.

● ● ●

I spent the rest of the afternoon at the construction site near where we'd found G.I. Jane. When I returned to the Cadmean Building at dusk, the two small dark women were back on the street corner side by side in the same motionless positions, with the same shopping bags beside them. Nearby Sergeant Brenda Moore and our forensics photographer Chuck Grant headed for a squad car at the curb. They were an odd pair—she, short, plump, African-American; he, tall, gaunt, self-described redneck.

"Know what those two ladies are doing over there?" I called to them.

Chuck stared, shrugged sardonically. "Hookers?"

Brenda nonchalantly raised her hand at him, then lowered each long, multicolored nail until only the middle finger was extended. She glanced at the women. "They're looking for work."

I was puzzled. "Work? Work from whom?"

Brenda opened the driver's side of the black and white cruiser. "Whomever, Justin, just about whomever." As she started her engine, she said, "Big Hair's after your ass again." She drew an imaginary box around her head with her hands and grinned with parodic sincerity.

I knew who she meant. And sure enough, Carol Cathy Cane from the Channel Seven "Action News" came hurrying with her bearded cameraman down the broad stone steps where a small line of picketing sanitation workers was parading back and forth. The TV diva wasn't much interested in the strike. It was me she was after.

CeeCee, as Ms. Cane was known to Hillston, had a personal stake in Cathy Oakes' and G.I. Jane's killer. Back in March she'd named him. What if—CeeCee had suggested with zest—what if the killer had put the label around G.I. Jane's toe "mailing" her to Cuddy and me because he was daring us to solve the puzzle before he murdered again? What if he had put Guess T-shirts on his naked victims to *taunt* the police with his crime: Guess who I am? What did I think of that idea? Without waiting to find out, CeeCee had christened him "The Guess Who Killer" on the spot—she was adroit at the sound bite—and by the following evening all the Piedmont news shows were calling our unknown murderer the Guess Who Killer, and by the weekend, all the television anchors were advising women not to go out jogging alone until the police caught Guess Who.

I tried to slip past her cameraman now by dodging behind a Civil War cannon near the steps, but CeeCee ran over and blocked my path.

"Lieutenant, Lieutenant!"

"Oh, CeeCee, I'm sorry, I didn't see you."

Carol Cathy Cane had big hair, long legs, and a breathless enthusiasm for the ephemeral that had finally freed her from the late-night wrap-up, where she feared the networks would never notice her, and promoted her to the coveted evening news spot at Channel Seven. She and I knew each other well, but in our interviews she always pretended she'd never seen me before and had never asked me the same questions a dozen previous times. Now she spun her finger at her cameraman and opened our exchange, as she always did, by warning her viewers with solemn glee that a homicidal maniac was still stalking the Piedmont and when was I going to apprehend him?

I smiled just as solemnly. "As soon as I find him."

I heard an ugly laugh. Sheriff Homer Louge, who appeared to spend very little time at the County Sheriff's Office across town, stopped beside us on the steps and stood there listening with crossed arms and a smug grin. He was tall and thick with a face that looked as if a truck tire had rolled over it.

CeeCee was asking why a homicidal maniac had singled me out as G.I. Jane's "friend." Was it because I was Justin Savile the Fifth? (The "V" had been emphatically added to my name on the label attached to the corpse's toe.) "Your family has always been very prominent in North Carolina. Could this be a class-hatred thing with Guess Who?"

Sheriff Louge gave another barking laugh and ambled up the steps past us, melodramatically shaking his head as I told CeeCee I had no reason to assume the killer had ever heard of my family or had any personal feelings about me or Chief Mangum either, one way or the other. "The label was addressed to me because I'm the head of homicide here."

Bored with that possibility, CeeCee said that we were all aware, from sources like *Silence of the Lambs*, of VICAP's criminal profilers at the FBI and she wondered why we didn't ask them to help us since we obviously needed help. Maybe they had other Guess T-shirt cases in their files. I told her we had worked closely with two FBI consultants in Raleigh who said our evidence fit the pattern of no known killer. CeeCee turned grim and dramatically hushed. "You mean serial killer, don't you, Lieutenant?"

"No, I don't," I insisted.

She wasn't listening. "He's killed twice. He'll kill again, won't he?"

I assured her that if so, the best way to stop him was to find out who G.I. Jane was, and once more I urged anyone with information to come forward. CeeCee wondered, since HPD had mishandled both the Professor Norris murder case and the G.I. Jane case, if maybe the *Hillston Star* was right today and it was time for Police Chief Cuddy Mangum to step down, even if he was winning the state's Raleigh Medal tonight?

"CeeCee, I don't think we've mishandled anything but the media." And I gave her my friendly nod, dodged through the hot, tired, listless picketers, and hurried up the steps.

• • •

Cuddy was leaving his office, reading through his endless pink phone messages. He punched at the elevator button, gave it five seconds to open (which it never did), then started at a trot down the marble stairs.

I caught him. "A construction crew dug up a running shoe near the murder site but no help with our shoelace. It was a Nike. Man's size nine—"

He bounced a message off the wall like a tiny basketball into a wastebasket. "So you just back here to defend the Old South from momentary homogeneity?"

"All I said was that's why we don't know Jane's name—"

"Lots of women got murdered back in your great-great grand-daddy's day, and nobody even *tried* to find out their names." He balled up another message. "But these women were mostly of a non-Caucasian persuasion."

"Don't start in again about all my genocidal landgrabbing ancestors."

"Justin, I don't believe I called all your relatives genocidal." Reaching out a lanky arm, he gave my bow tie a pat. "Just Governor Eustache P. Dollard." We trotted downstairs, past the floors of town and county offices, down toward the courtrooms off the lobby.

I said, "The governor was not personally responsible for the deaths of those Cherokee Indians."

"Well, now, personal responsibility." Cuddy bounded along, slapping various city officials and police officers on the back as we passed them on the stairs. "When Eustache Dollard and Andy Jackson told a tribe of—and we don't call them Indians anymore, you got to catch up—told a tribe of Native Americans to take a fast hike across the Appalachians to Oklahoma, you think they figured they'd all make it there, no problem? Old folks, women and children, just jogging to Oklahoma, 'stead of freezing to death on—"

"I get it." I nodded. "It's this Raleigh prize they're giving you tonight. You're down on governors."

"Oh am I?" We stepped into the lobby of the Cadmean Building, a handsome domed octagonal space with a floor of black and white marble, just as the big double doors to Superior Court banged open and the crowd scurried out of the afternoon session of the Tyler Norris murder trial.

For months the *Star* had been sniping at Cuddy not only about the G.I. Jane killing, but also about this Professor Norris. A young star of the mathematics faculty of Haver University, a recipient of a Haver Foundation genius grant, Norris was the only son of one of the most eminent families in the area. We had arrested him for shooting his pregnant wife in the face with a shotgun last New Year's Eve. He said a burglar had shot her, and most people believed him. I'd been the arresting officer. Back in February I had walked into Norris's parents' sixteen-room Greek Revival estate on Catawba Drive and taken him out of it in handcuffs. His father, whom I'd known all my life, had followed us to the squad car and asked me, "Justin, how could you?" The editor of the *Star* seemed to feel the same way. For the first time in years, the town of Hillston was not happy with its police department and the newspapers and television channels were losing no opportunity to say so.

The Norris trial was almost over. Pushed forward by a confident defense (the famous Isaac Rosethorn had come out of retirement to take the case), it had moved along quickly under the brisk gavel of a young female judge. Cuddy stopped now to get the news on the day's proceedings from Miss Beatrice Turner, the court clerk, who was seventy-one, wouldn't admit it, and dared Age to imply otherwise by inflicting on her any of its typical advertisements like poor eyes or stooped posture. "Going okay in there, darlin'?" he called to her.

"Good afternoon, Chief Mangum. Justin, how's your mother doing, bless her sweet heart?"

"Still in the hospital, but much better, thank you, ma'am."

Miss Turner was as sharp-eyed, plump-breasted, and self-possessed as a robin, and like that bird had no idea how small she was: despite the stiffness of her blue hair, she fit easily under Cuddy's arm when he hugged her as he asked, "How far'd Isaac get today?"

"He's through. They're done except for summations."

"Darlin', talk to me. Is the good side gonna win?"

Miss Turner fluffed the old silk violets pinned to her full bosom. "Depends on which side of the church you're sitting on."

"The bride's side, the bride that got her face shot off, I'm sitting on Linsley Norris's side, Bee."

"Then I'd say you were destined for disappointment," she told him matter-of-factly. "Isaac Rosethorn has got the whole state convinced that we are dealing with a burglar, and I don't know how many times I've seen him on Channel Seven going on about how they finally proved Dr. Sam Sheppard was innocent of killing his wife after all those years in prison because it turned out it *was* an intruder, and how we don't want another decent useful life ruined in another terrible miscarriage of justice." Miss Turner did a recognizable imitation of Isaac Rosethorn, with whom reputedly she had been in love for forty years. "I bet if you polled that jury this afternoon," she added, "they'd acquit and go home."

Cuddy kicked something invisible. "Damn it. Now, Bee, Professor Norris killed his wife and shot himself to cover it up. I know he did."

"Well, the State better start proving it, because the jury believes Tyler caught that North Hillston burglar robbing them and the burglar picked up the rifle he'd planned on stealing and shot Tyler in the stomach after he'd already shot Linsley in the face when she came through the door."

"Norris shot himself!"

She shook her head firmly. "That jury doesn't think so. Isaac keeps telling them you don't have a motive, and you don't. For a man to kill his wife when she's about to have their first child, he's got to have more of a motive than they had an argument at a dinner party. Plus, your crime scene was a contaminated mess!" The implication was that the police had wasted Miss Turner's time by arresting the defendant in the first place.

"Sheriff Louge's boys trashed the place before HPD ever got there."

"I don't care whose doing it was."

"Well, hell." Cuddy didn't question her assessment; in more than forty years of trials she had studied the faces of thousands of jurors.

Across the lobby, Isaac Rosethorn lumbered out of the courtroom doors with his arm around his client, the defendant Tyler Norris. Cuddy pointed at him. "That old bastard ought to be ashamed of himself. He knows Norris is guilty as sin. I know he knows it."

Rosethorn was fat and tousled as a bear. Norris was slim and tall, his brown hair cropped, his brown loafers polished, his khaki suit pressed. He looked like thousands of other well-to-do young Southern men who'd gone from good families to good schools to good jobs. His distinguished-looking parents followed them out, arm in arm, walking through the lobby, stoic in undeserved adversity. They were followed in turn by Norris's dead wife's parents, who had been on television insisting they would never believe their son-in-law had murdered their daughter. All four parents shook hands solemnly with Rosethorn as a reporter took their picture.

Then Rosethorn shuffled away in his rumpled black suit with his snowy head buried in the loose papers he was reading, oblivious to people dodging out of his path as he made his way to the revolving doors. He stood there blocking the exit until a woman behind him impatiently pushed him through the doors ahead of her. He never noticed. Cuddy sighed. "Why doesn't he stay retired? Christ, he's older than God."

Miss Turner puffed up. "Well, he's not too old to make a shambles of you and the D.A.'s office."

Cuddy swooped over to pick up a candy wrapper someone had dropped and to stuff it down in an already full trash can. "The fact that Isaac is still alive is a slap in the face to the Surgeon General, Alcoholics Anonymous, and the American Heart Association all three."

With an exasperated cluck Bee Turner turned from watching Rosethorn try to retrieve his bamboo cane from the revolving door in which he'd jammed it. Then she instructed Cuddy, "Do us all proud tonight at the governor's, you hear me?" and she patted him between his shoulder blades as if he were a baby being encouraged to burp.

"I hear you, darlin'. After I do this prize thing, you want to go shagging with me at the Lush Life Bar?"

With a sharp poke at his ribs, she turned to me in mock horror. "I don't have an idea in the world what 'shagging' means. But I know what it sounds like it means."

Cuddy laughed. "Does that mean you will come, or you won't?"

As she scooted around us to head up the stairs, she pinched my arm. "Justin, you found yourself such a smart pretty young woman to marry you. Why can't you locate somebody like Alice for your friend here? Bye now."

I called after her, "I keep trying, but Cuddy's still in love with you."

"She knows that," he yelled up the stairs after her.

Cuddy grilled everyone else he could reach coming out of the courtroom for feedback on how the trial had gone today. It was unanimous. The defense was beating us. Our medical examiner Dick Cohen wandered out yawning—he's insisted for years that he hasn't had a good night's rest since he left Brooklyn. He mumbled, "Kiss this one off, Cuddy. They're licking the dirty sugar out of Rosethorn's fat old hands." He added, heading for the doors, "But what's that to you? Raleigh prize tonight anyhow, right?"

"Right. Let 'em eat a whole cake full of dirty sugar, Dick, what do I care?" Cuddy waved Dick off, then used his raised hand to yank on his thick shock of nut-brown hair as if he were impatiently improving his posture. "I said this was going to be a bad year when I woke up New Year's morning in bed with a priest," he growled. "For a heterosexual atheist like me, that gives you the unsettling feeling you're losing control."

I laughed. "You got sick and Paul didn't know where else to put you."

"Justin, you be sure to mention that incident if they ask for any little Chief Mangum anecdotes tonight at the banquet."

Cuddy was the North Carolinian chosen to receive the Raleigh Medal tonight at the State capitol for "distinguished service to the state." The medal was given at one of the social highlights of the year—the Governor's Gala—and the governor nominated the recipients. Everybody at the Hillston Police Department appeared to be happy that Captain Mangum had won this prize, except Captain Mangum. And I was probably the only person who knew why. All the reasons why.

Of course, one reason was that Cuddy felt responsible, if not for the whole world, certainly for Hillston and every human life in it. Secondly, he was very media sensitive, and embarrassed by the awkwardness of his receiving a prize for eradicating crime in Hillston when he obviously hadn't done so. In his early years as police chief he had been such a success, such a symbol (even in a national magazine like *Newsweek*) of the youthful, modernized, computerized, affluent equal-opportunity New South that he'd grown accustomed to having the media fawn all over him. He wouldn't admit it, but it mortified him that (because of the Norris trial and the unsolved G.I. Jane homicide), for the first time in his regime the press was treating the Hillston Police Department with the same irreverent derision that they'd shown his idiotic predecessor Captain Van Dorn Fulcher (V.D. for short.) The press was pointing out publicly that we weren't perfect, and maybe Cuddy had thought we were.

But there was another reason he didn't want the Raleigh Medal. He didn't like the governor who'd be handing it to him. He hadn't liked the very popular, good-looking, charismatic governor Andrew Brookside (an acquaintance of mine) even before Andy had been elected. He hadn't liked him even after Andy had stepped in front of an assassin's bullet that had been meant for Cuddy himself (although at the time, everybody thought the future governor was the target). Not liking the man, Cuddy let people go on thinking Andy had saved his life, and Andy had used the assumed assassination attempt to help win the election, and I suppose Cuddy thought that made them even. It wasn't Brookside's politics that Cuddy objected to. He hadn't liked Andy Brookside before he ever met him, for a very personal reason that he and I had never talked about.

I didn't talk about it now. I said, "You're mad because you don't want to want that medal."

Cuddy stared at me, then looked away to watch people shivering as they moved from the muggy heat outside into the icy air conditioning of the lobby. After he rolled up his blue shirtsleeves, he turned back nodding. "Justin, when you're right, you're right."

"I'm right?"

"Yep."

"This is an historic moment. I'm right and you're not?"

"I want that prize and I don't want it." Walking to the gigantic varnished portrait of the dead textiles king Briggs Cadmean that dominated the lobby, he gave the old bald millionaire a salute. "As B.M., the capitalist hog, my old personal patron up there always advised me," he puffed out his thin cheeks and deepened his voice to a sonorous rumble, "'Son, concede the irrefutable.' Well, what he actually said was, 'Son, if you jump up on your high horse when they've got your pecker nailed to the floor, it's gonna hurt.' That was the kind of advice it was hard to argue with, and I never did."

Cadmean, Hillston's dead patriarch, the man who'd left me Manassas in his will, had left Hillston the municipal building, the name of which had been changed to honor him. (He was holding up the blueprints in the painting, as if to make his generosity absolutely clear.) He'd thought that he owned everybody who worked in the building, including Cuddy, and had always boasted that he had personally made Cuddy police chief, an exaggeration Cuddy had never contradicted because it was useful; he still referred to Cadmean as his "patron" years after the old man's death.

I pursued my advantage. "You admit that's why you're badgering me."

"Well now, no, this badgering," he pulled the gray matted rabbit foot of his key chain out of his pants pocket, "is about you locating the Guess Who Killer ex po fasto." He took the wad of messages from his pocket and ruffled them at me. "Because the mayor and the D.A. and Ward Trasker, our suck-ass attorney general, are leaning on Redial in a half-nelson kind of way, wanting to know who slit that woman's throat and cut out her tongue and mailed her body to you to give to me. They are not asking me for your theories about how there wouldn't even be these homicides if we all could trace our ancestors back to the alluvial mud and just revere the glorious Southern past together—"

"I've got a seven hundred and forty-page murder book. I've done a hundred-twenty-eight interviews—"

"And I can't keep telling them we don't need the FBI or the SBI or the damn sheriff because we can do it ourselves when we're *not* doing it ourselves. They want a suspect. I want a suspect. I don't even care if it's you. I want this case closed. And the *least* I want is that fiber analysis on the T-shirt from NCBI that I asked you for two weeks ago—"

I threw up my hands. "It hasn't come back yet! You know, your hostility to the past is damn perverse for a man with a Ph.D. in history—"

He gave me his ironic blue-jay wink. "This is not about perversity. This is about power, pure and simple, in which struggle, Justin B. Savile the Fifth, you are seriously outranked by Cudberth the First—"

"Cuddy, babe. Justin, hi." Judge Margy Turbot hurried out of Superior Court and squeezed Cuddy's arm as she rushed away. "Congratulations."

He blew her a kiss. "Thanks, Margy. Well hey, the rumor mill is grinding you to glitter. I hear you're the next attorney general."

"Leave you and move to Raleigh? No way, you big hunk of love!" she sent a kiss back over her shoulder.

He shouted after her. "How's it going in there?" Margy was the judge on the bench in the Norris trial. Without turning back, she lifted her arm and waggled her hand ambiguously.

"Norris did it!" he called after her, then grumbled at me. "How could she let Isaac talk her into giving him bail? Even O.J. couldn't get bail."

I shrugged. The judge's decision hadn't surprised me. "Margy knows Norris isn't blowing his daddy's million dollar bond by going anywhere."

"He's going free, that's where he's going. We're about to lose this trial, Justin. And you better find out who did G.I. Jane before that happens. I don't wanna hear CeeCee Cane on the same Action News show telling the whole Piedmont how we pulled in the wrong guy on the Norris case, and no guy at all on G.I. Jane."

He watched Judge Turbot—trim, good legs, blond pageboy hair—laughing with a federal marshal near the doors. "There goes the best-looking judge in the district."

"You said she was too healthy for you. You said she admitted she'd never had a Big Mac and never planned to."

"That's true," he nodded.

"On the other hand, I wish you'd marry her. I've had your wedding present ready for over ten years, just waiting for a bride."

"I hope it wasn't a case of Twinkies."

"Why, don't they have a shelf life of a century?"

Cuddy grinned. "Maybe Alice'll come home, wake up, and realize she should have married me in the first place, instead of a guy without air conditioning." Cuddy's grin vanished abruptly. "Well, great!"

I saw the reason for his frown, and for the crowd, and for Carol Cathy Cane's presence outside. She hadn't been there for me after all. Governor Andrew Brookside had just walked into the building. His press secretary Bubba Percy was easing him past the herd of reporters as they all slipped around the striking sanitation workers and through the doors, jostling to stay close to the fast-moving, good-looking man known to everybody in the state as "Andy." CeeCee must have already gotten whatever sound bite she wanted out on the steps because she hadn't followed the crowd inside. She looked down on print journalists anyhow. She was a personality.

I muttered, "Take it away, Chief," as Cuddy tossed his jacket over his other arm, smiled, and held out his hand.

Tall, crisp, and handsome, in his early forties, with the deep tan of the athletic rich, Governor Brookside had always had a brightness to him, as if he wore armor made of all the silver trophies and gold medals, bronze statues and brass plates he'd ever won in his lifetime. The more glory, the more Andy seemed to throw off light. Light gleamed from his polished shoes and his luminous tie and his radiant hair as he strode toward us now, his golden hand outstretched. He stopped when he reached us, and the whole circle of reporters stopped with him, leaning into his light. As he rubbed my shoulder, he shook my hand. "You and Alice coming to the banquet tonight?"

"Alice is still up in the mountains visiting family, but I'll be there."

"Good. And you tell Alice I don't want to hear any more about her not running for re-election in November. We count on her voice in the General Assembly." Only then did the governor turn his profile slightly as a camera flashed, and reach for Cuddy's hand. "Captain Mangum, congratulations again, see you tonight, you'll be at our table."

Cuddy said, "Looking forward to it, Governor," and withdrew his hand from Brookside's. We all knew that the "our" in "our table" meant Andy's wife Lee, the first lady.

"How is Lee?" I asked.

"Lee is perfect." The governor smiled. "Always. She looks forward to seeing you, Cuddy, it's been a long time."

The governor's wife Lee Brookside had been born Lee Haver, as in Haver County, Haver University, billions of Haver Tobacco Company cigarettes smoked, despite the warnings, by millions of people; as in Haver keys to open Carolina doors for Andy to sprint into the presidency of Haver University and from there to vault into the governor's mansion. No one doubted that without the first lady, Brookside would never have won that election, a close ugly race against the then current Lieutenant Governor, a cousin of mine. But nothing had ever stopped Andy Brookside from getting where he wanted to be. Maybe, like the old heroes, he had a goddess for a mother who wrapped him in magic and kept him safe.

First Lady Lee Haver Brookside was the personal reason why Cuddy didn't like the governor. He was in love with her. He always had been.

Chapter 3

Bubba

There are two things Cuddy and I never talk about, even after all this time together. They both have to do with love.

One is the death last Christmas of my infant son Copper and the weight of that loss on my marriage to Alice.

The other is Cuddy's love of Lee Haver Brookside. They fell in love when they were in their teens; her parents broke it up and I'd always suspected he'd never gotten over her, even during his short marriage to somebody else and his short engagement to Briggs Cadmean's daughter.

I'm certain that Lee and Cuddy started seeing each other again after he became police chief and that they were seriously involved during Andy Brookside's first gubernatorial campaign. I suspect that Cuddy asked Lee to leave Andy and marry him. Cuddy Mangum is not a man who has affairs. I think the relationship was ended by the assassination attempt that sent both Cuddy and Andy to the hospital and almost sent Andy to the morgue. The affair was over, I mean, not the feelings. Cuddy is also not a man who stops loving someone he has loved as long as Lee. Alice and I used to speculate about what had happened. I had never asked him. But I'm a good detective and I notice things.

"I'm here to see your mayor." Brookside smiled in his easy confidential way.

Cuddy nodded. "Well, Carl's in a real bad mood about this strike. I hope you came with a box of cigars."

Cigar-addicted Carl Yarborough, Hillston's first African-American mayor, was Cuddy' partner in what *Newsweek* had called "the booming, bustling, fresh and flourishing New South." It hadn't been so fresh this morning when Carl had arrived at the Cadmean Building to find trash bags piled in front of his office by Hillston's mostly African-American sanitation workers, who had also left a large sign accusing the mayor (unfairly) of contemptible indifference to his racial brothers in the matter of a 6 percent raise. After the protestors had returned to their picket line, I'd seen Carl in the men's room puffing away in a blue smoky funk.

Andy Brookside winked at the press. "With my family connections, I guess I could lay my hands on a few cheroots for Carl." The young reporters laughed with him at the fact that he'd married into tobacco billions. Andy started for the stairs, and then he turned, dropping like a flirtatious handkerchief the possibility that he might have something interesting to say to the press tomorrow, why didn't they swing by the Capitol to hear it? His teeth and eyes and shirtfront sparkled as he waved good-bye.

But Shelly Bloom, a young woman at the *Sun*, scooted up the stairs and blocked him: Was Brookside changing lieutenant governors in his upcoming campaign for reelection? Is that why he was here to see Carl Yarborough? Because Shelly had heard rumors....

Someone handed Andy a cell phone; he took the call and gestured to Bubba Percy to handle Shelly. Randolph Prewitt Percy—Bubba to us all—a reporter himself before he quit to become the governor's press secretary, quickly elbowed a path through the crowd and pulled Shelly away from the governor. "Shelly," he said, "I've heard rumors that you're got Eric Clapton's name tattooed in a heart on your fanny, and it's Hewitt here who's spreading those rumors." Bubba threw his arm around a disheveled grungy old-timer from KWWB-FM, who collapsed in an embarrassed coughing fit.

Shelly patted Hewitt's back. "Percy, don't you think it's time for you to join the grown ups?"

"Not yet," Bubba said and made as if to kiss her. "First I want to give you a hickey." As the press snickered, he moved among them, a smart, conceited man, large and pretty, with peachy freckled skin and just on the good side of pudge. "Hi, boys and girls. Who started this little press conference here in the lobby?" He slid next to Cuddy and slapped his back. "Captain Hog! You announcing you finally caught that Guess Who Killer? About time." Bubba checked his wavy auburn hair in the glass display behind him. "Here you and Mayor Yarborough turn Hillston into Paradiseville, get us profiled on *20/20*." He turned to Cuddy, grinned knowingly. "And then all of a sudden Hillston's got mad dog killers on the loose and the streets are full of garbage. Doesn't look good. Make an arrest?"

Cuddy glared at him. "No, we haven't made an arrest."

Bubba did some loud tsk-tsking sounds. "No? Man, I bet it tears you to bits to have women scared to go out jogging, scared ole Guess Who's gonna give them a buzz cut from the neck up." The youngest reporters laughed.

"Bubba, it tore me to bits for women to go out jogging when *you* lived in Hillston." The reporters laughed again. Cuddy then gave Bubba a long friendly squeeze on the shoulder at the trapezius muscle, pinching a nerve until the big man's smile broke and he jerked loose.

Ending his call, Andy Brookside asked us if there was still a possibility that G.I. Jane was a local girl. Bubba threw his arms out with a sardonic chortle. "Well, if she *was* local, she didn't have enough friends, and if she was just passing through, southern hospitality's sure not what it used to be."

The press chuckled, but without much enthusiasm; most of them aren't native, and for them, Hospitality is just the name of a fast food chain on the interstate. At this point, Bubba's cell phone rang. Reporters tried to listen in as he briskly answered it, but he stepped away, moving the governor off to the side with a nod that must have conveyed a clue as to who was calling, for

Brookside grabbed eagerly at the phone. After Bubba blocked the reporters' path, they turned on Cuddy and me. Shelly, the *Sun* reporter who was always giving me a hard time, took the opportunity to do so again. With her short wings of rich black hair, her sharp nose, and huge inquisitive eyes, she swooped down on me like a small pretty falcon, wanting to know why I was busy turning the homicide division of HPD into a local joke.

"Seems to me you're the ones doing that," I said.

Shelly abandoned me and tried Cuddy. "Come on, Mangum, is murder the only crime you *can* get away with in Hillston? What if there's another G.I. Jane, what if there's another *dozen*, before you stumble over the guy because his taillight's burnt out and there's a woman's body in his trunk?"

Cuddy told Shelly he wasn't sure what her question was, but that if she was implying we were dealing with a serial killer like Ted Bundy, she shouldn't be provocative. Despite the two Guess T-shirts, it was possible the Neville and the Balmoral Heights stabbings were isolated. Out of the corner of my eye, I was watching Andy Brookside, who seemed to be passionately engaged with whoever was calling him. From all the way across the room, I could feel him pouring his (considerable) seductive power into the phone. Then he laughed happily and handed the phone back to Bubba, who continued the conversation with the caller.

Meanwhile Shelly was rubbing Cuddy the wrong way by smiling as she asked if he'd read Fulke Norris's full-page ad in last Sunday's *Star*. In it, North Carolina's eminent "philosopher poet" had charged the Hillston police with vindictive harassment of his brilliant math professor son, a loving heartsick husband who had emphatically *not* murdered his wife. The elder Norris was a "state treasure": Emeritus at the University, he wrote pretty books of spiritual poetic advice illustrated with pastel drawings and printed on handsome creamy paper. They sold in the millions (my mother had a shelf full), and Norris's plangent voice could be heard reading them on public radio from time to time. Norris's ad (accusing Cuddy of incompetence and bias) had probably precipitated the *Star* editorial calling for his resignation.

"I understand Mr. Norris's reluctance to believe in his son's guilt," Cuddy said. "But I think we caught the right man."

Shelly couldn't leave it alone, darting forward with her thin avidity, like a bird snatching at a string. "When are you going to admit you can't catch Guess Who at all?"

"I'm not. There are no unsolved homicides in Hillston," he said flatly.

"Sixty-five percent of homicides in America *are* unsolved."

Cuddy wheeled around on her. "I don't know where you're getting your statistics, Shelly, but there will be *no* unsolved homicides in Hillston as long as I'm head of HPD. That's zero percent. Is that clear enough?" The hardness of his voice caught her off guard; his style with the press tended toward the casually facetious, but now he was even jabbing his finger an inch from her startled face. "And hey, about Professor Norris? Why don't we let a jury decide on his guilt or innocence instead of you folks and his father? Isaac Rosethorn can flit around like a fat old Tinker Bell throwing fairy dust in your faces, but if Norris shot his wife, I don't care if he invented algebra and his father is goddamn Billy Graham!"

The huddle of reporters stared at him, even Bubba Percy and the governor looked over. Cuddy caught himself and laughed. "Please don't tell Isaac I called him a fat old Tinker Bell." Everyone looked relieved as he went on in his normal, wry, easy style. "I apologize, Shelly. But I don't want to hear how you can get away with murder in Hillston. There's nobody smart enough to do that. I will catch Guess Who. I guarantee it."

Bubba grinned, walking toward us. "But it must sting, Chief, Guess Who just rubbing your nose in it, leaving that toe tag telling Savile here to bring you the body. So can you put a date on closing the case?"

Cuddy looked across the lobby where Brookside paused to listen. Then he turned back to the reporters, "That woman's killer will be in custody by the Fourth of July. That's a promise. By the Fourth of July."

The reporters vowed to hold Cuddy to his pledge, then

congratulated him on the gala tonight. He nodded impatiently. "The Raleigh Medal's honoring the Hillston Police Department, not me. So excuse me, I've gotta go get prettied up. And why aren't y'all over at the Sheraton interviewing our rock'n'roll queen instead of me anyhow? You'd think Janis Joplin was back in town." A few young reporters didn't appear to be really sure who Janis Joplin was, but they knew Cuddy was talking about Mavis Mahar's final concert at Haver Field, her last appearance in a fifteen-city U.S. tour. Scalpers in Hillston had been selling even bad seats for a hundred dollars each. The reporters jokingly confessed they couldn't get anywhere near the rock star. The police chief was much easier to hound.

Our impromptu press conference broke up and the lobby emptied. Bubba Percy, who was following the governor upstairs, called down to us from the first landing, his voice bouncing around the marble rotunda. "Mangum, you think you're so smart. You think compared to you, Einstein and Madame Curie would be too dumb to figure out long division together! And you call me conceited?"

Cuddy tilted his head, tapped the side of his temple. "I'm not conceited, Bubba, I *am* smart. You're conceited because you're not smart and you think you are."

"Well, you better hope I.Q. doesn't stand for I Quit when they ask for your resignation, Porcus Rex."

"You better hope there's a long future in kissing the governor's ass," Cuddy smiled back, but I could tell Bubba had stung him.

The press secretary knew it too. He grinned. "There's always a future in ass kissing. Happy Fourth of July, Chief. That's, let's see, that's about two weeks from now. Shit man, you'll probably confess you whacked Jane yourself before you'll admit you're clueless." Laughing, Bubba bounced up the stairs and disappeared down the hall toward the mayor's office.

Cuddy and I stood alone a moment in the empty lobby. "Fantastic," I snapped at him. "Why'd you let Bubba goad you into a deadline?"

"So meet it," he said.

I looked at him awhile. "It's arrogance, thinking you're to blame for everything. You know what the difference in us is?"

"Yep." He gave me his mean smile and counted, touching his key chain to his fingertips. "You've got old money, old manners, old school ties—most of them, I'm sad to say, bow-ties with stripes and dots—"

"I've got looks. Everybody always said I had looks."

"True. You've got looks, smart pretty wife used to be in the legislature, except she doesn't seem to be around much lately and you don't seem to be doing anything about that." I flinched. He stared at me a long minute, his face slowly softening. "Hey, look. I'm sorry. I'm in a rotten mood."

I stepped away. "Don't worry about it."

"I know this Guess Who mess hit you right when you were trying to deal with...with Copper. I guess I've been hoping the investigation would help pull you out of the hole."

He almost never mentioned by name my baby son who had died half a year ago. Cuddy, his godfather, had nicknamed him "Copper" for the bright color of his hair and in humorous reference to our profession. Copper had died in his sleep just before Christmas, when he was thirteen months old, so young that friends thought to comfort Alice and me by telling us that had we lost our child later in his life (when he would have been "more real" to us), we would have loved him more. But Alice and I loved him with all the love we had, and all we shared. He was born with a hole in his heart that couldn't be repaired, and his loss left the same defect in us.

I tapped Cuddy's shoulder, acknowledging his kindness. "I'm sorry too. I wish I could clear this case for you by tomorrow."

"July third will be just fine." He grinned and headed for the door.

The elevator opened and Sheriff Homer Louge emerged, tall and thick with his flat mean face. He always wore a fresh uniform and a close crew cut. The hair had gone grisly gray but was still in the style he'd worn the night he'd intercepted a pass in the high school football game that had made the Hillston Cougars state champions and made him sheriff of Haver County for apparently as long as he wanted to be, despite two failed marriages and a racial-bias suit against his department by a local branch of the NAACP.

Cuddy called to him. "Hey, Homer, you and Carl settle the garbage strike, I hope?" Louge moved his mouth but just kept going. He walked at a tilt, possibly in admiration of John Wayne. Cuddy tried to help him out. "Oh, you could say lots of things. Like, 'If I had ended the strike, there'd be at least one thing done right in Hillston.'"

Louge paused long enough to drop a gum wrapper on the floor.

Cuddy picked it up. "Well, I wish I could go on discussing this with you, Homer, but I gotta get dressed in a tux and head to the capitol for this Raleigh Medal prize they're giving me and not you." Louge quickened his pace and was at the revolving door when Cuddy called, "I appreciate your good wishes.... Hold on, Homer. Door turns to the right. There you go."

After the sheriff stomped off, I said, "I don't know why you have to rile him. He doesn't take it well. So you're really wearing a tux?"

Cuddy loosened his tie and pulled open his shirt to show me the Elvis Presley T-shirt underneath. "How about with this?"

"Sure. As long as it's with black tie too."

"Now look at that, speaking of ties...." He gestured and I turned to see Officer Nancy Caleb-White just coming out of the elevator; she was in uniform, but with her collar open, tieless. Shaking his head, Cuddy pointed at his own tie. "Nancy, put it on." Then he spun backwards though the revolving door, calling to me, "Pick me up at eight and don't be late as the big-eyed girl said to the Big Bopper. Well, they're all in rock'n'roll heaven now and left this cold old world a whiter shade of pale."

One of the few women on the force whose slender long-limbed body wasn't defeated by those hideous boxy trousers and squared-off shirts, Nancy, in her twenties, my junior partner, could never make herself wear the full uniform unless coerced.

Pulling her truant tie out of a pocket, she muttered, "What's he bugging me for? I saw that Elvis thing he had on."

"That T-shirt of Cuddy's is famous. He wore it in *Newsweek.*"

She nodded morosely. "Four years ago."

"According to our captain, Elvis is timeless."

"Zeke says Elvis had Indian blood." Nancy recently married a young sergeant of ours, Zeke Caleb, a Cherokee from the North Carolina mountains, presumably descended from one of the few survivors of my great-great grandfather's governorship. For some reason, they'd added Zeke's last name in front of hers and she was now officially "Nancy Caleb-White."

I centered the knot in her tie. "Didn't your husband also tell us Frank Sinatra hired Sirhan Sirhan to kill Bobby Kennedy to get back at him for killing Marilyn Monroe?"

Nancy laughed. "Zeke reads these magazines." She held up a tabloid. "Listen, Justin, I got something for you on Guess Who."

"That's good, Nancy, because the Hillston *Star* just called for Cuddy's resignation, and Bubba Percy just maneuvered him into telling a dozen reporters we'd have Guess Who locked up by the Fourth of July."

"Sure, no problem." Nancy aspires to the rank of a homicide detective, and she works hard, except for refusing to take her exam. It reminds her of school and scares her. Nothing physical has frightened this former East Hillston girl gang leader since she hit her stepfather over the head with a hammer when he tried to rape her. "NCBI just called," she said. "Fiber on the Guess T-shirt? It's car carpeting, gray, but they can't make the model yet."

"So he moved Jane?"

"I knew we were in a rut figuring Jane was out jogging when the perp grabbed her. I always thought those shoelaces were *his*. He offs her, puts the Guess shirt on her, drives the body out to Balmoral Heights after dark. Maybe he burns her, cuts out her tongue there, gives her sunglasses so it looks like a day hit. First time, with Cathy Oakes, all he did was put the T-shirt on her and add the roses. With Jane, he's getting fancier."

"How can a girl like that die and nobody miss her?" I slapped my hand on a glass case in the lobby.

"Hey, watch it." Nancy rubbed carefully at the glass beneath which she and her husband had arranged a display labeled, "Crime and Punishment. Hillston Police 1883–1953." They had come across the dusty case packed with artifacts that had figured in homicide cases solved over the past half century. These murderous items had been exhibited at the old courthouse, but in one of the many moves of government offices, they'd been relegated to the basement. Zeke Caleb, a fervent historian of the state that had exiled his ancestors, put the display up in the lobby. Among the still carefully labeled weapons were old guns, a hatchet, a bludgeon, and a straight-back razor, all stained with rusty human blood. There was even the "Hangman's noose used to execute Miss Idele Straithorn on March 1, 1901, in the yard of Hillston County Courthouse for the murder of Mrs. Boone Hackney."

When he saw it, Cuddy had disgustedly suggested that Nancy and Zeke take the restored display back to the basement. "Or hey, bring it up to date. Stick G.I. Jane's bloody T-shirt in there too." But the case had stayed in the lobby, and every day people stopped to peer into the murderous past it contained. Old violence was almost as good as fresh carnage.

Nancy pointed now at a brown bottle labeled "POISON." "I bet it was easier to catch them back then."

I agreed. "In 1901, Hillston didn't have Jane Does lying around dead in the woods for months." I looked down into the case. "That's weird. Did you rearrange these guns?" I showed her where a 1947 Italian pistol was missing and a long-nosed Colt revolver had been moved into its place.

She leaned over to look. "Well, the case is still locked. Probably Zeke lent that Bernardelli to the Historical Society."

The Hillston Historical Society ran a little museum in a former tobacco warehouse that they shared with a Thai restaurant and a ceramics arts gallery. But their displays ran to the bourgeois and decorative—the malachite shoe buckles worn by a debutante flapper—and it didn't seem likely that they would borrow the Italian Bernardelli PA thirty-two with which Big Bob Futton had killed a prostitute at the Piedmont Hotel in 1949. Nancy said she'd check with Zeke.

She wanted to tell me an idea she'd had about Jane. Opening her tabloid, she pointed to a grainy photo of the Irish rock star Mavis Mahar being hauled into a patrol car apparently wearing nothing but a Nashville police officer's jacket. Her hair was in the buzz cut she had worn in the magazines in Cuddy's office. Nancy said, "What if Guess Who didn't saw off a lot of Jane's hair like he did Cathy Oakes? What if she already had a buzz cut and it had just grown out a little, and this guy wanted it to look like he'd shaved off a whole lot of her hair and maybe kept it, so he used the knife on what little she had? I mean, lots of models get buzz cuts. See, Mavis had one. Now she's grown it back." Nancy pointed at the Irish singer's fuzzy skull, beautifully shaped, pressed against the policeman's jacket.

When I told Nancy that I'd spoken to Mavis Mahar this afternoon in the Tucson, she was devastated that I hadn't gotten an autograph for her niece Danielle, who was a fan. She yanked at her braided ponytail, tightening its rubber band. "But how can I blow off the Chief's big night tonight, just so Danielle can get fucking crushed by a zillion blotto rock freakheads."

Everyone at HPD knew that Nancy was taking her niece to the Mavis Mahar concert tonight but that she hated to miss seeing the governor pin a medal on Cuddy, whom she adored. She'd been fretting for a month about her dilemma to anyone who'd listen: not attending Cuddy's ceremony would show him a lack of respect. Attending would mean giving up tickets she'd bought *last winter.* I said, "Hey, give me the tickets, I don't mind skipping Cuddy's getting one more civic prize."

She sighed. "I figure Mavis won't even show up anyhow."

It was true that of the forty thousand people who would be at Haver Field tonight, there was some doubt that the star would be one of them. The magazine had said that as a result of "a drinking problem" for which she'd been in and out of Windrush Clinic here in the Piedmont as often as the man delivering the mineral water, Mavis Mahar had started a riot when she'd walked off the stage in Houston, had canceled her concert in Atlanta (the promoters were suing her), and just last night in Hillston had been so late fans were close to assaulting her weary band.

"Sixty-seven-fifty each for these tickets," brooded Nancy. "Mavis Mahar is like my niece's personal idol. Danielle was at the Sheraton downtown—that's where Mavis and the Easter Uprising are staying—at five o'clock this morning waiting to catch her coming out. My asshole brother don't—doesn't— even know it, but Danielle's seeing a lot of me, and this is important to us." Nancy's alcoholic brother, Danielle's father, hasn't spoken to her since she married Zeke Caleb, whom he oddly called a "half-breed," although Zeke was proudly 100 percent Cherokee.

"I've got to go talk to forensics. Nancy, take Danielle to the concert."

"I bet the Chief wishes he could blow off this whole thing too."

"I doubt it," I said. "Cuddy's worried the press'll get sarcastic about Norris and G.I. Jane, but he'll get his face in the TV camera and blow smoke 'til they roll the credits. How many times have we heard him on the news saying how Hillston's got the lowest per capita felony crime rate in the South? And how the hell does he even know that?"

Nancy didn't like any criticism of Cuddy. "Studies. They do studies."

As I headed to the elevators, I added, "Well, Guess Who's cost our captain his A+ on the test, and I can assure you that the glorious summer of his bonhomie will not be making a return appearance until we're back to ground zero in the world of unsolved homicides."

Nancy spun her finger at the side of her head. "Justin, most of the time I don't even know what the fuck you're talking about, and neither does anybody else around here."

"I'm saying Cuddy will boot some butts if we don't collar Guess Who before the Fourth of July." I held the elevator door.

"He won't fire his friends."

"Sure he will. You want me to say I saw you at the Gala?"

She shook her head, the long black braid flicking a shoulder. "No thanks. Lying just messes me up. But I gotta think this through; I hate to blow off the Chief's big night—"

I distracted her quickly. "That eyebrow earring on the shoelace, tied around the neck of the victim? Remember I thought it was like the old custom where a girl wears a boy's high school ring on a chain around her neck because they're going steady? That's young romance, like the roses on Cathy Oakes, right? I'm thinking maybe Neville PD focused too much on her johns. I want to check Cathy's high school book. Maybe this psycho went to school with her and Jane. And you ask around the local hair salons, see if anybody like Jane maybe got a buzz cut back in January."

Her face brightened. "Yeah, let's grab this squirrel. Me and Zeke can't even get a beer at the Tucson without somebody cracking some lame joke."

My only suggestion was to stay out of cheap bars.

• • •

The defense lawyer Isaac Rosethorn was leaving the dilapidated Piedmont Hotel, where he had lived on the top floor in unbudgeable clutter for forty years while gentrification swept around him with the stimulating hand that Cuddy and the mayor called Progress. Walking with Isaac was his current client, the accused wife-killer Professor Tyler Norris. Isaac was holding forth with energetic gestures as if arguing some point with him. I watched as they passed through a nearby pedestrian alley where years ago an undercover sting had gone awry and almost killed Cuddy and me both; on damp days my right leg still stiffened around the ingenious little pieces of steel that held it together.

I drove to the other side of the alley just as the lawyer and his client emerged and paused to talk near the door of the Tucson bar. Norris's bland clean-cut features grimaced as he swatted at the smoke from Isaac's cigarette. They made a distinctive pair: Norris with everything so tight and pressed; Isaac with his flowing white hair and white rumpled billowing shirt looking like a fat polar bear wearing trousers. Suddenly Norris spotted me in my car and, frowning, turned his back; Isaac was too busy talking to notice. I waited until they'd left before stopping at the Tucson. It was nearly six o'clock and the black limousine was still waiting outside. I noticed the driver asleep at the wheel. I thought about going inside the bar to see what Mavis Mahar was doing but it was a dangerous urge and I knew it. The two small dark women were back at the dumpster looking through the garbage bags. Sheriff Homer Louge came out of the Tucson and shooed them away.

• • •

Later that evening when I drove on the new winding streets to Cuddy's River Rise condominium complex, the white sweep of searchlights criss-crossing the sky lit up the bridge over the Shocco River. The day's second hard rain had just ended and the bridge still had a lush wet shine. The lights were coming from the Mavis Mahar concert at Haver Field. I imagined her standing in those lights, her pale arm raised, her hand filled with red tulips.

Cuddy was waiting outside his unit, leaning against an ornamental street lamp, wearing a black tie and a white dinner jacket. In all the years I'd known him, I don't think he'd ever looked better. Despite his jokes about how in high school he'd resembled Abe Lincoln with a flat top, Cuddy had never been anywhere near as homely as he boasted, but tonight there was a remote, handsome edge to his looks. The sweeping lights had an old nostalgic war look about them, and as Cuddy watched them arc across the night, with the big silver moon floating past the Shocco, he had a trace of that imperturbable forties cool that makes the disenchanted so alluring.

When he didn't seem to hear me brake, I rolled down the window of my new car (new to me, it was a thirty-year-old Jaguar sedan), and called out, "You'd think the governor would send you a limo."

He patted the Jaguar hood. "So you finally got Miss Moneypit out of the shop? How long this time, a month?"

"Thoroughbreds are more trouble, okay? Well, you are classic."

His grin broke the spell. "Classic what?"

I don't know why I said what I did, after years of pretending not to know about Lee. "Classic, like you're getting ready to say, 'Of all the gin joints in all the towns in all the world, why'd she have to walk into mine?'"

Cuddy looked at me with the familiar head-tilt but there was a wary curiosity in his eyes as he tried to figure if I meant by my quotation what in fact I did mean. Then he said, "Don't mix us up. You're the short romantic guy in this duo, not me. Look at your car. Old, everything's gotta be old."

"Don't forget beautiful."

"Looks like a car JFK put the make on movie stars in."

I slid the sedan into gear. "You're right, you're no romantic."

"Didn't Alice and I tell you buy U.S.A? Don't you know driving around in this old Jaguar won't bring back the splendor in the grass, boy."

"What will then? Because it sure is gone." I drove out of the lot. I couldn't say to him that Alice didn't tease me about anything anymore, that since Copper's death my wife and I have found ourselves standing on either side of a fissure of grief that we were so unable to bridge that she left our home and I let her go.

Alice and Cuddy are very close and I was wondering what she might have told him about our separation when he suddenly asked, "So how long is she staying in the mountains?"

"I told you I don't know."

He surprised me by coming close again to the unspoken subject: "Alice's gone to her family for comfort. She wasn't getting it from you." He held up his hand at me. "And I know, you weren't getting it from her either. But somebody needs to take a step here. Love's the wrong thing to waste."

I didn't say anything as I drove toward the Raleigh bypass, and finally to fill the silence Cuddy started bragging about his new Ford. Relieved to change the subject, I pointed out my new sound system and clicked on what I expected to be the FM university jazz station. Instead, the tape deck started playing a bouncy Elvis Presley number. My fingers froze on the knob as the dead rock star sang, *"Won't you wear my ring around your neck..."*

Cuddy turned the sound louder. "Now that's real friendly of you, Justin—"

I knocked his hand away. "Shut up!"

"What the hell's the matter with you?"

I swerved off the road and slammed to a stop. "I didn't put this in here! I've never owned any Elvis tapes."

Cuddy didn't get it. "Well, don't be bad-mouthing the King."

"To show the world you're mine by heck..."

I shouted at him, "It's Guess Who."

"Are you nuts?"

"The thing around G.I. Jane's neck. Won't you wear my ring around your neck? It's Guess Who. Cuddy, get out of the car!"

Chapter 4
Andy

The skeptical, the stubbornly sanguine, the slow—all have their reasons to resist cries of alarm, but even a cynic like Cuddy won't press his luck if there's an easy alternative. He didn't believe me when I shouted that there could be a bomb in my Jaguar, but he jumped out and let me drag him across the road. We stood in our dinner jackets on the shoulder of the interstate, stared at by rubber-neckers, until the tape had ended. Although, as Cuddy gloated, there was no explosion, I insisted we call HPD to send somebody to check out my car. While we waited, Cuddy kept arguing that I was wasting his time. The old lawyer Isaac Rosethorn had once complained that if Cuddy Mangum had been Moses he'd have stood tapping his foot on top of Mount Sinai telling God to hurry up with the Ten Commandments.

It was Cuddy's idea that before Alice had left for the mountains, as a joke she'd gone over to Imports Garage and had the mechanic put in the tape cued to the song, "Won't You Wear My Ring?" But I knew that these days Alice would never go to the trouble to buy an Elvis tape in order to tease me about not liking rock'n'roll. Cuddy called the garage on his cell phone anyhow. Naturally, no one was there; they rarely were. Next he located Alice at her grandmother's family reunion in Highlands. I'd called her the day before myself, only to be told by an aunt that

Alice couldn't come to the phone just then, that she'd call me back, which she hadn't done. But she did come to the phone for Cuddy and told him that she hadn't put the tape in my car and had no idea who might have done so. He told me that Alice had been on her way out the door and she sent her love. He claimed that she'd joked about hoping that he was the only Elvis fan I was driving around in my Jaguar while she was gone. It was something the old Alice might have said, and it felt like hearing a familiar voice after a long silence. Maybe she found it easier to talk to me through a translator.

After I admitted that I'd misplaced my keys earlier, Cuddy jumped on the idea that someone at HPD had taken them in order to plant the tape in my car (parked in the lot behind the Cadmean Building), someone to whom I'd talked about my "high school ring" theory on the G.I. Jane homicide. "You ever have a single solitary thought you didn't blab to anybody would listen to you?" he churlishly asked.

I was tempted to reply, "Yeah, I never told anybody I thought you were sleeping with Andy Brookside's wife." But I didn't say it. I said, "This is Guess Who, Cuddy. I can feel it, I've been feeling something getting closer."

He started down the highway, walked back. "Don't start that psychic googoo with me again. Don't start imagining things."

"That's what they told Jimmy Stewart in *Rear Window*."

He threw up his hands. "Life's not a movie."

"It wants to be."

"Oh, Jesus." He stomped off again and started picking up trash off the shoulder of the highway. This was a man determined to clean up the world.

Old cravings suddenly rushed over me. I wanted a cigarette and a drink. I had an odd but pleasant image of myself on the dock at Pine Hills Lake with Mavis Mahar, both of us smoking, sharing a bottle of wine, watching the sun settle in the water. But I was married and I'd given up smoking long ago, and my well-documented drinking problem had been for years, by all accounts, entirely under control.

Out of the heat-fogged night came the spooky whirring bubble light of the HPD tow truck and behind it our indefatigable head of forensics, Lt. Etham Foster (an African-American still known to all long-time college basketball fans as "Doctor Dunk-It"). He unraveled from the squad car to more than six and a half feet of laconic self-possession, crossed his lean long brown arms, and frowned at us. "Got a problem?" he said.

Etham and I were friends. I think. It was hard to tell with him. In his bass monotone he rumbled at Cuddy, "Raleigh?"

Cuddy nodded. "I know, I ought to be at the capitol getting my prize. My night of nights, and Justin decides the Guess Who Killer's trying to blow up his old Jaguar with Elvis tapes."

"Um hum." Etham turned, ambled over to the sedan and leaned down to talk to the explosives specialist now checking under the hood with a flashlight. After a few minutes, he strolled back to us. He could cross the whole road in four steps. "No bomb," he told us. "Tape's been wiped."

Cuddy said, "It's just a stupid joke. Guess Who is not hanging out at the Cadmean Building looking for a chance to break into Justin's Jaguar."

They towed my car back to the HPD garage to dust it for prints. I borrowed the black and white HPD cruiser that had brought Etham to the scene and drove a silent Cuddy to Raleigh at ninety miles an hour with the blue barlight flashing. I was thinking that the tape was a challenge, like the tag on G.I. Jane with my name on it, thinking it was a warning that another woman was going to be killed.

Cuddy was thinking about Lee Brookside. I knew him so well I suppose it didn't matter that he kept things to himself. He had bought that white dinner jacket to wear to the Gala because Lee would be there, laughed at himself for doing it, didn't want to be late, didn't want to go. As we took the downtown exit, I glanced at him grabbing one clenched hand by the wrist. The prospect of having dinner with Lee tonight was bound to break loose feelings that he'd long kept locked away. It was possible that they hadn't spoken once in private since she and Andy had moved to the governor's mansion three years ago. He stared fixedly ahead at the state capitol as we drove toward it. The gold dome shone in the moonlight like all the treasure of the New World heaped into a dowry that the richest woman in the South had given to her husband Andy, a dowry of houses, planes, cars, paintings, friends, universities, and the whole state of North Carolina.

• • •

In front of the capitol building, a parking valet, puzzled to see two guests in dinner jackets step out of a patrol car, apprehensively accepted the ignition key from me. Cuddy and I took our places at the end of a slow-moving river of guests as they streamed up the steps and through the columns of the portico and under the banner announcing the one-hundred-and-third Governor's Gala inside. Camera flashes flared at us as we climbed the marble stairs. Halfway up, Cuddy was nabbed by a mike-swinging Carol Cathy Cane, looking tonight more like a lounge hostess than a news anchor in an orange one-shouldered sheath, with a wide hairdo the same color. She cut Cuddy out of the herd like a rodeo champion. "I'm here on the Capitol steps talking to Hillston Police Chief Mangum, tonight's Raleigh Medal honoree. Captain Mangum, you must feel the irony. Here you are accepting congratulations for your low crime rate, when Guess Who's out there in the dark stalking his next victim because you can't find him even after the taxpayers almost doubled your police force. *And* your salary."

He took the mike right out of her hand. "CeeCee darlin', you've been staying up too late at night watching slasher movies on cable all by your lonesome. You need to get out more and you'll see that nobody's stalking anybody. There's nothing for anybody in Hillston to worry about."

She laughed skeptically. "Except a killer wandering around loose who already slit two women's throats."

"Hillston has the lowest crime rate in the Southeast."

"Well, maybe it used to—"

"CeeCee, have you heard these rumors about Judge Margy Turbot?"

She jumped at the bait because she couldn't bear not to prove that she knew as much as he did. "They're saying state attorney general Ward Trasker is going to retire after the election this fall to become President of the Haver Foundation. Judge Turbot's on the short list to replace him."

Cuddy smiled as if CeeCee had just gotten a hard word right in a spelling bee. "I think she'd make a great attorney general. Judge Margaret Turbot. Always a real pleasure, CeeCee." He kept walking.

I had moved ahead, catching up with an oddly distressed Bubba Percy (usually he was as buoyant as a rubber ball), who fell in beside me. I tapped his tuxedo jacket. "Dollyland Souvenir Shop?" My horror at Percy's taste in clothes was an old joke between us. Tonight he sported a chartreuse silk tie and a vest embroidered with gold roses. "Sonny Bono estate auction?"

He was so upset he didn't even take offense. He'd lost track of the governor and his wife. He'd assumed that our cruiser was leading in Brookside's entourage and seemed to be blaming me that it wasn't. Glancing down at the street, I shook my head. "Andy's kind of big to lose, Bubba."

The press secretary bit at his mouth. "Andy and Lee both! They're forty-five minutes late, and the driver said they never called for the limo."

I checked my pocket watch. It was 8:58, cocktails had started at eight, and the brief ceremony itself was scheduled for 9:15. "What do they need a limo for? Don't they live next door?"

"Jesus, Justin, the governor and the first lady don't walk anywhere. You can check into the twentieth century now that it's over."

"Well, I'm sorry. Cuddy and I were a little late ourselves."

"Everybody's fucking up tonight!" Bubba kept telephoning people (thick-skinned ones, I hoped) on his cellular, shouting at them, "Shit!" and clicking off.

I tried to distract him, fingering his flowered vest. "Big Boy

Discounts at River Rise Mall?"

He gave the vest an angry tug. "Savile, don't start with me and the class struggle or you'll be watching your head roll down the blood-soaked streets of Paris while I sit knitting R.I.P. on your silk scarf like Madame Defarge in drag." Proud and breathless after this retort, he stuffed the slender phone in his tuxedo pocket and calmed himself with a quick comb through auburn locks dampened by sweat in the heat.

I brushed a speck from his sleeve. "Bubba, you're always so much more literate than I remember you."

"I said don't start. I'm going down for the third time here, I've got sharks chewing off both my legs and sea gulls crapping on my head." According to Bubba (whose vivid personal style bore no relation to his bland press releases about the Brooksides), Andy had fucked the schedule for tonight's Governor's Gala the same way he'd fuck anything in a skirt except Rob Roy. Tonight would make the Titanic look like a great vacation plan. His TV crew was tearing around shitting their pants like dogs on a diet of Mexican beans because they were shooting the Brooksides live in ten minutes and there were no live Brooksides to shoot. His drama queen banquet coordinator was off somewhere with his face in a paper bag because guests had sneaked into the State dining room and changed the place cards at the bad tables, the press had broken into the champagne hidden under the bar, and Bubba was sorry he had ever left journalism in order to accept Brookside's invitation to "Go the Distance" as his press secretary.

Why hadn't he instead married Edwina Sunderland, the flirtatious seventy-eight-year-old who had once capriciously vaulted him over the heads of his superiors into the managing editorship of the Hillston Star (which she'd owned along with Channel Seven)? "Hey, so she was pushing eighty and couldn't keep her arthritic fingers off my fanny. You know what? Muff-diving Edwina would have been a sweeter-smelling job than state politics, Jesus, and besides, she dropped dead and I'd have all her money now."

"Bubba, your vulgarity is in a class by itself." He probably thought that was a compliment. "And by the way," I added, "Edwina Sunderland never would have married you, you were just a Pretty Boy Plaything to a Ruthless Dowager. The rich are very different from you."

His cell phone rang, and he flipped me the finger as he answered it. "Yeah?... Yeah?..." And he hung up. "Okay, Andy's here. He took a different car. Jesus, I'm too good-looking for this kind of stress!" He ran back down the steps toward the approaching sound of sirens. Two police motorcycles led a long black sedan into the cul de sac. Andrew Brookside sprang from the back seat and waved to the crowd. But no Lee followed him out of the car and I noticed Bubba struggling to mask his surprise as he moved in close. Andy spoke to him hurriedly. The limousine looked familiar, but the windows were so dark-tinted I couldn't see the driver. However, as the car sped away I saw the license plate, and I'd seen it before. I'd seen the same limo outside the Tucson waiting for Mavis Mahar.

The governor moved through the swarm of eager guests like a skillful fakir dancing along a path of red hot coals. When he reached me, Brookside paused and we shook hands. He said that Lee had come down with a sudden high fever and that he'd insisted she stay home tonight. I said I was sorry to hear it. After Andy moved off with Mayor Carl Yarborough and his wife Dina, Bubba told me I was to take Lee's place at the main table. I'd be next to tonight's other medal recipient—the "Hot Hat Barbecue Widow," who was receiving the Virginia Dare Prize for donating five million dollars to two North Carolina colleges. Bubba said she had been "close" to my late uncle, U.S. Senator Kip Dollard, a handsome, incredibly stupid old man with a beautiful voice, long lovely sentences, and absolutely nothing to say.

"Is there anybody in politics you're *not* related to?" sneered Bubba.

"You, I hope."

Staying outside on the portico, I called Etham Foster. He had asked around at HPD. Nobody had admitted taking my car keys to rig the tape player to blast out "Won't You Wear My Ring?"

"But I wouldn't admit something that dumb either," growled Etham. He added that Wendy Freiberg from SBI documents had called to confirm that the snake tattoos on Jane's ankles had been drawn with the same red magic marker that had written the label addressing the corpse to me. "Guess Who drew those tattoos."

"Wonder why?"

The forensics chief said, "I do *what*. You do *why*."

"I wish I was doing why faster," I said.

The taciturn Etham surprisingly confided something: "I got a friend tight with the Mayor, says Homer Louge is spreading bad junk about Cuddy, and folks on the city council are listening. Council's had a lot of flack about y'all arresting Tyler Norris. Something needs to break on Jane soon." In other words, should Sheriff Louge succeed in his smear campaign, I would be to blame for Cuddy's downfall.

• • •

My mother's family has held office in this state for a long time, and my wife was in the legislature for a term, so I know most of the people who show up at political receptions. It took me a while to make my way through the familiar flushed faces and recognizable high-pitched laughs in the crush of babble. In the crowd, former Raleigh Medal winners milled about wearing their medals on blue ribbons. Among them was the poet, Fulke Norris, father of the math professor on trial. Accustomed to being adored (he'd been one of the youngest and most decorated heroes in World War II), he now looked like Robert Frost and knew it and made sure everybody else did too: his carefully disheveled white hair looked exactly the same tonight as it did on the jackets of his twenty-three books of inspirational verse.

The Norrises turned ostentatiously away from me as I approached their area. Frankly, I was surprised to see them here, since the evening was to honor the chief of the police department that had arrested their son Tyler. But perhaps they felt that their absence would be construed as fear bred of guilt.

Slowly I squeezed past them toward the far side of the rotunda where I saw Cuddy backed against a Corinthian column shaking hands with pudgy businessmen. Tall and lanky in his white dinner jacket, he stood under a huge painting of a few ragtag Tarheel Revolutionaries defeating the entire British army. He was smiling but looked strained. Maybe he was disappointed that Lee wasn't coming to the ceremony tonight. Or maybe her absence was a relief to him.

"I saw where the People's Poet cut you dead." He pointed at Fulke Norris. "Your mama's got a bunch of his books right there by her hospital bed. I checked one out. A *Chorus of Comfort*. Terrible. Anybody who rhymes 'Dalmatian' with 'salvation' and 'offspring' with 'golf green,' it's no surprise his son's a killer." Cuddy waved his jacket flaps. "This air-conditioning needs to fight harder."

Sergeant Zeke Caleb joined us and pumped our hands, glad to find familiar faces. Six-foot-three and 220 pounds, he took shallow breaths in order not to explode out of his rented tuxedo.

Cuddy patted his ruffled shirt. "*Oh-see-yoh. Toh-hee-joo.*"

Zeke grinned at him. "*Oh-sah-dah. Nee-hee-nah?*"

Cuddy grinned back. "*Oh-sah-dah. Wah-doh.*"

I asked, "What's that all about?"

"Zeke's teaching me Cherokee. You just heard everything I know. 'Hi, how are you? Fine. How 'bout you? Fine. Thanks.'"

Zeke stopped smiling before he popped his collar button. "We got a deal. He's teaching me Spanish. I bet I get a lot more use out of mine."

Suddenly a state militia guard marched over, saluted us, and barked, "Captain Mangum. Please follow me, sir."

Cuddy said to me, "Good-bye, old friend. It's a far far better place I go than you have ever been. Or are likely ever to get to go."

Zeke said, "Chief, Nancy just wants you to know she's sorry she had to blow off your big night, but she had to take her niece Danielle to the Mavis Mahar concert."

Cuddy smiled. "I know, Zeke. I got all twenty of Nancy's messages."

I looked at my watch. The Mavis concert must have started. I wondered what song the Irish star was singing at Haver Field right now. And how she looked. And whether she'd sobered up since she'd told me she was filled with music and wanted me to stay at the Tucson to hear her song.

Five minutes later, on the crimson dais, Cuddy bent his head so Governor Andy Brookside, whom he intensely disliked, could place around his neck the wide silk ribbon, Carolina blue, that held the gold Raleigh medallion. Andy then read out the plaque praising "Captain Cuthbert Randall Mangum, Chief of Police, Hillston, North Carolina," for his nationally acclaimed law enforcement department, and he talked a little about all Cuddy's achievements (United States Army Purple Heart and Bronze Star, Ph.D., LL.D.), and Cuddy thanked him and everyone applauded. It was true that Cuddy had passed a miserable nineteenth birthday in a flak-dodging helicopter while Army medics pumped blood and morphine into him. It was true he had an honorary degree from his alma mater as well as a Ph.D. from Haver University that had taken him years of night classes to acquire. But it was not true that his name was "Cuthbert." While Cuthbert is what most people assumed his name was, actually his mother, a country woman, had told the nurse in the maternity ward her baby's name was "Cudberth" and she had proudly called him Cudberth all her life.

After the brief ceremony ended, the special guests trooped into shuttle buses to be ferried half a block away to the Governor's Mansion for dinner in the State Dining Room. Among the few of us who insisted on walking, Cuddy strolled ahead with Carl Yarborough, talking of strategies to deal with Hillston's sanitation workers. I think Cuddy and the mayor cared more about the well-being of Hillston than they did about anything else in their lives, and I suspect Carl's wife Dina, following along beside them, thought so too. Thinner and much lighter than her stout husband, Dina had startling green eyes and a short Afro that was almost blonde. She and I were distantly related but had never talked about it. We were chatting about a community play we were both in when Zeke loped over and pulled me aside. Nancy had just called him from Haver Field. Mavis Mahar, scheduled to follow her warm-up act at nine o'clock, hadn't shown up. It was now 9:40 and her band The Easter Rising was still on stage without their lead singer. The band was very good, but they were not what forty-seven thousand fans had come to see. Nancy told Zeke that when she'd run into Sheriff Homer Louge and asked if he wanted reinforcements from HPD, he'd told her, "No thanks, honey," as if she were a waitress asking about a refill. She was concerned about security at the stadium.

I agreed with Zeke that it was best not to mention the concert to Cuddy now. The university police were working with the county sheriff's people and had already told HPD they didn't need our help. "Let the Stooges handle it," I said. (At HPD we called Sheriff Louge "Stooge," and his deputies "the Stooges.") Zeke was fretting. "But if this Mavis situation…. You know how the Chief likes to stay on top of everything."

I shrugged. "She's been late before. Wasn't she late last night too?"

"I guess." Zeke said Nancy's niece Danielle would be heartsick if she missed Mavis. "I'll tell you this, I read where Marilyn Monroe entertained the troops in Korea with a 103-degree fever. The old timers had a sense of responsibility, not like these young stars today." (Zeke was twenty-seven.)

I said that actually Marilyn Monroe was late all the time.

"But she didn't let folks down like Mavis does. But what it is, is, I read where Mavis has got a real problem with alcohol."

"Yeah, that's what I hear too."

"It'll mess you up."

"It sure will." I thought of the winter sun tediously moving across the ceiling of my small room in a Blue Ridge Mountains sanitarium—so many years ago that I'm sure Zeke Caleb knew nothing about my own real problem with alcohol. I thought of Mavis Mahar on the Tucson stage, swaying from drink, her beautiful arm raised in the dusty afternoon bar light, reaching high for the next note with her outstretched hand, a ring on each finger….

"Reeee-lease me…and let me love again." How long had she stayed there singing for seventeen people instead of forty-seven thousand? Where had she gone next in the black limousine? To meet Andy Brookside? Was he the man all the sad songs were for?

Zeke yanked off his clip-on black bow tie and, pulling open his stiff collar, took a long deep breath of the night air. "Well, I'm proud of the Chief and I'm out of here. This is worse than desk duty. I tell you, I'm trying for a K-9 division job. I'm waiting for my dog. She's in Holland getting trained."

"Ah, a Dutch girl, huh?"

"Yeah, I'm going to call her Heidi."

"Okay." I asked him to check back with Nancy and then to page me with any news. I knew he was right: if things did go wrong at Haver Field, or anywhere else in Hillston, Cuddy would take it personally. As he left, he handed me an envelope he'd found on Cuddy's desk. "Chief Mangum, Private" was typed on the front. "Probably just congratulations," he said.

As I moved back toward the Yarboroughs, I heard Carl oddly snap at Cuddy. "It's the last thing I need on top of this fucking garbage strike."

Cuddy said, "I bet it's the last thing that girl he killed needed too."

"Well, if Savile can't handle it, get some damn help."

"I have every confidence in HPD homicide."

Dina, embarrassed, started talking effusively about *Measure for Measure*. Then Carl abruptly excused himself from Cuddy and moved away to join a group of men smoking on the mansion steps. They included the current Attorney General Ward Trasker and the majority whip of the state senate. Cuddy was left walking alone.

I joined him and handed him the envelope from Zeke. Distracted, he opened it. There was nothing inside but the clipped editorial from the *Hillston Star* calling for his resignation. The paper's front-page banner was attached with the word "STAR" circled in red and a large red question mark beside it. He started to toss it in a nearby trashcan. I took it from him.

"Hey, Justin, a lot of people want me to resign. What are you going to do, sue them?"

I asked him where else he'd seen red magic marker used to send him a nasty message. Wasn't it on the label tied to the toe of G.I. Jane's corpse?

Chapter 5
Dina

In the State Dining Room, everyone circled pretty tables set with gold-rimmed plates, finding their places by the numbers on replicas of the gold Raleigh Medal sticking out of garlands of tiny roses, gardenias, and miniature orchids. Because of Lee's absence, I'd been moved to Table One with Cuddy, Andy, the Yarboroughs, a college president, and today's other prizewinner, Mrs. Boodle. Fulke Norris and his wife were at Table Two with other former Raleigh Medal winners; everyone ignored the fact that the Hillston police officers who'd arrested their son were seated only five feet away.

It was an elegant meal. Despite Bubba's disparagement, the "drama queen" banquet coordinator had prepared a dinner for sixty-four that looked better organized than most military campaigns. Effortlessly, lobster bisque changed to grilled quail changed to pork medallions, champagne changed to wine to coffee, and welcoming speeches changed to raucous small talk.

Andy devoted himself mostly to Carl and Dina Yarborough. That the mayor and his wife were seated this close to the governor and that he was being this attentive suggested that Shelly Bloom of the *Sun* had heard the right rumors: Brookside was going to drop Horace DeWitt, the old party regular he'd needed in the first election, in order to offer the lieutenant governorship to Carl. (Poor DeWitt wasn't even here tonight.)

An African-American running partner would be a risky choice. But Andy loved taking chances. Some years ago, a group at the Hillston Hunt Club had founded the Carolina Polo Regulars. We had just enough players to make up a match. The first time we played, Andy got whacked in the temple with a mallet while forcing his way at a gallop between two other horses. Blood streaming down his face, he made his goal and I'd never seen him happier. Afterwards, we were in the stable grooming our horses. Mine was Manassas, the former champion that the old eccentric industrialist Briggs Cadmean had left me. Andy owned two Arabian polo ponies, bought with Lee's money. He could have bought a cavalry. Leaning into my stall, he suddenly asked, "What excites you most, Justin?"

I was brushing Manassas's black forelock past his wild watchful eye as I thought about it. "Human gifts, I guess. Talent. Beauty." Since my answer appeared to puzzle him, I asked, "How about you?"

Andy replied immediately: "Danger excites me." Manassas, as if he agreed, shook his head free and kicked out at his stall door with a foreleg. "I like upping the risks. I played Russian roulette once."

"I hope once was enough."

"Well, it takes you to a different place."

Picking Carl as his running mate wasn't as dangerous as Russian roulette, but it was certainly going to add risk to the governor's chances of winning the election next fall. Because no matter how much Hillstonians might love their mayor, this state was still crawly with bigots who'd be muttering did we really want a Yankee and a black man running North Carolina together, and what if the Yankee dropped dead?

Andy was now raising his crystal glass. "Gentlemen, we are privileged to be at the First Ladies' table tonight. To Dina, the First Lady of Hillston." He toasted her. Then he toasted the college president, "First Lady of Frances Bush College for Women." Then the wealthy widow Inez Boodle, recipient of the Virginia Dare Prize, "Our First Lady of Philanthropy." After that,

Carl toasted the absent Lee, "First Lady of North Carolina." And after that, Andy suddenly asked Cuddy if he really believed, as he had claimed to reporters this afternoon in the Cadmean Building, that there was *no* killer smart enough to get away with murder in Hillston?

Dina Yarborough said with her wry sweetness, "Do you think *you're* smart enough to murder somebody, Andy, and not get caught?"

"The Governor's *too* smart to murder somebody," Cuddy told her. "Mostly murder's for the freaked-out and dumb as dirt. The ones that are mad at their girlfriends, mad at the convenience store clerk, so high they'll shoot their own mother for the fun of hearing the gun go off. These folks have a serious, what we call today, attention-deficit, lack of impulse control type personality."

With his earnest look, Andy nodded. "We have to get rid of the guns."

"I wish you would." Cuddy smiled at him. "It won't stop people killing each other, but it sure will slow them down some."

Shimmering tiny diamonds in his brilliant white shirt, the governor leaned to include Dina in the conversation. "Planning a murder is where the brains come in."

"I'd certainly use mine if I knocked off Carl," Dina smiled.

Cuddy patted her hand. "Then don't inject him with dry cleaner fluid you borrowed from your brother-in-law. That's the kind of plan I hear about."

Dina thoughtfully sliced off a quail's wing. "But isn't the governor right? Whoever killed that girl G.I. Jane in the woods took pleasure in it. There'll always be murderous hearts out there, getting a rush from killing."

Cuddy nodded. "Yep. A few. And I'll always catch them."

"Ah," Brookside grinned. "So *no one* can get away with murder?"

"Not in Hillston they can't." Cuddy smiled back at him.

As waiters interrupted with mango sorbet, my pager beeped. It was Nancy. I stepped out into the foyer of the Governor's Mansion to return the call. A policeman (his arms crossed as if he dared anybody to challenge him) stood guarding the base of the wide cantilevered staircase that led to the private quarters above. I wondered if Lee were up there, feverish in her bed, or if Andy had lied to us about why she was skipping the banquet.

Nancy answered from her car. There'd been a riot at the Mavis Mahar concert. When the already frustrated audience was told that the star was "ill" and that her performance would have to be rescheduled, some inebriated teenagers started throwing whatever was handy down onto the field. After driving her niece home, Nancy had returned to help out the ill-equipped sheriff's deputies and university police move forty-seven thousand angry people through the exits without their killing each other.

By the time Zeke found Nancy, six people had been rushed from Haver Field to the hospital. While nobody was seriously injured, three were being held for observation. Among them was Sheriff Homer Louge himself. He'd had what might have been a mild heart attack when two teenage girls defiantly bared their breasts at him, displaying little rings in their left nipples just like, presumably, Mavis Mahar's.

"Where's Mavis?" I asked. "Is she seriously ill?"

"Don't make me laugh," snapped Nancy. "Probably still where you saw her, in the Tucson. Or try the By-Ways Bar. Danielle was crying her eyes out!"

"Find out what happened to Mavis and call me back."

"What do you care?" Nancy asked. It was a fair question.

"Just call me." I hung up.

Back at the banquet, Cuddy was being chastised by Mrs. Ward Trasker, wife of the attorney general, for "peddling" Margy Turbot as the A.G.'s replacement "before poor Ward has even started thinking about leaving."

Cuddy smiled at the small mean woman. "But SueAnne, everybody's already saying Ward's retiring after the election and you know it's gonna take him at least six months to get all that golf equipment out of his office."

Mrs. Trasker rebuked him strenuously. "Ward has given this state the best years of his life. When he heard you telling

Channel Seven how you wanted this woman judge to get his job, he couldn't believe why Channel Seven didn't ask him who *he* wanted, isn't that right, Ward?" She turned to her husband for confirmation. "You couldn't believe it, could you, Ward?"

The stocky Trasker, purple-splotched from embarrassment or rage or both, grunted non-committally and informed her in a warning way, "Captain Mangum has every right in the world to his own opinion, now you know that, SueAnne, why don't you pass me a little more butter?"

Dina leaned between them. "I think all Cuddy was trying to do was express his admiration for Margy Turbot, and if you got to know her I bet you'd like her too."

"Hmmph," said Mrs. Trasker with a smile as greasy as the butter her husband was stabbing into his roll.

Seated on Cuddy's other side was the Frances Bush College president, who wore a floor-length plaid kilt, a scoop-necked sweater and a velvet jacket, as if in formal imitation of a school-girl's uniform. She also came to Cuddy's defense, commending him for supporting a female candidate like her close friend Judge Turbot in so traditionally male a position as State's Attorney General. He rewarded the president for her support by frequently re-filling her wineglass. Staring at it, she suddenly launched into a description of a scotch-tasting party that she'd recently attended and went on at such wistful length that he finally offered to hop out to a package store and get her a bottle. I could tell the president liked him; she was unmarried (she'd made that clear), nice looking, and she loved to laugh. But if she was making a play for the police chief tonight, she was running onto a field of romantic war that had already been won by the absent first lady. I'd seen two other women defeated by that same ghostly warrior.

On my right was Inez Boodle, recipient of the Virginia Dare Prize, widow of the Hot Hat Barbecue king, a sly loud woman in her sixties with yellow-tinged bangs and a low-cut black-beaded gown that somebody should have advised her not to wear. "I know what you're thinking," she told me.

I said I doubted it.

"'Why in the world would ole Inez marry a man with a ridiculous name like Boodle?'" She guffawed robustly, throwing up her arms to express bewilderment. "I have *no* idea. That man's name was the least of his problems. I'll tell you something, Justice—"

"Justin. Justin Savile."

"Oh, right, Peggy Savile's boy. How is your poor mama?"

"Still in the hospital, but better, thank you."

"That's good. Justin, I used to tell people, when I said I married a Boodle, I meant it! Pete was loaded! I don't mean snockered either. That man loved barbecue and barbecue loved him. Why at the Hot Hats, the damn phone number spelled out HOT PIGS. He loved to make it and eat it and sell it and he sold oodles and oodles!" Her laugh rattled her ice water and I'm surprised it didn't shatter the glass.

Mrs. Boodle had received her Prize for her philanthropic support of college education, as displayed by her five million dollar gift to Hillston's Frances Bush College for Women (her alma mater) and her five million dollar gift to King's, a small African-American college in the eastern part of the state, Carl's alma mater. She merrily told Dina that if her husband Pete hadn't already dropped dead of a massive coronary while on a tour of his Hot Hat Barbecue franchises, he would have done so instantly on hearing this news, for Pete had always believed that the rise of women and black people was the source of everything that had gone wrong in America, ever since the slave Sally Hemings had seduced Thomas Jefferson. It was hearing on CNN that Sally Hemings's descendants had tried to use their DNA to get into the Monticello Society that had shot Pete's blood-pressure through the ceiling and brought on his last and fatal heart attack. The first one he had blamed on Jane Fonda.

"Go, Jane," Dina mumbled at me.

I flashed back to a red poinsettia pinned to my mother's mink when my parents came home from a neighbor's Christmas party and argued in the hall. My father had indignantly left the party because their host had tried to convince him that Martin Luther King worked undercover as a Communist agent for the Soviet Union. Had their host that night been Mr. Boodle?

Inez hee-hawed. That was Pete Boodle, all right! She remembered that Christmas party and how Fulke Norris—over there at Table Two right now—had tried to keep Dr. Savile from walking out in a huff. Pete had always refused to believe that Martin Luther King and the U.S.S.R. were both as dead as these pigs on our plates and not off plotting together to bring down America. Mrs. Boodle stabbed a pork medallion with her fork and shook it at Dina. "I wish I could slip past the pearly gates for long enough to let Pete Boodle know I gave half his Hot Hat millions to a women's school and the other half to a college named after Martin Luther King!"

Dina placidly laid her napkin on her plate, and asked, "Why in the world do you think your husband's gone to heaven?"

Mrs. Boodle stared at her a moment, then belly-laughed. "You are absolutely right! Thank you, Mina, for setting me straight."

"It's Dina," I said futilely.

Over dessert, Mrs. Boodle, who seemed to have no idea that I'd been the person to arrest Tyler Norris, told me that arresting Tyler Norris was the most "asinine, insane, and idiotic thing the Hillston police ever did." Like most people in town (particularly the well-to-do), she was sure a burglar had "panicked and shot Tyler and Linsley both," just the way Tyler's defense attorney had described. "What was his name? Rosenberg?"

"Isaac Rosethorn," said Dina. "It's so hard to keep those Jewish names straight, isn't it?"

"That's right, the Rosenbergs were that poor couple Pete blamed the Cold War on. Well, I was right there at Fulke and Mary Norris's for New Year's when Fulke got the call from Tyler that a burglar was in his house and he drove over and found him lying on the floor. Well, Mary's whole life has been one long nightmare. You know she almost burned up in a house fire. Where is that idiot waiter?"

Mrs. Boodle was more disposed to believe in Isaac Rosethorn's scenario of an interrupted robbery because two years ago she and Pete had been robbed of a portable gas grill they'd kept in their garage, and if you could be robbed on Catawba Drive, Lord knows you could be robbed in Balmoral Heights. "Hillston has gone to pieces," she announced. "Robbing and killing and cutting up strangers and chopping off their hair and their tongues." Out of patience with the missing waiter, she lit her own cigarette with a candelabrum that almost set fire to her bangs. "Not when I was a girl. We didn't put up with that kind of violence."

Dina said quietly, "Well, the last public lynching in Hillston was in 1932. And they sold postcards of it in Machlin's Pharmacy."

"Good god," gasped the college president, overhearing. "1932?"

"Would earlier be better?" Dina asked.

Mrs. Boodle frowned disapprovingly; she obviously thought it would be politer to discuss the mutilation of G.I. Jane than to bring up Hillston's racial problems in 1932. "Well, this Guess Who hates women," she told us. "So did Pete Boodle. Pete was always telling me he'd like to blow my head off just to shut me up." She suddenly squeezed my hand as if she suspected me of trying to steal her watch. "I know what you're thinking, Jordan! You wish ole Inez *would* shut up and hand you that champagne bottle you keep looking at." For the first time Mrs. Boodle had read my mind.

I was ready to go home, but at the other end of the table, Cuddy was telling the President of Frances Bush the most hilarious jokes she had ever heard. I looked at my watch (11:33) and then glanced down the long noisy row of gilt-glistening tables just as Bubba Percy walked back into the room. Something was wrong with him. He had the greenish look of a drunk back from being sick in the toilet. I watched him lean against the door wiping his hand against his usually pink sanguine face.

Then suddenly he hurried over to our table. When he squeezed past, I stood to ask him what was wrong. He ignored me, crouching behind Andy Brookside's chair, whispering in his ear. Frowning, Andy stepped away from the table. Bubba put his hand on the governor's forearm and said something else in a low intense voice. With a rapid intake of breath, Andy stared at him. Bubba nodded. Running his hand through his famous hair, Andy spoke urgently to Bubba who hurried off to the exit as Andy returned to our table, looking troubled. I wondered what unsettling news he might be going to tell us. I said, "Andy? Is Lee okay?"

"She's fine," he said distractedly. "I mean, she's not well. The flu." Then composing himself, he said he had an unexpected problem to deal with, thanked us for coming, wished each of us a cordial goodnight, and within thirty seconds had disappeared from the room.

"Was it something you said?" Cuddy asked the college president.

This set her off laughing and then into a coughing spasm. Mrs. Boodle rushed over to hit her vigorously on the back. Had Mrs. Boodle not recently given Frances Bush College for Women five million dollars, its president might have objected to these blows, or at least moved out of their way, but apparently she felt obliged to endure the violence in hopes of further donations. The Attorney General Ward Trasker stopped his wife from inviting her to join them for drinks at The Fifth Season, the overpriced resort in Hillston, and our table broke up.

Tired guests were being marshaled out of the State Dining Room by a phalanx of large men dressed in white jackets who looked like moonlighting highway patrol officers and probably were. Two of them were blockading the stairs. Maybe someone was worried that, left on our own, we'd scavenger through the Governor's Mansion slipping priceless antique bijoux into our pockets. As we passed into the foyer, Cuddy stopped suddenly, turned, and stared up the curving green-carpeted staircase leading to the Brooksides' living quarters above, as if he were dreaming of racing up the stairs like Heathcliff and carrying Lee over to look one last time out the window of her bedroom at the moors before she died of this sudden high fever.

I stopped beside him. "Cuddy?"

He didn't answer or move as the crowd stepped irritably around us. I was about to reach for his arm when abruptly, unexpectedly, Lee herself came through a door on the second floor landing and stood looking distressed at the top of the stairs. The timing and suddenness of her appearance gave me the strange sensation that Cuddy had summoned her there, purely by the intensity, the longevity, the fidelity of his desire.

"Mrs. Brookside," he called to her, "are you all right?"

Chapter 6
Lee

Lee Haver had always been an elegant, lovely woman. Even as a teenager, she had dressed in subdued colors and classic lines and worn her silver-blonde hair in a chignon, knowing even then how she would need to look as a public figure for decades to come. Nature had made her attractive and the Haver millions had done the rest. Now she wore a simple gray dress the color of her eyes that undoubtedly cost thousands of dollars. She wore a simple diamond bracelet that cost tens of thousands more.

No one else in the crowd seemed to have noticed her yet. She and Cuddy just stood there staring at each other; it was probably only a few seconds, but it felt forever to me, so heaven knows what eternities passed for each of them. I called up the stairs, "Hello, Lee. How are you feeling?"

As half a dozen other guests turned to look as well, a young woman wearing headphones by the exit rushed up to the second-floor landing where Lee was standing. Both state troopers moved to the middle of the stairs to block anyone from following her. Lee looked away from Cuddy and she smiled the way people like her are trained to smile when crowds are watching. "Justin, hello, how are you? Captain Mangum, congratulations."

There was no smile on his face. "Are you all right?" he said again.

"Much better, thank you." As the young staff worker reached

her side and reached for her arm, Lee stepped back from her and turned silently to walk across the landing and out of view.

• • •

On our drive back to Hillston, Cuddy sat quietly, his hand touching the gold medallion that hung from the bright blue ribbon. He kept staring out at the black rush of pines on the one dark stretch of old highway between Raleigh and home, the only forest that had managed so far to hold off the waiting future of plastic-wrapped tacos and discounted sweat suits indistinguishable from all the others in all the other strips girding the nation. Cuddy was staring, I assumed, into his own irrecoverable past.

I too was thinking about Andy's wife Lee, but about why she hadn't come to Cuddy's ceremony. If Lee had a fever so high she couldn't fulfill her duties as first lady (and I suspect no one knew better than Cuddy how much she was willing to sacrifice to those duties), then why was she wandering about the Governor's Mansion dressed in a cocktail dress and diamonds? And if she weren't ill, why hadn't she come to the banquet? Why had both she and Bubba looked so distressed? I thought about Andy's arrival alone in the rock star's limousine and then his abrupt departure from our dinner. There were growing rumors about strains in the Brookside marriage that Bubba denied with such pontifical sincerity to the press that they were sure the governor and his wife would divorce tomorrow if they could.

But of course, they couldn't. There was no doubt that if Mrs. Brookside left her husband before the November election, his first term as governor would be his last. Lee Haver had been the first lady of North Carolina long before she'd married the "Yankee" Andrew Brookside; she had been born into that title and (no matter what her husband did or did not do to serve the state that had adopted him), she would die with that title inscribed in gothic letters on her tomb in the fan-vaulted crypt of the Haver Mausoleum. My family the Dollards might have run North

Carolina, but the Havers had owned it for over a hundred years. Andy could not afford to lose her.

As I drove us home, I tried to talk about my sense that we were getting messages from Guess Who. I elicited not even a monosyllabic response from Cuddy. From a man who talked in paragraphs, the silence was scary. Finally I gave up and made a call from the cruiser to Etham Foster at his home. Etham said I could go pick up my Jaguar; he agreed with Cuddy—some HPD practical joker had planted the Elvis tape. And please stop calling him; he was in bed watching *The New Detectives* on A&E, and if the phone woke up his wife again she was going to make him turn off the television.

As Cuddy plainly had no interest in talking, I switched on the AM radio. The cruiser we'd borrowed was one normally assigned to a young cop on downtown surveillance and his dial was set to a rock station; I was surprised by the surge I felt when the sound came on in the middle of a long pulsing bluesy refrain sung by Mavis Mahar, whose voice I recognized instantly although I'd never heard the song before. It was the same strong melodious voice, but rawer and more sensual than when she'd been singing in the Tucson. Even before the song ended in a long low groan, it was overlapped by the startling intrusion of the D.J. "That was 'I Want You More' by the First Lady of Rock'n'Roll, Five-Time Grammy Winner Mavis Mahar! Mavis, they sure wanted you more at Haver Field tonight! Fans in the hospital! Too bad you couldn't make it! *Mavvvvisssss*, where *arrrrrre* you?!"

Cuddy lowered the volume. "People in the hospital? Call the desk!"

I explained what I'd already learned from Nancy and Zeke about the scuffle at the stadium, including the sheriff's "heart attack." I said that I'd decided not to bother him with it during the Raleigh Medal banquet. Cuddy exploded: "Don't you *ever* withhold HPD business from me again! Somebody sticks a mike in my face and wants to know my take on the riot at Haver Field tonight and I go, 'Duh, I was off gettin' a medal for law enforcement so I told them to hold my calls about any riots going on in the town I'm supposed to be enforcing the law in!'"

"Man, it's like Wendy Freiberg said!" (Wendy was the documents examiner at the North Carolina Bureau of Investigation who'd done the Guess Who analysis for us.) "You get so twisted about bad news these days, it's like you've got poison ivy in your shorts."

"Well, tell Wendy Freiberg to drag her mind off my private parts and go find me some *good* news, go find out who wrote that label tied around G.I. Jane's damn toe asking you to bring her to me!" He impatiently waited for the HPD dispatcher to call him back.

"You know what you need, Cuddy? A wife and a life."

"Hey, worry about your own wife, not mine. I've got a job, a thankless job, a job where my division heads don't bother to tell me things. I don't have time for a life. Don't miss the turn."

The squad car radio buzzed back with word that Sheriff Homer Louge's apoplectic reaction to the breast-baring teenage girls had caused no lasting damage. The five injured fans had been dismissed from the hospital with minor injuries and the Haver University provost was already out looking at the vandalism inflicted on the stadium. Apparently the injured fans were going to sue the university and the university was going to sue Mega Records, who had sponsored the concert, and Mega was going to sue Mavis Mahar. Cuddy sighed, "Maybe I'm going to sue God for the Fall of Man. It's caused me serious and irreparable emotional distress to have the sins of the fathers visited on me in downtown Hillston when I could be lying around Paradise munching on pomegranates and philosophizing with angels."

At least he was talking again.

• • •

Cuddy's home, River Rise, is a post-modernist village of ninety cheerfully painted clapboard two-storied apartments strung together in tiers along a ridge above the Shocco River.

Each apartment has curving concrete walks divided by busy landscaping, with patios separated by redwood fencing and with narrow cement balconies, in some of whose heavy glass sliders moisture had already condensed, blurring the view. All it had to recommend it when Cuddy moved in was that it was brand new, and now it didn't even have that. To me, the best thing about it was its huge vista of pine forest and the willow-banked river below. But as he says, "You like old."

Until recently, whenever even good friends came to Cuddy's door, his ancient little white poodle Martha Mitchell (nearly blind) would block their path in a frenzy of barking until she recognized your scent and even then she would usually bite you. But now Martha was deaf and lame as well as blind, and tonight when Cuddy turned on the lights, she barely moved her head off the pink satin bedding near the heating vent that he called her boudoir.

"Hey Martha, look at this," he told her, placing the gold Raleigh medallion down beside her wobbly head. "I won this for doing some good." She lifted her dirty white frizzy head (he'd named her for her resemblance to Martha the deceased wife of Nixon's attorney general John Mitchell, and claimed that the soul of that maligned and discredited lady had transmigrated to his dog). Sniffing the Raleigh medal without interest, Martha turned away. He stroked her black nose softly. "Honey, you are so right. We got to remember that virtue is its own and its only reward." He turned to me. "My Ph.D. didn't impress her either."

Cuddy listened to his messages. Most were congratulations on the Raleigh Medal. Three were about the trouble at Haver Field; one from a reporter wanting a comment. Cuddy glared at me. One was from our chief county prosecutor, District Attorney Mitchell Bazemore, wanting to double-check some details about the Norris homicide case that he needed for his summation at the trial tomorrow. Cuddy reluctantly phoned him back (they hate each other), and was surprisingly told by a sleepy Mrs. Bazemore that Mitch had been called out on business, she couldn't, or wouldn't, say where.

"Our Mitch out on midnight business?" mused Cuddy as he headed upstairs. "Could Mister Bible Camp have a mistress?"

"I doubt it." I stretched out in the living room on a ten-foot-long beige leather couch. The whole first floor of Cuddy's condo was a big open space with cinnamon-colored wall-to-wall carpeting, an entertainment system that took up one side of the room, big low leather furniture, and a glass coffee table as large as a single bed with two chess sets on it—one chrome cubes and one Lucite bars. Cuddy loved it all.

While he was upstairs changing (not happy unless he's in jeans), Nancy called my cell phone. She'd checked for me; nobody appeared to know where Mavis Mahar was, or at least if they did, they weren't saying, and that included the star's staff, her band, and the management of the downtown Sheraton. If she was in the hospital, it wasn't under her own name. If she'd left town, it wasn't in the Mega Records private jet still sitting at the Triangle Airport. I told Nancy to call the hospitals back and describe Mavis; had they admitted anyone who looked like her?

"Thought you didn't like rock'n'roll." She hung up.

Then, "Very funny," Cuddy shouted down from upstairs. "When'd you do this?" I heard him above me in the study between the two bedrooms.

"Do what?"

Something sailed over the stair rail, spinning to the floor below. "Stick this on my study slider."

The spiraling object landed on the glass coffee table. It was a gold glittered cardboard star about the size of a dinner plate. I picked it up; on the back was a sticker that had attached it to the glass door. "I didn't," I called up the stairs. "I haven't been over here since you ordered those horrible take-out ribs two weeks ago."

In jeans now, he leaned over the rail. "Are you sure?"

"Of course I'm sure." I ran up the open stairs and found him in the study where books filled wall-to-wall, ceiling-high shelves and spilled out into piles stacked against each other around the floor. He gestured at a small telescope on a tripod that stood near the balcony sliders pointing up at the sky beyond them. "Somebody moved this up here." Grabbing the cardboard star from me, he slapped it against the glass so that it was positioned directly in the telescope's line of vision. "The star was right there. What was your point, I like gazing at my own stardom?"

"I told you, it's not me! You didn't leave your telescope out in the middle of the room like this?"

Cuddy said he hadn't used that telescope for years; he'd bought it way back when he was dating old Briggs Cadmean's daughter, an astronomy professor, and after they'd broken their engagement he had stored the telescope in the utility room off the kitchen. He hadn't touched it since.

Together we checked through the apartment. The utility room opened onto a rear patio downstairs. Its door was unlocked, but Cuddy admitted he might have left it that way himself. I used a print kit he kept at home to dust the doorknobs; they'd been wiped. So had the telescope.

Cuddy tried to convince himself that the cardboard star was like the Elvis tape rigged in my Jaguar—a joke played by some cop at HPD, who had sneaked in to tease him about the Raleigh Medal by pasting the star up and pointing the telescope sights at it. Half the Hillston police force knew that Cuddy kept an apartment key under a potted azalea on his little brick patio. He even came up with a suspect: Sergeant Brenda Moore, who was given to practical jokes like the hidden tape recorder she'd inserted to make the water cooler scream "Take your hands off me!" whenever the faucet was twisted. When I admitted that I'd seen Brenda in the HPD parking lot as I'd parked my Jaguar there this afternoon, he took it as confirmation that she was the probable culprit behind the Elvis tape and the cardboard star both.

Back downstairs, looking into his refrigerator for wine, I said, "You may be the one with 162 I.Q., as stated in *Newsweek* four years ago," no one would let Cuddy forget this, since who but he could have given them the exact number?, "but I don't see why a jokester at HPD would bother to wipe that tape and your door knobs clean." All I could find was some Chianti. "You got any wine that's not in a half-gallon?"

He was eating cold pizza. "You don't need any wine, you already had four glasses of champagne tonight. For somebody who quit drinking years ago, that seems a little absent-minded."

"Champagne and wine aren't the same as hard liquor."

"Sure. Right."

"What are you, my mother?"

"You ought to go see your mother. Poor thing in the hospital."

"I see her every day." Cuddy's wine tasted the way it looked—economical. "I can't drink this."

"Good." As he opened a can of Coke, he shook his head mournfully. "If I'd been Peggy Savile, you'd have gone to the public schools like the rest of us, and not in a Triumph convertible either. Want some pizza?"

"In eleven years, have I ever eaten your pizza?" I poured myself a beer.

"See, spoiled." He added, "Probably Cleopatra wiped off those door knobs herself."

Cleopatra Skelton was the name of Cuddy's elderly and increasingly narcoleptic cleaning lady. Age *had* withered this Cleopatra, subjecting her to nearly as many infirmities as Martha Mitchell. She and the poodle appeared to spend most of their time napping together in front of Cuddy's fifty-five-inch television and I suspected they would go on doing so until they passed away, for Cuddy would never get rid of either. He was always rushing one or the other of them to a clinic for emergency medical treatment.

I was obliged to point out that Cleopatra didn't appear to have wiped off the kitchen counter, much less the door knobs. Saying so, I ran my hand over his stove top, which was splattered with tomato sauce.

"I spilled that this evening," he claimed. He always defended her. "I don't see why you're not crazy about Cleopatra. She's *old*."

"I do like her, she just didn't wipe these door knobs."

"She's having a rough time. Her husband's in the hospital with diabetes."

"I'm sorry to hear it. Look, somebody waltzed into your house and slapped that star on your sliders. Somebody put a tape in my car."

"It's Brenda. Last week she Saran-wrapped the men's toilet bowls."

"You think Brenda Moore sent you a *Star* clipping calling for your resignation? No way. I'm going to have that red magic marker checked."

He snorted. "What's the possible point of Guess Who's sticking a star up in front of my telescope?"

"He's saying, 'Hey, Big Star, look at what's right under your nose.'"

Cuddy was now scrubbing at his stovetop to preserve Cleopatra Skelton's reputation. "What's right under my nose besides you?"

Suddenly, the doorbell rang with a manic impatience so shrill that even Martha heard it and raced angrily barking at the noise, driven by outrage beyond the pain of rheumatism; as I opened the door, she lunged at Bubba Percy's tuxedo leg. But Bubba was already so upset he didn't even react. Still sallow faced, he now looked disarrayed as well, his bright-green flowered vest unbuttoned, his wavy auburn hair flattened with sweat and tangled on his forehead, a sight I don't think I'd ever seen, for Randolph Prewitt Percy would stop to comb his hair even in the middle of our basketball games. "What are you doing here?" he brusquely asked me as he pushed past.

"No, that's my line. Your line is, 'I'm sorry to bother you at...'" I looked at my watch. "At one-fifteen in the morning but...But?'" I stopped him with a hand on his ruffled shirt; it was damp with perspiration, although the night was almost chilly after the early evening rain.

The press secretary's voice was hoarse. "Cuddy? I gotta talk to you."

Cuddy walked quickly from behind the kitchen counter. He'd known Bubba a long time. "What's wrong?"

I said, "Is this about the Brooksides?" The truth is, I

wondered if Lee was going public with a decision to leave Andy, if that's what all the whispering and sudden departure had been about, if she and Andy had had a sudden break-up. If so, there went the election.

Reaching for my beer, Bubba took a long gulping swallow. "I've got a big problem. I need help."

Cuddy stared at him. "What problem?"

Bubba sat down on the couch, pulled off his chartreuse tie, and threw it on the coffee table. "I'm putting my nuts in your hand here."

Cuddy snorted. "That's the kind of help I'm just not prepared to give, pretty as you are, Bubba."

He ignored the crack. "You know the rock star? Mavis Mahar?"

Cuddy walked around the big glass coffee table to face him. "Yeah? I heard she didn't show tonight at Haver. You know what happened to her?"

Bubba looked up, rolled the can of beer across his forehead. "She's dead."

Chapter 7
Agnes Connolly

I'd seen Mavis Mahar in person for less than an hour of my life, yet I felt loss sweep over me so strongly that I had to sit down. I reminded myself that thousands who'd never seen her at all would, at the report of her death, mourn as if they'd lost a loved one. And I suppose they had. On television tomorrow, there'd be an orgy of bereavement. When stars die suddenly it's as if they give us our chance to grieve over Death itself, at how fast it can come and come too soon, at how much it can rob us of grace. I saw the Irish singer leaping perfectly through the morning mist into lake water. I heard her voice flying toward me like a bird of paradise.

"I don't understand why nobody called me about this!" Cuddy was griping to Bubba. "Car accident?"

The big redhead laughed without humor. "Accident would have been better."

Cuddy, flipping channels on his muted television, wasn't much interested. "Overdose?"

Bubba rubbed the cool beer can against his forehead. "Shot herself. In the head."

His words brought me to my feet. "Mavis Mahar? I don't believe it. Bubba, is this a sick joke?"

"Right, Justin, I made it up for fun."

"How do you know?" He just stared at me until I went over and shook him by the shoulder. "How do you know!"

Cuddy turned from the news, fixing hard blue eyes on the press secretary. "Talk to us, Bubba. Why is this *your* problem?"

When Bubba looked up—his long lashes wet, the smug irony usually in the corner of his mouth wiped away—two things came clear. One, he'd seen her dead body. No secondhand report could have shaken him like this. And two, I knew why he needed help. I flashed to the limousine waiting outside the Tucson for the rock star, then to the same license plate on the same black car as it sped away from the cul de sac at the State Capitol after the governor had leapt out of it. Then I saw the look on Brookside's face when Bubba was whispering to him at the banquet.

I turned to Cuddy. "Andy," I told him. "Andy Brookside. That's why it's Bubba's problem." When Cuddy looked puzzled, I pointed at Percy. "Right, Bubba? The governor's mixed up with her?"

Bubba glanced at me, alarmed at my knowledge, but finally he nodded, dropping his sweaty auburn head into his long pink fleshy hands. "Fuckin' unbelievable. You heard too."

"Just a guess." Strangely I felt a bone-sharp reluctance to believe that this woman who had called so seductively to me across the empty space of the Tucson bar this afternoon should have gone the same evening to a tryst with Andrew Brookside. How involved were Mavis and the governor if what happened at their meeting had been so emotionally distressing that afterwards she'd taken her own life? Had whatever happened between them led to Lee's not showing up at the Gala? I nudged Bubba's foot. "Was it Andy who found her body?"

"No! God, no!" Bubba took a breath and his press secretary voice emerged. "The governor is not romantically involved with Mavis Mahar. But he did visit her briefly at her hotel suite this afternoon. I mean, her suicide didn't have anything to do with the governor, let's get clear on that." He added with real despair, "I admit the timing sucks." As Bubba frowned earnestly at Cuddy, I watched him fighting to keep desperate sincerity in his voice. "I hate what I'm asking, but I *am* asking, Cuddy, I'm gonna beg you—"

Cuddy scoffed, "I don't like it already—"

But Bubba hurried ahead. "Can't we keep the governor out of this? It's gonna be a media circus. They get a whiff of Andy and the re-election's fucked!" The thought seemed to make Bubba's hand shake, sloshing beer on his ruffled wrist.

"Does Mrs. Brookside know about them?" Cuddy looked through his glass sliders at the black moonlit woods as he asked. "Is that why she wasn't at the banquet?"

Bubba turned prim. "She had the flu."

With a growl Cuddy stalked over to the kitchen counter, lobbed his Coke can into his recycle bin. "Can't that idiot ever learn anything?"

He was referring, I assumed, to Andrew Brookside's past recklessness with women. Shortly before his first gubernatorial election, the opposition had made a videotape of Brookside having sex with an exotic "model" whom the opposition had hired for just that purpose. His opponent, my cousin Julian Dollard, was mortified by the existence of the smut tape, having had no idea what his campaign workers had been up to on his behalf. (Julian had almost no ideas about anything.) Being a gentleman, and vulnerable himself because these same campaign workers had also supplied with stolen guns a team of white extremists who'd killed a man, Julian had suppressed the tape.

A month later, Andy beat him in the governor's race by a margin of 45 percent to 41 percent; the other 14 percent voting for a television evangelist. Julian was doubtless much happier playing golf all day than he would have been running North Carolina, and Andy was doing a fine job. Over the years, I had heard no rumors of any further womanizing on his part, and all of us had assumed that his near-misses in the past had taught him if not temperance at least discretion. Obviously not.

Cuddy came back to Bubba with a paper towel for the spilled beer. "How much does the press already know? What's on the news?" He pointed at the television. Actually what was on the muted late local news right then was not about Mavis Mahar at all (which suggested they didn't know about it yet), but a clip from the Governor's Gala at the capitol. In it, Carol Cathy Cane was interviewing Andy Brookside and looking at him as if she wished they were in a small bed on a long cruise together.

Bubba said, "Nothing's on the news and if it stays that way I'll take Jesus on my knees as my personal savior."

Cuddy grabbed his phone. "Okay, Bubba, I'll see where things are. Who took the call at HPD? Who went out there? Anybody you knew? When'd she go to the morgue?"

The press secretary's jaw dropped. "*Nobody* went out there. I fucking found her by myself and you're the first person I've told! I went over there after the banquet had finished up to see if she was okay. I just about fell over her body and then I came straight here to you. I didn't call anybody. She's still out there."

Now it was our turn to stare at him. It had not occurred to either of us that Mavis Mahar's suicide wasn't already in the hands of professionals, her body already in the city morgue. Appalled, Cuddy actually ran at Bubba. "You didn't call 911?" He speed-dialed his telephone. "You didn't get her an ambulance??!!"

Bubba peered hopelessly down at the bows on his patent-leather pumps. "What for? She blew her fuckin' head off! She's dead, she looked like something in a freezer, she's dead!"

Cuddy had the receiver at his ear, already connected to HPD. "*Where? Where is she, Bubba?*"

"The Fifth Season, you know, North Cove. A bungalow." Bubba's teeth started chattering. "Either of you got any Valium or Xanax?" He was now shaking so hard he had to hold his arms.

"Here. It's shock." I threw Martha Mitchell's plaid lap robe at him. But lying there blind in her cushioned bed, the old poodle kept up a horrible growl until I pulled the robe back off Bubba, returned it to her, and tossed him instead the Tarheels blanket lying on Cuddy's TV-watching chair. Bubba tucked it under his chin as if he were going to ask somebody to shave him.

I said, "What was Mavis Mahar doing at The Fifth Season? Nancy told me the whole entourage was staying downtown at the Sheraton."

Bubba muttered into the sheet, "The Fifth Season was secret; she'd rented it under the name Agnes Connolly. I don't know why. She was dead when I got there, Justin. It's not like I left her there and she was alive!"

Cuddy was telling the on-duty supervisor to rush an ambulance and patrol officers over to The Fifth Season. He said we had a suicide; he didn't say whose, just that he wanted the victim's room sealed off as fast as possible. While he was talking, I crowded Bubba on the immense leather couch. "What time was it really," I asked him, "when you went over to The Fifth Season and saw her dead? It was way earlier than you said, wasn't it?"

Burrowed to the nose in the blanket, Bubba turned his back with a truculent shrug. "No, just before I drove over here. What a waste, man.... Though they didn't really know each other well, the governor will be shocked and saddened when I call him," he added as a sort of trial press release.

Cuddy yelled at him from the phone, "What's the bungalow number?"

"Eight. The one down by the lake."

I kept at Bubba. "You're telling me that right after you saw her dead, you drove straight over here?" I looked at my watch.

"Yeah." His nose twitched and he rubbed at it angrily. He was lying.

"You sure you didn't tell Andy at the banquet tonight, around 11:30? I saw you come back in, looking green in the face, and you hauled Andy out of there. You knew she was dead then, didn't you?" I shook him.

"What's with you, Justin?"

"You just walk over her body and drive back to the Governor's Mansion for some pork medallions? Jesus!" I shoved him away from me.

He muttered something obscene at me.

"Don't fuck with us, Bubba," I yanked him around to face me. "You not only won't get any help with your 'problem,' you'll spend some unpleasant time where there won't be any mirrors to comb your hair in."

"Back off, Savile." He jerked away from me again, huddling with my beer behind the Tarheels blanket. "It's freezing in here!"

They'd transferred Cuddy. Now he was ordering a team from the ID section to hurry to the resort.

I stepped around Bubba so he'd have to look at me. "Why'd you go to The Fifth Season to see Mavis Mahar?"

"To find out why she'd missed her concert."

"What do you care why she missed her concert? And how'd you know about this 'retreat' if it was so secret? You over there to check on her for Andy? Andy having an affair with her?"

He shook his head vehemently. "He knew her casually, from a few fundraisers."

"Yeah sure, Bubba."

I heard Cuddy on the phone now to Dick Cohen, the medical examiner, waking him up.

Bubba faced me. "I swear. I'd gotten word she'd skipped out on her concert at Haver. None of her people could locate her, so I told Andy. That's what you saw me doing at the banquet. Then afterwards, I thought I'd go check on her."

"I repeat, what's her skipping a concert to you or Andy?"

"Andy facilitated Haver's letting Mavis sing in the stadium. They were worried there'd be problems. He felt responsible."

I said, "Bullshit." He glared at me. "You hop in your car past midnight to check on this woman all the way out at The Fifth Season just because she's a political acquaintance of the governor's and he's looking out for Haver University?" No answer. "If Mavis Mahar was already dead, how'd you get into her bungalow?'"

He grumbled into the Tarheels wrap.

"What?"

"The door was open."

"Rock stars don't leave their doors open."

"Well, it was. But I was figuring she'd let me in."

"Even though you and Andy didn't know her very well?"

"Don't start with me, Savile." He stirred himself into indignation. "Look, I could have just gone home and crashed and kept my mouth shut."

"You haven't told anybody? You didn't tell the governor?"

He looked away from me. "No, nobody."

Cuddy was holding the door open, "Let's go. "

I kicked Bubba to his feet.

We sped along the Old 28 in our borrowed cruiser, this time with siren and barlight flashers, on our way to the northern shore of Pine Hills Lake. Cuddy's apartment was on the opposite side of town; the ID team and the M.E. would get there sooner than we would. Bubba perched forward in the back seat, fingers squeezed into the wire mesh that separated us, insisting that he hadn't done anything wrong, and that if I threatened him with jail again he'd have my badge. He represented the governor of this state for fuck's sake. This was a suicide by Mavis Mahar, a world-famous recording artist; this wasn't some cheesy carhop mattress-banger ODing on a big bottle of discount aspirin because some poonhound with a Kmart franchise had gone back to his wife.

Cuddy wheeled around in his seat. "Bubba, shut up. We ask you a question, you answer it, you don't do anything else." There was something in Cuddy's face that scared even the impervious Percy because at least for a while he did exactly that. Not that his answers to Cuddy's questions bore much relation to the truth. He persisted in his claim that the governor and the rock star had been no more than political acquaintances with a shared affinity for saving wildlife and housing victims of ethnic cleansing. His press secretary voice had a syrupy sincerity to it that made him sound strangely like Ronald Reagan. "Well, what Andy and Mavis shared was all the causes they were both committed to and that's all they shared."

Cuddy said, "Bubba, don't practice on us. I swear I'll book you for leaving the scene. Was Brookside alone with her in that bungalow?"

Bubba admitted that the governor had dropped by Mavis's Fifth Season suite alone, briefly, twice. Yesterday afternoon, to say hello. Was he responsible for the star's hour-late arrival at her first Haver concert? Absolutely not. But the governor had been concerned about her not showing up at her second concert and he'd asked Bubba to go check on her.

Cuddy asked why Miss Mahar would share with a casual acquaintance like the governor (and his press secretary), the address of her secret hideaway. Bubba shrugged; Mavis was friendly and unpredictable. She had once given a Cartier watch to the maid cleaning her hotel bathroom.

Cuddy nodded. "Mmmm, that does sound friendly. I'm sorry I didn't meet Ms. Mahar in time to scrub out her sink. How 'bout today? When was Brookside there today?"

The governor's second visit this afternoon had been even briefer than his first. In fact, Bubba was willing to tell us that the governor had found Miss Mahar so "inebriated" and "on edge" that he had left The Fifth Season almost immediately and had never seen her again.

Maybe it was true that Andy had left immediately. Maybe he had finally grasped the folly of spending time alone with an alcoholic diva capable of *inviting* the tabloid paparazzi to photograph her, as she had done with the congressman on the steps of the Nashville landmark. If Andy had the slightest interest in preserving his career, not to mention his marriage and presumably his self-respect, from the same media meltdown that had vaporized this politician in Tennessee, he must have known it was time to tell Mavis Mahar good-bye and god bless.

I called over my shoulder as I raced the cruiser toward the resort. "You keep saying Andy went back over there this afternoon?"

Bubba threw out vaguely, "Yeah, three, four...."

I glanced in the rear view mirror. "Make it earlier or later, Bubba."

"What are you talking about?" he snarled.

Cuddy also peered at me inquisitively. I checked the press secretary's face in the mirror as I said, "I'm talking about my seeing Mavis Mahar in downtown Hillston at three o'clock. In the Tucson, entertaining the kitchen staff with country songs. She was still there at quarter-to-six."

Cuddy, who was eating some of the cheese crackers he carried in his pocket, wanted to know why I'd been hanging out in the Tucson bar from three to quarter-to-six. I said I hadn't been hanging out. Walking home for my keys, I'd seen a limousine at the bar door and had wondered what such a car was doing at a place like that. Mavis was inside. The car was still there when I drove past three hours later.

"Her limo?" he asked.

I said I didn't know whose limo it was, but the one waiting for Mavis Mahar outside the Tucson had the same license plate as the one that had delivered Governor Brookside—late—to the Governor's Gala tonight.

Bubba's throat noises grew increasingly violent; this one sounded like he was being garroted. "That's not true."

I nodded at him in the mirror. "Yes, it is. The plate number is BAC 5768. It wasn't the official state limo, which is NC 1. It was a private car. By the way, Bubba, I've noticed your license plate too. RPP 241. Cute. Randolph Prewitt Percy. Two for one. Two what for one?"

Bubba mumbled. "Leave me alone."

Cuddy twisted around to say to Bubba, "Start over. Try the truth."

"I'm telling you the truth. I drove all the way over to your place to tell you the truth."

"Bubba, you wouldn't drive to River Rise at one A.M. to tell me I'd won the Nobel Prize unless we had a deal to split the money. There's something you can't handle, which is why you need me to keep Brookside out of it. Otherwise, you'd have stepped over Mavis's body and let that maid with the Cartier watch find her in the morning."

"I'm trying to do the right thing," he whined.

Cuddy replied with his sardonic snort. "You don't have a clue what folks trying to do the right thing do when they walk in on a woman who's shot herself. They call 911. They hang around 'til an ambulance gets there."

"You're police, I came to you. Can I have one of those crackers?"

Cuddy said the packet wouldn't fit through the mesh. "So

what puts Brookside too close to wiggle out of? She leave a note blaming him for this?"

Bubba gagged loudly. "Oh Jesus fuck, I hope not!"

Cuddy nodded at me. "Well, I guess it's not that."

I said, "Maybe somebody saw Andy with her there tonight."

Cuddy watched Bubba. "Maybe that's why the maid got the watch."

Bubba turned sullen. "I'm not answering any more hostile questions."

At that moment, I was jackknifing into the turn for The Fifth Season Resort, whose stone gateway was so discreet that it was almost impossible to see it until it was too late. I cut the siren and slowed down enough to flash my badge out the window at the security guard. He waved us through with such a lack of surprise that Cuddy said, "Our folks already got here."

We drove past the main house of the resort; despite the late hour, lights glowed from the windows and its large parking lot was filled with luxury cars. We could even hear a group of people laughing on the verandah. Obviously, they didn't know that one of their fellow guests had killed herself, or if they'd heard, they didn't care.

A decade ago, a hotel-resort like The Fifth Season would have been inconceivable only five miles from Hillston, North Carolina. But as soon as it opened, would-be cosmopolites, looking for the rich life in a hurry, booked every room before the Frette sheets even went on the Biedermeyer sleigh beds. Now reservations need to be made a year in advance. That's how fast new money has come to our area. In The Fifth Season, at an exorbitant fee, the middle class can live for a few luxurious days the way glamorous people presumably live (according to shelter magazines) all the time. The main house had lobbies and bars that mimicked an English country manor and offered guests an anglophilic fantasy of convivial cocktails with Lord Title and Lady Hyphen. There were dozens of deep soft plaid and striped armchairs beside dozens of glossy end tables and round tables and gaming tables, on top of which were hundreds of china pugs and porcelain grenadiers and leather hat boxes. On the green lacquered walls hung nineteenth-century oils of nobody's ancestors in particular.

Bermuda might have been a more fitting site than Pine Hills Lake for the resort's crescent beach with its imported pink sand. The huge lake had never been as exclusive as my great-grand-parents would have liked, and now it was even less so: most of the big private houses on the north cove, with their gazebos and hundred-year-old trees, had to look over at the south cove's lit-tle summer rentals with their aluminum boats tied to rotted wood poles and their tether balls hung from poles on scruffy lawns. But The Fifth Season had completely blocked any view of the south cove with fast-growing evergreens. Hidden in those trees were pink plastered, tile-roofed bungalows dotted about the ten private acres—many with their own pools and hot tubs. These bungalows in the pines provided the sort of sumptuous protected privacy needed by people like Mavis Mahar.

Bubba directed us along the clandestine gravel drive to Bun-galow Eight on so dark and convoluted a lane that, as I swung into the last turn, I nearly hit a black Lincoln sedan I didn't expect to see there. In fact, none of us—and that includes Bubba in the back seat muttering "What the fuck?"—expected what we ran into. As Cuddy had predicted, one of our HPD squad cars had already arrived on the scene, but it was a latecomer. Parked between it and the bungalow, five other official cars sat helter-skelter under the landscaped trees. On a terrace beside the bun-galow, tall young men milled aimlessly around beneath outdoor lights. They looked as if they'd been playing basketball when somebody had suddenly run off with their ball. I recognized two deputies from the sheriff's office.

"Okay," said Cuddy. "What's going on, Bubba?"

The press secretary banged his head on the mesh between him and the front seat. "You think I know? Jesus Christ, fuckin' Barbara Walters could be in there taping! Somebody called the cops. And it wasn't me."

It wasn't the Hillston cops they'd called either. It was higher up. Yellow tape with the Haver County Coroner's seal on it crossed the front of Bungalow Eight. Under a small covered entryway, wearing the same too-tight tuxedo in which he'd been squirming earlier tonight at the Gala, stood Ward Trasker, the attorney general of the state. With him in the open door was Hillston's district attorney, the strenuously virile and fervently moralistic Mitchell Bazemore, a courtroom warrior who was always asking for the death penalty and usually getting it. Seeing Mitch there was a surprise. I'd never known him to visit a suicide scene, yet here he was at two in the morning far from home checking out Mavis Mahar's death. Clearly this was the "business" that the D.A. had already been called away on when Cuddy had spoken with his wife.

And that meant Mitch had been called away long before Bubba arrived at Cuddy's, and that meant somebody had told Mitch about Mavis Mahar long before Bubba claimed to have been the first person to find her body, and that meant that Bubba was lying about the time he'd found it. But we already knew Bubba was lying. What we didn't know was who had called Mitch and told him to come out here. The look on Bubba's face suggested strongly that he wasn't to blame. In fact, I'd say he was more upset to see who was there than we were.

Chapter 8

All the King's Soldiers

Cuddy jumped out of the patrol car and hurried toward Nancy Caleb-White as she ran from her cruiser. She was shouting, "I heard it on the dispatch so I came out. Nothing I could do, Chief—"

Cuddy asked her, "Our ID team inside? And where's Dick?" (Dick Cohen, our medical examiner.)

"They sent him back. And they sent the ambulance back. They said they already took Mavis away." Nancy shook her head. "I swear, they'd sealed the whole place and told us to back off, how they're handling it and we're out of our jurisdiction, so when our ID guys got here, they just turned around and left, and me and Roid were waiting for you!" Nancy gets hyped when she meets resistance. "They won't let us in. Right, Roid?"

Detective Sergeant John Emory ran toward us. "Right, I tried, Chief," he called. "But the attorney general's here!"

The word "Roid" had long ago lost its origins (it was short for Hemorrhoid as well as a play on "Emory"). Nancy had given John the nickname in his early days at HPD. She said she'd never met anyone so anal as this bookish middle-class African-American with a military school background. He and Nancy were better friends now, and both passionately loyal to Cuddy Mangum, the only police chief under whom they'd ever served. Nancy added eagerly, "But we told them you were coming, Chief, and you weren't gonna take their shit."

"Who's them?" Cuddy asked, still moving toward the bungalow door. Bubba, by sprinting ahead, was already inside. "Who
sealed off the scene? Who brought the coroner in?"

Roid, in an immaculate taupe linen suit with perfectly knotted chestnut tie, stopped himself from standing at attention as he
answered. "Sheriff Louge is here. He says it's county business.
D.A. Bazemore came with the coroner. I don't know why Ward
Trasker's here."

"Any press?"

"Not yet."

I asked, "And the body's definitely gone?"

"Way before we got here."

Cuddy patted Emory's shoulder. "Back the press off if they do
show. Radio the ID guys, tell them to turn around, come back.
Call Dick Cohen too. And Nance, get me a timetable, I want to
know exactly who showed when."

Fiercely improvisational, insubordinate, and slapdash, Nancy
may have had trouble with hierarchy, but there was no one better
one-on-one in the ranks; everybody liked her. Hurrying over to
the nearest sheriff's deputy now, she threw her arm around him.
"Hey Frank, how you doing, buddy?" I could hear her starting in
about how she'd tried to take her niece Danielle to the Mavis
Mahar concert tonight and how Danielle was in tears, and now
wait'll she had to tell Danielle that Mavis was dead! So why'd
they bring all these big shots over on a suicide anyhow?

Cuddy called me away, "Justin, get in there, okay?"

I ran to keep up with him.

At the bungalow door, D.A. Mitchell Bazemore was blocking
our way. He showed us his biceps folded over his chest. Mitch lifted
weights in his office and kept his shirtsleeves rolled high so everybody could follow the results. He and Cuddy clashed all the time.
Mitch blew out the words, "Mangum, what're you doing here?"
Perhaps he pumped so much iron he breathed that way without
thinking. "We've got a suicide and the sheriff's handling it."

Cuddy looked around, then mildly asked, "How's the sheriff
doing that, Mitch, when he's in Haver Hospital in ICU?"

"Well obviously Homer was discharged," Mitch addressed his remark to me as if I'd been the one who'd challenged him; he disliked me more than he did Cuddy. Once he'd oddly told me—after I'd been employed by the Hillston Police Department for twelve years—"At least Mangum works for a living." I suppose it was an uninformed jab at my family background (he thought we were rich), and what he really meant was, "At least Mangum *has* to work for a living." The D.A. confused class with wealth—often the case with those who lack the former.

Cuddy was peering around the bulging district attorney in order to see into the room as Mitch added in the repetitive way habitual with him, "The sheriff's department will deal with this. This is outside Hillston limits."

"Actually, it's not." Cuddy shook his finger in a teacherly way at the D.A.'s nose. "Actually The Fifth Season has a Hillston R3 zone and a City of Hillston registered liquor license." (I'm always amazed that Cuddy knows these kinds of details. But, as I say, he loves the town; it's the world to him.) "So it's HPD business, I do believe. And it's a big fucking stick of dynamite that I don't think we want Homer Louge blowing up in our faces."

Mitch puffed out annoyance. "Don't curse at me, Mangum. What's there to blow up? We've got a simple suicide."

"You've got a crowd, Mitch, is what you've got." In the room were two state troopers, a young field agent from the State Bureau of Investigation, whom I knew to be the county coroner's nephew, and two deputies who'd followed us inside and were huddled around Sheriff Louge. Cuddy waved at Attorney General Ward Trasker across the room, now urgently insisting on something to Bubba Percy. Bubba didn't look happy. Signaled to leave by Trasker, the state troopers stepped through the french doors to a secluded swimming pool that I could see lit up beyond the patio. Once outside, they stood gazing at the water as if they'd love to jump in it.

Cuddy started jotting the names of the people there in a little spiral notepad he always carried with him. As he did, he asked Mitch Bazemore, "So, if it's no problem and if the sheriff's handling everything, what's a Bureau agent doing here, and state troopers, not to mention the attorney general, not to mention you, Mitch? Your wife said you were out. But she didn't say you were out here in the woods, way past the midnight hour."

I smiled at the district attorney. "Yeah, why *are* all you people here?" He couldn't control his eyes and they flicked over to Ward Trasker and back.

That chain of command was obvious. Who else but a high-ranking man like Attorney General Trasker could have brought so many different state officials to an unreported suicide in a private hotel suite in the middle of the woods after midnight? But who had sent Trasker? Not Bubba; he wasn't that good an actor. Could Andy have called the attorney general himself?

Homer Louge, in full uniform and still wearing his white plastic hospital bracelet, heard my question and ambled over. "Y'all the ones don't need to be here," he told us, "So say good night."

Cuddy looked around at the crowd. "Homer, sorry to hear you had a heart attack—"

"No, I didn't."

"Well, you can't keep a good man down. Maybe I'm just a Mavis fan too, folks, came out here to join y'alls candlelight vigil over the body. Where is the body by the way?"

I pushed past Bazemore and Louge while they frenetically tried to read what Cuddy was writing. Cuddy followed me, still taking names.

Number Eight Bungalow was in Art Deco style and evoked a *Flying Down to Rio* set—white ceiling fans, tile floors, and lacquered cabinets. It had a living room large enough to do the carioca in, polished heart-of-pine floors, and the sort of curvy blonde and black deco furniture that Fred and Ginger might have tossed each other across in one of their finales. Except tonight it looked as if Fred and Ginger had used it instead to call the whole thing off. Chairs were knocked over, lamps broken, drawers askew. On the near wall there was a gigantic 1920s poster of Le Train Bleu steaming through the Riviera. Its glass was shattered. On the far wall there was a great deal of blood. It darkened both the floor and the hemp of a sisal rug. The chalk outline of a body drawn on the floor looked small and bleak. I tried hard not to see Mavis Mahar lying inside those lines.

Cuddy knelt down and touched the stains on the floorboards. I pointed his attention to a blood-smear streaked sideways across the plaster a foot above the baseboard. A trace of blood that looked scrubbed could be faintly seen on the wall that led to the bedroom. Cuddy called to the sheriff. "So where's Miss Mahar, Homer? Bubba claims there was a body in here, and it sure looks like he was right. Bubba, didn't you say you stopped by, saw Mavis Mahar dead on the floor and left her here, just a little while ago?" Cuddy pointed at the chalk outline. "Was this it? Body was right like this?"

Bubba mumbled back, "Why don't you talk to the attorney general here? He's your host, not me."

That seemed to be the case. Attorney General Trasker stepped in front of the sheriff and D.A. both. He started off in a friendly way with a sorrowful nod. "Cuddy, this is real sad situation we've got here. She was a big star, and this is a big loss. For some unhappy reason she held a gun to her face and pulled the trigger. Terrible thing, suicide. But these rock stars, just seems to keep happening to them, doesn't it? A flash across the sky, then they're gone." He was moving slowly through the room, picking up strewn clothes, looking behind chairs and tables. "Sheriff Louge here has things under—"

Cuddy interrupted, his arms crossed in a stubborn way I knew well. "This is a suspicious death within the Hillston city limits. Last I heard, I was chief of Hillston police." His words fought past his clenched teeth: "I'd like to know why this room doesn't even look dusted. I'd like any video and Polaroids of the body."

"There's no video," Trasker looked hard at the young NCBI agent who nodded back in agreement.

"No video? Great. That's great." Cuddy wrote in his notebook. "Who removed her body, Ward?"

Trasker nodded with mournful affability. "Well, Homer called…"

Louge said, "We had Pauley and Keene take her away."

Cuddy's eyes turned to blue ice. "Pauley and Keene? You gave her to a private mortuary? You gave a body with a gunshot wound to the head to a private mortuary before the Hillston M.E. looked at her?!"

The A.G. turned to the D.A. Mitch tightened his grip on his biceps. "Osmond Bingley examined her and released her."

Osmond Bingley was the Haver County Coroner. He was an old nepotism appointee with no training in forensic pathology, and he did whatever Mitchell Bazemore told him; he even went on wilderness hikes through the Pisgah National Forest every August with Mitch's Clean Teens for Christ Club, something Mitch's own children refused to do.

The two sheriff's deputies were now wandering around admiring the knickknacks. One of them stepped in a pool of blood.

Cuddy turned and yelled at him, "Back off, kid! Now!" The young deputy froze, looked down at the tiles where a red imprint of his shoes had followed him like the Invisible Man. Embarrassed, he stepped backwards.

Homer rubbed his gray flattop furiously. "Don't you order my boys around."

"Then stop these imbecilic ox-heads," he pointed at the sheriff's men, "from stampeding through a crime scene with no gloves on, tracking blood on the goddamn floor!" Cuddy raised his voice loud enough for the state troopers on the terrace to hear. "Ward, you want to stop looking for whatever you're looking for and tell me why you guys are even over here?" He moved closer to the A.G. "You want me to guess who sent you? Want me to guess why? Want me to start talking *real loud* about that particular individual right here and now in front of all these troopers and deputies?"

Everybody stared at him. Trasker quickly instructed the curious deputies to go join the troopers outside by the pool. Homer turned sullen when he was told to go with his men. Then the A.G. closed the french doors firmly behind them, leaving only himself, Bubba, and Mitch in the room with Cuddy and me. Trasker smiled in a queasy way. "Let's everybody calm down. I don't know why Mr. Percy here," he glared at Bubba who had opened the minibar and was pouring the little bottles of liquor he found there into a big plastic go-cup, "thought it necessary to bother you about this, Cuddy, but this is not a Hillston police matter."

"This is just a suicide," Mitchell Bazemore reminded us yet again.

Cuddy turned to him. "You came an awful long way at an awful odd time for a suicide."

Ward Trasker smiled with remarkable inappropriateness. "She was a big star. There are sensitive media issues."

"And it's even odder all of you got here in time to do all the things you've done. Because Bubba tells me he was the first person to see Mavis Mahar lying on the floor of this room in a mess of blood and that it was half-past midnight when he left her lying here and he didn't tell anybody and he drove straight to River Rise to let me know we needed to keep Andy Brookside out of it."

"Cuddy, for Christ sake!" Bubba sputtered.

"What's Mangum talking about?" Mitch's head snapped back and forth like flies were chasing him. "Why's the governor have to be kept out of this?"

It was clear that Bazemore had not been fully briefed. It was equally clear that Ward Trasker knew about the affair from the way he was furiously glaring at Bubba Percy while Mitch stared baffled at him.

Just then Bubba's cell phone rang loudly; he scurried with it to the end of the room, then with a flushed look gestured furiously to Ward Trasker to join him. Trasker looked at the phone as if it were a tarantula he was supposed to pick up and put to his ear.

Cuddy moved over beside the D.A. "Mitch, come on, don't be their patsy. You've got a room looks like a cyclone hit it, you've got a dead body with her brains smeared on the walls. That's a suspicious death, you treat it the way you would a homicide. The body goes to our M.E. at our morgue. It doesn't go to

Pauley and Keene Funeral Home! You secure the scene, you dust, you video. Look at this! Homer's Bigfoot boys slipping and sliding in blood, just like they did at the Tyler Norris house. Is that what we want?"

Cuddy was rubbing salt in a wound. Bazemore took pride in his conviction rate, but odds were that he was going to lose the Norris case, in part because his great enemy Isaac Rosethorn had successfully—and gleefully—offered proof that the state's evidence had been contaminated by the sheriff's men who'd been first on the scene.

"Come on, Mitch, do we want *another* case blown from the get-go?"

"It's a suicide." Mitch's body tightened defensively. "Ward and all these officers were already here and already told me it was a suicide when I drove over with Osmond—"

Cuddy nodded. "It was Ward who told you to bring Osmond?"

Mitch blinked, worried. "Ward wanted the body someplace safe and settled before the press got hold of the news. That made sense to me. You know what those vultures are like with celebrities. So he asked me to bring Osmond. I saw her lying there with a gun in her hand. There wasn't any question in Osmond's mind about suicide."

Cuddy's mouth twisted ironically. "Well, now, as I recall, there's rarely a question or an answer either in our county coroner's mind. Didn't he tell us John Wintergrass had drowned himself when it turned out he'd been shot four times before somebody dumped him in the reservoir?"

Mitch's thick line of eyebrows furrowed. "You think this wasn't a suicide?"

"How would I know? That's what investigations are for." Cuddy waved his arms around. "Was everything torn up like this when you got here? Has anything been removed? Besides the goddamn body?"

Mitch shook his head on its thick corded neck. "Nothing. Nobody's taken a single thing."

The A.G. Ward Trasker tried to keep an eye on me but was distracted by Bubba's handing him the cell phone. Whatever was said to him was said fast because he turned immediately purple, then handed the phone back, sat down, and put his head between his legs. While Cuddy drew Mitch into a corner and started writing down what he said, I pulled on a pair of latex gloves.

The red tulips Mavis had been holding at the Tucson lay in a wilted tangle on a dresser. The black top and black jeans I'd seen her wearing lay in a pile on the floor. Empty bottles—wine, whiskey, beer—cluttered a pale blue rug in a bay window, looking like messages floating on the sea. Someone had swept glass from a broken bottle into a neat pile in a corner. There were flamboyant clothes and bizarre jewelry all over the bed and the chairs; the strangest was a straw hat in the ribbon of whose brim was stuck a circle of small white candles.

Carefully I made my way through tangled sheets and stale room service meals into the master bathroom where a chaotic jumble of strewn make-up covered the counters. A trail of used towels led to a frosted glass shower door. I opened it. By lying on its tiled floor, I could see a miniscule thread of blood around the cap of the shower drain. Also interesting was a chunk of gouged-out grout and a big crack spidering through the tiles in the back wall of the stall. Luxury places like The Fifth Season don't let their accommodations get rundown. I gave the shower walls a careful look with a flashlight.

When I finished, Bubba was off his cell phone and hissing at the A.G. "Well, he sure as fuck didn't figure you'd invite in the National Guard! He says get all these people out of here *now*."

Trasker had a green scared look. "None of those officers know anything about this except it's a celebrity suicide."

Bubba was skeptical. "Yeah, and I don't know you were boffing your brother's wife at the Charlotte Marriott either."

Now the attorney general went dead white as Mitch and Cuddy turned to stare at him. Quickly Ward stepped out to the terrace and spoke to Louge, who started hustling troopers and deputies back through the room and sending them out to their cars with thanks for helping out, everything was under control now. Everyone but Bubba went outside to watch the exit as the puzzled lawmen drove off into the night, leaving only Nancy and Roid under the trees with the HPD forensics officers who'd just arrived. I saw our medical examiner Dick Cohen grouchily join them in his Bermuda shorts and baggy T-shirt, his long thin hairy legs as pale as they had been the day he'd first come South twenty years ago and announced that he'd never go outdoors in this heat if he could help it. Cuddy was pacing under the terrace lights, yelling at Bazemore and Trasker, while Homer Louge leaned against a pine tree and smirked. I heard Cuddy threaten Ward Trasker with a call to Channel Seven if the A.G. didn't instruct Mitch to get on the phone to the brain-dead coroner and have Mavis Mahar's body transferred immediately from Pauley and Keene mortuary to our city morgue.

As I came back into the suite, I caught Bubba crawling on the floor under the bed. He dragged out a balled-up man's rain-coat, stood casually, and draped it over his arm as if he'd walked in with it. I had no doubt that the once nice Italian coat belonged to Andy Brookside, but I pretended not to notice what Bubba was doing with it. When I touched his arm, he jumped. "Bubba, you need to straighten some things out for me. Do you know what this is all about?" I pointed at the straw hat with the candles.

He looked at it. "Jesus, I've got no idea. But Mavis was a total kookamonga. One minute she won't even wear silk because it's not fair to the worms. Next time you see her she's got on a zebra belt and ostrich feathers in her hair."

"Let's start back at the beginning. You got here, you knocked, nobody answered, and—"

"Justin, Christ, I already told you all this!"

"Tell me again. You know what they say: we can do it here or we can do it downtown."

As Bubba babbled out his story, I could tell he was simulta-neously thinking through his very messy situation and how he best might be able to get himself out of it. "So Andy had told me she'd been wasted when he saw her and I heard she'd missed her concert, so I thought maybe she'd passed out inside. I could hear her CD going when I got here. It was old blues junk. Mavis had told Andy how Janis Joplin got 'Ball 'n Chain' from this old black woman so Andy had me find her the CD—that's the kind of crap I do in my job, can you believe—so he gave it to her yesterday and that's what was on."

"Music was playing when you opened the door?"

"Yeah." Bubba pointed at a CD player on the bar. "Nobody but her would have been listening to that shit, so I went in."

I said, "I wouldn't call Big Mama Thornton 'shit.'" I looked at the CD player. The volume had been turned completely down, but the machine was actually still on and still programmed to keep repeating the Thornton *Vanguard Complete Recordings*. I turned up the volume. Thornton was wailing "Hound Dog."

Bubba snapped back into focus. "Well, hell, Justin, take the damn CD. Mavis won't be needing it anymore."

I hit "Stop." "Bubba, I've got a problem. I bet you know what it is. The way you described things to Cuddy and me is not the way things looked when we got here. You agree?" He kept his eyes on his go-cup cocktail. "Now you said the lights were off when you walked in?"

He folded the raincoat over twice, but not before I saw the bloodstain on its liner. "But the bedroom light was on. That was enough to see her."

"Propped up and facing the front door so you could see her face?"

He started for the patio again. "Stop bugging me about this."

Grabbing his arm, I pulled him over to the chalk outline. "Bubba, come on." I pointed down at the floor. "This isn't even where you saw her, is it?" He just glared at me. "And where was the gun?"

"The gun?"

"If she shot herself, there was a gun, right, Bubba?"

He flushed. "Of course there was a gun. It was, yeah, I guess it was lying on the rug somewhere."

"Not in her hand?"

"I don't know."

"What did it look like?"

He stared at me. "Like a gun. How should I know?"

"Big? Small? Black? Gray?"

He thought. "I don't remember."

"What was she wearing?"

Bubba flinched and chewed at his lip. "I'm not sure."

"Clothes? Naked?"

"I don't remember! Leave me alone!"

Voices rose. Cuddy's two ostensible superiors, the Haver County district attorney and the state's attorney general, barged back inside with him, all arguing loudly. Cuddy was shaking his cell phone at them, saying that this was a Hillston case and he was the chief of the Hillston police, and if Bazemore and Trasker didn't back up and back off, he'd go straight to CeeCee Cane at Channel Seven. He'd apparently wormed out of the terrified NCBI agent (Ted Bingley, the coroner's nephew) that Ted had taken Polaroids of the scene and before Trasker could stop him, the young agent had handed them over to Cuddy. Cuddy now passed them angrily to me. There were only two shots of the body, both poorly done from the same angle. Mavis had a large raincoat over her that covered her head, but her legs and arms looked bare. She lay where they'd drawn the chalk outline, on her stomach with her arm outflung. There was a small silvery gun in her right hand.

I handed the pictures back to Cuddy. "I thought Mitch said nothing was moved from the scene besides the body."

Bazemore yelled at me, "Nothing's been removed from this scene! Absolutely nothing but the corpse! What do you think, public officials are robbing a dead woman?"

"Well, that too," I nodded. "Because a while ago I saw Deputy Eddie Boggs walk off stuffing a gold scarf of Miss Mahar's in his pocket. But what I more had in mind was, if Mavis Mahar shot herself, where's the gun?"

Chapter 9

Dermott Quinn

It is axiomatic that suicides do not dispose of their weapons after the fact, and certainly not after they've been photographed dead holding the weapons. Nevertheless, a thorough search produced no gun anywhere in Bungalow Eight. Mitch assumed it had been bagged before he arrived. Ward Trasker called in Homer Louge who said he'd seen a gun in the victim's hand but couldn't say where it was now. The attorney general and the district attorney accused the sheriff of allowing an underling to remove the suicide weapon from the premises; they did so with such vehemence that I was convinced neither of them did know where the gun was. After they finished blaming Homer, they called in everybody who was left—none of whom had even been inside the place until that moment—and blamed them. Then Homer, Ward, and Mitch all three turned on Bubba Percy and accused him of removing the gun for obscure reasons of his own.

Bubba indignantly denied having taken the weapon. In fact, he now confessed that he hadn't gotten within fifteen feet of the dead woman and wasn't sure if he'd noticed a gun at all. I forced him to look at the Polaroids of the body and he turned green.

Cuddy was advising Mitch to call Pauley and Keene mortuary to see if they'd taken a weapon along with them in their goddamn van. Or call the goddamn half-wit Osmond Bingley—

maybe the coroner had kept the gun as a souvenir. The young NCBI agent mumbled rather wistfully that he didn't want to hear Cuddy insulting his uncle. Cuddy told him that insulting his uncle would be a fucking impossibility.

Mitch was rattled. "I'm sick of your cursing at us, Mangum! It's offensive."

Cuddy was steaming. "Offensive? What's *offensive* is the criminal activity being committed in this room by state officials! Come on in, Dick." Cuddy pointed a disgruntled Dick Cohen at the suite's bedroom while Ward tried to keep the HPD forensics team behind Dick from entering the premises.

Bubba Percy hurried out the terrace doors with the governor's raincoat in one hand and his drink from the minibar in the other. Assuming he wasn't going anywhere far, I let him leave and followed Dick Cohen into the bathroom. The M.E. was annoyed. He'd been brought *twice* to the middle of nowhere in the middle of the night and then told there was no body out here anyhow and he needed to get the body from a funeral parlor that was only half a mile from his house! While Dick was grousing, I showed our forensics photographer Chuck Grant the thin line of dried blood on the shower drain and the shattered tiles on the back wall. I pointed out what looked like strands of short gold-brown hair. We bagged them. He took photos.

Cuddy stuck his head in the door. "So we saying she got shot in here and was moved later?"

I gestured toward the living room. "Yeah, I think she was moved *after* Bubba saw her. So if the killer moved her, he was still around when Bubba waltzed in and he's damn lucky he's not at Pauley and Keene's too."

Cuddy pointed at the crack in the shower wall. "No slug in there?"

I said somebody had chiseled it out of the tiles, either the killer or the crowd in the next room. "But I don't know why they'd do it unless—"

He nodded. "I know why they'd do it. Go see if Bubba's too deep in this muck to haul him out."

"My pleasure."

Out on the landscaped slate terrace, the night sky was so clear I could see the full moon in the water of the swimming pool. The press secretary stood staring at it sadly. I said, "Bubba, running off with Andy's Armani won't solve your problem. It's got her blood on the liner." Startled, he dropped the coat on the glass table beside him. "And despite Ward's best efforts, don't you bet Andy's prints are going to be all over this bungalow, not to mention other more personal residue of his here and there?"

Bubba had the decency to blush—either at my sexual implication or at my catching him with Andy's raincoat—until his whole freckled face was nearly the color of his auburn hair. "Savile," he snarled tiredly, "why go testing for Andy's semen? She shot herself."

"Not if there's no gun."

"Of course there's a fucking gun! Chuck Pauley probably slipped it into his hearse and he's off hawking it on eBay right now, same as that deputy's doing with her gold scarf!"

I sat down on the blue-cushioned teak deck chair next to his. "And she didn't shoot herself in two different rooms either. That's just too hard to do, even for a superstar."

"I don't know what you mean!"

"Yes you do. Somebody moved her body from the shower to the living room. Before you saw her. Or after. Which?"

Not only did Bubba look terrible (his skin clammy, his eyes webbed with blood-veins), but he was actually ripping out little curly strands of his beloved hair. "I'm fucked up here," he finally confessed, sounding almost poignant. "All I wanted was to get a discreet official closure on her suicide without bringing in a mob of yahoos. That's why I came to Cuddy. I wanted to keep Andy out of it and then tomorrow, you know, somebody would quietly announce she'd passed away."

"'Passed away?' Well, I suppose that's one way to put having your face shot off. So what happened to your idea?"

Bubba sighed. "About what would happen if you stuck dynamite up a duck's ass. Ward says somebody anonymous, some guy, called the manager here at The Fifth Season and told him to go check out Bungalow Eight, so he goes and he sees her body."

"The manager goes?"

Bubba tore off his jacket and tossed it on the patio. "Yeah, I guess somehow the manager knows Andy's been here visiting Mavis—Christ, they probably run camcorders through the walls in these suites—and when he sees she's dead, he flips out. He just saw Ward Trasker sitting right there in his lobby having a drink."

"Tonight at The Fifth Season?"

"Ward and SueAnn came back here after the banquet instead of driving so late to Pinehurst—and you can guess who's paying their tab, you and me, bud. So the manager runs back to the lobby, grabs Ward, and tells him there's this problem of Mavis being dead. Bam bam bam. Stormin' Ward takes the ball and—" Bubba shook his head in sad amazement.

"Who tipped off the manager?"

"No clue. Says the caller didn't give a name, just told him he better go check out Bungalow Eight."

"Maybe it was Andy himself who called the manager."

Bubba gagged. "Why would he do that?"

"So her body'd be found." I took his drink from him, sipped it, and spat the contents into a bed of white peonies. "Jesus, what is that!?"

"It's all she left in her minibar—rye, Drambuie, and Chianti." He shrugged, taking back his vile concoction. "I call it The Lost Election."

I noticed a condom wrapper under Bubba's deckchair and brushed it out with my foot. "Bubba, can we drop the 'Andy was Adlai Stevenson and Mavis was Eleanor Roosevelt' party line and admit he was sleeping with her? Can we also admit you were over here checking up on her a lot earlier than you've told us? If we could start there, maybe we could get some place."

He gave me an earnest look. "Justin, help me out. We're in Ollie North Cover-Up Country in there."

"We?"

"For Christ's sake, I'm your friend!"

first lady • 115

"Okay, my advice is, if you can get out of the country, Bubba, do it fast."

He laughed sharply. "Fine. How?"

"Step by step. Start here. At 11:30, when I saw you walk back into that banquet room, you'd already seen Mavis Mahar dead and you were telling Andy she was dead. True?"

Bubba stared at the condom wrapper, then at me, then he took another drink. "Okay," he said. "True. I'd already seen her, about 10:45."

"And then what?" I sat in a deckchair and pulled it over beside him.

"Andy and I talked it over. My first thought was just leave it alone. Somebody'd find her sooner or later."

"Good god, Bubba."

"Right, blame me. I got you and Cuddy here, didn't I? Who knew it'd be like the bumblefuck L.A. cops at O.J.'s house!"

"Wouldn't have happened if you'd called 911 in the first place."

"Could we do this without the moral commentary?" He slapped at the folded coat on the table as if he blamed it for his dilemma. "Then Andy remembers his fucking raincoat. By then it was too risky to go back for it. So I said I'd go ask Cuddy's help in keeping things quiet."

I asked him with real curiosity, "How in hell did you think you could keep it quiet?"

He laughed in a tragic opera way. "Well, it sure wasn't by having Ward Trasker yell May Day to all the shits at sea. Who knew he was going to round up every moron in his Rolodex—the D.A., the sheriff, the coroner and his fucking nephew, and tell them to rush right over?"

"Okay, Ward's in there spring-cleaning the place without telling poor Mitch what they're spring-cleaning for. Here's the big question. Did you or Andy ask Ward to come over and destroy evidence of Andy's presence?"

"I not only didn't ask Ward, I didn't know he'd be here!"

"Did Andy ask?"

Bubba gave me a disgusted look. "Are you kidding? He was reaming Ward through the phone just a few minutes ago for ever coming in here."

"Doesn't mean he didn't want it done, just that he wanted it done better."

Exasperated, apparently past bearing, Bubba twisted himself out of his chartreuse vest and ruffled shirt, and with a skipping trot peeled down to his black bikini shorts. Then he cannonballed into the pool, splashing me with a round billow of warmed water.

I called to him as he stroked a long crawl across the black water. "Was Andy's raincoat lying on top of Mavis when you saw her at 10:45?"

Bubba powered back to the pool's edge, where he stared up at me morosely. "No, she was naked. And she was propped up the way I said, not on her stomach like in the picture."

"And her body wasn't where the chalk's drawn, right? She was back in the bathroom, right? Was she in the shower?"

Slowly he nodded. "Jesus, yes. And she'd shaved her head."

"She'd what?"

"She'd shaved off her hair. I mean, I know she'd done it before, but this was a shock."

"So you had to walk through the living room to see her. How close did you get to her?"

"Just to the bedroom door. I could see into the bathroom, into the shower stall. The straw hat with the candles was sort of half on her head."

I shook my head at him. "But you didn't go in the bathroom? You didn't go find out if she was dead or alive."

"Justin, she was dead." He ducked under the water, came up and shook his head as if he hoped to shake out all the memories. "She was naked and that weirdo hat was kind of slipping off her head. She was facing me."

I walked to the pool edge. "Look at me. Was there a gun in her hand?"

He squeezed his eyes shut. "I honestly don't know." He hoisted his body from the pool, shook himself like a big dog, and grabbed a towel lying in a chair. "Here's the rotten break of it, it was totally in the toilet anyhow, then this crap had to happen."

"Does that translate that the affair between Mavis and Andy was already over?" He nodded, rubbing at his hair. I looked back at the suite where I could see Cuddy now bidding good-bye to Dick Cohen. "Yep, a rotten break, okay, especially for Mavis Mahar."

"Savile, don't make me out some hard-hearted Mr. Pitiless."

"I wouldn't dream of trying. But Bubba, you're up to your furry nipples in what the Irish call shite."

The press secretary adjusted his black bikini briefs, found a cigar in his brocaded vest, lit it, and studied first the sky, then my face. Finally he leaned back in the deckchair.

I sat in the one beside him. "So why did Ward's guys move her body?"

"The hell I know. I wish to God somebody'd cut Andy's willie off."

When I asked him how Andy had ever met Mavis, Bubba did his Pagliacci laugh and thumped at his chest. "Through Randolph Stupid Percy! That's how they met! Through me."

"Tell me all about it, Bubba. We're not going anywhere."

• • •

A few years ago, Bubba Percy and the Irish rock star had sat out a thunderstorm together in the VIP lounge of Triangle International Airport and had fallen into conversation. Mavis was leaving North Carolina after a stay in the new Windrush House, a very private resort clinic where clients with a drinking problem and a lot of money could get rid of both. She headed off to Sardinia to honeymoon with a Spanish tennis player whom she'd married during the bender that had sent her to the clinic. Five months later, she and the tennis star divorced as suddenly as they'd wed; he went to Wimbledon and she came back to America on a concert tour. During this tour, the singer ran into Bubba again at a fundraiser in Atlanta where she was performing for free, as she often did when charitable causes caught her eye. The press secretary introduced her to the notoriously handsome governor. Now compared to Mavis, Andy was about as left-wing as Jesse Helms. Still, he had a reputation as one of the great young hopes of Southern liberalism and that was enough to make the radical Mavis want to meet him. A little while is all the seductive Andy ever needed. "Half my job's beating them off Randy Andy. Mick Jagger never had it so good."

"So an affair started around the first of the year?" I said.

Bubba rubbed the towel over his hair. "I have no idea," he claimed. "But I don't think they led into it with months of stuffing envelopes for the Southern Poverty Law Center. These type people don't have time for foreplay. All I know is, rumors started spreading like grass-fire and I had to suck a lot of dick to blow them out."

I said, "Do me a favor, Bubba, don't get into your personal life."

"Justin, you want to hear this or not?"

He said the affair between the governor and the singer was more like a three-week fling, never serious, and was over when Mega Records ran into a snag about two Mavis concerts scheduled for Haver Field here in Hillston, the last stop on her southeastern tour. The Haver University administration suddenly expressed concerns about the mayhem at earlier concerts at other colleges. They wanted to cancel. So Andy, former president of Haver, made a call to the new president, persuading him to let the star appear at Haver Field. Of course she would behave herself, the governor had apparently promised the university. In the meantime, Mavis started drinking again and if she'd ever planned to behave, she changed her mind. There was a riot in Houston, she was sued in Atlanta, she spent a night in a Nashville jail. By the time she flew into Triangle Airport three days ago, Mavis Mahar was so famous, so wild, so addicted to the spree, so dangerous, that Andrew Brookside couldn't have found anything more risky with which to play games unless he'd tried Russian roulette again, this time with bullets in five of the six chambers.

The evening before Mavis's first performance at Haver Field, the governor went to see her at the secret Fifth Season bungalow. According to Bubba, he went there to ask her to perform at a huge campaign party for his fall election. If so, he didn't deliver the news well. They had a fight—she'd been drinking heavily— and she was an hour late to her concert. Then, apparently to attempt a "nicer close" to their relationship, Brookside had gone back to see her at the bungalow again for a second time, this evening. "Don't ask me why," Bubba shrugged.

"Because she's dangerous."

"Try not to be epigrammatic, Savile, all right?" Bubba was licking at his long, expensive cigar. "Well, Andy says he waited here for her from six-fifteen to six-thirty. She came back so drunk she started a fight about his, get this, centrist politics—" He gestured at the wrecked room behind us. "And the kicker—she flushed his fucking car key down the toilet. Then she passed out and he left in her limo."

I asked him what time that had been.

"Andy said he left her conked out beside the pool at seven-thirty. He had her driver rush him back to the Governor's Mansion. That's the limo you saw I guess. He was late for the Governor's Gala."

I thought back to Andy's flurried arrival at the capitol without his wife. I asked, "So when he got to the Governor's Mansion to hop into his tux, he had a fight with Lee? That's why she refused to come to the banquet?"

Bubba shrugged. "I don't get in the bloodbath with them."

During the banquet, Andy had asked Bubba to return to The Fifth Season to retrieve his car; he couldn't risk sending anyone else. Bubba sighed. "I was a Morehead scholar. I was a *Rhodes* scholar." He blew cigar smoke into the air, it drifted away like all his old dreams. "Can you believe this is my job? Mop up service?"

I shrugged. "Well, you wanted to be close to power."

"Right. But not because I was wiping their butts."

So he'd taken a taxi and an extra key to Brookside's Mercedes and headed for The Fifth Season. It was actually only 10:43

P.M. when he'd opened the bungalow door and found Mavis dead in the bathroom. He immediately drove back to Raleigh in the Mercedes, pulled Andy out of the Gala Banquet, and told him the singer had killed herself. For forty minutes, they'd discussed their options. At one-fifteen A.M. Bubba arrived at Cuddy's place claiming he'd driven straight there after discovering the body. He and Andy had decided it would be cleaner not to have to explain the missing time.

"Oh much cleaner," I said.

But what Bubba (and, he assumed, Andy) hadn't known was that while they were still mulling over options after the banquet, The Fifth Season manager had gotten an anonymous call, had found Mavis, and had asked Ward Trasker to help preserve the privacy of a dead star, who—he suspected—was sleeping with the governor. Ward had called for reinforcements, and by the time Bubba brought us there to look at the body, the body was gone.

I looked at the big redhead carefully. "You think Andy killed her?"

He shot upright, flicking live cigar ash on his bare stomach and hissing at the pain. "Are you fuckin' serious?"

"It didn't cross your mind when you walked in and saw her body that Andy had sent you over there to see it?"

"No way." Bubba appeared to be genuinely shocked.

"But you've got to think it crossed Ward Trasker's mind. Why else all this rearranging?"

"Why should Andy kill her? What's she gonna do, tell on him? So what if she does?"

I gave him a skeptical look. "'So what'? Didn't you just name your drink 'The Lost Election'? So he loses the state and his wife leaves him. That's so what."

"Lee hasn't left him by now, why start?" He stared morosely at his drink. "Course, it'd be just my luck if she did."

As Bubba subsided into a self-pitying sigh, I heard a car leaving on the other side of the bungalow. When the splatter of gravel faded, I picked up a different sound: a slow crunching noise nearby in the dark behind the landscaped shrubs. It sounded like someone carefully walking on the expensive mulch that was piled high around the plants bordering the pool. The noise was steadily moving closer. I stood quietly as Bubba wiggled around in the deckchair with his hideous cocktail and his cigar, muttering, "You think there's a chance I could get my old job back at the *Star* if I gave them the Mavis Mahar suicide as my first lead? I could let it rip how she was banging the governor."

I grabbed Bubba's tuxedo jacket from the patio floor and strolled toward the shrubbery. "Excuse me just a second—" Wheeling around, I flung the coat at a shadow hunched behind a small spiral juniper, then leapt at the shape and grabbed it. The shape screamed as I dragged it back to the pool.

When I yanked off the jacket, Shelly Bloom came out swinging. The thin pretty young reporter from the *Sun* was a whirl of terror, her short black hair an unruly tangle, her large black eyes shocked wide open. She wore black Spandex pants, a black tank top, and black Reebocks. It may have been her notion of night camouflage. She was hard to hold on to. Fighting her off, I grabbed her camera and tapped out the canister of film. "What do you think you're doing!" she wanted to know.

"Shelly, crawling around in the bushes out there, did you notice a lot of official-looking yellow tape with DO NOT CROSS on it?"

When I gave her back her camera, she hurried over to Bubba who was quickly pulling on his tuxedo pants. She told him not to get dressed on her account, and added that he wasn't as out of shape as she'd figured he'd be. He zipped up his trousers. "That it, Shelly? You drive out here to caliper the body fat on my abs?"

Shelly admitted that she'd gotten a tip from a buddy in the sheriff's office that Mavis Mahar had checked into The Fifth Season and that something big had happened to her, that she was maybe dead. So Shelly drove out here, parked on the highway, and crawled over the stone wall. Wandering around the grounds, she saw this geeky little Irish guy that she thinks worked for the rock star. He was calling "Mavis" over and over, so she figured she was in the right place. But when she tried to talk to this guy he ran off and a few seconds later she saw two hotel security guards run after and grab him. She made her way over here where she'd spotted all the barlights flashing on cars. "Is she dead?" the reporter asked eagerly.

Bubba was fishing around for his dress pumps. "Is who dead?"

"Mavis Mahar! Did she kill herself?" She said it as she might have announced that she'd just won a forty-million-dollar lottery.

"How long you been listening, Shelly?" he asked her.

"Long enough to hear you say Governor Brookside was having an affair with her." She nodded eagerly, combing her tangled hair with her hands. "Come on, I've been good to you. Is the body still in there?"

Behind us, Cuddy suddenly stepped through the bungalow doors onto the patio. "Hey, Justin, wrap it up, okay?" He called over to the couple in the shadows. "Hi there, Shelly and Bubba. Pool party? Justin, would you please escort Shelly out of a sealed police scene? And Bubba, if you know any lawyers that haven't been disbarred, you might want to ask one along when you come to HPD tomorrow at eight A.M. Shelly, good-bye or you'll be joining Mr. Beefcake there in needing a lawyer." He turned back inside.

I handed Bubba his shirt. "Maybe Shelly will give you a ride home." Taking the governor's folded raincoat off the table, I waved it at him. "Maybe you could marry her if she'll find you a job on *her* paper. At least you could give her your Porsche."

Shelly tried to see into the bungalow as she said, "No to the marriage, yes to the car. I've already had a husband, I've never had a Porsche. That's Mitch Bazemore in there. So the Chief of Police *and* the D.A. are here?"

Bubba forgot his troubles in his incredulity. "No way, Bloom. Married to who? I don't believe it."

Shelly sniffed indignantly. "I was married three years. Who to's none of your business. Don't try to throw me off with insults."

I left as Bubba used his syrupy Reagan voice to ask for her help in saving a career.

"Brookside's?" the reporter asked.

"No. Mine," he said.

• • •

Inside, everybody from HPD had left but Cuddy and Nancy. Nancy had her arms around a short, skinny, over-wrought young man wearing an orange and baby blue antique velour leisure suit from the 1970s. He had skin as white and dull as cheap paper, an almost shaved head, and at least eight tiny gold studs stuck through various features—ears, nose, lip, and tongue. His face was blotchy with acne scars as well as tears and he was now crying so hard he had trouble breathing. He proved to be the person Shelly had seen the security guards chase down on The Fifth Season grounds—Mavis Mahar's dresser and makeup man, Dermott Quinn. Nancy had just told him that Mavis had killed herself.

Quinn grabbed at Nancy's hands. "She'd not do a bollocks eejet thing like that. It's a fuckall lie, a lie," he kept gasping in sobs.

Nancy hugged him tighter as his emaciated frame convulsed into spasms. "Hey, Dermott, hey, I know, I know, it's okay."

"It's bloody shite. Kill herself? Mavis? Not Mavis. *You're liars!*"

Cuddy pulled the little Irishman away from Nancy and stood him upright. "Mr. Quinn, you need to help us here. Can you do that?" His hand tilted Dermott's chin to look up at him, until finally the dresser nodded, slowing his breathing in long shudders.

"Yes, I want to help, I do, I'm all right."

"Okay. What made you come out here?"

Quinn told us that none of the Mavis Mahar entourage had known about this bungalow at The Fifth Season, including him, and that this was the first time Mavis hadn't shared with him the whereabouts of her secret place because they were very close good friends and she told him everything. So he'd waited for her in her dressing room at Haver Field until half-an-hour before she was scheduled to go on stage and then he'd started trying to track her down: calling the Sheraton, checking the local bars. It was not the first time Mavis had disappeared, but they'd always been able to find her before. Now they couldn't and the Mega Records reps were "going bleedin' ballistic." Some of the band wanted to call the police, but Bernadette (her manager) didn't want any more bad publicity.

Frantic by now, Dermott had gone off on his own to look for the star. He'd come up with the idea that she might be staying somewhere under her real name, which was Agnes Connolly, although he'd never known her to do so before. (He was the only one of the group who knew her real name because they'd been friends, best of friends, since their Temple Bar days singing on the streets of Dublin, and she'd kept that name quiet.) So the dresser had slipped away from the others and phoned every hotel in the area until he'd reached The Fifth Season, where an innocent night clerk put him through after he asked for Agnes Connolly. However, to his surprise, a strange man had answered the phone in the bungalow and then hung up on him. When he'd called the desk back only a few minutes later, the same clerk had told him that there was no Agnes Connolly registered there and that he'd been mistaken before. Now alarmed, Dermott had taken a taxi from downtown Hillston out to the resort, where he had started searching the grounds for her. But hotel security had caught him and brought him here.

I asked Quinn if Mavis owned a gun. A fresh burst of tears shook him. Nancy sat him down beside her. He whispered, "I told her not to fool with that feckin' poxie gun. I hate the guns."

I pressed him. So Mavis did own a firearm? He told us that her ex-husband, the tennis player Matteo Garcias, had once given her a pistol for a birthday present. The dresser had no idea what caliber it might have been, only that it was small and had a white handle.

Cuddy showed him the Polaroid photo of the body that he'd confiscated from the NCBI agent Ted Bingley, and Quinn gagged before finally identifying the pistol in her hand as looking like the one Mavis had owned. I asked him if she'd ever attempted or talked about killing herself.

"No. Never." The small man refused to accept even the possibility. "She wouldn't send her soul to hell, doing away with herself so."

"She's Catholic?" asked Cuddy. Quinn nodded.

"Practicing?" I asked the Irishman. I doubted it. Mavis Mahar was so famously angry with the Catholic Church that they'd banned her songs.

Dermott Quinn wiped his nose on his sleeve. "Tisn't much *that* matters," he said stubbornly. "She never would." But he admitted that Mavis might have shot herself by accident while drunk, although he thought it more likely that a sick fan had killed her. "It's terrible the tossers we have to put up with." For example, in Amsterdam they'd found a naked man under the covers in Mavis's hotel bed, and a girl in Houston had cut out the letters of Mavis's name into her arm with a razor blade and then jumped in front of her limousine to show her the bloody tribute.

Quinn also had suspicions of Mavis's ex-husband, Garcias, who was a "fuckall mental" and who had shot at her with a crossbow once. Everybody knew the Spaniard was a jealous maniac. He had broken Quinn's nose with his tennis racket when the dresser was just lying on the couch in Mavis's arms and anybody with a brain could see that they were only good friends.

Cuddy shook his head at me. "It's not Garcias. He was live on ESPN in a tennis match televised from Barcelona tonight."

Quinn started picking up and straightening Mavis's clothes strewn on the floor. I told him to put them back, that he mustn't touch things. Pointing out the straw hat with the candles in its brim, I asked him if the star wore it on stage. He looked it over curiously, then said that unless Mavis had acquired it since he'd left her this afternoon, the hat didn't belong to her. He'd never seen it before and he knew all of her clothes by heart. The small man suddenly spun around and clung tightly to Nancy. "Where did you take her? Oh, let me go to her. She needs me. Oh, what'm I to do to do to do?" Nancy walked him away from us, stroking his back.

Cuddy walked me toward the terrace. "You break Bubba's story out there?" I nodded. "It took you long enough."

"He likes to talk. He admits he lied. He was here at 10:45, told Brookside at 11:30. When Bubba saw the body she was propped up in the shower, naked with that straw hat on. He doesn't know who moved her body or why." Cuddy gave me a quizzical look. "No, I think Bubba really is clueless on what Trasker was up to. The coat over her in the photo is this one." I held up the Italian raincoat, showed Cuddy its front and back. "It belongs to...." I left the sentence unfinished.

Cuddy nodded. "Yeah, I know who it belongs to. Call him."

I moved him further away from the others. "He's the governor. He's got more lawyers than the tobacco industry. He's got the *same* lawyers. And they're not going to let me talk to him in the middle of the night. I'd have to tell them the alternative was a subpoena."

"Then tell them. And tell Mr. Brookside that his raincoat's got his girlfriend's blood on it."

Chapter 10

Woman in Gray

We let Nancy take Dermott Quinn back to his hotel as soon as a new HPD team arrived to safeguard the bungalow. Then Cuddy and I walked over to the lobby to see the manager. Barricaded in his office in pajamas and robe, the petulantly defensive Mr. Rochet said he had nothing to add to what he'd already told the attorney general: at eleven P.M., he'd happened to be at the front desk and had answered the phone to hear an anonymous caller say only a few words to him: "You've got a real problem with Mavis in Bungalow Eight. Look into it before somebody else does." Then the caller had hung up.

No, there were no tapes kept of phone calls. No, Mr. Rochet doubted he could identify the voice again. It was an ordinary male voice, nothing unusual about it: neither elderly nor juvenile, unaccented. The manager had hurried immediately to the bungalow. When he saw the dead star's body, he hurried back to turn matters over to Attorney General Ward Trasker, who happened to be a guest.

He was happy to take us into the lobby to show us the front desk and the phone. But when asked to describe the body he'd seen and exactly where he'd seen it, the manager tightened his lips as if we were trying to force vinegar down his throat and told us he had nothing to add to what he'd already said to the attorney general. Cuddy asked him, "You didn't call the police?"

Mr. Rochet said that the attorney general was after all the highest law enforcement officer in North Carolina, wasn't he? Wasn't that even better than the police? His fervent hope was that in this tragedy we could all work together to preserve the privacy of Miss Mahar.

"She's dead," said Cuddy.

"I would hope here at The Fifth Season we could protect a guest's privacy even after her death, Captain Mangum."

Cuddy leaned across the man's french provincial desk. "I would hope you wouldn't break the law to do it. I would hope you understand it's against the law to withhold evidence in a homicide investigation. Let me start again. Did you know Andrew Brookside was here in Bungalow Eight this evening visiting Miss Mahar?"

The manager shuddered as if he'd swallowed the vinegar. "I'm sorry. Unless you have some legal order that obliges me to talk to you, I have nothing to say." He hurried off, pausing to straighten a bowl of marble eggs beside an antique leather letterbox.

• • •

It was past three A.M. when Cuddy and I took the Raleigh exit to the Governor's Mansion. To my surprise, Andy Brookside had agreed to see us. Led into his immense office, we discovered him seated in a Sulka bathrobe behind a desk weighty with state affairs, as if it were his regular habit to catch up on paper work in the small hours of the morning. From silver frames on his desk, both his wife and the president smiled across at him, reassuring him that all would be well.

Andy introduced us to two lawyers (one from the state justice department, i.e., Trasker's office, and one who was Brookside's personal attorney as well as a legal counselor of Haver Tobacco Company). They leaned against a wall that glowed with warm cherrywood paneling. Despite the hour, they were both crisply dressed in their summer suits. They stood there casually but as poised to leap forward as two hunting dogs waiting for the signal to run. An elderly African-American in a white jacket entered, pushing a cart gleaming with a silver coffee service. No one wanted any and he took it away.

One of the lawyers told us that the governor would not be answering questions but that he would be giving us all the information we might need to understand his part in tonight's events.

"Good," said Cuddy. "His part in tonight's events is what I'm here for."

The other lawyer told us that Governor Brookside was making this extraordinary gesture because of his respect for the deceased artist Mavis Mahar and because of his personal regard for the two of us. Then he placed a tape recorder on the desk, turned it on, and nodded at the governor.

Andy looked only at me as he spoke. Cuddy looked only at him. The governor spoke with a quiet sorrow that would have been completely convincing except there was something in his eyes energized and excited and not terribly sad. I recalled his telling me that what he loved most was the thrill of risk. I recalled his telling Cuddy that a smart man could get away with murder and might enjoy doing so, just for the rush of winning.

Rubbing at the bright hair that was the icon of his fame, Andy began, "First of all, this is a heartbreaking waste. Mavis Mahar was a gifted young woman whose music was important to millions of people. Let's not have the aftermath cause even more damage."

One of the lawyers interrupted. "Has this been leaked to the press?"

"Not by us," Cuddy said, adding that we didn't know whether anyone else had leaked it or not.

The other lawyer nodded at the governor. Andy said, "I knew Mavis. I liked her. We shared in a political agenda. I visited her this evening at The Fifth Season Resort because I was concerned about her tardy appearance the night before at Haver Field, for which I bore some responsibility. I arrived at the bungalow at 6:15. She turned up fifteen or twenty minutes later, intoxicated and," he paused, whether really searching for words or not, I don't know, "violently emotional. She asked me to leave and I did so at 7:30. I have not returned to The Fifth Season Resort since then, nor did I see her again, alive or dead. When I was told that she had failed to show up at her concert, I asked my press secretary, Randolph Percy, to go to her bungalow to check on her. He returned and told me that she appeared to have committed suicide. We agreed that he would communicate this news directly to Captain Mangum here. We had every faith," said the governor, "that in dealing with this suicide, Captain Mangum would do what was right and best...for everyone involved." Brookside looked at Cuddy for the first time. They stared very carefully at each other. Then he turned his eyes back to me. "I am now told that Attorney General Ward Trasker was notified by the hotel management that Miss Mahar was dead and took independent steps to deal with the matter."

Cuddy interrupted. "Who told you this?"

"Randolph Percy telephoned me from the bungalow. Mr. Trasker had apparently felt he should take immediate action to handle the tragedy. Naturally, everyone wished to control the kind of media feeding frenzy that Miss Mahar's suicide would inevitably cause. Mr. Trasker did not inform me that he planned to involve himself. Nor do I know what he might have done. That's all I can tell you. I admired her talent and her political passion. I'm very sorry she made this tragic choice."

"The problem is, I'm not sure the choice was hers." Cuddy spoke quietly. "When you saw her, had she shaved her head?"

Brookside looked startled. "Shaved her head? Good god, no."

Cuddy unfolded the blood-stained Italian raincoat that he'd brought with him. "Is this your raincoat?" Andy looked at it, saw the blood stain. One of the lawyers told him not to answer any questions.

Brookside said, "Yes, it's my raincoat. I must have left it there."

Cuddy put the coat back in the bag in which he'd brought it. "Did you ask Bubba Percy to remove this coat from Miss Mahar's suite?"

"We said no questions," answered one of the lawyers.

Cuddy ignored him. "Mr. Brookside, not only was Miss Mahar's body moved after her death, there is also the strong possibility that the gunshot was not self-inflicted. Did you kill Mavis Mahar?"

"How dare you!" snapped the Haver Tobacco Company man.

"That's it! This meeting is over," snarled the justice department man.

"No, I did not." Andy Brookside stood and faced Cuddy. "And I'm offended that you should ask me."

Both lawyers now moved quickly to open the large paneled door. Brookside walked briskly through it without looking at us again. Five minutes later we were escorted out of the mansion by polite state troopers on duty in the foyer. As we left, Cuddy turned to stare up the wide carpeted stairs into the darkness above, where guarded halls led to the private quarters of the first lady.

• • •

"Without sounding unduly cynical," I remarked as I sped us along the highway, back to the Cadmean Building in downtown Hillston, "You really think a popular governor running for re-election and married to one of the richest women in the country is going to shoot a rock star one-night-stand in the face and leave his raincoat tossed over her dead body?"

"What would *duly* cynical sound like?" Cuddy wanted to know. "Really thinking that the state's attorney general would destroy evidence at a possible crime scene, move a dead body, and hide the governor's raincoat?"

I said we might as well agree that it was more than a "possible" crime scene. "She didn't kill herself. Dermott Quinn's right. She wouldn't kill herself. Not Mavis Mahar."

"How the hell do you know?" He was on the radio, trying to reach Dick Cohen, our medical examiner.

How did I know? I thought about it then told him, "Because I saw her, you just had to see her once."

"Oh for Christ's sake."

But it was true. Maybe it wasn't a husband or a fan who had murdered her as Quinn thought, maybe it wasn't Brookside either, but it wasn't suicide. Cuddy shrugged. "Maybe it was Dermott Quinn. Who knows how long he was wandering around those grounds."

I shook my head no. "It'd be like killing himself."

"Justin, I hope you're not taking night courses in abnormal psychology and charging them to the department." He shook the car radio mike. "Come in, damn it!"

Cuddy's threat earlier to go to the television news had bullied Mitch Bazemore into having the coroner transfer Mavis's body to the city morgue. Dick Cohen had grouchily driven over to Pauley and Keene Funeral Home himself to make sure it happened. When the HPD dispatcher was finally able to put Cuddy through to Dick, he had already started to work on the body in the autopsy room.

Dick growled through the crackly speaker: "Good news, we got a gun. Turns out Pauley did waltz off with it. Swore it was 'pure accident.' Says it must've got itself wrapped up in the bag with the body. Hell, maybe he's even telling the truth. Down here, anything's possible except a decent meal. I'm in a diner, I ask for lox, woman tells me, 'Go to a hardware store.'"

I said, "Dick, that happened to you two years ago."

"I can't forget it."

Cuddy interrupted us. "And what's the bad news?"

"This gun's a .22."

"Does it have a white bone grip? Mavis Mahar owned one like that."

"Sure does. It's been fired too. And there's a twenty-two slug in her cerebellum. Medial medullar lamina. Right between her eyes. Slug's soft, messed up, but Etham thinks they can match it to the gun."

Cuddy rubbed at his hair. "That's the bad news?"

"No, the bad news is, it's not suicide."

I muttered, "Told you so. Suicides do it here or here." I pointed my finger first at my temple and then inside my mouth. "Not in the face, and they couldn't do that kind of damage with a .22 anyhow."

Cuddy told me to keep quiet. "Dick, you don't buy suicide?"

Dick yawned into the speaker. "Not unless she shot herself through the brain with one gun, dug the slug out of the shower tiles and swallowed it, threw the gun out the window, and after she died, shaved her head, then went in the living room and shot herself in the face with another gun, and then crawled under a raincoat just to be modest."

"Dick, I know you don't stay up late enough to try out as a late night comedian, so how about just do it straight?"

His voice crackled at us. "Two different entry wounds, two different bullets. The .22 between the eyes. But post mortem. Probably a .38, .32 killed her. Entry wound up through the lower jaw. Exit wound high on the back of the skull. So I don't buy suicide unless she killed herself because she was pissed off about some s.o.b. murdering her."

Cuddy looked at me as he tapped the mike against his cheek. "Well hey, Dick, something like that is enough to put you in a real bad mood."

• • •

I parked in front of the Cadmean Building behind a gray Mercedes that someone had left in the No Parking zone. In the eerie hollow echo of the marble lobby, Cuddy and I walked past the empty courtroom where tomorrow Tyler Norris would probably go free. While we waited for the elevator, we watched a *Hillston Star* delivery truck slow down outside and a bound stack of newspapers come flying from its rear doors. He yawned. "So what's *this* morning's headline? 'POLICE CHIEF TO CITY: DROP DEAD EVERYBODY'?"

"Well, if Shelly Bloom has her way, the *Sun* won't be talking about you at all. It'll be 'MAVIS DEAD IN GOV'S LOVE NEST.'"

He picked up cigarette cellophane off the marble floor and tossed it in the trash. "This homicide's got to get closed, Justin. We're entering O.J. land. The press was already killing us over G.I. Jane and Linsley Norris and neither one of them was a rock star on the cover of *Time*. The *world* press will rampage through this town like it was Pompeii and the streets were full of lava."

"I guess by the end of the day you want me to bring in somebody yelling, 'I did it, I did it!' Well, you already accused the governor."

A cleaning woman came out of the courtroom carrying brooms and mops. Cuddy waved hello to her and then smacked the elevator button again. "Just find out fast if he did or he didn't."

I held the door for him. "*Can* we pull Andy in? Maybe he'd have to be impeached first?" Cuddy didn't answer me. Silently we rode up to the offices of the Hillston Police Department. A few minutes later he came out of the men's room looking scrubbed and awake and ready for the day. He'd always had the ability to recharge himself. He said, "All I'm telling you is, we are—how can I put this?— shooting down the rapids blowing air into the flat rubber raft that we are sitting in."

"I get your point."

At the front desk, Sergeant Brenda Moore was tiredly listening while a red-haired young man swore to Jesus that he'd thought it was his cousin Kobe's Toyota Tundra he'd hot-wired and had been selling its parts just as a joke. Cuddy walked over to him and patted his back. "Griffin, you be sure to get your eyes checked out by one of our fine prison optometrists soon as you get settled, 'cause just a few months back you were swearing to Jesus you mistook a Ford Explorer for an old Plymouth belonged to your mama's Bible club."

The boy grinned before he could mask his pleasure at seeing Cuddy.

Cuddy grinned back. "And how is your mama?"

I recognized the sullen shifty blue of the boy's eyes. He looked like one of the Popes, a large local family who'd been marrying each other and robbing everybody else since before the

Civil War. Cuddy was the only person not closely related to them who could keep their genealogy straight.

I asked, "Is this a Pope?"

"Yep."

The boy said with stiff disdain, "Mama left Daddy."

Cuddy patted Griffin's thin tattooed arm. "Paula'll come back by the time Graham's out on parole. Your folks'll be together again."

"I could give a fuck," their son boasted.

"Good god," I said, "a new generation of Popes."

"Always," Cuddy nodded as Brenda handed him a stack of the pink memos. She gestured that there was someone waiting to see him, adding, "She's been here a while."

"Who?" he asked her, his body tightening.

Brenda looked at him solemnly. "Chief, I think you want.... She said it was private."

"I hope it's not the press already because—" But I was talking to no one because Cuddy was almost running along the corridor toward his office.

Brenda and I shrugged at each other, then I left her asking the boy for his full name. He said, "Griffin Torii Pope. Two *I*s in Torii. Just please don't phone my mama, okay? She'll fry my ass."

"Occupation?" she asked. And he told her, "Musician," and she wrote it down without believing it.

Out of the dark at the end of the hall, someone stepped softly toward Cuddy. A woman in a gray suit. She moved from the shadows with the stillness of a ghost. A slender woman, pale blonde hair, a cool soft voice I would have known without seeing her. As I came up behind Cuddy, she said politely, "Justin, hello." Her suit was the color of her Mercedes outside.

"Lee, good god, what are you doing here?" I asked.

She wasn't looking at me. "Cuddy, I'm sorry to trouble you."

He stared at her as if she'd hypnotized him as she moved closer, gestured at his office door. Then with a sudden lunge, as if compelled, he threw open his door for her. I saw Lee noticing the raincoat that Cuddy still carried. I saw her recognize it as Andy's.

Then she stepped around us and walked inside the dark room.

I pulled Cuddy from the door. "This case will be under a microscope. Everybody in it. Okay? Don't do for her what you wouldn't do for anybody else. Why do you think Andy sent Bubba to you? How do you know he didn't send *her* to you?"

He shook free of my arm. "Go do your job, Justin."

"Yeah, you too."

The door closed in my face.

Chapter 11

HPD Homicide, Female, Caucasian

I spent the next hour at the wearisome paper trail that wanders through the databases and file cabinets of modern police departments. From the news about Mavis, the lack of sleep, the unaccustomed number of drinks, I had a horrible headache. Coffee didn't help as I wrote a long report on the crime scene at The Fifth Season. In it I put everything I'd seen going on in Bungalow Eight tonight, plus everything that Bubba had told me out by the pool. I have a very good memory if I don't wait too long. I locked the report in my desk. I didn't know what Lee was going to ask Cuddy to do for her husband, nor could I be absolutely sure what he would agree to, or not to, do. I thought I knew. I thought I could wager my life on Cuddy's integrity. But even the purest knights in Camelot were tempted by love, and the next thing they knew there was a war going on and the whole place was in flames.

Crossing the annex to the autopsy room, I heard the clatter of wheels banging through the doors into the corridor. Two bored attendants yawned as they shoved a mortuary gurney around a corner. In disposable paper scrubs, Dick Cohen stumbled sleepily along beside them.

I caught up with the macabre procession. "Is that Mavis Mahar?"

Dick nodded, tapping a clipboard lying on top of the body. "A shame, somebody like that, got it all. Great cardiovascular system, stomach, kidneys, lungs, perfect. Even her liver. Thought you said she was this big boozer."

I tried not to look at the gurney. "She was. High alcohol content in her system, right?"

The medical examiner shrugged. "Not at all."

"What?" Surprised, I followed them into the morgue. "Dick, she was already plastered when I saw her in the afternoon. And there were so many empties in her suite it looked like the French Quarter at Mardi Gras."

"Well, you and I should have such a liver." He shook his head. "We'll have a toxicology report on the chemical stuff tomorrow."

The bored attendants chatted about whether they should give up on cable and buy satellite dishes as they lifted the gurney off its trolley, slid the body into the refrigerated compartment, and left Dick and me alone in the morgue with her. I felt grief fall on me like the heavy weight of water, stopping my breath. How could everything that Mavis Mahar had been lie so still beneath the white sheet, how could all those colors and all that song slide without a sound into so small an opening in the wall? Could it really have been only this past dawn when a beautiful stranger had dived through the mist into the lake and then burst back into the morning air, smiling at me? That moment felt as distant and alien as some lovely foreign city briefly visited and left forever behind.

Dick was talking about "livor mortis lavidity of the face and chest as well as lavidity of the back and hip." It meant that she'd been moved—and turned from her back to her stomach—as much as four hours after her death.

"Any chance she was still alive when Bubba got there at about 10:45?"

"No way." From rigor and body temperature, Dick put the time of death as early as nine, even eight P.M. I said it didn't seem likely that a killer would hang around 'til after Bubba left and then drag his victim into another room and flip her face down. Dick flexed his arms, his white hairy fingers laced. "You don't know what's 'likely' with these nuts. They'll chop up their mothers and then sleep with her body parts 'til they rot. If I could take my kids and move to the moon, I'd do it." (Dick was divorced and gloomy and often said that if he'd been his wife, he'd have left him too, for moving her down here from New York.)

Shivering, he rubbed his skinny arms. "So are we done?"

"Just a second, okay?" I reached for the stainless steel door.

He grabbed my hand. "It's not pretty."

"I know."

He scratched his beard. "You think you know. Her eyes are gone."

"Gone?"

He pulled me back from the door. "Cut out, both eyeballs, neatly, with a sharp knife. The bozos at the scene didn't catch it, I guess, 'cause of all the gunk from the face wound."

I stepped back to look at him. "Before or after she died?"

"Postmortem if that's any consolation." He grumbled, "And I'm right as always. The .22 slug's definitely postmortem too. Muzzle was held about two inches from the nose bridge. Augie called from the lab, says there's just her prints on the grip. But some creep stuck that .22 between her eyes after she was dead and pulled the trigger."

"So death was—"

He rubbed at his stubbled cheek. "Death was immediate from the larger caliber weapon—I don't know what, but not a .22—right under the mandible and into the cranium."

I thought about this. "So she's in the shower. He opens the door, holds the gun under her chin, shoots her. The slug goes up through the brain and exits into the tiled wall behind her, blows out the grout and cracks the tiles."

Dick nodded. "Then he takes out her eyeballs in the shower."

"The eyes weren't left at the scene. At least not when we got there."

"Maybe he ate them," Dick shrugged. "Remember the nut in Wrightsville that ate that Marine's penis?"

"Dick, can't you ever press 'Clear'?"

He shook his head. "They're always telling Jews, 'Press clear.' After the pogroms, 'Press clear.' After the Holocaust, 'Press clear.' No, I can't. For all we know, this nut sits around that bungalow a couple of hours watching TV and nibbling on her eyeballs. Then he hauls her into the living room and sticks the .22 in her face, blows it to bits. You wanna know what? I'm sick of humans. I am. I like bonsai. I like koi. I'm okay with some of the quieter cats. But I don't like humans."

"I don't think the same person did both shots," I said.

His eyebrows twisted wryly. "Oh gee, now I feel a whole lot better about the species."

"It wasn't Mavis's killer who dragged her into the living room and threw the raincoat over her and shot her postmortem to hide the eye mutilation. I think they planted the .22 in her hand so we'd go with suicide."

He snorted at me. "They who? And how dumb can they get? We're not going to notice she was moved postmortem? We're not going to notice she was shot twice with two different guns? Who's this they?"

"*We're* going to notice. But that idiot Osmond Bingley and those coffin peddlers Pauley and Keene aren't going to notice… Dick, this is between us—"

He laughed. "Who am I gonna tell? My wife left me and my kids won't listen—"

"It was Ward Trasker using Homer Louge and his boys."

"Sure, the A.G., right. The A.G. shot a corpse."

"No, I'm telling you. Ward Trasker goes in that bungalow, sees Mavis Mahar is murdered and mutilated and she's got this weird hat with candles stuck on her head, and he freaks. Even if…if the governor didn't kill her himself—"

"Cheez, Justin, what the fuck are you saying?"

"Dick, he was in there. It was his raincoat on the body."

"Holy shit."

"Even if he's cleared, he'll be hauled in as a witness on a celebrity homicide and the press'll eat him alive. But if it's suicide, and they quick get a death certificate from a coroner like No-Brain Bingley and they quick get her to a private funeral home and buried, nobody knows what happened and maybe they can keep the governor out of it."

Dick stared at me a long time. "I shoulda stayed in Brooklyn. They wanted to get rid of somebody, they just dumped them in a canal. Simple, tidy, professional, no problem."

He backed away as I reached for the cloth covering the corpse. I paused and took a breath. Then I pulled the sheet away from her head. I've seen a hundred dead bodies. This was the hardest.

"Sorry." Dick steadied me. "Warned you."

I looked for a long time at the roughly cut and shaved skull, the blasted shattered face, the empty eye sockets. Slowly I turned her head to one side, then the other. Then my heart kicked at my chest. Quickly I examined her naked shoulder, held up each of her hands and studied them.

Dick leaned over the corpse. "What? I miss something? You gonna tell me they poisoned her too just to make sure?"

I pulled the sheet back over the young woman's body. I told the medical examiner not to leave. I was going to bring Cuddy down to the morgue in five minutes. We had a problem.

● ● ●

Cuddy was alone in his office, standing in the dark by the window, intently watching a jet's lights blink across the blue-black sky, as if Lee Brookside had left him and he was watching her fly off in her private plane. When I flipped on the light, he turned around startled.

"You okay, Cuddy?"

"Yeah fine." He said nothing about his visit from Lee and neither did I. Instead, I told him I'd just gone to look at the body they'd taken from Bungalow Eight at The Fifth Season tonight. I asked him to come down to the morgue with me right now.

He interrupted me. "Look at this first." He stepped to his desk and pointed with a pencil at an eight-by-ten black-and-white photograph inside a clear plastic HPD evidence bag. With the pencil's tip, Cuddy twisted the photo around so it faced me. It was a commercial shot of Mavis Mahar's face, one of the thousands that are given away in promotions and sold in concert lobbies. But on this one, the words "GUESS WHO" were scrawled across her mouth in red letters. And in the same blood-colored marker someone had completely blotted out both her eyes.

He said, "You know her eyes are gone?"

"Yes. I saw the body. That's what—"

"This was under my door," Cuddy said, pulling the photo back.

"When you and Lee walked in here?"

"Yes. I didn't open it until after she left. No one seems to know how it got here. I haven't been in since six, so it could have been shoved under the door way before the murder. Augie checked it for prints, but it's clean." Clean except for a tiny speck of gold glitter on the back of the print—as if it might have once been in an envelope with the kind of cardboard star that had been stuck on Cuddy's slider. "You know what you call this type photo?"

I picked it up. "It's a head shot," I said.

"Right. A head shot. A star's head shot." He snapped the pencil in two and threw the pieces across the room into the trash. "Cute pun, huh? Head shot, shot in the head? Keep your eye on the star, I'm going to shoot her in the head. And he did, goddamn it." Cuddy was talking about the cardboard glitter star he had found stuck to his study slider at River Rise earlier this evening. The star that his telescope had been pointing at. The star he'd thought was only a joke of Brenda Moore's.

I leaned over to study the photograph of Mavis. The block letters spelling out GUESS WHO across her mouth looked similar to those on the label that had been hung months ago from Jane Doe's toe telling me to deliver her body to Cuddy. "Cuddy, you need to come down to the morgue."

He slid the evidence bag into his briefcase. "I don't know about you, but to me this photo means our killer's not Brookside, it's Guess Who."

I stood to hold open the office door for him. "The victim's not Mavis Mahar either."

He stopped, his hand still reaching for his intercom. "What do you mean it's not Mavis Mahar?"

"That's what I came to tell you. That's not her body down in the morgue."

Chapter 12
Lucy Griggs

The police chief and the medical examiner had never seen Mavis Mahar in person and had no reason to doubt me when I said that the woman in the morgue was somebody else. But they had invested in their preconception and so it took a while to persuade them to listen. Their preconception had been shared by a lot of people. It had started with Bubba Percy's assumption that Mavis Mahar had killed herself. Of course as Bubba had later admitted, he'd never gotten anywhere near the corpse. The next person to assume the corpse was Mavis was the hotel manager. The anonymous caller had told him that Mavis Mahar was in trouble in Bungalow Eight and so when he looked into Bungalow Eight and saw a woman's dead body in a blood-splattered shower, he understandably assumed that this was the trouble referred to.

Next, Ward Trasker, and then the other law officials who gathered at The Fifth Season, reinforced the mistake. They saw a corpse in the place where they'd been told they would find Mavis Mahar's corpse, so they assumed the corpse was hers. Why shouldn't they? The young dead woman was the same age, the same height and build, the stubble on her shaved head was the same tawny color, the nail polish and jewelry looked the same. Moreover, she was naked in the rock star's private hideaway, so who else could she be but the rock star?

But the young woman lying on the gurney in the Hillston city morgue was not Mavis Mahar. I'd known it the minute I'd looked closely at her body. Just as Dermott Quinn would have known it, or Andy Brookside, or even Bubba perhaps, if he'd bothered to examine her closely.

Patiently I showed Cuddy and Dick the unblemished spot in the crook of this corpse's neck where there ought to be a birthmark of a small dark-red pointed star and there wasn't. I showed them how this young woman wore fewer rings than Mavis had, and how these rings were cheap imitations of the gold and silver ones on Mavis's fingers. I said this corpse didn't have strong enough muscles in her arms to be a musician as Mavis was; that her fingernails were long—useless for playing the piano— whereas Mavis's nails were short and blunt. I said that you could tell from stubble left that this woman's hair was cheaply dyed, and that while Mavis might, like the corpse, have a pierced nipple, she did not have, like her, a shaved pubis.

Cuddy shook his head smiling at the medical examiner. "My my, Justin only caught a glimpse of Mavis singing in the Tucson Lounge, or just think of all the other things he could have told us. Dick, that's what I call detection."

For some reason, I didn't want to say that while out riding Manassas at dawn, I had seen the singer standing naked on the dock at Pine Hills Lake.

Cuddy and Dick looked together at the body for a long silent minute. "You're sure about this," Cuddy finally said.

"Very sure."

"Good enough." Cuddy covered the corpse and told Dick that she wasn't Mavis Mahar.

Dick Cohen scratched at his beard. "Here I was finally going to impress my daughter, telling her how I did an autopsy on Mavis Mahar. She plays those CDs of hers all the damn time. Now you're telling me the victim's not a superstar."

I said the purity of the corpse's liver should have been a clue.

"Well what do you want from me, Justin? You think I read in magazines about the vital organs of the rich and famous? How would I know Mavis Mahar drank?"

Cuddy said, "Dick, that's like saying you didn't know Di was bulimic."

"Di? Who's Di?"

"Diana, the Princess Diana!"

Dick nodded. "Oh, Diana, she's dead. She died in a car crash."

"Good, Dick. You keep up." Cuddy patted him on the back.

• • •

Back in Cuddy's office, Brenda brought the two of us doughnuts made of air and sugar. Cuddy bit into one as he said, "Justin, you better pray to God the Stand-Up Comedian that this dead girl is not another Jane Doe."

"She's not. She's a waitress at the Tucson."

He stared at me. "For somebody who claims he didn't even go inside that bar yesterday, you sure know a lot about it."

I told him, "When I saw this girl yesterday she was dressed like a Xerox copy of Mavis Mahar. And her hair was mid-length, like Mavis's. I was in the doorway of the Tucson and I heard her asking Mavis if she could get their picture taken together. I can tell you her name...." I closed my eyes, saw the thrilled smiling girl as she leapt up on the band platform to hug the singer. I heard Mavis ask the girl her name. "Her name's Lucy," I told Cuddy.

It took us only half an hour to find out that the waitress Lucy Griggs was twenty-three, single, and lived at home with her divorced mother and her younger brothers when she wasn't living in a low-rent downtown apartment with an indeterminate number of transient roommates. She had dropped out of Haver University after two years of very good grades in order to pursue a career as a singer. She might have pursued it, but she hadn't caught it. She worked as a waitress at the Tucson because the owner let her perform there on slow nights with a local band called Mood Disorders. ("Worst garbage you ever heard in your life," groused the crabby owner, whom we'd admittedly awakened before dawn.)

Yesterday, Lucy had walked out of the Tucson at six P.M., right in the middle of her shift, despite being told that she'd be fired if she skipped out on work one more time. She'd left because Mavis Mahar had offered to take her for a ride in her limousine and Lucy would have sacrificed a far better job than waiting tables at the Tucson for a chance like that, although she (probably) wouldn't have sacrificed her life had she known what was going to happen to her if she went to The Fifth Season with the star.

Nobody had seen Lucy since she and Mavis drove off together. However, her mother, Mrs. Jackie Griggs, rarely saw her daughter from one week to the next anyhow. As she gave us the names of some of Lucy's friends, she didn't appear to be unduly alarmed by a predawn phone call from the police asking about the girl's whereabouts, but then I didn't tell her why we were calling. That sad task was being carried out now by Nancy Caleb-White.

The fact that the fingerprints of the corpse in the morgue did not match those of Mavis Mahar, obtained by fax from Nashville (where she had been booked after her arrest at the Parthenon) was a confirmation of something we had already accepted. We'd identified the wrong victim. The question was, had her killer done the same? The cardboard star, the word "Star" circled in red marker on the clipping from the newspaper, the disfigured head shot of Mavis, all delivered to Cuddy, suggested that Mavis was the intended victim.

It was almost dawn when Cuddy and I headed down in the elevator to leave the Cadmean Building. But as soon as the doors opened at the front lobby, Cuddy pulled me back inside and banged the "Close" button. The large marble space was jammed with reporters and television cameras. "Damn it, damn it!" He pushed hard at the "Up" arrow. "It's leaked!"

"No fooling."

Cuddy returned to his office, wrote and sent down to the lobby a brief press release about the real identity of the murder victim. Then we left through the underground HPD garage and headed toward my Jaguar. He righted a trashcan as he passed it. "Okay," he said, "Let's go on the assumption that this guy thinks he killed Mavis Mahar. Or he thought so at the time. Or maybe he still thinks it's Mavis he killed, we don't know—"

I saw that Etham Foster's lab had looped a neat forensics envelope through my car's door handle. The key was in the ignition.

A HPD cop named Fisher was walking toward us, sipping coffee, reading a newspaper. He stopped when he saw us and held up the morning edition of the *Sun*. The entire front page had only three words on it: "MAVIS IS DEAD!"

Below the headline was a picture of the Irish star performing two nights ago at Haver Field. Affable Ralph Fisher whistled. "Here we go again. See Hillston and die, right?" He offered us doughnuts from a bag he carried.

"I wouldn't be joking with the chief right now," I advised him.

Without ceremony, Cuddy snatched the paper out of Ralph's hand. He had always been the fastest reader I'd ever seen; now it was almost comic how quickly he skimmed Shelly Bloom's "*Sun* Exclusive." He handed the newspaper back to Ralph, telling him to go upstairs right away and make sure Brenda Moore had sent the press in the lobby his statement about the identity of the victim at The Fifth Season and make sure that she had called the rest of the local papers and television stations too. Ralph should tell Brenda to call them all again immediately and assure them that the *Sun* was absolutely, and *irresponsibly* wrong, that Mavis Mahar was not, repeat, not dead.

"She's not?" Ralph's mouth opened and didn't shut. "She's not?"

"Ralph, give me those doughnuts and go!"

Ralph Fisher took off in a sprint, spilling a trail of Starbucks coffee.

I asked Cuddy if Shelly Bloom had said anything in her "exclusive" about the governor's sexual involvement with Mavis

Mahar. He shook his head. "Nada. But Shelly's out on a limb with what she did say. Especially since she's wrong and it's not Mavis."

"Maybe she was annoyed because Bubba wouldn't give her his Porsche," I suggested.

"Too bad. She could have used it to get out of Hillston." He checked his watch; cheap as it was, it never seemed to give him any trouble. "Okay, I want you to go scare Ward Trasker into telling us exactly what he did in that room, or what he told somebody else to do. Right now. Most of all, I want to know who stuck a .22 in a dead girl's face and pulled the trigger. Because even I'm shocked at that, and as you oughta know by now, I already had a view of this post-lapsarian world that makes Hieronymous Bosch look like Mr. Rogers' Neighborhood."

I told him I needed to find Mavis Mahar first. It was conceivable that the killer had shot both women.

"Not anywhere around The Fifth Season. Homer Louge's boys would have stepped on her. Get to Ward. Maybe they did do a video of the real crime scene before they moved her, just to cover their butts. See if you can find out. How about driving me to River Rise on your way?"

"You going to bed?"

He said, "No, I'm getting my car, taking this head shot to Raleigh, see what Wendy says about the handwriting." He picked through the doughnut bag, found a crushed-in chocolate concoction inside, and offered me half.

"No thank you," I told him. "So it's Guess Who."

"Yep, you were right." Licking chocolate from his fingers, he added, "And we're gonna get him and save our jobs. I love my job. Plus, I don't have money and looks to fall back on like you do, JBS Five."

I opened my car door. "Why does everybody think I have money?"

"Because you look like you have money and you—"

I told Cuddy not to get in my car.

His sigh was dramatically loud. "I am real tired, so please

don't say Elvis is about to blow up your Jaguar again because I just want to get to Raleigh."

"Fine. But I don't want you in my car until after you finish eating that chocolate doughnut."

He laughed, stuffed the rest of the pastry in his mouth, and wiped his hands on his jeans. "Oh good lord. Peggy told me you were like this even when you were little. She said when you were four years old you asked for a lock on your bedroom door so your baby brother couldn't crawl in there and mess up your toys."

I rubbed my hand on the backrest. "These seats are Cordova leather, thirty-five years old. I look like I *had* money."

He laughed. "In the South, son, it's the same damn thing."

• • •

When I stepped into Cuddy's apartment with him for some aspirin, his elderly cleaning lady Cleopatra Skelton, large, sooty black, with wild white hair like Don King's, was sitting on the couch with his poodle Martha Mitchell watching *Sunrise Gospel Hour* on cable. She had her legs up on an ottoman and a hot water bottle over them. I asked her how she was feeling.

She moaned softly. "Mr. Savile, I am feeling just like that Etta James song. 'If it wasn't for bad luck, I wouldn't have no luck at all.'"

"I'm sorry to hear that."

"My husband's got the sugar. They're taking his leg tomorrow."

"I'm so sorry, Mrs. Skelton."

"Well, I got this neighbor Nonie Upshaw, she's been trying to run off with my husband for the last ten years and him not havin' a leg gonna make it a lot harder!" She laughed, then asked me for some of the aspirin and then for a glass of water. After she took the pills, she politely inquired about Alice.

"She's still with her family in the mountains."

She nodded. "Well, if you got family, then you always got a light in the wilderness. The police chief needs some family."

"That's very true. Well, I'll see you then."

She waved her hefty arm at Cuddy's collection of jars. "But you need your health too. Mine's gone and how am I suppose to git all this done?" A few years ago Cuddy had improved his interior by removing the photo mural of Cape Hatteras and the life-size cardboard cut-out of Elvis that offered guests a bowl of bite-size Snickers, and by replacing his collection of different beer cans by an almost equal number of indigenous pots from Costa Rica and Guatemala. They probably were very arduous to dust.

"You're right, it's a lot of do. You didn't happen to take Cuddy's telescope upstairs to his study, did you?"

"That old heavy thing?"

"I didn't think so. Nice to see you, Mrs. Skelton."

As Cuddy yawned walking me to the door, I asked him, "Why don't you get some sleep, send somebody else to Raleigh."

Buttoning his fresh shirt, he said, "I'm going to fix this mess myself before we all get fired and poor old Martha Mitchell and Cleopatra over there have to cut down on the gourmet treats."

I pointed out that both his poodle and his cleaning lady were seriously overweight anyhow.

"Shhh," he whispered.

• • •

My instructions were to interview Ward Trasker, but that isn't what I did. I drove to North Cove. And not to ride Manassas around the bridle path, pretending I was leaving behind the familiar things when I was moving in a circle and not getting very far. This dawn I knew exactly where the something new would be. I was there in time to see the sun swelling above the lake like gold. I was waiting there at the edge of the crescent beach in time to watch the morning sky streak across the long wooden dock. I was there because I knew sooner or later that would be where I'd see her.

The seventeen-foot O'Day sailboat came tacking beautifully nearer, its white hull and gleaming white mainsail filling with the morning air. On its next sharp tack, I saw her at the stern, her strong slim arm holding the line. She was dressed in a loose white shirt, and light sparkled on the luminous skin and on hair the color of lions.

I stepped onto the deck and waved until she saw me. She called, "Hi there, boyo!" Her voice was always like a song. Then suddenly the Daysailor caught a quickening breeze and, sailing fast before the wind, the foresail full out, she came flying at the dock like a great swan. At the last minute, she brought the boat sharply about, laughing as she ducked under the beam, and I grabbed the bow and pulled her to me.

"So where's that great black brute of a horse of yours?" she asked me. She looked shockingly rested, carefree, untroubled.

"Miss Mahar, did you know we thought you'd been murdered?" I tied the bowline to the dock post.

My question surprised her. It was obvious that she had no knowledge of the events of the past twelve hours. I held up for her the front page of the *Sun* with its banner headline, "MAVIS IS DEAD!"

Cupping her hands, she squinted into the sun to read the print, then she frowned. But only for a moment, then she laughed and jumped from the boat. I caught her in my arms. "I'm Lieutenant Justin Savile," I told her. "I take it you haven't been back to your bungalow since last night?"

She stayed inside my arms as she said, "Am I killed then? To tell God's truth, there's been days I wouldn't be sorry either." She pulled back from me to look at my eyes. Her own really were— as the magazines said—the color of violets. She smiled the famous smile. "Mavis dead? Now do you believe that at all, Lieutenant?" Soft and slow her hands pulled my face down to hers. "Here's life," she whispered and she kissed me full on the mouth.

Chapter 13

Lady of the Lake

When Mavis stepped out of the sailboat and kissed me, the image I saw was my wife's face. Sharp, clean, clear as autumn air in the North Carolina mountains of her birth. I saw Alice, since our marriage the only woman I had kissed, although before Alice there had been in my prolonged bachelorhood a great many women, some wanting to marry me, some already married, some wanting only entertainment or company or a respite from whatever really mattered to them. Too many women, Cuddy Mangum was always telling me before there was Alice. Too many women and too many drinks in one vague hazy lost weekend a decade long. But when Alice moved into my life—frank and fresh as apples red as her hair—everything that was clouded fled like ghosts from an exorcism. And the ghosts stayed away from our house until the death of our baby son brought them howling back.

I knew there had been more drinks and more men in the briefer life of Mavis Mahar than she bothered to remember. I knew that my responding to her kiss would cost her nothing and might cost me a great deal. For a star like Mavis, seduction was an easy gift and an old habit. Seduction on a grand scale had become a multimillion dollar business, and sex in her private life was notoriously both as casual and as continual as her drinking. I knew all this and reminded myself that I was investigating a homicide with Mavis tangled at its core, tangled by her affair with our state's married governor—a man I saw socially and whose wife Lee I had always liked. I told myself I'd been living without Alice for weeks and without sleep for a day and a night and that in their absence I was likely to be tilted out of balance. And knowing all this, I went right on kissing Mavis Mahar until my wife's face turned from me and faded away.

The old dock moved beneath us as we stood there together embracing, the O'Day Daysailor nudging with a gentle thump into the padded post. Neither of us spoke. For my part, I was certain that if I said anything, even spoke her name, the magic in which I was telling myself I was spellbound would disappear— like the lady of the lake—beneath the mist.

But finally noise did break the spell, the very loud sudden noise of a Channel Seven News helicopter. It was circling above The Fifth Season's grounds, closing in on the bungalows beside the crescent beach. Quickly I led Mavis across the pink imported sand into the pinewoods where the cameraman leaning out of the helicopter couldn't see her. Beneath the pines, a meticulous path bordered with silvery shade plants curved upwards for a hundred yards and then opened near the pool of Bungalow Eight where she had stayed. Holding her out of view, I waited until the helicopter drifted back toward the main house, then said I had to ask her some questions.

"About a kiss? Well, it was a surprise, wasn't it?" she smiled at me.

"Somehow I don't think you were surprised at all," I told her. "But my questions are about a homicide in your bungalow last night."

She gestured at herself. "But do I look murdered?" She spun to show her trim healthy body in the man's shirt that she wore with only white boxer shorts beneath. "If I answer the questions, will you find this poor killed lady a drink now and a bite to eat?"

I said I would and then sat her down on a stone bench on the path. I said that first I needed to know at what time she had left her suite last night and where she had gone. And I needed to know what had happened with Andy Brookside before she left.

Only a few flicks of the famously long eyelashes suggested that she was startled that the Hillston police knew about the governor's visit to her hotel suite. Nor did she challenge why I was asking her. She began instead by laughing: "So it's about Andy. Well, let's see. Last night." She looked out over the lake. "I was pissing drunk, and wild mad, and Andy tried quieting me down and, well, you might as well light yourself with napalm entirely, and dive into a tank of petrol—" She slid her hand up between my legs and touched me. "Don't forget that, will you, darlin'?"

I moved her hand away. "Diving into a tank of petrol isn't in my plans."

"Isn't it now?" She smiled. "You have a different look to you. Well but right you are, it's a dangerous habit."

I walked away from her to the edge of the path. "So you and the governor had a political argument and tore up the bungalow?"

She grinned, movie star teeth that would look perfect on screens a hundred feet wide. "You might say. Andy and I had long since come to the end anyhow. Only did a blackout instead of a fade. Got a fag?"

"I quit years ago. I quit smoking and drinking both. Quit all my dangerous habits."

"Ah, did you for certain?" She took a crumpled pack of Lucky's from her shirt pocket, found one bent in half and tenderly straightened it. "So I chucked a whiskey bottle at Andy's gorgeous head of hair and waved this little gun at him. Just for the drama's sake, you know. I've got my reputation. Poor sod tried not to look too bloody relieved and off he goes in my limo.... *Auf wiedersehen, a bientôt,* bye-bye." She kissed the air cheerfully.

"And the time when you closed your cabaret?"

She held up beautiful arms, the white shirt sleeves falling, leaving bare wrists. "Don't know. No watch. Can't bear the ticking. I could sing you a thousand songs about the time but I never know what it is."

I asked, "And Andy drove directly off The Fifth Season's grounds?"

Her shrug had an elegant indifference. "Could be. Myself, I had a wee bit of a vomit on the beach, swam somewhere, and—so they tell me it's getting to be a habit—passed out." Frustrated, she gave up trying to strike some damp matches to light her cigarette. I found the old Zippo I kept in my jacket pocket and lit her cigarette for her.

"Did they think Andy murdered me then?"

"It crossed our minds."

"Just because my place was a bleedin' wreck and the gun was lying there on the bed?" She smoked deeply, enviably, shaking her head. "No. If Andy Brookside's a killer, it isn't day yet and no mistake. He's a fucker, that's what he is." I wasn't sure whether she meant by the word a bastard or a fornicator; in either case it seemed neither insult nor compliment. "It's not much for murder to come into your heads, is it?"

"Oh somebody was definitely killed. It just wasn't you." I explained to her how at first we'd thought she, Mavis, had shot herself in her bungalow last night, then had discovered that the corpse was in fact that of a young woman named Lucy Griggs whose body had been mistaken for the star's. Mavis blew a startled burst of smoke upwards and with it came unmistakable shock. "Girl named who?"

"Lucy Griggs. The waitress at the Tucson Bar, the place where you were singing? They told me there that you'd brought her back to The Fifth Season with you, promised her some clothes?"

Recognition flooded her face. "Jaezus mother of God, *that* girl? Last night? Here?" Mavis searched my face. "But you don't think she killed herself? Or could be she did, this girl Lucy? Could be she came to my place to do herself harm?"

I told her no, it was unmistakably murder.

She smoked a moment. "Who would kill her? Do you know then?"

I explained carefully, "No, we don't. And it's highly possible that the person thought he *was* shooting at you. If so, you may still be in danger." As she took this in, I asked, "Any ideas about someone who might want to kill you? Jealous husband, lover, fan?"

"Expect so," she said, preoccupied.

"Which?"

"All, I suppose."

But of her three husbands, the third was the tennis player who'd been in Barcelona. The second was an English movie star now famously married to an American movie star with whom he had just made one of the summer's top-grossing movies; it was unlikely that he'd taken time off from publicizing it to come murder Mavis. And her first husband was still in a Belfast prison. "And don't go thinking Brad Pitt in the IRA neither. This shite so-called record-producing sod stole eight million pounds of my bloody royalties before they locked away his ass and God willing he'll rot there."

Pressed, her only suggestion was that recently there had been "a pest of a stalker," who had followed her from Houston to Atlanta where hotel security had threatened him with the police; I could get details about the incident from her manager, Bernadette Davey, who could also give me access to Mavis's fan mail.

"Okay, lovers then?" I asked her. "Besides Governor Brookside."

She carelessly tossed her cigarette onto the path where I quickly ground it out before the pine needles caught fire. "Is it the whole list of my lovers you want?" The seductively murmured implication was that there wasn't world enough or time to compile such a list. Then with a wistful irony, she added, "If you go to it, Lieutenant, there wasn't a murderer in the whole sorry lot of Mavis's lovers but one, and that one it was himself he was wanting to kill and finally managed it with a leap into the Liffey." She gestured a dive.

In fact, I'd read in Cuddy's magazine about the suicide of the young Irishman who'd written her first hit song. I said, "I'm sorry."

With Mavis, one had the feeling that she said nothing that wasn't perfectly staged—each gesture, the delivery of every line, was under her control—yet at the same time that everything she said was perfectly and irresistibly true and—the best trick of all—shared with you alone.

Had she noticed anyone on the grounds near the bungalow? She paused, then told me no. Had the governor and Lucy seen each other when both were at the bungalow? She thought again. She wasn't sure. When she'd arrived at The Fifth Season with the waitress, she'd found Andy waiting there "shitin' thunder," so she'd quickly gotten rid of the girl—presenting her with an outfit of stage clothes as well as money for a taxi back to town. Mavis had told Lucy to walk up to the main house and have them call the taxi for her. Apparently, the girl hadn't done so.

Her recollection of the young waitress's conversation during the limousine ride was sketchy; she'd heard too many of these gushing confessions of idolatry to be much interested in their details. But she did recall thinking that Lucy's infatuation wasn't a sexual come-on, as some approaches from women turned out to be. Instead, Lucy had a strange conviction that she and Mavis were "the same person in two identical bodies." The waitress's passionate delusion (along with their striking physical similarity) had sufficiently intrigued the intoxicated Mavis for her to offer to take the girl back to her hotel to give her a souvenir of her clothing. In the limo, Lucy had snapped another picture of Mavis with her camera. She'd also begged Mavis to listen to a tape of her singing. Mavis wasn't sure what had happened to the camera or the tape; probably both were in Lucy's purse, which she remembered as a large loose-weave yellow bag. As for a straw hat with candles in it—Mavis had no idea what I was talking about. It wasn't hers and she hadn't seen it on Lucy either.

Slowly I pulled details from Mavis's memory. Most of the car ride had been spent with Lucy prattling on with all her proofs of their being "soul twins." How they'd been born only a few days (and years) apart, how neither had ever known their fathers, how both had been in love with married men and both had been stalked, and how both had started their own bands and so on. No, Lucy hadn't told her anything about this married lover, just that there'd been one. She'd amused Mavis by saying that the man's name was "a deep dark secret."

How about the "stalker"? Who was stalking Lucy Griggs?

Mavis pressed at her temples and pulled her hands hard through her hair. "The thirst is on me for certain. Darlin', you don't smoke but you've got yourself that lighter. You don't drink and I'm wondering if maybe you have a shot of whiskey in that pocket of yours as well?"

I said I knew just how she felt. A few more questions, I promised, and I'd see that she got her drink. "Did Lucy say anything specific about this stalker of hers?"

Mavis remembered that the girl and she had laughed about something. "Ah now, what was it? She threw someone over and he took it terrible hard. It was his name, he had a funny name. Scotch. Johnny Walker. That was his true name, she said. He was a stalker and his name was Walker. John Walker, like the scotch."

As she spoke, Mavis looked toward her bungalow. Something she saw there made her suddenly leap up and run forward. I stopped her from rushing to the terrace by gesturing at the helicopter now circling back until it was directly above us. The motor's uproar awakened the small blue and orange figure she'd seen curled up sleeping on the stones of the patio just outside the suite. It was her dresser, Dermott Quinn, faithful sentinel at the tomb—or so he thought—of his dead mistress. She had spotted him there by the doors and suddenly realized he must have thought she was dead. "Let me loose! It's Dermott! He's destroyed."

"I'll send him to you." I pointed out to her the crowd in the parking area above the bungalow; through the landscaped shrubbery you could identify camera trucks and police cruisers, and at the edge of the gravel walk at least fifty people were milling near the yellow DO NOT CROSS tape that stretched from tree to tree. Some of them carried flowers. They still thought Mavis had killed herself and they wanted to be where it had happened.

In the past twenty-four hours, dozens of mostly careless men—law officers, agents and deputies, coroners, government officials, hotel personnel, morticians—had wandered around Bungalow Eight since the shooting, and as a crime scene, it was completely compromised. At this point it was impossible to tell the aftermath of the fight between the Irish singer and the governor from the movements of the killer or for that matter from the pandemonium of the investigators. Trace evidence and prints had already been tampered with before our ID section team had stepped inside the room. If there was ever a suspect and ever a trial, it wouldn't take an Isaac Rosethorn to tear the prosecution apart. Furniture, clothes, even the body itself had been moved by the crew that Ward Trasker had brought in to help him protect the governor because he wanted the governor to appoint him the new head of the Haver Foundation. Now two Hillston police officers and two Haver County sheriff's deputies guarded the murder scene and each other.

Tear-stained, pocked, and dirty, Dermott Quinn looked even more ravaged than he had the night before. My sudden shake of his shoulder scared him into a little shriek. As I shouted in his ear over the helicopter's noise, my news so shocked him that his legs buckled and he fell against me. He searched frantically in my eyes. "She's not dead? Not dead!?" I grabbed a bottle of Jameson's whiskey from a bureau top, handed it to him, turned him toward the path on the other side of the pool and pointed. When he saw her, he shot out the french doors, tripping over his blue platform shoes. The sheriff's deputies whispered to each other and laughed. Through the pines I could just make out Dermott's clumsy leap as he flung his thin legs around Mavis, knocking them both over.

Malik Xavier, still in his first year with HPD, was worried about the whiskey bottle leaving the scene, but I pointed out that every single object in the suite had now been dusted at least twice and that most of the prints we'd found had belonged to the sheriff's department anyhow. The HPD officers laughed and the sheriff's deputies glowered at me. Malik whispered that these sheriff's men had already been told to leave by Chief Mangum but that they had refused to go, although all they did here was try to get their faces in front of the TV cameras or use the hotel phones to call their families.

I arranged with the hotel to forward inquiries to a police hotline where callers would be told that Mavis Mahar was in fact alive and that anyone who had seen or heard anything suspicious last night at The Fifth Season should telephone HPD, but should not come to the hotel. They came anyhow.

I had Malik's partner check the crime scene inventory for a large loose-weave yellow bag that the victim had allegedly had with her last night, and that contained a camera and an audio tape. We couldn't find anything that resembled it. Nor had anyone been able to find the slug that had shattered the shower tiles.

According to The Fifth Season desk, the attorney general Ward Trasker and his wife had checked out earlier in the morning and were presumably driving home to Pinehurst. I left messages at the A.G.'s home and at his Raleigh office. Then I called Cuddy Mangum.

He was in his car on his way back from Raleigh. The Cadmean Building, he said, had been overrun by reporters—most of whom were demanding to talk to him about this latest murder. Because of the media siege, Margy Turbot, the Superior Court judge in the Tyler Norris murder trial, had adjourned proceedings until tomorrow morning. Isaac Rosethorn pitched a fit.

Cuddy said he had just hung up from talking with Bubba Percy, who had passed on to the governor the good news about Mavis Mahar's being alive. "Bubba's so thrilled he's really going to take Jesus as his personal savior, right after he gets Shelly Bloom fired: he says Shelly had promised him not to leak the Mavis story. That big wuss has forgotten how the mix-up wouldn't have happened if he hadn't been too wimpy to get close enough to see if that girl in the shower was dead or alive."

The word from Raleigh was that Wendy Freiberg was confident that the handwriting on the Mavis headshot photo matched the handwriting on the G.I. Jane tag telling me to deliver her body to Cuddy. Forensics thought the red marker used on both was a probable match with the red marker used on the editorial from the *Star*. It looked as if we had another Guess Who homicide. And that was the last thing we wanted the local press to find out any sooner than they had to. Cuddy asked, "So what was the deal with Ward? I assume he's denying he had somebody shoot the corpse."

I told Cuddy that I hadn't spoken with Ward Trasker yet, but I'd left messages. I added that I'd found the rock star. She'd passed out by the lake all night and had no idea that anyone thought she was dead.

There was a long pause, then he said, "Can we keep in mind, somebody *is* dead? Lucy Griggs is dead and Nancy had to tell her mother that. All because Mavis Mahar wanted to play Lady Bountiful."

"Well, come on, that's a little—"

"Are you with Mavis Mahar right now?"

"Yes, we're here at The Fifth Season and it's crawling with press too."

"Did you get a statement from her about last night?"

I filled him in on what Mavis had told me about her encounter with Lucy Griggs and with Brookside. I said, "She can't stay here. I thought I'd take her somewhere—"

He interrupted me. "That woman has at least twenty people traveling with her and they're paid nice salaries to watch out for her. Why don't you let them do it, and you go do what I asked you to do? I don't want messages left for Ward Trasker. I want Ward Trasker questioned. Also, I've set it up for you to take the governor's statement at five this afternoon. I need the real timeline on what happened in that bungalow—from Brookside's arrival 'til you and I got there. I want it typed up by six-thirty tonight."

"Nancy was going to meet me—"

He interrupted bluntly, "Nancy's going to be working with me."

Nancy had been on my investigating team for months. I asked, "What do you mean working with you?"

"Look, Justin, I'm stepping in on this. I'm running a task force out of HPD. While I was in Raleigh, I had a talk with Rhonda and Bunty. They're coming over." Rhonda Weavis and Bunty Crabtree were female special agents of the FBI, working out of the Raleigh field office, regional-based and specialist-trained at VICAP in Quantico. Their specialty was serial sex-related homicide. They lived together in a big new house in a gated community. Some law people thought they were a couple and others thought they were just splitting the mortgage on five thousand square feet with two Jacuzzis and a club pool. Those of us who liked them called them "R&B." Or "RhoBu." I'd also heard them called "Weavis and Bunthead," "the Bureau Bitches," and persistently by Sheriff Homer Louge, "those two Lesbionic girls."

Cuddy was saying, "The task force's gonna meet in 105. They're setting it up now. We'll need all your files by this evening."

It was obvious that I wasn't in charge of the Guess Who homicides anymore. "So, am I going to be answering to R&B?"

He told me I was going to be answering to him.

I said, "You're not a homicide cop anymore. You're the chief of police."

"And while I'm in my office writing pep talks for Kiwanis buffets, some psycho's slicing out women's tongues and eyes. And the 'homicide cops' can't figure out who. Mavis Mahar, hey, no trouble finding her. But the son of a bitch that *told* us he killed these women, him no clue. When I was in homicide, we *caught* the killers, you remember that?"

His sarcasm infuriated me. "You want somebody to blame? Fine, go for it, Cuddy, be my guest. You and RhoBu go catch Guess Who."

"Don't you think that'd be a good thing for a change?"

"Just do it by the Fourth of July. That's two weeks. Oh, and since you're so focused on Lucy Griggs—now that I've told you who your victim is—maybe I should also tell you that Lucy was being stalked by her old boyfriend. Could be he followed her out here. Could even be he meant to kill Mavis out of jealousy. Check on a local musician named John Walker. Just a thought." And I dropped the phone into the receiver.

• • •

Dermott Quinn slipped inside the french doors from the bungalow terrace and tugged at my sleeve. "She wants to talk to you," he whispered so as not to be heard by the four young men—ours and the sheriff's—still keeping an eye on each other from opposite sides of the suite.

I gave a pat to his bony chest. "You were right, Dermott. She didn't kill herself."

Tears wet the dresser's straight pale eyelashes. "Aye. But I feel bad for the other one, the waitress. Just a fan and some fucker does her so." He showed genuine sympathy but little curiosity about Lucy Griggs. All his focus was on Mavis. A second news helicopter had joined the first; they were swarming above the bungalow. Wrapping a pear and apple from a gift basket into a napkin, he gave them to me, begging me to get Mavis away and keep her safe. He'd deal with the "bleedin' rats-ass" media. I saw there was no need to warn Dermott Quinn against them; he'd lived for years with a superstar and knew more about the press than I ever would. He explained that Mavis wanted to make a statement—but at her own time and under her own terms. He was going to call her manager who was to set up a press conference at the Sheraton in time for the evening news. The manager would also start negotiating with Haver University to reschedule the cancelled concert. Taking the fruit from him, I picked a round of cheese from the basket and asked him if he had a knife. He found a room service tray and handed me a dinner knife. I told him I'd meant a sharp knife, like a Swiss Army knife, did he own one?

"Knives or guns neither, I want nothing to do with them myself. I don't like anything dangerous about me."

"Except Mavis Mahar?"

He looked at me a moment then slowly nodded. "Ah, for certain. Except Mavis."

I gestured out the doors at the police and the press. "Is this what her life's usually like? Except for the dead body?"

Dermott Quinn gave me a smile a little condescending about my naïveté. "Dead bodies too. There was a student in Singapore hanged himself in a tree outside our hotel, last December it was."

"Over Mavis?"

The dresser raised his scrawny shoulders. "Prove his love is what he said in his letter. She's waiting in that boat for you. You'll take good care?"

I told him protecting people was part of my job.

"That's why you're good for her. See she's at the Sheraton at half past three." A bee had flown in through the terrace doors; he very carefully and gently waved it back outside with a folded magazine. Moving closer, he looked seriously at my face. "You know, you look a terrible lot like Niall."

"Who?"

"Niall Mahar. She took his name. Wild man he was. Played a beautiful guitar, but drank himself silly and went lookin' for fellows to fight 'til they kicked in his face. He taught Mavis a bit of music and he wrote her a gorgeous song. It was the first time she went platinum. 'Light at Midnight.'"

I said I'd heard it.

"But that song was the death of them. He wasn't in her class and knew it and couldn't live with it. Ah, but she loved that poxie fucker."

I asked if Niall Mahar was the one who had killed himself by jumping off a Dublin bridge into the Liffey River.

"He did indeed, the eejit. She said you're going for a sail." Dermott Quinn pulled a pink rosary from his tight pants. "Give her this. It'll do her no harm. And leastways, they say you can't drown on St. John's Eve."

• • •

As I walked toward the woods, the news helicopter swooped around to see if I was worth following and decided I wasn't. So I made my way across the beach to the dock and, casting off the O'Day, jumped aboard. Mavis was lying hidden in its hull. "May your fire never go out," she said, raising her whiskey bottle to me.

I didn't have time or ballast in me for this sail and I doubted she did either. But I didn't care.

Out on the lake, I accepted her offered drink and moved away so she could take the rudder. The whiskey burned my throat and memories rushed back. It had been a long time.

"I'll have you on the cigs again as well soon enough," she predicted. Rightly as it turned out.

I asked her, "You want everybody to share your sins?"

"Oh, not everybody," she smiled.

When I gave her the rosary from Quinn, she wrapped it around her wrist, making a bracelet of it. "So it's St. John's Eve today. Poor Dermott's a country boy and believes all that shite.... Midsummer's Eve you know. That's when you go lookin' for flowers that will tell a girl about her future fellow.... Dermott'd like to see me with a good strong safe married man." She took my hand and tapped the gold wedding ring on my finger. "Isn't that you, Lieutenant? A good strong married man."

I swung the rosary in front of her. "I'd say your friend was determined to save you from hell."

She tilted her head and spit whiskey out from her mouth in a playful spray. "And I'm determined to go there."

"Well not today, I hope. Not with me, I hope."

She just smiled and took a bite from her pear.

Chapter 14
Queen of the Night

The Irish whiskey was warm, the cool morning wind fresh, the sky Carolina blue and racing with white clouds. I'd sailed Pine Hills Lake since my boyhood, but Mavis had a feel for its water as sure as mine. We were good together. Heeled over, sail snapped taut, we leapt across the deep water, sheering foam. She told me she'd practically lived in a boat until she was eight, sailing daily on Bantry Bay with her older brother. His name was Willie Connolly. Nearly every day Willie had taken her out in his skiff. He'd found the wooden boat smashed up in a rocky cove, fixed it, and made a business from it. For a few pounds he took tourists out to photograph the seals sunning on the islands in the bay. She said Willie was a wonderful sailor "and the sweetest soul ever lived altogether," but that he was big and shambly with epilepsy and a funny twist in his face that put off the tourists. So he brought along his baby sister Agnes because she was pretty and good for business, especially with the Americans. They'd give her as much as five dollars for singing "I'll Take You Home Again, Kathleen" and even more for "Danny Boy" with a tear in her voice. With Agnes drumming up trade, they'd made a success. Willie called her his lucky angel.

"Some luck, some angel," she sighed, leaned over the gunnel and splashed water in her face and her hair. "Ah, I miss him still."

"He's dead?"

A shake of her head and water drops in the sun flung like crystals around her. "So he is." She told me the story as I'd read it in the magazine. "We'd dropped off the German couple and were going home and all of a sudden one of Willie's seizures came on him. He fell out of the boat and I couldn't pull him back, try though I did 'til my heart was bursting out of my chest, so big he was and myself so little, a girl of eight. He drowned then and there, my brother Willie, nineteen years old." She pushed the rudder away from her, swung the beam about, turned the bow before the wind. "And I never loved another so."

After a while I asked, "Your only brother?"

"Only everything. There were but two men in my life that left me—well, me shitebag da, but him I don't count—two men and both by drowning." She sipped again from the bottle and sang softly, "'It's been a long time comin' but a change is gonna come.'...Sam Cooke, ah, Willie loved that Sam Cooke. 'There's no music but the American blacks,' he'd say. I took his records with me when I ran off; seven albums he had, Motown hits. But myself I like it all. Country, R&B, blues, especially early blues."

"So I heard from Bubba Percy."

"Ah, him." All poor Bubba's deficits modulated through her two monosyllables.

I pointed out an inlet ahead where a large gray shallow-roofed summerhouse with wide verandahs sat above a green lawn. On the lakefront, a white gazebo was shaded by two huge willow trees. "Head her there," I said. "It's my family's summer house."

She raised an eyebrow. "So?"

"So I've got .78s by Sippie Wallace and Ida Cox. I've got Louise Bogan's 'Tricks Ain't Walkin' Tonight.' I've got the 1925 original of Bessie Smith and Louis Armstrong doing *St. Louis Blues.*' And I've got very nice cheese for your apple."

Two could play at the seduction game.

• • •

Although christened "Nachtmusik" by my Mozart-loving father because of all the windchimes my mother hung in its willow trees, the lake house had belonged to my maternal family the Dollards since the 1880s. In their typically unimaginative way, they had always called it simply "Summer Place." Since my father's death, my brother Vaughn and his wife Jennifer—who thank God live in Chevy Chase—had been trying to trick our mother into selling the house ("It's just sitting there. Just list it, just see what you could get, the market's through the roof, just call a realtor..."), but I had relied on Mother's fluttery indecisiveness to keep them at bay. Now since her stroke, she didn't even remember that she owned the lakefront property. I've kept putting money in savings so that when Vaughn and I inherit Summer Place, I can buy his share from him. As Cuddy says, I like old things.

Mavis wandered everywhere through the large rambling house, with no notion of possible trespass. For coolness, all the rooms had tall windows and large french doors and opened— Louisiana style—onto the verandah or above onto a balcony. There was less furniture than there'd been in my childhood because everyone in the family "borrowed" from Nachtmusik whenever in need of a wicker chair or a pine hutch. Actually, the more they removed, the better I liked it: the present spareness of the furnishings had a soothing effect on me. With Alice off in the mountains, I'd taken to spending some of my nights out here. One reason was that Summer Place is closer to the stables where I keep Manassas. The other reason is that my baby son Copper didn't die here.

I was eating Stilton cheese and an apple when finally Mavis skipped down the wide stairs from the bedrooms and flung herself into an ancient Morris chair. She took a slice of the green apple from me. "So what was your *winter* home, a palace maybe?"

I said my family hadn't been rich but they'd been comfortable for a long time.

She laughed. "You American sods never think you're rich. Now do you know what I'm going to tell you? My mother cleaned a hotel in Glengarriff not so big as this and too much for her bad feet it was at that." The singer poured herself a glass full of her whiskey and took it to the small white spinet where I'd left out sheet music of the Scott Joplin that I played too slowly. The piano had been my mother's; she called it "The Summer Piano" and she and my father, an amateur violinist, played Mozart duets here in the long August evenings when he came home to us from Haver Medical School, which he ran. It was my mother who gave me piano lessons. A sudden rush of memory took me back to sitting with her on this white wooden bench, her hands patiently guiding mine to form the chords, our tanned bare legs side by side, in our summer shorts, my legs then shorter than hers that now seemed so small and frail to me.

Mavis's fingers raised nonchalantly over the keys and suddenly a strong sad rolling stride of bass melody shook the room. She sang from an old blues that I'd heard before, "When I…came in…to this ole world, I didn't come here to stay. / I didn't bring nothin' into this ole world. / And nothin' I'll carry away." The music stopped as suddenly as it had started. She waved her whiskey glass around the room. "Darlin', you and Mavis got more than we can carry away, that's for certain. I am terrible, terrible rich."

I said I would imagine so.

"All of a sudden I had more money than time. And that's surely a curious situation in which to find yourself at twenty years of age when you grew up with a poor mum longing day and night after a ratty plastic reclining chair collecting dust in a cheap store window."

I expected her to tell me some tragic way in which her sainted mother had died—starved or clubbed by British soldiers or eaten by venereal disease—but instead she said that as far as she knew, her bitch of a mother still lived in County Clare; at least somebody at the rest home was cashing the checks she sent. She said frankly she had never liked her mother, who was "righteous religious." "Always lighting the candles to these bloody martyred saints of hers that got burned up and raped and chopped to bits, their tongues pulled out and their heads whacked off." The mother had even told her son Willie that his fits were signs of sin and his own fault.

The war with Mrs. Connolly had driven Mavis to run away when she was eleven. She stole the money to take the bus to Dublin to find an aunt of hers whose name was Mavis. Her mother asleep in the lumpy bed that morning as she robbed her purse was the last sight she'd had of her. "Always smackin' me. 'You're the spit of Mavis and the twos of you will be burnin' in hell together for all eternity.' So I say, 'That's fine by me, Ma, for I'd rather be damned with Aunt Mavis and the devil in hell than sittin' with you on the high cold throne of God.'"

I laughed. "That's a mouthful for an eleven-year-old."

"Not for the Irish, me boyo. We've done bollocks all but talkin' at each other since the Middle Fuckin' Ages."

When I asked what had been so damnable about her aunt, she said that the original Mavis was either a junkie hooker or she'd let a Protestant get her pregnant, or both. The young Agnes had never been able to locate her aunt in Dublin, but she had taken her name and made it famous all over the world. And as soon as she'd made the money to do so, she'd hired a detective to find her relative. The detective learned that her aunt had recently died of cancer. After he found the grave for her, Mavis had her aunt reburied in County Clare beside Willie under a marble tomb that cost ten thousand pounds. "My aunt used to say when we'd go by that church, 'This cemetery's shite. I want a stone so grand and gorgeous the Mother of God will be proud to come calling, and please Jaesuz, she'll bring champagne and caviar.' That was her dream of heaven, someday sitting down to champagne and caviar."

I helped myself to a glass of her whiskey and toasted her aunt with it. "To the two Mavises. May your fire never go out either."

"Ah," she grinned as she watched me sipping at the whiskey, and when I finished the glass and poured another, she said strange words in a raspy voice. "Aithníonn ciaróg ciaróg eile."

I asked her if it were Gaelic and she nodded that it was. "It's an old proverb. 'One beetle recognizes another beetle.'"

I knew what she meant and didn't bother pretending I didn't. "Then you've never seen your mother since?"

She drank from my glass. "Never once. But I can see her still, with her brown kerchief tight knotted under her chin and her black purse in her fists and her legs locked together, waiting at the bus stop." She looked at me and smiled. "So this is Nacht-musik. Am I the Queen of the Night then?"

"What do you think?"

She turned back to the piano and started singing in a raw throaty voice:

I don't want you to be no slave.
I don't want you to work all day.
I don't want you to be true.
I just want to make love to you.

She circled slowly around and looked at me. I asked her if she would like breakfast, although I was sorry I couldn't offer her champagne and caviar.

"I wouldn't be sorry for an egg," she told me. "But I hate to leave just yet." Her left hand played a slow blues beat. She looked at me again "Not when I've come to such a handsome place with such a handsome fellow."

I moved to the fireplace, lit the newspaper I kept ready beneath the logs. "We don't have to leave. I'll cook you some-thing. There's food here." The month-old newspaper in the fire was the *Hillston Star* and I noticed the small headline, "POLICE ADMIT NO PROGRESS ON G.I. JANE HOMICIDE," before the words flamed into ashes.

Mavis smiled at me, not watching her hands as they moved slowly over the keys. "You cook then, do you, Mr. Savile? Ah, quite the catch you'd be. You sail...you ride...you send the bad fellows off to prison...." After every phrase, she played the slow rhythmic beat. "You get the girl." She turned again on the bench, leaned toward me. "Do you get the girl?"

The fire leapt up behind me. I said, "Yes I do."

She stood and walked toward me. "At home on St. John's

Eve in the country, the fellow and his girl they're supposed to take hands, you know, and jump over the fire, and that'll tell them if they're meant for one another or not."

"Here's the fire," I said and pulled her down toward me.

• • •

Afterwards we slept for an hour and it was two-thirty when I cooked the omelette while she listened to my old blues .78 recordings. She asked for pencil and paper and wrote things down as she played the Bessie Smith song again and again. In the hall, the old black dial phone suddenly rang.

No one knew that I came here to Nachtmusik but Alice and Cuddy. I didn't want to talk to either one. I let the phone ring. There was no answering machine in the house. Finally it stopped.

• • •

Back on the lake, the wind had died and I lowered the sails and used the outboard motor to speed us along. We were in a hurry now, late for our lives. Mavis was listening to voice mail on her small cell phone. I'd left my car near the bridle path and had decided we'd go straight there and avoid The Fifth Season. I'd take her back to the Sheraton where her entourage was waiting for her. For safety's sake, just in case, I asked her to promise to keep her people around her at all times.

"Ah," she smiled ironically, "'people around me at all times.' Wouldn't that be unusual now? Eight years ago, I woke up one noon and I was a celebrity and there were people all around me, who knows where they came from, and there've been people all around me ever since. Combing my hair and patting my face and hauling me along halls onto stages and into cars and onto planes and under lights and stand here and move there and hold it please. I can't go sit in the loo without people shoving their autograph books under the stall door at me. I haven't bought my own pair of knickers in fuckall because I can't go strolling in the shops. You know, I heard where in Memphis they'd open up stores for Elvis in the middle of the night like they do for the bleedin' Queen. Maybe Dodi's dad would do that for me at Harrod's, what do you think?"

"I think stars are famous because they want to be. They like it."

She laughed like a song. "Of course I like it! I feckin' love it."

We were coming close to The Fifth Season. I could see the outdoor ring of the stables where I boarded Manassas; it bordered the resort on one side. I had assumed the Daysailor belonged to the resort, but when I asked her if the resort had a boathouse so I could return the sailboat later, she said she hadn't taken the boat from the hotel. She had seen the O'Day tied to the small dock of some cottage that she'd swum past this morning. So she'd taken it for a sail. There'd been a duffel bag down in the hull with clean clothes in it—that had been where she'd gotten the white shirt and shorts. She wasn't sure which cottage it had been. Painted blue, she thought, but maybe not.

She sat in the bow, resting on her arms. She'd thrown open the white shirt to feel the afternoon sun on her breasts. Like everything about her, they were beautiful. Contrary to all the reports in magazines, neither nipple was pierced. I could see the red birthmark of a star on the side of her neck, the stigmata of her destiny, the mark that hadn't been there when I'd looked at the body of Lucy Griggs.

I said, "You just stole it? Somebody else's boat?"

She turned back to me and laughed. "Well, darlin', I'm not planning to keep it forever, am I?"

It was a warning. Or should have been.

part two

On the Devil's Horn
Thursday, June 21–Friday, June 29

Chapter 15

New Deal Tavern

At dawn when Mavis kissed me, the media had only just begun to hear the first whispers that she was dead. Through the morning, grief raced across the world. People cried in the streets. In our global village of strangers, our strongest feelings may be for celebrities we've never met. But by noon, the *Sun* had apologized and CNN had explained to the world that the rumors were false and that nobody had been murdered but a waitress who was nobody. And then the world that had sighed and cried and rushed to heap altars of flowers and cuddle toys at the star's death site, now sent up a cheer, reprieved by the happy news flashing on television screens across oceans. Mavis Mahar was alive. It had been thrilling that she had killed herself and it was thrilling again that she hadn't. In fact, her quick resurrection was even more satisfying. For there is one discontent in what is otherwise a thoroughly enjoyable gobble at the trough of public grief: after the shock subsides, people are forced to notice that the celebrity they are mourning really is gone. Gone for good. There will be no new footage. Never again will those particular stars do the glamorous dangerous things that made us all so fascinated with them in the first place. Never will they be messily divorced or noisily adulterous or drunkenly arrested or caught in the nude by paparazzi in their Mediterranean love nests again.

Of course, Mavis had taken a risk by being alive. Early death has its advantages for stars. It makes them endlessly young. Out of the imperishable rerun of their self-destruction comes their immortality. A Marilyn, an Elvis, a Diana—and maybe someday still, a Mavis Mahar. She was reckless enough. But for now the magic of Mavis was her escape from death. Here she was, so recently excitingly a suicide (or better yet, so gruesomely murdered), the newspapers still on the streets around the globe screaming:

MAVIS E MORTA!
SÄNGERIN MAVIS MAHAR BEENDET SICH.
LA MAVIS SE SUICIDE!

And then only hours later, here she was again *not* dead. Here she was waving at her fans live on the news, alive to sing for them and wreak havoc for them once more. Alive to make the question of who may have *tried* to kill her international news, and so a nightmare for Cuddy Mangum.

As for the young woman who actually had been killed in Bungalow Eight at The Fifth Season Resort in a small city in the Piedmont of North Carolina, she was only an ordinary person and the world didn't care about her. Ordinary people get themselves murdered every day. Lucy Griggs' only claim on even a minute of the world's time was her bad luck that the killer had mistaken her for Mavis Mahar.

The governor's press secretary Bubba Percy was feeling, as he boasted, "pumped." We'd just watched Mavis on television making a live statement to as many of the media as could squeeze into the ballroom of Hillston's largest downtown hotel. Quietly dressed, beautifully made-up (Dermott Quinn must have been waiting when I dropped her off at the Sheraton), the rock star was somber about the murder of Lucy Griggs, she was charming about being alive herself, she was apologetic about the missed concert at Haver Field—while leaving the effective if erroneous impression that it was the homicide itself that had somehow caused her failure to show up.

And she was irresistible in her pledge to redo the concert whenever the university would let her. She'd do two concerts and she'd sing all night! But as she spoke, the person I kept seeing wasn't this celebrity on the television screen, but the woman with whom I'd been making love only hours earlier. A troubling passionate private woman, who was now performing the part of Mavis Mahar the rock star.

Meanwhile, as far as Bubba Percy was concerned, the best thing about the singer's appearance was her complete silence on the subject of Governor Andrew Brookside. Equally miraculous to him was the fact that no one else mentioned Brookside's name in the cacophonous burst of questions shouted at Mavis as soon as she finished her statement.

"You Riverdancing bitch, I love you!' Bubba told the television set hung above the bar at the New Deal Tavern. "Home free!"

It was amazingly true. With the single exception of Shelly Bloom's *Sun* exclusive ambiguously talking about "unconfirmed rumors" linking Mavis Mahar to "a second high-ranking Southern politician" (the first presumably the ruined Tennessee Congressman), not a single leak had tied Brookside to the Irish star in any way. (At least not publicly—half the crowd here in the New Deal were trading rumors about the affair right this minute, but they were all "in the business.") And not even this in-crowd seemed to have a clue that the governor had been in Mavis's bungalow on the actual night of the murder.

According to Bubba, it was possible that the only people who knew the truth knew that it was in their best interests to keep their mouths shut. Admittedly, this group was not small: in addition to Mavis, the governor, Bubba, Cuddy, and myself, it included at the minimum the N.C. Attorney General and Brookside's two crisp lawyers, the Haver County D.A. and the coroner, the sheriff, an SBI agent, the reporter Shelly Bloom, the hotel manager, the murderer, and (I suspected from her predawn visit to Cuddy's office) the governor's wife, Lee Haver Brookside. Of course, if someone in this group happened to *be* the murderer, that cut the number down by one.

The potential danger in this free-floating knowledge did not seem to bother the press secretary at all. He chortled, "Jesus loves me and I love Him," still fooling with the born-again vow to which Cuddy had earlier referred. Elatedly he slapped the bar in front of him and crowed, "Come on, Justin, I'm buying," to the astonishment of the local politicians and press corps around us, all of whom knew him to be notoriously cheap.

The state auditor hit his arm. "Bubba! And after I heard you were so tight, you shut off your mother's defibrillator to save on the electric bill."

A columnist called to me, "Don't turn your back on him, Savile. Last time Percy bought somebody hard liquor in here, he tried to fuck her before she could drink it."

But their ribbing rolled like water off the oil of his slick self-regard. "Mock on, mock on, Voltaire, Rousseau," he told them cheerfully as he led me past a loud table of state legislators over to a corner booth.

The New Deal was only half-a-block from the State House, and since 1938 had been serving increasingly expensive Italian food to government officials and the reporters who got paid for talking about them. Low and wide, it had two dark noisy dining areas—the original one in which Democrats traditionally gathered and the "New Room" for Republicans (where, rumor was, prices went even higher). The walls of each were entirely filled with photographs of famous patrons shaking hands with three generations of New Deal owners. Giuseppe DiSilio with Harry Truman and a governor. Joe DiSilio Jr. with JFK and my uncle Senator Kip Dollard. Scott DiSilio with Bill Clinton and Andy Brookside. Bubba pointed at this last picture as we passed it. "Two lucky bastards," he grinned.

I reminded him that his boss was by no means free and clear. Brookside was still a material witness in the Lucy Griggs' homicide, if not a suspect. The same, I noted, could be said for Bubba himself.

Bubba told me blandly that he'd never met or heard of Lucy Griggs and neither had the governor. If the person who'd shot her had done so thinking she was Mavis Mahar, the killer was not Andy, but one of the "Slut Queen's" ten thousand other lovers.

I stopped myself from saying, "She doesn't think much of you either," and pointed out that even if Brookside was innocent, it was conceivable that someone had killed (or thought they'd killed) Mavis Mahar in order to implicate the governor, knowing that he'd been there on the night of the murder. The homicide still might prove to be a political vendetta against Andy Brookside in an effort to derail his reelection bid. Or it might be an act of more personal revenge. Either way would mean that the lid, which Bubba had gloated about keeping so tightly in place, was about to blow off and splatter the whitewashed walls of the Governor's Mansion.

Brookside's press secretary gave his auburn hair a quick comb. "Hey, don't even try heavying up on me, Savile. Your Cuddy-buddy Porcus Rex had me in a damn interrogation room today. Not his office, an interrogation room! Like he was trapped in some Jimmy Cagney flick and hadn't heard you can't slap the suspects around any more. You can shoot them but you can't slap them around. Does he really think we're going to roll over?" He gestured at a waitress, both his arms waving like some Balinese dancer.

I'd had one hour's sleep in the past thirty-two and the scotch was numbing me. I said I wasn't sure what he meant by "roll over."

"That crazy arrogant bastard of yours—"

"Stop saying of mine."

"—told me I had two weeks to resign as State House press secretary." Bubba swung a passing waitress around by the arm to stop her and got himself rapped on the head with her pencil. "Oww! Honey pot, two more of the same."

"You got it, Septic Tank," the big bottle-blonde told him matter of factly and kept going.

Unfazed, Bubba went on. "Porcus was on a roll, you didn't know? Told your coroner to resign, told the sheriff and the D.A. to resign, ditto that kid SBI agent, ditto Ward Trasker."

I was abruptly awake again. "But isn't Trasker retiring after the election anyhow?"

"According to your God Almighty Police Chief, Trasker hasn't got 'til November. He has to resign in two weeks. Now get this. Your boss gives me a letter to give Andy telling *him* to resign!"

"You're kidding."

"No way. He wants the fucking governor to resign! And if we all don't squat over and spread 'em for ole Saint Thomas More Mangum, he's charging us with conspiracy to obstruct justice by tampering with a crime scene and destroying evidence in a felony homicide, and even hinting about the big kahuna—accessory after the fact."

I sat back and whistled, then toasted him and sipped the last bit of my scotch. "Well, frankly, Bubba, it's all true, isn't it? I mean maybe not you yourself personally—all you did was lie, cheat, and try to steal a raincoat. Well, you ran out on a girl lying in her own blood, that from a safe distance you mistook for somebody else."

"That girl, whoever she was, was already dead!"

I looked over at the television. Local news was now showing footage of the helicopter's aerial shot of The Fifth Season bungalow; bizarrely enough, I could see myself walking across the lawn from the terrace to the woods where Mavis was waiting. "Isn't what Cuddy says the truth?"

He spluttered at his beer foam. "Don't make me quote you Pontius Pilate on the truth, Savile."

"I guess that's part of being born again, Bible quotes? Why shouldn't they resign?" I leaned forward to keep my voice low. In The New Deal, you always had to be careful. "Bubba, they did destroy evidence, they did obstruct justice. You know it."

He shrugged. "So they took her out of the shower and picked up a few condom foils, so what?"

"So what? For Christ's sake, they took a .22 pistol and *shot* the poor girl between the eyes with it after she was already dead!"

He gagged on his beer. "What!"

"Man, you *are* out of the loop. They shot Lucy Griggs in the face, and left her on the floor with Andy's raincoat over her. They shot her because whoever killed her had gouged out her eyes and even our sieve-head coroner would have known that wasn't suicide. Not that you noticed, but then I guess you didn't really look all that closely."

Bubba's eyes opened wide, then wider. His face changed color so fast that his freckles stood out like a sudden attack of measles. "Somebody cut out her eyes?"

"Right, then in comes Ward and, like the hotel manager—and like you—he mistakes the victim for Mavis. Ward either thinks Andy killed her or he thinks *any* kind of involvement in a sensational murder won't look good on Andy's résumé."

"You think it would?" Bubba asked with a trace of his old sarcasm.

"So they wipe down the bungalow and Ward gets somebody to shoot the corpse with a gun of Mavis's that was lying on her bed. They stick the gun in her hand. Osmond Bingley is hauled in and signs the death certificate 'self-inflicted gunshot wound.' They rush her out to Pauley and Keene Funeral Home where they figure those bozos won't even notice her eyes are gone and that if you have a bullet still lodged in your brain, you don't have an exit wound through the back of your skull."

He whispered, "Are you shitting me? Don't shit me, Justin."

I leaned back. "I have to keep remembering you were a teen campaigner for George McGovern. I know you've been selling out ever since, Bubba, and I know you think you're complete jaded scum, but, buddy, you're seriously out of your league."

The waitress came over with our new drinks. Bubba took the opportunity to collect himself. When he gave her a dollar tip and she sardonically asked if he wanted change, he told her to "just bank it for the next time I drop in." His caustic eyebrow back in place, he leaned forward and told me, "Okay, so maybe I'm a little surprised they'd go that far. I saw Ward was cleaning the place up, but I figured it was cosmetic."

"You could still call it cosmetic, I suppose."

"I figured they threw the raincoat over her not knowing it was Andy's. That it got shoved under the bed when they bagged the body."

I said, "Frankly, resigning may be the least of people's troubles."

Now Bubba's smugness returned, full smirk. "You're the one out of your league. The only resignation on the table here is going to have C.R. Mangum's name written on it. These guys aren't about to mess up this reelection. I don't care if they stuck the .22 between her eyes while she was *alive* and pulled the trigger. They'll come up with a spin that'll smear your pal Mangum so bad his own mama wouldn't let him in her house."

It was certainly true that Ward Trasker was stonewalling me: his wife had said he was at his office, his office had returned none of my messages, and when I'd showed up there an hour ago had told me Ward was home with his wife. I said, "It'll be hard for them to ignore a warrant for arrest."

The press secretary snorted. "They'll call Mangum's bluff. He backs off or he's out of there. Where's a police chief that's been booted going to get a warrant from? Besides, Mangum loves that job too much. He lives for that job. He'll do what he has to to keep it."

All of a sudden the contents of an entire pitcher of beer flew at Bubba's face. Spluttering and flailing he leapt up, knocking his own beer into his lap. "What the fuck!"

"You shithead!" It was Shelly Bloom, the *Sun* reporter, in a rage so intense her whole slender body trembled, even the short black wings of her hair, as she shook the last drops of the overturned pitcher onto Bubba's head.

There were hoots, cheers, and applause from our end of the dining room where the blond waitress shouted at her, "You go, girl!"

"Sit down, Shelly!" I stood and slid her ahead of me into my side of the booth. Bubba was frantically wiping beer out of his eyes and hair with his pink Versace shirt.

"You got me fired!" she hissed at him. "I kept Brookside's name out of it and you still got me fired!"

"Lower your goddamn voice. Who told you that?" He grabbed a wad of paper napkins from the dispenser and wiped himself down.

She snorted. "Which? That I was fired or that you arranged it?"

"Well, both," he said as he shook beer from his comb and used it on his hair. "Listen, Shelly, you're sniffing the wrong luggage on the carousel here."

"What?" She turned to me. "What kind of lame metaphor is that? Sniffing the luggage on the carousel? I can't believe this man was ever the editor of the *Hillston Star!*"

"Mrs. Edwina Sunderland owned it and she was in love with him," I threw in. "According to him."

The waitress tossed Bubba a large towel. "Don't bother to tip me again," she told him. "Your dollar's still good."

"Thanks, honey. Listen, bring this young lady another beer. Just a glass." Bubba patted himself down. "Listen, Shelly, I was sorry to hear you got the boot, but I figured it was because you fucked up and went front page on a bad lead."

I had to hold her back from lunging across the booth to shake him. "You bastard, you're the one gave me the bad lead! You told me Mavis Mahar shot herself!"

He shrugged. "You told me you'd hold the story for twenty-four hours." They glowered at each other.

I interrupted the staring match to ask Shelly if she'd seen anyone lurking in the vicinity of Bungalow Eight last night while she was out there lurking herself. She said no, she hadn't, and don't bother to ask. Mangum had already had her hauled into a police cruiser this morning, dragged to HPD, and questioned for over an hour. The city would be lucky if she didn't sue them as soon as she finished suing the governor's staff for forcing her out of her job because she knew too much.

Bubba tried humor. "If you're out of work, you probably shouldn't have spent fourteen bucks on that pitcher of beer."

"You think I'm kidding, Percy?" she seethed. "I'll work twenty-four hours a day 'til I blow your reelection back to the Stone Age."

He shook his head with a paternal smile. "Shelly, you've got the wrong idea about modern journalism. It's not about investigation, it's not about truth, it's not about *work*. It's about looking good when you carry the press releases of the powerful to an ignorant public with the attention span of a gnat. You're a good-looking spin toady, sweetheart."

"Maybe you are."

He grinned. "Hey, thanks. You noticed."

I stood, wiping beer from my jacket's sleeve. "Excuse me. I have a meeting with the governor under discussion."

Shelly laughed bitterly. "Be sure you have it before November or it'll be with the ex-governor."

Leaving the booth, I could hear Bubba telling Shelly that if she'd treat him to dinner at Pogo's, he'd slip her a hot lead about the gubernatorial race that would get her her job back at the *Sun* for sure.

"You're fucking amazing," I heard her say.

"I think so," he replied.

On my way out of the New Deal, I saw Margy Turbot, the woman Cuddy called the best-looking judge in the state, in a tête à tête with Ken Moize, the former attorney general whose decision to quit to run a human rights organization had made it possible for the assistant A.G. Ward Trasker to ascend to the post. I'd always liked Ken Moize. I couldn't decide if he was advising Margy to run for A.G. on Brookside's ticket or to avoid his mistake by saying no. Or maybe the two of them were just having lunch.

I approached them. "Hey, Margy. So the problem wasn't media interference, after all? You really adjourned the Norris trial so you could come over here and drink Cosmopolitans with Ken."

Moize, recently divorced, laughed. "I wish. All she talks about is Cuddy Mangum."

Margy patted his arm. "What can I say, I'm a sucker for a Raleigh Medal winner." At any rate, she cared enough about him to ask me to pass along a message. "Tell Cuddy to watch his back, okay? Ken's hearing things." Ken nodded at me. "And so am I."

I asked her what things, but the judge shook her head. "Just tell him, watch his back. And after this trial, maybe we could all have dinner."

"Sure. You figure the Norris jury'll be out fast?"

She shrugged with non-committal discretion. "You never know with a jury. That's why I love the system." But we both knew it was likely that Tyler Norris and his jury both would be home tomorrow in time for dinner.

By the door, three members of the General Assembly stopped me to ask about Alice, who'd served two terms with them. I said she was still spending time with her family in the mountains. Her grandmother was getting old and.... I let the inference fade away. The young congressmen immediately began speculating that Alice might actually be up there canvassing votes, she might be thinking of switching districts, maybe even running for state senate. For politicians there are no innocent acts. I smiled secretively and let them think what they would. "You never can tell." I didn't know what else to say.

• • •

The scheduled interview that Cuddy had instructed me to have with Andrew Brookside had been postponed twice by the governor's office. Now once more I waited in his anteroom until finally a polite secretary floated in and whispered to another polite secretary who then told me that someone would see me in the Havana Room. A third secretary led me through the Mansion to an attractive waiting room with a bay window where a large table was covered with magazines to read while you waited. It was called the Havana Room because another Dollard governor had brought back from the Spanish-American War the two Toledo swords and the huge Spanish map of Havana that hung on the wall across from me. I studied the map, thinking about the strangeness of its being here on a wall in North Carolina, this relic of the death of Spain's empire in the New World, this birth of our American imperialism. The map was dated January 1898. I pointed at it and said to the young secretary, "Only a month before the *Maine*."

"The main what?" she asked, and when I just shook my head, politely left me alone.

No one came for me, so I made another phone call to Ward Trasker. This time I told his secretary to say I was in the governor's office. This time he took my call. When I told him he had conspired to obstruct justice by disguising a murder as a suicide, he accused me of having lost my mind. He denied categorically that he had wiped prints or altered a crime scene by moving the body he'd thought was Mavis Mahar's. He denied vehemently that he had shot some poor girl in the face. He hadn't covered up a damn thing except the corpse. It was true, he had put a coat over the corpse. It seemed the decent thing to do. If it was a crime, he'd like to know which one.

I asked, "Did you instruct anyone in the room with you to move the body or remove anything from the body? Like a hat with candles in it?"

The A.G. expressed amazement that I wasn't in a mental institution and hung up the phone.

I looked out the large window at the Mansion grounds where old trees heavy with lank summer leaves shaded grass that no one walked on but its caretakers. Finally the two lawyers who'd seemed so brisk and crisp in Andy's office at four in the morning suddenly appeared through a side door, now even crisper. One of them handed me three neatly typed pages. The other one said that the pages were the governor's fully cooperative effort to assist the Hillston police in our investigation of the Lucy Griggs homicide. If I had any further questions, I should telephone their office and someone would be glad to help me. I glanced down at the typescript and read at random:

> I called upon Miss Mahar to discuss the importance of her timely appearance at the second Haver Field concert. She arrived in her hotel bungalow accompanied by a young woman who somewhat resembled her. I was not intro-duced to nor did I speak with this person. The two women went inside the bungalow together. I remained on the ter-race and don't know what was said or done inside the suite. When I did enter the bungalow, Miss Mahar was there alone; she said the young woman had already returned to town in a taxi. I expressed concern about Miss Mahar's inebriated condition....

The lawyers waited with affable impatience while I glanced through the rest of the document. Then I ruffled the pages at them. "A, not an interview," I told them pleasantly. "B, not signed. Captain Mangum set up an in-person interview." A quick flick of the eyes at each other, superior, amused, before they solemnly gazed back at me. The first lawyer said Governor Brookside sent his apologies for missing a chance to say a personal hello and sent his thanks to the Hillston police for their efforts to resolve this unfortunate matter. The second lawyer said he'd show me out.

As I was hurried along the hall, I passed an open door and, noticing Dina Yarborough, I broke away from my escort to talk to her. She was seated by herself on a silk couch whose pillows she was idly rearranging. Dina's green eyes were always startling in her cinnamon-colored face, now the more so because she wore a suit the same green. She said, "Good lord, are you okay, Justin? You look awful."

"Sleep will fix it," I said. "I guess you heard we've got another murder. Carl must be as flipped out about it as Cuddy. And just a year ago they called us, 'Hillston, A Bright Star in the Flag of the New South.'" I was quoting a bumper sticker. She glanced past me anxiously, then she stared silently down at her long slender feet in their beautiful shoes. I tried again. "You look elegant, Dina. First Ladies Lunch?"

"Thank you. No."

"Something wrong?"

She appeared to make an abrupt decision; reaching up for my hand she said, "They're going to announce in an hour so I guess it's okay if I tell you. Carl and I just had a meeting with Andy. They're still up there talking."

I knew exactly what she meant and nodded. "Ahhh…"

She stood and smiled. "Carl's on the ticket. Lieutenant Governor."

I reached out a hand, then instead quickly embraced her. "Congratulations, Dina. Alice'll be thrilled. Andy's made a great call. But what's Hillston going to do without the mayor?"

She wryly raised her exquisitely manicured hands. "If I can do without Carl, Hillston can. Cuddy saw more of him than I ever did, and I swear if I couldn't play bridge, I'd have never seen either one of them."

"Carl and Cuddy did great things for Hillston," I said, noticing that the remark made her take an angry breath.

She nodded solemnly. "They certainly did. They did great things."

"Let's celebrate. Pick a night, we'll go to Pogo's. Nicer. Pine Hills Inn."

Now she glanced evasively at the fireplace mantel. There was a plaque there saying a freed African-American named Thomas Day had designed the mantelpiece in 1832. Dina said, "Great. Let me check with Carl."

"I don't want you to move to Raleigh."

"You'll miss me."

"I sure will. It doesn't mean you have to quit the Hillston Players, does it?" Dina was an enthusiastic member of our amateur theatrical society. She was one of the best actresses we had and was scheduled to play the lead this fall in *Measure for Measure*.

She touched her pale Afro. "They better not ask me to give up the Players. My hair's bad enough." I asked what she meant, give up her hair. With the quiet acerbic smile that confused people, she said, "Andy thought this was a dye job and wondered why I didn't let it go natural. When I said it *was* natural," Dina laughed, "he wondered if maybe I should dye it black!"

We both knew the ancestral reason for Dina's hair color, an ancestry that she and I shared but had never discussed and probably never would.

Her husband Carl hurried into the room to find her. Chunky, bald, pleasant-faced, the mayor was normally so effusively friendly that his aloof behavior now was startling. My presence seemed to embarrass him and he looked stiff and awkward. When Dina said she'd told me about the reelection ticket and when he thanked me for congratulating him, he didn't once look in my eyes. Nor did he ask about the murder at The Fifth Season despite all the confusion and press coverage of the last twenty-four hours. Nor did he mention Cuddy, with whom he'd spent every day of their shared professional lives for the past eight years. Instead, reaching for Dina's arm, he led her so quickly out of the room that she had to twist awkwardly backwards to say good-bye to me. My first thought was that Carl was just annoyed with his wife for telling me he was on the ticket before the announcement.

I had my second thought as I was walking through the large impersonal lobby of the Governor's Mansion toward the front doors. An entourage came hurrying down the stairs from the private quarters above. Two of the house staff (both African-Americans, wearing white jackets) carried four large suitcases while two young secretarial-looking women (both white, wearing black suits) walked behind them, carrying small bags. Behind these women came Lee Haver Brookside carrying nothing but a purse. She was dressed for travel in that style of comfortable casual sophistication favored by the well-to-do. She was also wearing sunglasses, even though she wasn't yet outside, and when she didn't take them off as she paused to speak with me, I had the feeling she'd been crying.

"Taking a trip, Lee?"

"Hi, Justin. Yes, I'm late for the airport." She stopped herself from sounding rushed (Lee was unfailingly gracious), and added that she was speaking at a conference on children and the arts in Washington, D.C.

I gestured at the luggage being carried outside. "Long conference?"

She told me she was leaving directly from the conference for London, a small vacation. She wished me well, moved toward the door, then, after her escorts had passed through, turned suddenly back and quickly handed me an envelope she took from her purse. There was nothing written on it. "Please give this to Cuddy," she said hurriedly. "Tell him," she looked at me as if the words were somewhere hidden in my eyes, "that he mustn't hurt himself for me. Will you tell him that please, Justin? Thank you."

Lee knew that I would do as she asked. She didn't wait for

my answer but moved ahead of me through the great doors of the Governor's Mansion. The house belonged to the state that had made her family phenomenally wealthy and she had always felt that such gifts imposed obligations on her. She had always felt that she belonged to the state.

As the long black limousine moved smoothly away, the entourage headed back up the steps. Behind them bounced Bubba Percy returning from the New Deal Tavern, looking disturbed and puzzled. He stopped beside me and watched the car drive off. "Jesus fuck my ass!"

"Bubba, I don't think that's what they mean by taking Jesus as your personal savior."

He bit frantically at his lip. "I saw her luggage. She's not leaving him, is she? Did Lee look like she was leaving him?"

I shook my head. "She'll be back in two weeks."

"You wouldn't be so sure, Savile, you heard the names her maid said she was calling Andy in their bedroom Friday night just before she didn't show at the banquet."

"Bubba, breathe. She won't leave him." I squeezed at his arm. "Now you tell me something. What are they trying to do to Cuddy in there?"

He rolled his eyes at me. "Trying?" And shaking his head at my naïveté, he hurried inside.

Of course, not even the attorney general could fire Cuddy. Only the Hillston mayor and city council could do that.

And that had been my second thought about why Mayor Carl Yarborough, now Brookside's running mate, hadn't looked in my eyes.

Chapter 16

19 Tuscadora Street

Sunday night the 24th of June, I fell asleep after a long talk with Alice in which I told her about all the betrayals except my own. I was back in our Queen Anne house on Tuscadora Street after spending the rest of the weekend hidden in my family's lake house with Mavis Mahar. I'd only been home an hour when Alice had called me. Instead of asking where I'd been, she apologized for not responding sooner to my call the week before. She said she hadn't felt she'd be able to talk. As she spoke, I looked at our wedding picture on the mantel, our laughter happy as angels, Cuddy, the best man, beside us, his arm around my smiling mother. Then Alice said she had called Nachtmusik once; she'd thought I might be out at the lake. I said no I hadn't been there at all. Ashamed, hung-over, I walked to the mantel, took down our wedding portrait, and put it in the desk drawer where after Christmas I'd hidden from view all the photographs of our baby who'd just died.

"So what have you been up to?" Alice asked.

I told her things at HPD were in chaos. We'd had another homicide since Cuddy had called her about the Elvis tape. The second case might be tied to Guess Who as well, although we didn't want the press to find that out. If our murderer was Guess Who, he apparently thought he'd killed the rock star Mavis Mahar but actually he had shot a young waitress instead. Mavis was alive and still in Hillston. I opened the bottle of Calvados I'd bought.

"Mavis?" said Alice.

"Everybody calls her Mavis," I said.

"But that's because they've never met her."

"Very funny." I poured a drink, saying that Andrew Brookside had once been involved with Mavis, that people close to him, under the mistaken impression that the singer had been murdered, had tampered with evidence and that Cuddy was demanding their resignations. I said that Bubba Percy was hinting heavily that these people, who included the A.G. Ward Trasker, were going to protect their cover-up by having Carl Yarborough fire Cuddy.

Alice was a politician. She jumped immediately to a motive: "So Andy did give Carl a spot on his ticket."

"You think Carl will sell Cuddy out to be lieutenant governor?"

"'But for Wales, Richard?'" Alice quoted her favorite line from A Man for All Seasons. Her voice was sad. "I don't know if Carl will or not. I don't know what anybody will do anymore."

I didn't know if she meant anything personal by this remark, and I didn't want to know. I told her of Dina Yarborough's odd awkward behavior toward me and of Carl's evasions. And of Margy Turbot's wanting me to warn Cuddy to "watch his back." She asked about Cuddy's response to these "hints." I told her that I hadn't conveyed them. He'd replaced me as head of the homicide investigation and we hadn't spoken for awhile.

"Replaced you? Who with?"

"With himself." I said that when I'd called his office, no one seemed to know where he'd gone, or at least if they did they weren't telling me. He hadn't returned my calls at home either. Finally I'd left a message saying that I had an urgent letter for him from his "old friend in Raleigh." I told Alice of Lee's request that Cuddy not "hurt himself" on her behalf.

Alice said that if all this was going on, there was probably no need for me to warn Cuddy. He wasn't naïve. "The best thing you can do for him is find out who killed these women as fast as you can."

"I just told you I'm not in charge anymore. He's doing it all himself."

"Justin, come on, all that means is he's near panic. Stick with him. The harder he pushes you away, the closer he needs you. You know that."

"It's tough."

"You're a tough guy," she said with the old sweetness. And as we were hanging up, she added cryptically, "Take Lee's advice yourself."

"What's that?" I was falling asleep.

"Don't do anything that'll get you hurt."

I heard myself mumbling, "Alice, why don't you come home?"

"I don't think you want me to. Good night, sweet dreams"

But my night was restless and my dreams were anything but sweet.

I was awakened by the moon. The phone rang. I thought it was Alice again, but when I answered I heard a different woman's voice, beautiful and strange, whispering, "*Codladh sámh, a chuisle mo chroí!*"

"Mavis. Are you all right?"

"I'm fine. Would you like to know what that means? 'Pleasant sleep, oh pulse of my heart.'"

"I'd say more likely it means, 'Oh pulse of Irish blarney,'" I mumbled. "What do you want?"

"You, I suppose."

"Do you have people around you? Don't be alone."

"Isn't that what we're all wanting? Not to be alone."

I sat up and knocked over the bottle of Calvados. "I'm going to say good-bye and go to bed."

"You know in the Gaelic, Lieutenant, 'good-bye' is different if you're the one staying or the one going. If you were going and I was staying, I'd tell you '*Slán leat*' for good-bye. But if I was leaving you behind, it's '*Slán agat*' I'd say to you. So which is it you're saying to me now?"

"I have no idea," I told her. "Let's just say good night." I hung up.

Asleep again, I dreamed of walking beside the lake toward Mavis. She stood on the dock waiting, her warm flesh luminous as the full moon above her. But then just as I reached her, she suddenly burst apart in a flower of blood. Blood as red as the silk robe she'd dropped from her shoulders to dive into the morning mist the first time I'd seen her.

I was awakened again at dawn by nightmares of endless dives of my own, down to the oozing silt floor of Pine Hills Lake where my child Copper lay twisted in weeds, drowning before I could free him.

• • •

At eight o'clock Monday morning Cuddy Mangum was leaning on my front door bell. The ringing echoed loudly through the large high-ceilinged bare-floored rooms and worsened my headache. Cuddy looked rested but tense. To my surprise, he was dressed in his captain's summer dress uniform, so starched the creases hardly moved. "What's with you?" I grumbled, still in my underwear from the night before and still half asleep. "Is there a funeral?" Parades and funerals were the only times I ever saw him in a dress uniform.

"Some folks are planning on it," he said tersely as he walked in. I saw him notice the empty Calvados bottle on the coffee table by the couch. He pointed at it. "Just tell me you spent the weekend at a cooking school and you were practicing Cherries Jubilee."

"You never ate a cherry that wasn't in a Pop-Tart." I followed him to the kitchen. "I don't guess everybody from the governor on down has turned in those resignations you've been asking them all for?"

He stared at me a moment, then nodded. "Oh, Bubba told you. No, not yet." He held up a McDonald's bag. "Sorry, no latté and quail's eggs."

I shook my head. "Thanks anyhow. How about *your* resignation? Carl ask for that yet?"

"Well hey, JB Five, you do have your ear to the railroad track."

"According to Bubba, the Dixie Comet's barreling down that track and you're tied to the rails. Didn't you get my message?"

"'Bout an hour ago. Bunty and I flew to Atlanta to talk to Samuel Chang. He's a friend of Bunty's." Dr. Chang was a nationally famous forensic pathologist. Bunty Crabtree was the FBI agent who had obviously taken over my investigation. He said, "I'm going to dig up G.I. Jane and Cathy Oakes both, have Chang examine them. Spaghetti for breakfast?"

I was warming some spaghetti carbonara I'd made myself for dinner and hadn't eaten. I was headed back to the place where I'd rather drink than eat. "It's bacon and eggs, what's the difference? Cuddy, people are dropping hints like slabs of concrete, they're saying the Brookside folks are going to bury what happened at The Fifth Season right on top of you."

He nodded nonchalantly. "Yeah well, in the game of chicken somebody could get their jacket sleeve caught on the handle of the car door and I see myself more in the James Dean part."

"You push them, they'll fire you."

He unwrapped his sausage biscuit. "So I push them, they fire me. They fire me, I go to the press. We'll all be out of jobs. This morning everybody's backing down, thinking that over. Even if they decide to pull the trigger, it'll take Carl a little while to gut it up to do something he'll hate himself for. And a lot can happen in a little while. Where's Lee's letter?"

I staggered back up the steep stairs to get it.

When I came down to the kitchen showered and dressed, Cuddy was listening to someone on his cell phone as he leaned against my refrigerator. He was moving around the tiny magnet words that you arrange into poetry. The fragments hadn't been touched since Alice had put them there shortly before Copper's death and they were still crazily jumbled together in a clump.

On the bleached oak refectory table sat a cup of espresso

Cuddy had made me. He pointed at it while listening to someone on the phone. "You're the prince of dark roast," I told him.

He was saying to the person on the phone, "*Gracias. Me has
ayadado muchissimo. Hablamos despues. I love it. Adios.*"

"Good news?" I asked.

Eduardo Vega in forensics had his first findings from the vac-
uuming of The Fifth Season bungalow. He had definite gray car
carpet fibers that looked like a match for the fiber taken from
G.I. Jane's T-shirt. There'd been a few loose short hair strands on
the floor as well and they proved to be a match for Lucy's hair.
The killer had obviously collected most of her hair as he cut it
off and had taken it away with him.

Cuddy said Bunty Crabtree and her FBI field agent partner
Rhonda Weavis were putting together a profile of Guess Who,
basing it on the assumption that he was responsible for the Lucy
Griggs as well as the Cathy Oakes and G.I. Jane homicides, and
assuming also that he'd thought Lucy was Mavis Mahar when he
killed her.

Cuddy wanted me to turn over to these two agents my homicide books on both cases and all my files. I reminded him that
he'd always warned me against inviting in the FBI, because once
inside the fort, they had a tendency to lower your flag and raise
their own.

Finishing his second biscuit, he carefully swept the crumbs
into his hand. "Yeah well, if you don't mind my running off with
your metaphor, this fort is under siege, plus it's on fire, plus it's
surrounded by Apaches and we just ran out of ammunition, and
there's no chloroform for sawing off our gangrene. So if all of a
sudden I hear the cavalry riding up, I'm not about to say, 'Thanks
anyhow, don't need your help.' Because I don't want this to be
remembered as Cuddy's last stand. I want Cuddy's last stand to be
in about 2020 when my retirement kicks in." He dropped the
crumbs in my trash.

"Why did I worry when you were just staring out the window?"

He grinned. "Back me into a corner and I come out talking."
He looked at his watch. "And I hope we can say the same for our

pal Mitch Bazemore, because he's starting his summation in an hour and if he doesn't shake up that jury, they're going to acquit Tyler Norris, and that's going to make me out a liar when I said you can't get away with murder in Hillston."

I handed him the envelope from Lee and told him I had a verbal message from her as well. "She says, don't hurt yourself for her. I assume you know what she means." He opened the envelope as if he didn't want to harm it. I added, "She was leaving for D.C. with plenty of luggage. Bubba's freaked she's not ever coming back. I told him she was."

Cuddy sat down across from me, gently slid out the blue notepaper and read it. After he'd put it away in his jacket without speaking, I asked, "Just one question. Does Lee have any reason to think Andy killed the girl, either mistaking her for Mavis or not? And would you tell me if she did?"

He frowned. "She knew Brookside had been over there at the bungalow and she knew why and what it could do to the re-election. She was scared Mavis had killed herself."

I poured a pitcher of milk. "So she wanted the same thing from you that Bubba did. Keep Andy out of it. When you saw her last night, she asked you to leave the cover-up alone."

A long silence. But then I hadn't asked him a question. I sat with a bowl of raspberries and took my time pouring milk over them before I said, "I almost told Lee she shouldn't be leaving the state when she's a possible suspect in a homicide investigation herself."

He looked up at me. "You know damn well she never shot anybody, whether she thought it was Mavis Mahar or not."

"I didn't say she did. I said she was a possible suspect. Just for the record, since you've made it clear I'm no longer running the homicide division, Lee had motive. Her husband was having an affair that could ruin his political career. She had opportunity. She wasn't at that banquet and she wasn't in bed with a fever either. She had means. You can buy pretty much anything you need with a few billion dollars, including a gun or somebody to use one. Just for the record."

I kept slowly eating as he walked to my kitchen door. In the doorway, he stopped. "Take yes for an answer. You said this was all about Guess Who. You were right. Oh, and thanks for the tip. I had Nancy pull in this punk John Walker, Lucy's ex-boyfriend. He's a mean little bastard—got bounced out of the Tucson twice for coming in there high and smacking Lucy around. We had him in for that, plus misdemeanor breaking and entering, communicating threats, second-degree trespassing."

"I thought I'd seen him at HPD."

"It was all about harassing Lucy. But she wouldn't press charges and that was the end of that."

"Think he blamed Mavis for Lucy's dumping him? Followed them out there and shot her?"

"It's a possibility. Nancy and Roid went over to talk to Walker. He made it easy. Had a bag of hash and ten crack caps in a knapsack shoved under the couch in this mildewed pigsty they're all living in—the band, the so-called Mood Disorders. He's high-wired and waves a goddamn air pistol in Nancy's face when she goes for the knapsack."

"Did he fire it?"

"Nah. She broke his arm before he could. We put a nice cast on it and we're holding him for forty-eight on the narcotics. Okay, Carl's called a meeting. It's either the garbage strike or I'm fired."

"Good luck." I took the bowl to the sink.

He nodded a few times. "Listen here, Justin, I don't want you off the case. All I want is you to cooperate with R&B. We had three months to solve Jane, and we didn't do it. Can we stop picking on each other?"

I heard Alice saying, "Stick with him." I nodded. "We can do that."

He sighed in ostentatious relief. "Good. Be in Room 105 at 11:30. Oh, and type up your best guess on what the crime scene looked like before Ward Trasker redecorated it. Something for them to read against what it looked like when we got there. Also could I get that timeline—who was there when? We need it at HPD in about an hour."

"Jesus, is that all?"

He jiggled the doorknob. "No. This plate's loose; your handle's going to fall out. Got a screwdriver?"

I asked him if he felt like he had to fix everything in the world.

He looked at the ceiling as if considering. "Yep. I sure do."

"Would you please go to your meeting?"

He grinned, put on his captain's hat, saluted, and left.

Returning the milk to the refrigerator, I noticed that Cuddy had moved all the jumbled magnet words into neat rows. They now said things like:

Sun on a stone wall.
Day in a dark room.
The summer road runs forever.
Love was.

I didn't know whether he hadn't had time to finish the last line or that was all he had to say on the subject.

• • •

Overnight a cold front had blown through the Piedmont and the weather now was crisp and clear, one of the rare June days that tricks you into believing that this summer will be different. I spent the morning typing the new crime scene report against the notes I'd kept locked in my desk. After I dropped it off at Cuddy's office, I started interviewing people who'd known Lucy Griggs. They all agreed on three things:

One, she had more brains than talent and should never have left college to try to make it as a singer. She'd done better at Haver University than she had on the stage at the Tucson Lounge.

Two, she'd abruptly dumped John Walker in the middle of what had looked like a "hot" relationship and he hadn't taken the rejection well. She'd complained to everyone about Walker's following her around, telephoning her at all hours, and creating such tension in the (apparently aptly named) Mood Disorders band (assaulting her in the middle of a performance at the Tucson one night) that the other musicians had agreed to throw him out of the group he'd started. He hadn't taken that well either.

Three, Lucy had hinted to several friends that the reason for her break-up with John was another man, "the love of her life," about whom no one knew anything. She'd been deliberately mysterious. A young worn-out-looking barmaid at the Tucson told me, "Lucy worked hard at being mysterious. She'd drop these hints to try to, like, make us jealous or whatever, okay? She was always going to be a big star and, like, know big people."

"And she never introduced you to this 'love of her life'?"

"No way. I bet he didn't even know she worked here." The barmaid waved an anemic arm around the cheap empty tables of the dimly lit bar. "This wasn't Lucy's real life, this was for losers like us."

No one I talked to seemed to have much liked Lucy Griggs. The young barmaid went so far as to comment with a chilling blandness, "Well, at least getting herself killed's made Lucy famous for a couple of weeks."

Walking back from the Tucson I saw the two short dark women standing on the street corner across from the Cadmean Building again, patiently waiting. Along the sidewalk curb, mountainous piles of black and green plastic garbage bags reached as high as their heads, making it look as if they were standing in a hilly fecund jungle. The women kept looking up and down Main Street expectantly. When I nodded at them as I walked past, they moved closer to each other, alarmed. One had a rosary in her hand, which she was ritualistically fingering. I asked them in English if I could help in any way. Either they didn't understand or were too frightened to answer me. I tried to reassure them, but they backed away. One of them tripped on the piled garbage and fell down, dropping her rosary. I picked it up and tried to give it to her but terrified, they both ran across the street.

The rosary was made of cheap plastic beads, but it also had

curious tiny feathers and what looked like a dried bird claw attached to it. I let the women see that I was placing it on top of the post box at the corner. They watched but didn't acknowledge me.

The Catholic beads made me think of the rosary Dermott Quinn had wanted me to give Mavis. It seemed unlikely the rock star would be saying her prayers with it as avidly as this woman on the street corner had been doing. Suddenly I recalled Mavis's hostile outburst at the lake house about her mother: "Always lighting the candles to these bloody martyred saints of hers that got burned up and raped and chopped to bits, their tongues pulled out and their heads whacked off." Even worse fates, it occurred to me, than what Guess Who had done to Cathy Oakes or G.I. Jane or Lucy Griggs.

• • •

I walked past the Cadmean Building down to Southern Depot, an upscale interior mall in a huge brick Victorian train station. In the midst of open rows of trendy shops—Laura Ashley linen dresses, Asian antique cabinets, highly priced cheese and wine, beautiful fish, imported wallpaper, rare books and prints—was a leafy atrium café trying with its green metal park chairs to look like the Luxembourg Gardens. At a table beneath a large potted birch tree sat the lawyer Isaac Rosethorn with the Norris family (Tyler and his parents). They had finished their lunch and the fat old lawyer was smoking vigorously.

Norris's homicide trial had resumed this morning after being postponed by Margy Turbot because of the media circus surrounding the "news" of Mavis Mahar's death. It was clearly now in recess. Fulke Norris, the philosophic poet, was lecturing Isaac with emphatic bobs of his beautifully disheveled white hair, which was even whiter and richer and more famous than Isaac's own trademark mane. Mrs. Norris wasn't involved in the conversation, nor was Tyler, although it was probably about him and today's events at his trial. Tyler and his mother never looked at each other.

With a final jabbing tattoo of his finger on the tabletop, Fulke Norris abruptly stood up, took his wife firmly in hand, and walked away, calling to Tyler to come along as if he'd been five rather than thirty-five. As they paused in front of a shop called Gifts and Goodies (where there was a window display of a dozen different volumes of the elder Norris's inspiration verse), a middle-aged woman came running out with a book in her hand for him to sign. I don't think I'd ever before seen so extreme a contrast in human facial emotions as I now saw between the courtly smile with which Fulke Norris unscrewed the cap from his enormous black fountain pen and the scowling grimace with which his son watched him do it.

The Norrises' clothes (blue blazers, tailored silk dress) hung on them so perfectly that they might have been a trio of mannequins in a Brooks Brothers window. Isaac Rosethorn, rumpled, littered with lunch crumbs and cigarette ash, was another study in contrasts.

"Hi there, Isaac." I pulled over a chair and sat down with my take-out espresso. "The poet of the people didn't look too happy when he left you."

Rosethorn scowled, his beautiful black cocker-spaniel eyes tearful from the smoke of the unfiltered Chesterfield hanging from his mouth. "Why should he be happy? His son's life is at stake. If Margy Turbot hadn't seen fit to adjourn my trial, I'd have finished my summation instead of having to listen to Mitchell all morning and then be postponed 'til after lunch."

"And you hate waiting."

"Justin, I despise waiting. But alas alas alas, you fellows had to turn the press loose on this dead Irish dancer like a herd of jackals on a rhino carcass."

I pointed out that Mavis Mahar was neither a dancer nor dead. It was a Tucson Lounge waitress who'd been shot.

"Yes, and a shame you didn't discover the difference before the ravening barbarians of television stormed into the Cadmean Building and terrorized the pusillanimous Miss Turbot into adjourning." He sighed.

"Well, murder is a problem, Isaac."

"Now I'm hearing rumors you think Guess Who is back. I've never defended a serial killer." He sighed again wistfully. "Too often their mad conceit leads them to insist on defending themselves."

I drank my espresso. "Too often they're guilty with a cellar full of mutilated bodies."

"Dear boy, no one is guilty until proven so. Your cellar might be full of mutilated bodies, your refrigerator might be full of human organs, your hands might be caked in human blood, and still, and *still*, you might be entirely innocent. Why, I can think of hundreds of reasons how you might find yourself, all unwittingly, in such an unhappy situation."

Isaac, "the grand old man," "the Beloved Cliché," as the papers called him, lived atop the Piedmont Hotel on unfiltered Dunhill cigarettes, Wild Turkey whiskey, and High Hat barbecue take-out. He had been threatening to retire for a quarter of a century, but never did it. The "Dixie Darrow" had a magnificent reverberant baritone that he'd used for decades to persuade juries of his clients' innocence. Words rolled up from his belly like gushers of oil, and made him rich. Not that you could tell it from his shabby clothes or his grubby suite in the Piedmont. You had to look closely at the first editions on the shelves and the Attic Greek pottery in the cases and the dozen antique chess sets, one of them originally the property of Henry VII, set out on tables.

The Piedmont Hotel had led an entirely undistinguished life except for two guests. One was Isaac who had now lived there fifty years. The other guest was a beautiful African-American movie star, who had spent half a night there in 1959 before the owner tried to evict her, saying that his clerk had broken the law by allowing her to register in a Whites Only hotel. That's when a young Jewish man named Rosethorn had come down to the lobby in his bathrobe and told the filmstar that he was a lawyer and she should refuse to leave. It was his first famous case.

"So have you any suspects?" Isaac asked me.

"If a serial killer comes along, I'll give him your card."

He ignored this. "Where's the pattern?" He was lighting another cigarette from a little box of wooden matches. "I don't see the pattern myself, not that I know more than the newspapers, but serial homicide is *about* the pattern, isn't that so? It's more than a modus operandi. These men kill precisely in order to reexperience the pattern." He put the match down in the ashtray with half-a-dozen others. "And yet two young women had their throats cut and one was shot; one was lying in a culvert, one hidden in the woods, one left openly in a hotel suite. Until you find the pattern, how can you find your way to the pattern maker?"

"Cuddy's set up a task force, brought in the FBI."

"So how is my Slim?" Slim had been Isaac's nickname for Cuddy since he'd first hired him decades back, when Cuddy had been a skinny brainy East Hillston ten-year-old and had run all the lazy Rosethorn's errands for him in exchange for the first real intellectual attention he'd ever gotten. Over the years he and the eccentric lawyer had adopted each other. Cuddy loved Isaac, but claimed he had no illusions about the megalomania of the gluttonous old bachelor. With Isaac, the universe was a place of personal possession. My Slim. My trial. My verdict. And usually, my victory.

I told him that his Slim was under pressure to resign for reasons I couldn't go into, but that Isaac should give him a call once the trial was over.

"Pressure from whom? That's outrageous. I'll call him tonight."

I reminded him that the bad publicity under which the Hillston Police Department (and most acutely Cuddy himself) suffered had begun with our arrest of Isaac's own client Tyler Norris. If Norris was now found innocent—

"Not if," he smiled sorrowfully. "If I know juries, and I do, they are eagerly, indeed impatiently, waiting to find Tyler innocent. I'm afraid the only question at this point is when."

"Afraid?"

He shrugged. "From your perspective." It was hard to tell with Isaac, he was such an actor and his large dark droopy eyes regularly had a tragic look, but I could have sworn I saw a genuine sadness in his face before he rubbed his large milky hands across his eyes and wiped the look away. "And your failure. You and Mitchell Bazemore offered no irrefutable evidence of guilt; in fact, thanks to Sheriff Louge's clodhoppers, offered little evidence of any sort. But most of all, Justin, you supplied no sufficient motive." He licked a finger and ran it around the rim of his chocolate sundae. "No history of more than normal unhappiness with his wife, no fat insurance policy on her, no secret amour, no motive—"

"Well, Isaac, you supplied no burglar, no evidence of any intruder—"

He waved his cigarette back and forth at me. "I didn't have to. You know that. I don't have to prove things. All I have to do is raise reasonable doubt." He lumbered to his feet in a shower of crumbs and ash. "And that's exactly what I've done. Tell Slim to come see me."

I watched the grand old man shuffle over to look in the windows of the rare books and prints boutique. There was a slight drag to the weak leg that, whenever he needed a jury's sympathy, suddenly worsened until he could barely walk. Behind the glass door, the owner waited in avaricious expectation as Isaac bent down to peer at some illustrated leather folio displayed on a stand.

I kept hearing his beautiful rolling voice. "Until you find the pattern, how can you find your way to the pattern maker?" Staring idly at the messy debris Isaac had left behind, I noticed all the burnt matches piled criss-crossed in the ashtray. A crude haphazard pattern. One by one I took them out and arranged them in an orderly circle, the burnt tips out, just the way the killer had arranged matches above G.I. Jane's shaved head. Just the way the candles had been arranged in Lucy's hat. And then I heard Mavis again: "Always lighting the candles to these bloody martyred saints of hers." An idea was somewhere just out of reach.

I pulled out the pocket watch that had belonged to my mother's father, and spun it on its gold chain while I was thinking. My grandfather's name had been Benjamin Virgil Dollard and his initials B.V.D. were engraved on the back of the gold watch, which amused my colleagues in the police department. B.V. Dollard had served as chief justice of the state Supreme Court. That was why, on the front of the watch, the maker had engraved a figure of Justice, a woman with sword and scales and blinded eyes.

The idea floated closer, fluttered away. I rubbed my thumb across the face, then snapped shut the watch and hurried back to Main Street. I was late to Cuddy's meeting.

Chapter 17

Room 105

Bunty Crabtree stood by a large white wallboard waiting with a pointer while her partner Rhonda Weavis pinned gruesome autopsy photos of the three murder victims to a corkboard.

Rhonda and Bunty had both grown up in the Georgia mountains and sounded like it. They'd known each other since kindergarten, gone to Western Carolina together. Rhonda had served in the Army while Bunty had worked her way through medical school. (She had a degree in forensic psychiatry.) They'd joined the Academy together and they were still together.

Rhonda, wearing gray gym pants and an FBI T-shirt, was a towhead with a wide friendly tan face and startling blue eyes; she had the stocky build of a fast-pitch softball player on a women's Olympic team—which in fact she'd been. Where Rhonda was ruddy and sturdy, her partner was pale and narrow; Bunty's nose, arms, and legs, even her black short hair looked thin. Today she had on a pink striped pantsuit with a black blouse that made her face look even whiter. Unlike Rhonda, who was friendly as a vinyl siding salesman, Bunty kept her distance, almost never making eye contact, moving through her thoughts with slow careful deliberation. Some thought she was a snob, but the truth is she was so introverted she really didn't notice the people whose greetings she ignored. Cuddy liked her because she was smart, almost, he thought, as smart as he was.

When I slipped into the room, Etham Foster was comparing a blown-up Photostat of the partial shoeprint we'd taken from the shower stall tiles to a computer printout of sample treads on men's running shoes. "I don't know," his assistant Augie Summers told Bunty. "It's close," Etham said.

Seeing me, Rhonda strode forward like she was going to pitch me a fastball; instead, she hugged me. "Hey there, JayJay, how's it going, buddy?" It was like being embraced by a friendly bear. Rhonda always called me "JayJay" and Cuddy, "Honch"— the latter short, I assumed, for "head honcho."

Cuddy held out his wrist to me. "Maybe you ought to get one of these modern doohickeys called a wrist watch."

I took off my seersucker suit jacket and rolled up my starched white shirtsleeves. "I was talking to Isaac Rosethorn. He says hello."

"What was the old bastard doing, spraying his throat with honey? He'll cry during his summation today, just wait. He'll beg that jury to send poor sad tragic widower Tyler Norris home to his lonely old house, which wouldn't have been so lonely if he hadn't blown his wife's head off."

"Isaac says Mitch did a 'fine job' this morning for the State."

Cuddy crumpled the paper he was doodling on. "There's the kiss of death. Okay, now that J.B. Savile the Fifth has dropped in, back to it, Bunty?"

Bunty shyly told the pointer she was using, "Hello, Justin." Dick Cohen the M.E., Etham and Augie from forensics, and Wendy Freiberg, the frazzled overweight State Bureau text analyst, made various, mostly caustic gestures in my direction. There were two other HPD detectives at the 105 conference table, plus Lisa Grecco, a young deputy prosecutor from Mitch Bazemore's office, whose well-developed body was the subject of all too many conversations in the HPD locker room.

Any representative from the sheriff's department was conspicuously absent. Before his falling out with Homer Louge, Cuddy had invited deputies to listen in on HPD brainstorming sessions, saying, "Even bad students will learn something in a good class, if they take it enough times." But no more.

This particular class was about Guess Who, how to identify him, how to apprehend him as quickly as possible. The task force had started with a few premises that Cuddy had written out on his blackboard:

G.W. [Guess Who] killed Cathy Oakes, G.I. Jane, and Lucy Griggs. He thought Lucy was Mavis Mahar.

We don't know if Cathy Oakes was his first victim.

G.W. is playing with HPD. He thinks he can't be caught. He can.

Here's what we need:

—ID on Jane
—ID on Lucy Griggs homicide gun (.32, .38, maybe .44?)
—ID on Guess Who would also be nice.

There was also a lot of information about the three cases on the walls of this room, but none of it mentioned Governor Andrew Brookside's being in Bungalow Eight with Mavis Mahar the night of the murder. Nor was there a word about state officials tampering with evidence and faking a suicide on a corpse. I sat down next to Etham; his legs stretched all the way under the table to the other side. "How you doing, Doctor Dunk-It?"

He grumbled, "Why do you folks keep calling me that?"

I said, "'Don't you like to be reminded that you were a big star?"

"You short white people like basketball more than I ever did. You and Billy Crystal." Around the table everyone made razzing noises.

I said, "Compared to you, Etham, everybody's short. And I think it's interesting that you could be so good at something you didn't even like."

Cuddy rapped his pencil on his Pepsi can. "Justin, do you mind if we save your analysis of ability and desire for another time? We're under a little time pressure here. Mitch Bazemore has already sent in a note telling Lisa to get back to the D.A.'s office—"

"Fuck him," said Lisa, and everyone clapped.

"—So can we go?"

"Go," I told him.

Rhonda took a swallow from her Classic Coke bottle after dropping some peanuts in it. "Hang on, Honch," she told Cuddy. "Let me catch him up. JayJay, we're inputting what info we've got so we can reconstruct these crime scenes, see if we can put together a sequence, and a repetition, you know. Sketch out some characteristics."

Bunty interjected, "Are time and place significant? Why those particular woods for Jane? That culvert for Cathy? Why that particular night for Lucy or Mavis? In fact, is it Lucy or is it Mavis we're talking about? And can we make deductions about our killer's physical build, any occupational clues from what we have?"

Rhonda summed up. "So that's where we're at, except for being told we shouldn't be here."

Cuddy said, "I just had a call from the FBI district director questioning whether R&B should join this investigation. I said we hadn't seen those ladies for weeks. Said they were probably in their Jacuzzi with piña coladas."

"Never met Piña in my life," laughed Rhonda.

Cuddy said, "So let me say it again, I appreciate y'all's showing up here, all of you, 'cause this is not the most popular party in town."

Wendy waved her arm around the room. "Has anybody noticed there's nobody in 105 today but women, blacks, and Jews? I mean, except Cuddy and Justin. I just point that out. If they fire us all in the next twenty-four hours, maybe we've got a class action suit?"

Augustine Summers, Foster's assistant criminologist, raised his hand. "I'm queer, if that helps."

Cuddy checked the door to be sure it was closed. Then he said we needed to get something out in the open. "Everybody in this room has heard certain things happened at Bungalow Eight *after* the murder, things that shouldn't have happened, like evidence tampering and conspiracy to obstruct justice. The people who did those things not only committed crimes, they've made our job harder."

"A lot harder," nodded Etham.

"Maybe they've even cost us a chance at a conviction if we catch the guy. But we're not going to talk about those things or those people except very specifically about what got moved when and where—like the body. Okay?" He looked slowly around the room until everyone nodded at him.

Rhonda said, "As long as we really do know those things."

Cuddy told her, "Justin's done a reconstruction of the crime scene the way we figure it would have been if those assholes hadn't fucked it. You're each getting a copy of that now." An officer passed out the stapled material.

I asked Rhonda how much profiling we were going to do of the *victims* as opposed to the killer? Bunty answered for her. "Well, we don't know who the second victim, Jane, even was. And the third one, Lucy, may have been a mistake. That makes it hard profiling them."

I wanted to know if she was assuming that the victims were strangers to the killer? Should we throw out the possibility that they might be acquainted with him or that they might even be well known to him? "At the risk of sounding like Carol Cathy Cane," I said, "are we definitely talking about a sociopath here?"

Cuddy asked, "As opposed to?"

"As opposed to some *strategic* motive for the murders: for money, for vengeance, to protect a reputation."

Cuddy yielded the floor to Bunty, who told me that at least for the purposes of our exercises today we were assuming a serial killer, someone who chose his victims not strategically but sym-bolically. That didn't mean the choices were random (any more than Ted Bundy's choice to murder young women with the same hairstyle as that of his ex-girlfriend was a random choice), but the victims weren't *specific* individuals. "He goes looking for somebody to kill; if one person gets away from him, he goes to the next one."

Rhonda flipped me a handout. "Okay, JayJay, a lot of this you and I already talked about back in March. It's regular old BSU and CPRP one-size-fits-all stuff." (She was talking about the FBI's Behavioral Science Unit and the Justice Department's Criminal Personality Research Project.) "So you know the drill: we're probably looking for a white male between twenty-five and late thirties. He probably had a frosty kind of mom and a not-there kind of dad. Our boy was a serious loner with a big fantasy life, lot of yanking the wank with nasty porno, setting fires—"

"Setting fire to the family cat," threw in Cuddy dryly.

Dr. Dick Cohen mumbled, "What was the name of that guy that poured kerosene on his two kids while they were sleeping, incinerated them and his wife and a couple of dogs?"

Nobody seemed to want to join Dick in remembering. He shrugged. "Must have been in Brooklyn," and sank back in his chair.

"Good ole Brooklyn," I sighed.

Dick hunched his thin shoulders. "At least our drug stores don't have whole aisles with nothing on the shelves but wart remover, lice egg loosener, and boil ointments. Geez, the South."

As Bunty called them out, Cuddy wrote headings on his blackboard.

GAMESMAN / MISOGYNIST /
ORGANIZED / ANTI-AUTHORITARIAN

Rhonda scooted her wide strong hand across the headings, clicking her fingers over each word. "One, our boy's all about dominance and control. GAMESMAN. He's manipulating us and gets a kick out of it. Two, MISOGYNIST. Call me crazy, guys, but I think he's got a problem with women." We laughed. "Three, ORGANIZED. He's got his shit together. I mean, he's not a drooler. Four, ANTI-AUTHORITARIAN. He hates folks in charge even more than he hates women. Way major hate. So let's recap the bureau's take on the organized type."

Bunty explained to the carpet that, unlike the chaotic, out-of-control "disorganized" serial killer, our murderer was intelligent, socially competent, might even be charming. He probably had a high birth order, was possibly married or with a partner. In other words, he would appear to be a functioning member of society. But at core he was emotionally dysfunctional and incapable of a healthy romantic relationship.

"No shit," said Lisa Grecco. She asked if Lucy Griggs had been raped.

Cuddy said no. Rape did not seem to be a factor in any of the homicides, but as we knew from the mutilations, sexual sadism was. He told us he had made legal arrangements to have the body of Cathy Oakes exhumed and the body of G.I. Jane returned by Haver Medical School (to which the city morgue had donated it). The forensic pathologist Dr. Samuel Chang was willing to examine all three corpses if our medical examiner had no objections. He looked over at Dick Cohen.

Dick shrugged. "Sure. If Bunty says he's the best, he's the best. I'm the next best." Dick grinned. "But Chang's got his own cable series."

Bunty smiled quietly, her eyes on the blackboard. "So on the profile? We're going to assume G.W. isn't transient. Some serial killers are, but the organized types tend to settle for a while. He's likely to be based somewhere in the Southeast, though maybe not in Hillston or even the Piedmont anymore. We know he has a car." She used her pointer to tap at a map of Neville, the town fifty miles to the west of Hillston where the prostitute Cathy Oakes had been found with her throat cut. "October. Outskirts of a mid-sized town; secluded but not rural. Public golf course culvert. Don't know if it's his first hit." She moved to a second map. This one was of Haver County; there was a red circle around the wooded incline near Balmoral Heights where we'd found G.I. Jane. "Late January or early February. Outskirts of a mid-sized town. Near a dirt road leading to a subdivision, few hundred yards from the construction company trailers on new building lots. So, isolated but not remote. We're assuming it's his second."

Rhonda interjected, "We haven't found any other victims in the data that fit the profile at all."

Bunty asked us to think about what had moved Guess Who from dreaming about murder to committing it. "Look for a big pre-crime stressor in early fall. Job loss, break-up, humiliation. Then look again for another big stress, maybe around Christmas or New Year's."

"He must have been at my house," mumbled Etham, who had four children.

Bunty made a try at a smile. "To Guess Who, the world's a hostile place and it would have gotten more hostile just before these killings. But when he kills somebody, you know what? It's a stress reliever."

Dick Cohen groaned. "He couldn't go hit a bucket of balls, drink a couple of beers?"

Bunty took his question seriously. "No. You could, but he couldn't."

Rhonda offered us all small Snickers' bars from a large bag as she picked up the thread. "So once G.W.'s done Jane and put the same T-shirt on her as he used on Cathy, he's got his nose glued to the TV because they're talking about him. He goes looking for where there's press around. He takes the name Guess Who straight from the media. He likes it. It puts him up there with Zodiac and Son of Sam. He hangs out in the Cadmean Building, we know that for sure. He's real savvy about this place. And savvy about forensics. He knows how to get around your procedures. We're not finding prints, trace, saliva, nothing. Except for the carpet fibers and one partial shoe print, all we've got is what he wanted us to have—the morgue toe tag, the tape, head shot, so on. They're his little calling cards and they're all left for the Hillston police." Bunty went back to the map and twirled the pointer around the Cadmean Building. "This guy's an expert on HPD. He knows names, he knows habits."

"So you think we already know this guy?" I asked.

Bunty shook her head slowly. "No, I'm not necessarily saying that. I'm saying you're a focus for him. Mark David Chapman knew John Lennon. John Lennon didn't know Mark David Chapman. It's the same with a serial. He may stalk a victim for a long time before moving in. He knows a lot about her, she knows nothing about him." Bunty's face whitened and was suddenly spotted with sweat. She put her hand out on the edge of the table to steady herself and then sat down.

I hurried over to her. "Are you all right?"

"I'm fine. Just tired."

"She's fine." Rhonda stepped in for her partner. "Not much sleep." Rhonda helped Bunty sit down. Everyone tried not to look curious. Then Rhonda took over the briefing. She said, "With these psychos, it's all about the fantasy life. In his own head, he's real tight with folks that wouldn't know him from the bagger at Wal-Mart. Which pisses him off." She handed Bunty a thermos, then walked over to a corkboard, pointed at a blow-up photo of the mailing tag:

LT. JUSTIN SAVILE V,
PLEASE DELIVER YOUR FRIEND TO:
CAPTAIN C.R. MANGUM

Wendy Freiberg said, "Obviously G.W. knew Justin ran homicide and that Cuddy was police chief, so they're the ones he's going to focus on. Plus, he knows they're friendly with each other—"

"Well, we were before Cuddy's promotion," I joked.

Bunty had finished whatever was in the thermos. She moved the marker northward on the map to The Fifth Season Resort where there was a third red circle. "So, Cathy was in October. Assuming Jane happened in February, and there's nobody in between that we haven't come across, G.W. waits four months between the first two victims and four months between the second and third. Does that interval hold or does it shorten?"

Rhonda passed out copies of the eight-by-ten, black-and-white headshot of Mavis Mahar with her eyes rubbed out with the red marker. "He scratches out her eyes and autographs it, 'GUESS WHO,' and somehow slips it under the police chief's office door."

Wendy Freiberg raised her hand. "I'm 95 percent sure the handwriting on that photo's a match for the tag on Jane. Check the Ss." We all looked from the words on the photo to the blow-up of the mailing label. She added, "Meanwhile, even with a clear disguise, this has got to be the most rigid vertical, evenly spaced, uniformly constructed script I've ever worked with. Bunty's right, G.W.'s a neat freak, ritualistic."

"OCD?" Cuddy asked about obsessive-compulsive disorder.

"Could even be in your league, Mangum." Wendy's relation with Cuddy was entirely ironical and I'd long suspected she had a crush on him. She never said anything sarcastic to me.

Cracks about Cuddy's "clean it and fix it" compulsions went around the room until Rhonda brought us back in line by whistling through her teeth. "So, first victim, Cathy Oakes, prostitute—no warning that we know of, no direct message to the local police, no follow-up. The signature—Guess T-shirt, a dozen roses thrown over the victim's body.

"Second victim, Jane—no warning that we know of, but a direct message, the toe label to Honch and JayJay here. The signature escalates, I mean it's like overkill—Guess T-shirt, necklace with ring and stone, tattoos, the matches around her head, the tongue, etc., etc., etc.

"By the third victim, G.W. is waltzing around HPD like it's home sweet home. This time he warns you ahead of time and he brags about it afterwards. He grabs Jay's keys off his desk, which means he knows who's drivin' what. Skips down to the garage and pops Elvis in the Jag's tape deck. He knows who's livin' where. He busts into the police chief's private home—pops the star on the slider and rigs the telescope in front of it."

Cuddy stopped Rhonda with a hand raised. "Okay, let's throw it out on the table now. Is Guess Who one of us?"

"One of us?" Wendy Freiberg looked at him puzzled.

"A cop, an ex-cop! HPD or County?" Cuddy took a thin folder from his briefcase. "Is this somebody works for the city? Is this maybe somebody with a grudge against me?"

Wendy said, "Apparently that could be anybody." We all laughed.

Cuddy repeated, "I'm serious. Was the clipping of that editorial asking me to resign from him? Do we think there's any chance it's somebody in the Cadmean Building?" He opened the

folder. "Here's the name of every current employee of the Hillston police, and any officer who was dismissed, quit, or retired
from HPD over the eight years I've been Chief. I put a check by
the names I think we can exclude." Slowly he grinned. "Everybody in this room got a check. But the only name I *know* I can
exclude is my own."

Everyone was quiet while we thought this over. Then Bunty
said, "We haven't worked out what we *do* know yet, Cuddy. I figure we oughta stay there for now. Hold off on this list."

Cuddy yanked at his hair. "I know you're right, Bunty, I just
want to get where we're going faster."

"We'll get there," she told him in her unhurried drawl.

Lisa Grecco interrupted to say that she had pulled a jacket
on an unsolved homicide down in Wilmington, N.C.—a young
white female's decomposed naked body had been discovered by
hunters in a marsh near a highway rest stop; she was naked, covered with silt. There were twenty-eight stab wounds on her body.
Her labia and nipples had been mutilated. She had ligature abra-
sions on her wrists and there was rope left at the scene. Could
this be an intermediate killing for Guess Who?

Bunty gazed out the window. "It's awful messy for G.W. He's
real precise." She said it with a kind of detached respect. "If he
left something at the scene, it's because he wanted us to see it.
Interpret it. Everything he sends you is a key to the code. Random stab wounds don't fit. Rope doesn't fit. He didn't need to tie
these women up. She's got long hair."

Rhonda interjected. "Remember, the significant part of the
code repeats. So what repeats? On victims one and two, a Guess
T-shirt. On victims two and three, cutting out body parts—the
tongue, the eyes. On all three, buzz cuts."

The voices of Isaac and Mavis suddenly ran together in my
head: "Until you find the pattern, how can you find your way to
the pattern maker.... Always lighting the candles to these
bloody martyred saints of hers."

"Light," I said.

"What, JayJay?"

"Light. The burnt matches around Jane's head and the candles on Lucy's hat."

Thoughtful, Bunty nodded at me.

Just then someone came in the room to tell Cuddy he had to take a phone call and the meeting momentarily broke up into small conversations. I leaned over to Wendy Freiberg. "Tell Cuddy I had to go to church."

• • •

In the lobby, reporters milled around the doors to Courtroom A. Latecomers, they hadn't been allowed inside to hear Isaac Rosethorn's summation in the Tyler Norris murder trial because the people crowded into Superior Court had already reached the maximum number allowed by the fire laws. Two of these reporters scurried over to me, eager to know if it was true that Cuddy had quit as police chief. Was it because he was beaten down by the negative press? Was it because Carl Yarborough was resigning as mayor to run for lieutenant governor? Had he been fired by Carl Yarborough because of the negative press? I said that as far I was aware, Chief Mangum had neither quit nor been fired. If he ever did quit, it wouldn't be because of the press, who shouldn't blame themselves because they weren't as powerful as they seemed to worry they were.

"Sticks and stones, Savile," smiled a young columnist from Greensboro. "So how's homicide? Looks like you just can't get your corpses straightened out these days. We hear you guys ID'ed a dead waitress as Mavis Mahar. How'd *that* happen?"

I had no comment and they hurried back across the lobby to see who was coming out of the big courtroom doors. They were disappointed that it was just Miss Bee Turner, carrying an empty cut-glass decanter in front of her like the holy grail. She was probably filling it for Isaac Rosethorn, who was probably pretending to have some kind of attack in the middle of his summation and in need of water to take some kind of life-saving pill.

Nearby, leaning his tall thick frame against the lobby display case that Nancy and Zeke had arranged of old weapons, Sheriff Homer Louge grinned at me. He had his thumbs tucked into his belt buckle like he was going to start a number from *Oklahoma*. "They giving you a rough time, Lieutenant Savile? Times change, don't they? Used to be, Mangum's boys could do no wrong. The rest of us had to just sit off to the side and watch him prancing around in the sun, TV and *Newsweek* kissing his fanny. Times change."

"Homer, you had a heart attack. Shouldn't you be at home?"

He scrubbed at his bristly gray crewcut as he watched me walk toward him. "You're the one might as well be home. Those FBI Lesbionics took over your case is what I hear."

"Not sure what you mean by 'Lesbionic,' because both Rhonda Weavis and Bunty Crabtree are American citizens."

"Well, they wouldn't be if I was running this good Christian country."

"Don't you like them? Why, they're always saying you're the most maladroit troglodyte they've ever met."

He frowned. "You're a little prick, Savile. You think your family makes you better than me?"

"Not at all. I think you have an inalienable right to be as good as I am. You just don't exercise it."

He flushed. "Laugh while you can. You and your smart-ass boss."

"I try. See you, Homer, I'm off to church."

"I bet."

Chapter 18

Trinity Church

Hurrying past the sanitation and cleaning service strikers, I made my way to my car and drove to Trinity Episcopal, the "smells and bells" Victorian Gothic church where Cuddy's friend Father Paul Madison was something of an authority on the subject I wanted to talk with him about.

Outside, Trinity looked like a mistake, like Exeter Cathedral dropped incongruously into a block of glass and concrete commerce. But inside, it was a huge, dark, vaulted, medieval sanctuary against the world around it, so large, so quiet that modernity was vanquished. My footsteps echoed on the stone floor as I passed the rows of empty varnished pews, the worn marble baptismal font, the red flickering candles, the photographs of a parish trip to rebuild a coastal town hit by last year's hurricane. Near the altar rail I found Paul crawling about on his hands and knees, tacking down loose carpeting in the choir stall.

The Reverend Doctor Paul Madison was single, small, and blond, and was often taken for a Catholic priest because of the collars and cassocks he wore. But as a matter of fact, he was divorced and always asking us to find him someone to date, since he was prohibited from dating most of the women he met because they were parishioners. Paul had a graduate degree in early church history and complained that he never had a chance to use it. I was going to give him the opportunity. I told him so after we'd chatted about the events of the past days. While entirely lacking in aggression himself (a problem for the rest of us on the Fuzz Five basketball team), Paul had the armchair detective's avid interest in violent crime and it was only by assuring him that my "theological question" was related to the Guess Who homicides that I was able to stop him from grilling me about the shooting at The Fifth Season. Taking a seat in the ornately carved stall, I asked him to listen to my description of the victim and then tell me if it made him think of anything.

He scrunched up his bizarrely youthful face, made the more cherubic by his blond curls. "My hands are sweating. It's like my Ph.D. orals."

"Just listen. And Paul, this is confidential."

He pointed at the old dark confessional in the corner. "Right, like that's a problem for me."

"Okay. Think of a young woman. A ring of candles around her head, she's shot through the neck, she's naked, and her eyes are cut out."

Paul just stared at me, horrified. "Oh my god, the poor woman."

"Yes…. So we're looking for any significance to the mutilation. Does it make you think of anything?"

He closed his eyes, then opened them wide. "You mean besides it's like the one you can't identify, the G.I. Jane one with her tongue cut out?"

I looked at him and slowly nodded. "Exactly…. Yes, besides that it's like that one. The ring of candles, the missing eyes."

He searched my eyes carefully. "Lucy. Didn't they say in the news today that this woman's name was Lucy?"

"Yes, Lucy Griggs."

He looked at me hopefully. "Are you asking me about Saint Lucy?"

I took a breath. "There's a saint named Lucy?"

He grabbed the altar rail as if there were information he could shake out of it. "Yes, Saint Lucy. She was blinded."

"Damn it! Of course. Luce. Light. I knew it was about light."

"Yeah, where was the old prep school Latin when you needed it?"

"Hey, a college major, too. *Lux et veritas*. How soon we forget."

When I asked him if religious painters ever depicted haloes as a ring of lighted candles around a saint's head, he said he couldn't think of a particular instance but agreed that the candles in the hat did resemble a halo. "Sometimes in the paintings, she holds a lamp or a candle."

"So what made Lucy a saint?"

Happy to be of help, Paul motioned for me to follow him into his office off the vestry room. "Like most of the virgin martyrs, her problem was she turned Christian before it got popular. It's always a risk to jump on a bandwagon before anybody else has identified it as a bandwagon. Just ask Otto Lillienthal."

"A saint?"

"A nineteenth-century German aviator. Flew over two thousand flights before he died in his glider and the Wright Brothers read all about him. Aviation's my hobby." In his dusty book-crammed study, Paul stood on a chair to reach down two volumes. "They tried everything to make Lucy give up her faith. They made her a prostitute, but Christ fixed it so nobody could get an erection around her and that way she stayed a virgin."

"Sounds like Christ had a sense of humor."

"Oh, a great sense of humor." Paul was searching through one of the books. "Then I think a judge gouged out Lucy's eyes. The problem is, all these virgin martyr stories get mushed together. They're all set on fire, raped, stabbed, fed to wild animals, decapitated. But with Lucy, it's definitely the eyes. Here, look at this." He showed me a painting of a slender blind woman in a white robe. She had a bleeding hole in her throat and stood placidly holding a large shell with two eyeballs in it.

"Are those her own eyes she's holding there?"

"Right." He was reading. "A sword through her throat, that's it."

I could feel my heart thudding. "Through her throat?" I pointed my finger under my jaw, in the trajectory through which the still unrecovered bullet had entered Lucy Griggs's neck.

Paul rubbed at his clerical collar. "Right. That's why Lucy's the saint of sore throats. And the saint of blindness. I could lend you these books." He flipped through the pages, pausing at an illustration of Saint Joan. Joan of Arc at her execution, her head shaved.

I startled the rector by hugging him. "God bless you, Father Paul."

He grinned, pleased. "Is that the answer? Saint Lucy?"

I told him it could be one of the answers. "Now find me a virgin martyr who had her tongue cut out."

• • •

An hour later, I slipped back into Room 105 without comment, except for a scowl from Cuddy. Etham Foster was asking Rhonda about the little stone that had been threaded through the shoelaces around G.I. Jane's neck. He'd thought it was some totemic amulet, but none of the many New Age stores in the area had been able to identify it. He wondered, could it possibly have been a clue already set back in February to lead us to Mavis. Rock? Rock star? Like the Elvis tape was to signal rock star.

Rhonda nodded. "It's an idea." She went back to reading out the items she'd written beneath the heading, "G.I. JANE."

—Victim WF, probably mid-twenties.
—Victim unknown; ID removed.
—No pre-crime warning or we missed it?
—Body moved (gray car carpet fiber) and hidden in shallow grave: wants it found but not right away.
—Probable no sexual assault but victim stripped of clothing, genitals left exposed.
—Weapon:
  –Probably hunting knife in the Colt Tactical Combat model category. Three stab wounds to neck, severed trachea, jugular, cracked vertebra.

—Postmortem mutilation:
  –Pierced eyebrow ring sliced from face.
  –Tongue cut out and removed. (Missing. Animals?)
  –Hair shaved.
  –Six postmortem burns to arms and torso.
—Evidence at scene:
  –Nine kitchen matches arranged around head.
  –Gray T-shirt with Guess logo, new, size Large.
  –Kenneth Cole sunglasses.
  –Nike white shoelaces tied together, strung with the
    eyebrow ring and small round gray stone.
  –Toe label addressed to Savile/Mangum.

Bunty turned to us. "We miss something?"

I said, "The snake tattoos."

Rhonda added the tattoos. "Right, on her ankles; looks like he drew them with the same red marker he used for the morgue label."

Then, on the right side of the board, Bunty pointed to another list she'd made under the words MAVIS MAHAR. "Okay, number three. Let's say G.W. got away with Cathy and then with Jane."

Cuddy spun his pencil through his fingers. "That's sure what every paper in the state's saying."

Bunty came over and silently patted him on the shoulder, an extraordinary gesture of intimacy from her. Then she walked back to the safety of the wallboard. "G.W.'s scared but he's also aroused. Murder's a high for him. He likes it. He remembers the feeling, he watches, he waits. My bet is, he goes back to the G.I. Jane scene between the murder and when you found her. Checks her out, fiddles with things, 'improves' them. He's a perfectionist, like Wendy says about the handwriting, a neat freak. Maybe the mutilation even happens days after the murder."

The way I was now thinking, Bunty's idea made sense.

"Weeks go by; months." Rhonda picked up the story. "G.W. gets cocky. 'Hey, I could do this again and again, they'll never catch me. And next time I'll do it even better.' Now if Bunt and

I are right, and this is about showing off and showing up the authorities, then G.W.'s thinking he won the first two games hands-down. But big whup, where's the satisfaction? Cathy Oakes was a low-class prostitute, not a single relative comes to claim her. G.I. Jane was some other nobody he ran into. Maybe another prostitute. You guys at HPD can't even put a name to her. And obviously she doesn't matter much to anybody because nobody's missing her."

Bunty said, "What we're suggesting is, he's thinking, if you want to stick it to the alpha males, take their women. The valuable ones. The ones they put a premium on. How 'bout a superstar? How 'bout Mavis Mahar? That ought to up the stakes."

I raised my hand. "What if he didn't think it was Mavis? What if he knew it was Lucy?"

Rhonda waved me off like a catcher's call. "No way, JayJay. It was set up for Mavis. Otherwise what do you do with his warnings? First he tells you he's back, he's the one that killed Jane— that's the Elvis tape. 'Wear My Ring Around Your Neck.' Like Etham said, Elvis is a rock star, so it's a pointer. Then he sets up the telescope and the cardboard star. 'Watch the star.' Then he kills the rock star. And just so you know he's the one who did it, he slips you her headshot photo with the eyes gone. He shoots her through the head. Head shot. Autographed, 'Guess Who.' He went after Mavis Mahar, screwed up, and killed the wrong girl."

"I don't think so," I said. "I think he knew her name was Lucy."

Cuddy leaned toward me. "Justin, will you please let them finish laying it out for us, okay? Then you can raise objections."

"Hang on one sec, okay, JayJay." Rhonda quickly read down the list under "MAVIS MAHAR":

—Victim WF, late-twenties.
—Victim known, famous.
—Pre-crime warnings—Elvis tape, *Hillston Star* clipping, glitter cardboard star & telescope.

—Body left on display; indoors, no attempt to hide it.

—No sexual assault but victim naked.

—Head shaved.

—Weapon:

   –Gun, (make unknown) missing from the scene. Single shot trajectory through lower mandible into cranial cavity.

—Postmortem mutilation:

   –Both eyes removed.

—Evidence deliberately left at scene.

   –Straw hat with four candles.

— Post-crime:

   –Headshot of Mavis with "Guess Who" autograph delivered to Mangum.

"Okay, now, what's your problem, Justin?" Cuddy asked. But before I could answer, the door to 105 burst open so loudly we all jumped. It was Nancy Caleb-White, not in uniform, but jeans and a sleeveless white blouse. As soon as she spotted Cuddy and me, she ran at us.

Cuddy asked, "Is the jury out? Is it over?"

"What? Oh, I don't know," she said distracted. "Listen, Chief—"

"Nancy, we're in a meeting. You ever hear of knocking? And why are you out of uniform?"

"It's my day off!" Nancy was nodding so energetically her long black braid swung wildly behind her. "I know who she is! This is her!" She held up a commercial photograph of a young woman's face. It was stamped "Shear Inspirations" and appeared to be one of those pictures that are taped up in the windows of beauty salons to show examples of haircuts. This young woman had a buzz cut. Looking closely, I saw what Nancy meant. Despite the differences in the way this woman looked smiling and made-up in a photographer's studio and the way she had looked after having her throat cut and lying dead in the wet earth, it was still possible to see they were the same person. The hair and ears, the wide cheeks, the mole on the side of the strong straight nose, the earring looped through the right eyebrow. It was the girl we called G.I. Jane.

Nancy beamed as Cuddy snatched the picture away and stared at it and then at me. I said, "She's right. It's Jane."

Cuddy swung Nancy off the ground. "Where'd you get this!"

"Justin told me to check hair salons—"

"It was her idea," I said. "Nancy had the idea Jane got the buzz cut *before* she was killed and Guess Who just hacked at it."

As the picture was passed around the room, Nancy eagerly went on. "So I've been checking places, asking them to go back in their records—which they mostly didn't even have, including this place called Shear Inspirations near Haver campus. But I'm there, kind of looking around and I flip through this stack of discard photos and there she is!" Her face fell. "But, Chief, they didn't know where they got the picture from. They say they get stacks of them in the mail. And they don't know her name."

I said, "I bet her name's Christine."

Chapter 19

Shear Inspirations

In the Protestant Bible-Belt South, there's Jesus, the Devil, and God. In that order. Very few people pray to saints, or indeed could tell you very much about saints, except that they've heard of St. Patrick's Day and St. Christopher medals. The notion of virgin martyrs is more likely to evoke images of sullen celibates than of the books that I was now passing around to a skeptical homicide team in Room 105: one book was open to a Venetian engraving of St. Lucy; another to a Flemish portrait of Saint Christine of Tyre. Another to a painting of Joan of Arc at the stake, with her shaved head.

"Bear with me," I asked Cuddy. "Bunty said if Guess Who left anything behind, he wanted us to interpret it like a code. That's what I'm trying to do." I described Saint Lucy's martyrdom (how she'd stayed a virgin in a brothel, how she'd been stabbed through the throat and had her eyes gouged out), and how on her name day still, in Sweden, the youngest daughter in the household dresses in white and wears a crown of burning candles. "We have the throat wound, the missing eyes, the halo of candles. I think he knew he was killing someone named Lucy. And now here's why I think he knew Jane's name was Christine."

I told them the myths about the possibly apocryphal Saint Christine: how the adolescent girl had renounced paganism, so incensing her father that he locked her in a tower. How she converted her twelve female guards overnight, and with them vandalized all the statues of the pagan gods they could find. How her father had her thrown into a bonfire, and when that didn't make her give up Christianity, he tried decapitating her, only to drop dead himself. How next they tied a stone around her neck and threw her in a lake, and after she wouldn't sink, burned her in boiling oils and sulfur.

I noticed that (except for Nancy, thrilled just to be in a room among celebrated investigators like Rhonda and Bunty) most people at the table were trying to keep smiles off their faces by freezing them into polite disbelief, but then Bunty put down her pointer and looked at the picture of St. Christine, which showed the young woman surrounded by flames, with a millstone hanging on a chain around her neck and snakes around her ankles. A pagan soldier had just sliced off her tongue and was holding it up. Encouraged, I went on, "They tried everything they could think of—flogging, a week in a white hot oven, poisonous snakes. But the snakes just *wrapped themselves around her feet*. Sound familiar? Finally, the only thing they could do to stop Christine from converting everybody she met was to *cut out her tongue*."

Cuddy flicked at his captain's hat, spun it in a circle on the table. "Paul Madison told you all this?"

"And lent me these books." I held them up. "Come on, folks. Just look at G.I. Jane's body. We've got burns with sulfur matches. We've got snakes drawn on her ankles. He shaved her head and nearly decapitated her. He put a stone around her neck. And, most of all, he cut out her tongue."

I knew Bunty was coming with me when she said (to the window), "Don't I remember those burnt matches looking like a halo around Jane's head?" I nodded yes. "So maybe G.W.'s doing the same thing again when he puts the ring of candles in Lucy's hat?"

I nodded again. "That's the repeat. Saints' shaved heads and haloes."

Cuddy asked, "What about dates? There're calendars of saints' days, right? Are these homicides tied to the calendar?"

I admitted the dates didn't work—St. Lucy's day was December 13, Christine's was July 24.

Cuddy shook his head. "And where's the halo for Cathy Oakes?"

I suggested that the Neville prostitute was the first crude step for Guess Who, a practice run. And for that reason he chose someone away from Hillston. The final touches came only with the second two victims. But I pointed out that flowers were often laid before images of saints (as they'd been strewn on Cathy Oakes's torso), and that Catherine was the name of a saint, a virgin martyr. I noted that if you looked back at the medical examiner's report on Cathy Oakes, you'd see that she had broken legs and broken ribs. In fact, the local police had speculated that her assailant had run a car over her.

Bunty knew where I was going. She held up a painted portrait of a young medieval woman who carried a wooden wheel. "Saint Catherine. Broken on the wheel," she said. "And her head was shaved."

I sat down beside Bunty. "And doesn't it feel orderly? On Jane, three stab wounds to the throat, six burns on the torso, nine matches around the head. Three, six, nine. On Lucy—"

"Whoa." Rhonda stretched her arms over her head. "This is a little out there, JayJay. He put a bullet in Lucy Griggs's throat, not a sword. And according to Dick here, it sure doesn't look like a case of a *virgin* martyr. And neither was Cathy Oakes."

"Still," said Wendy Freiberg looking at the pictures in a book. "A lot of coincidence here."

Cuddy asked us to keep in mind that any evidence could be made to fit any number of scenarios; all you need is a clever theory. The question always is, which theory actually turns out to be the truth. He walked across the room and tapped the photos of the crime scene in Bungalow Eight. "Here's what we know *without* a theory: Lucy Griggs was in Mavis's room, she was dressed like Mavis and she looked like Mavis, so much like Mavis that everybody thought she was Mavis. Somebody sent me a *Hillston Star* and a cardboard star and a Mavis headshot. I think the target was Mavis, candles or no candles, and I think G.W. made a mistake."

Augie Summer cleared his throat gruffly. He was a young, plump, sweet-natured person who'd fallen into the habit of mimicking his grouchy superior Etham Foster, but without any of Etham's saturnine affect. (Sooner or later, everyone who worked in forensics adopted the director's disgruntled tone, even instinctively pleasant people like Augie.) "Does anybody know how at Mavis concerts, fans hold up candles? She likes them to do it for the dead, like innocent victims killed in wars. It's like a candle-light vigil."

No, nobody had mentioned that.

"Did anybody mention," he added, "that she had a hit song a few years back called 'Prayers to Plastic Saints,' and it's all about how sick the Catholic Church is, fixating on the dismemberment of young women."

No, nobody had mentioned that.

"Well, there you have it," Lisa Grecco shrugged.

Cuddy said right now he'd rather I go back to the hair salon Shear Inspirations and push them on the name of the girl in the G.I. Jane photograph, instead of assuming her name was Christine because of some fifth-century saint. Next thing he wanted was for Bunty and Rhonda to take a look at John Walker (Lucy's jealous boyfriend) whom we were still holding on cocaine possession. We'd reconvene in an hour.

With a rub of a thin finger along her narrow nose, Bunty said quietly, "Maybe we can have both." We all looked at her. "Maybe Guess Who planned to kill Mavis, but walked in and shot the wrong person. If there's one thing true about this man, he doesn't like to make mistakes. More, he doesn't want anybody to *know* he made a mistake. Especially not you, Cuddy."

Cuddy frowned. "Hey, don't put this guy on me."

Bunty shook her pointer at him. "*You* put this guy on you. You're the one quoted in the papers saying nobody's smart enough to get away with murder in Hillston. Saying how you're going to arrest Guess Who by the Fourth of July." She studied him bemused. "And why you let yourself get quoted saying such a thing—well, if I saw private patients, I'd say you oughta make an appointment." (This rare bit of wryness drew scattered applause.)

Cuddy acknowledged the applause with an ironical bow, then asked her, "So you're saying Guess Who tries to fix it?"

She nodded. "The clipping and the cardboard star suggest he's planning to kill Mavis. So does the headshot. You said he could have slipped it under your office door *before* the murder, right? Then he sees it's *not* Mavis lying there, but somebody else, some nobody like Jane. He needs to get in control. He needs it to have been his choice. That's what I mean. So he takes the victim's purse—that mesh carry-all thing is missing, right?"

I said yes, it was missing. And with it a music tape that Lucy had given Mavis as well as a camera with film taken that night.

Bunty said, "So he gets her name off her DL, credit card, whatever. It's Lucy Griggs. Okay, if he's into saints, he knows what to do with Lucy. No hesitation, he slices out her eyes. Maybe Lucy already had the candles for the concert in her purse. We know she had a ticket to the concert. So he puts the candles in her hat. See? If we figure out it's Lucy, he's ahead of us."

Cuddy asked her, "If he's into virgin saints, why Mavis Mahar?"

Bunty said, "Justin's report says Mavis Mahar's real name was Agnes Connolly. If she's his intended victim, you can believe he's done his homework and knows that. It says in here," she held up one of Paul's books, "Agnes was another one of those teenage virgin saints, and she was set on fire and decapitated and all that bad stuff. And before that, she was also thrown in a brothel and anybody who tried to sleep with her went blind. I mean, any which way, this nut could be into virgin martyrs."

Everyone thought this through until Cuddy tossed his pencil in air. "Hey, Rhonda," he called to her. "This why your partner gets the big bucks?"

Rhonda wound up an imaginary ball and hurled it at him. "Damn straight, Honch. But I can spend it on home improvements as fast as she can make it. I am the original Gold Medal Black and Decker dyke."

Dick Cohen said, "God, I wish you'd come over and do something about my air-conditioning."

● ● ●

Cuddy had wanted me to check by Courtroom A on my way out of the Cadmean Building. I couldn't get anywhere near the doors because a crowd was pouring through them: the summations were over. I heard that Margy Turbot had adjourned the trial until Tuesday morning when both sides would offer rebuttals and she would instruct the jury. A reporter I recognized from the *Sun* was complaining to Shelly Bloom, "Turbot's dragging this out like they had her on Court TV. It's only 3:30. Why wait 'til tomorrow? I'm losing my time-share right on the beach at Hilton Head. Maybe I'll just go ahead and file my piece. We already know the verdict. Tyler Norris Not-Guilty, on to the next gig, right? I need a drink. Hi, Savile." He waved good-bye.

I cornered Shelly, looking curiously unlike herself in a soft green Talbot's dress as if she hoped to join the Junior League. "Back at the *Sun?*"

She told me, vividly, that she wouldn't work for the *Sun* if they begged her, which seemed unlikely since they'd just fired her. She was writing a freelance piece on the Norris trial for the *Hillston Star Sunday Magazine*. Bubba Percy had helped arrange it, either out of remorse at having Shelly fired or because she'd blackmailed him into making amends.

"So you're friends again, you and Bubba?"

"When were we friends?"

I asked her how she thought Isaac Rosethorn's summation had gone over. She predicted I wouldn't be happy to hear. Suffice it to say that one woman on the jury had been crying and that Judge Turbot had to use her gavel to stop at least a dozen spectators from clapping. Rosethorn finished by limping to the jury box in tears and swearing he would gladly give his own weary old life, worn out in long service to Lady Justice, if he could die in the knowledge that those twelve wise and decent jurors were no more going to take away Tyler's chance to live out his days, doing the good he'd always done—as a son, as a teacher, as a churchgoer, and as a member of this community—than they would strike dead their own living children.

Shelly said she would vote not guilty herself if she were on the jury. She had always suspected that we'd arrested Tyler Norris mainly because we didn't like his attitude and because we couldn't find the intruder and it was a high-profile case we needed to close.

"Thanks, Shelly."

She shrugged. "Well, I don't like him either. But that doesn't make him a murderer." Her cell phone rang. "Hello?" She listened, shaking her head in disgust, then said to her caller, "Grow up. You couldn't possibly think I'd find that proposal remotely attractive." She hung up. "Your pal Bubba Percy," she told me, "is a complete pervert. I won't repeat what he just offered to give me his Porsche for doing."

I said, "Please don't."

"Repeat it or do it?"

"Either one. I know how much he loves that Porsche."

• • •

Nancy was waiting by the HPD display case to drive me to Shear Inspirations. Near her I was surprised to see the two dark-skinned women I'd spotted so often on the street. I'd never seen them inside the Cadmean Building. They were emptying the trashcans into plastic bags. Nancy said she'd heard the city had unofficially hired some of these "migrants" because cleaning services had gone out on strike in support of the sanitation workers.

I'd never heard of migrant workers in Hillston, North Carolina.

"Yeah, it's been happening. 'Ninety-fivers,' that's what you hear them called, 'cause they walk Interstate 95, follow the crops, Florida to Maine. Then they turn around and head back. Like birds. Some of them don't have nothing like a visa neither, but the chief says to the guys on patrol, leave 'em alone. Ninety-fivers."

In fact, the two women bent above the cans with their shiny raven-black hair and rusty black clothes, did look like birds, like two large black crows huddled over the trash, dragging it away with them.

Shear Inspirations was a long low corridor between an Indian restaurant called Rajah and a Sam Goody music chain where Mavis Mahar CDs filled the windows under a hasty handmade banner that read, "SHE'S ALIVE!!" As a result, the hair salon smelled like curry and coriander and sounded—between the hip-hop booming through one side of the thin walls and the seventies disco thumping through the other and Frankie Lyman shaking the speakers inside—like the whole history of rock'n'roll being performed simultaneously. Most of the space in Shear Inspirations was a cluttered shrine to Marilyn Monroe—posters and photos and cutouts on the walls; statuettes, dolls, ashtrays, and clocks on the counters. In keeping with its fifties goddess, the temple was decorated with grimy flea market furnishings from the period, but the vinyl stools were too torn, the chrome tables too tarnished, the pink cone hairdryers too rusted and wobbly. On the floor, black and white linoleum looked as if it had been walked on more times than it could stand, and the female manager of the place looked as if she had too. This short overweight woman was a middle-aged baby boomer with dyed platinum Marilyn Monroe hair and light pink lipstick through which big pink gum bubbles kept popping. Forty years ago she might have looked good in her pedal pushers, tight pink horizontally striped sweater and wide stretchy belt, but at her current age and weight this outfit was the last thing she should have been wearing.

Nancy introduced me to Mrs. Doris Nutz, who immediately snapped, "No cracks!" emphasizing her point with a loud *pow* of her pink gum. Mrs. Nutz also had portraits of lesser fifties celebrities on her walls (Tab Hunter, Troy Donahue, Sandra Dee), but it was quickly apparent that she shared none of their energetic goodcheer. She didn't see why the hell Nancy was bothering her again; she'd already said she didn't know who the girl with the buzz cut was or from where the photo had originated. It was no wonder the Hillston police had such a lousy reputation when they would rather harass hard-working taxpayers than arrest the dregs of society.

Couldn't I see she was busy running a business? To prove her point, Mrs. Nutz held up her hands—puckered, shriveled, and white from years of immersion in various toxic liquids. I indicated with an arm wave that Shear Inspirations was currently empty except for one customer asleep with her feet in a basin of green glop. "Hell," she sighed, "between the Koreans and the Hair Cuttery chains, I don't know why I don't just stick my head in an oven."

Finally, Mrs. Nutz begrudgingly allowed us to talk with her two haircutters (one with cornrows, one with a purple pompadour, both in bowling shirts with pleated backs), who were off in the rear of the shop eating frozen yogurt while watching *All My Children*. Neither of these young men recognized G.I. Jane. But then even the one with seniority had only worked there for four months.

After a little more chitchat, Mrs. Nutz agreed to show me her old appointment book. While I looked through it, Debbie Reynolds' "Tammy" fought off the BeeGees from Rajah's and Mavis's "Coming Home to You" from the record store. Behind me, Nancy was checking shelves stuffed with old newspapers, magazines, and promotional photos, searching for any other pictures of G.I. Jane or any other model with the same studio wallpaper visible behind her head.

The white Shear Inspirations appointment book was inscribed "Wedding Guests." It had not been rigorously kept, perhaps to avoid troubling the IRS with too much income to tax. For if Mrs. Nutz had had no more clients over the past six months than those she'd recorded, it was hard to imagine how she could pay her two stylists to watch soap operas. The notations I did find in her ledger were so haphazard, I worried I was wasting my time even looking. On only a few occasions were the client's name, the haircutter's name, the desired treatment and the price all listed. Usually there was only a terse code, like "D–4." But I was lucky. I turned a page and saw the name "Kristin" on December 24. The word "buzz" was right beside it and after that the name "Bo." Kristin was the same name as Christine; "buzz" was the cut I was looking for. She'd had an appointment for one P.M.

Excited, I asked Mrs. Nutz to look again at the photo we'd brought back to her shop. Might this "Kristin" in her appointment book be the girl in the photograph? If she'd gotten the buzz cut here on December 24, was it possible that someone around here had taken the photograph that Nancy had found?

Mrs. Nutz didn't take time to think; she had no regulars named Kristin and couldn't be expected to remember a walk-in from six months ago. She said she'd already said that no one in her salon had ever taken any photos of haircuts. The hair product companies sent them and she didn't know where the one of G.I. Jane had come from. I asked her about the other name in the appointment book: who was Bo?

"A bitch and a thief," was the answer, fired back again with the accompanying gum pop. Apparently, Bo Derek (self-named after Bo Derek but "who's she kidding?") had robbed Mrs. Nutz on Christmas Eve of all the cash in the register, her Sony TV and camcorder, and a new lamb shearling jacket she'd accidentally left in the restroom. When she'd rushed over to the house on Whitcomb where this thieving employee had rented a room, she'd found Bo's landlady crying in the street because her Toyota Camry was gone. "She robbed us both on Christmas Eve. And Bo's landlady even had a little present waiting for her under the tree!"

"That's awful. I guess this Kristin would have been Bo's last customer."

Mrs. Nutz took back her appointment book. "Well if 'Kristin' was wearing anything that bitch wanted, Bo's probably the one that cut her throat." She looked at me thoughtfully. "There're too many people on this planet and half of them ought to be shot into outer space."

I pointed at Marilyn Monroe smiling down on us from the pink wall. "Doris, you think it was a kinder, gentler world back then in the fifties?"

Mrs. Nutz made a dismissive splutter through her pale pink lipstick. "No, I think it was the same pile of crap. I loved Marilyn, but I never had her innocence," she said. "I was more like Carolyn Jones in *King Creole*," she said. "Kind of bitter."

As I was writing down what information she had about the larcenous Bo, Nancy, behind me on her knees in piles of mildewed junk mail suddenly shouted, "Hey!" When I walked over, she handed me a faded photo Christmas card. "Look at that." On its glossy cover, I saw a half-dozen people standing in front of the Shear Inspirations sinks, all but one of them wearing Santa hats with pink smocks and holding up a string of tinfoil letters that spelled out "HAPPY HOLIDAYS." I recognized Mrs. Nutz, looking in her pink smock like one of her bigger gum bubbles, but I didn't see anyone resembling G.I. Jane.

"No, not her." Nancy pointed at the one person not wearing a Santa hat or a salon smock. It was a hostile young man, good looking, dressed in black jeans and black leather jacket, and not at all in the Christmas spirit. "That's John Walker," she whispered. "That's the guy we're holding. The guy was stalking Lucy Griggs. Her ex-boyfriend."

He was also the person I'd seen glowering at Lucy from the shadows of the Tucson band platform when she was getting her picture taken with her idol Mavis Mahar. I took the greeting card over to Mrs. Nutz and asked her about the young man sulking in the corner of her Christmas card. Had he worked here in Shear Inspirations? She avoided my question. Instead, she pointed out a big-boned muscular woman with a white streak in her feathered hair, who was standing with her arm around Doris just as if she wasn't planning to rob her in less than a month. The thief Bo Derek.

I said it was the young man I was interested in right now. She told me she didn't see why I had to waste her time. "Come on, Doris. You know who he is."

She abruptly burst out that the young man in the photo was her son John Walker from her rotten first marriage, and no, he hadn't worked here. Honest work didn't interest her son John. He was "a quote artist unquote." But in her opinion, what his band the Mood Disorders played wasn't music, and anybody with any talent from Percy Faith to Ray Charles would agree with her. Why were we asking her about John? Just because a kid got in trouble when he was a kid did we have to keep hounding him his whole life?

I asked if she was aware that her son was being held at this moment for questioning in the shooting death last night of Lucy Griggs. She looked at me shocked. Then she sat down in one of the pink metal chairs, carefully placed her hands on the knees of her pedal pushers, and stared at their white shriveled skin. She sat without moving for so long that finally I repeated my question, although I already knew the answer was no. She hadn't known that Lucy Griggs had been murdered. No, she hadn't known that her son was in custody. Is that what we were really here about? Was the G.I. Jane photo just a trick to get us in the door so we could try to pin something on her son?

Glancing mournfully around her shop—as if wondering why she bothered—Mrs. Nutz promised me that John had not killed Lucy. They broke up over a year ago and were out of each other's lives now. Yes, the break-up had been Lucy's doing and yes, Lucy had added insult to injury by trying to persuade her quote band unquote, whose other guitarist happened to be John's best friend since junior high, to throw John out of his own band. The other guitarist's name was Griffin Pope.

I suggested that this rejection by Lucy must have troubled her son. Not at all, claimed his mother. John could care less about Lucy; he'd had a dozen other girls since then. Mrs. Nutz— caught between protecting her child and casting as much blame as possible on the dead girl—went on proving that Lucy's mistreatment of John was monstrous and that John hadn't been in the least bothered by it, until she finally tangled herself in verbal knots and abruptly stopped, taking refuge in popping her gum at me. I borrowed the photo Christmas card and told her we'd be back. She wasn't surprised.

Chapter 20

Interrogation Three

On the way to HPD, Nancy nodded as she drove. "You're good with women, Justin. I couldn't get old Doris to open up at all."

"You're better with guys."

"It's this personal thing you do. Yeah, I'm like you that way with guys. You noticed?" She glanced over and the car swerved.

I asked her, "Hasn't Cuddy talked to you about having only one finger on the steering wheel?"

"A good finger," she said and used it to make the turn into the municipal lot. "But listen, where I'm best is young guys. You grow up in East Hillston and you got younger brothers, you better be. Let me do Mister Johnny Walker Black Leather, okay?"

"He's all yours."

• • •

Nancy's husband Sergeant Zeke Caleb was supervising the desk. He passed release forms to a remorseful DWI before acknowledging us with a stiff hello. (He and Nancy keep a formal distance between work and love, and if you saw them on HPD property, you'd never know they'd ever met, much less been married for years.) He told Nancy, "Officer, you got a phone call from a guy called Dermott Quinn, wants you to call him back after six, okay?"

"Okay, thanks, Sergeant," she said. "The Lieutenant and I are going to talk to this kid we're holding, John Walker. I'll take him to Three, Justin." She waved as she walked off.

I asked Zeke if the task force had reconvened in Room 105, and he said no. Cuddy was in the district attorney's office and some of them had gone out to interview the coroner, Osmond Bingley.

"I hope they ask him why he keeps ruling suicide on victims with multiple gunshot wounds to the head."

Zeke was too good a soldier to joke about city officials. He said only, "I hear there's a break on G.I. Jane. I hear you got a photo."

"Thanks to your wife," I said. He tried to stop his smile but couldn't.

• • •

We looked through the glass of Interrogation Room 3 at the pouty fidgety young suspect seated in the plastic chair with his lizard-skin boots up on the table, his arm in a cast. Nancy nodded at me. "Okay, go crazy, show me what you got."

"Just watch me."

It took only five minutes to scare the bravado off John Everett Walker's pretty face and replace it with a green jellyish anxiety. I knocked his legs off the table, cuffed one of them to the chair leg, and told him he was the best thing to happen to me in months because he'd solved two big problems of mine. I was under pressure to book a suspect on the Lucy Griggs murder and here he was—a prime candidate. Plus, I *really* needed to clear the Guess Who killings, and here he was again. I could tie him to G.I. Jane's homicide through his mother's hair salon.

As Walker fought to hold on to his skeptical sneer, I fell forward onto him and hit him hard with my elbow as his chair went over. "Lost my balance," I smiled.

On his side, trapped by the leg cuff, he held his cast in air and heaved for breath, shocked and gagging, his eyes darting desperately to Nancy. "What's the matter with him? I didn't kill Lucy! What's going on? First these two FBI bitches are all over me, now this freak?"

Nancy stepped between us and helped Walker pull himself upright in the chair, patting his back kindly as she did so. "Lieutenant Savile, hey, take it easy. You okay, John?"

I snarled, "This s.o.b. murdered three women and you want me to take it easy with him?"

She stared at me dubiously. "Think we can make him for all three?"

"Three women? Jesus, what the fuck are y'all talking about?" The young man looked like someone who'd suddenly been abducted by aliens.

I stepped close to his face, squeezed his chin in my hand and stared into his eyes. Flinching, he pulled his head back as far away from me as he could. "Yeah. He killed them all," I told Nancy. "I can see it all over him. It makes me sick, what he did to Lucy and Jane, butchering them like that, cutting out their tongues and eyes."

Walker's own eyes swelled, pushing open his thick-lashed lids. "You're crazy! He's crazy!"

"You think so? Give me a reason not to strap you down and slide the needle in. Give me a reason!" I shoved hard at his chair with every few words until I knocked it over again against the wall.

Tilted backwards, Walker twisted himself frantically toward Nancy. "Get him away from me! I didn't kill anybody!"

Nancy pushed me across the room, pleading with me to calm down, take a break, leave her to talk to the suspect alone for a while. Finally I was persuaded to go have a cup of coffee. As I slipped out the door, she whispered, "Better. I mean, you got a ways to go, but you're getting there."

"From you," I told her, "high praise."

Usually I'd be the one protecting the suspect from Nancy's outbursts. She thought her "mad dog cop" was scarier than mine, and she was right. The stepfather who'd tried to rape her when she was a teenager came out of the hospital in a wheelchair two months after he went in.

While Nancy was comforting John Walker, I checked by District Attorney Mitch Bazemore's office. There was no need to wonder if Cuddy was still in there because he exploded like a bull out of the closed door just as I walked by it. Mitch, swollen with anger, chased after him, waving a letter at his back. "You don't tell me! I tell you! There's a chain of command here and if Ward Trasker, the attorney general of this state—"

Cuddy wheeled around on Mitch. The veins in his neck were so distended I could see his pulse beating there. "Ward Trasker ought to be indicted and you know it, you goddamn coward!"

"If the attorney general tells me we're turning the Guess Who investigation over to the sheriff's department, then that's exactly what we're doing because there's a chain of command here! Turn your files over to Homer Louge." Bazemore suddenly realized he was in a public corridor and that I was in it with him. By a huge effort of will, he deflated himself as if he'd let out compressed air. "We'll discuss this later, Mangum."

Cuddy grabbed the sheet of paper from Bazemore and ripped it in two. "No, we won't." He threw the paper at Bazemore's chest. "The answer's no. Homer Louge has fucked this investigation already—"

"Don't you dare use that filthy language—"

"And I'm not turning a fuckshit paper clip over to him. And you fucks fire me you'll be seeing yourselves on the news more goddamn times than Monica Lewinsky!"

I walked past them. "Hi. How you doing, Mitch? Cuddy. Nice day. Good talking to you." I kept going.

• • •

The next morning, Tuesday the twenty-sixth, I arrived at Room 105 before Cuddy's brain trust assembled there. No one was around but Rhonda Weavis, perched on the conference table, eating some egg and cheese concoction out of a cardboard container. Oddly, she looked as if she might have been crying, which was startling in someone so habitually sanguine. As she hopped down to greet me, she forced energy into her voice. "How's it going, JayJay?"

"Fine, how about you? Where is everybody?"

"Caught in traffic probably. Bunty's lying down in Cuddy's office. She was here all night."

"She okay?"

Years of asking people questions they don't want to answer has taught me that the ones who don't like to lie have trouble with their faces when they do it. Involuntary eyelid flickers are a typical giveaway and that's what Rhonda did now as she said, "Sure, she's fine, just tired. Works too hard." She hurried over to some photographs on the conference table. "Good news, buddy!" Showing me a blow-up of the commercial photo of G.I. Jane that Nancy had found at Shear Inspirations, Rhonda pointed out a small insignia on the T-shirt that Jane wore, just visible at the bottom edge of the picture. Bunty had identified it as the logo of a cruise ship line. "We got her!"

"My god, Rhonda, you know who she is?"

"We sure do!"

I held out my hand. "I owe you an apology. I didn't want you two brought in. It was a slap and I resented it. But you and Bunty have gone further in four hours than we did in four months. Congratulations."

She looked at me with a quizzical affection. "JayJay, you don't know what resentment is. Some guys we work with act like we're shoving their heads down in a toilet full of menstrual blood. Sorry, that's a little graphic."

I smiled. "It makes your point."

She rubbed my back. "So I like working with you. And I appreciate your getting the ego out of it. Besides, hey, you guys are the ones who found the photo. You know how it is, sometimes you catch that first break and then it's chain chain chain, chain reaction." She opened a folder on the table and handed me a fax. "So, anyhow, can you beat it? Shipping line runs out of

Nassau, but it's a Scandinavian company." Rhonda pointed out the same logo above a famous cruise line's letterhead on the fax. "We fax their headquarters this photo and they match it to this ship of theirs that does island-hops in the west Caribbean. This wallpaper's in the beauty salon."

"Could they ID Jane?"

Nodding, she passed me another fax. I looked down at the fuzzy paper at a copy of a young woman's identification card as an employee of the cruise liner's "Atlantis Salon." She had worked there as a hair stylist and it was there that the photograph had been taken that Nancy had found in Shear Inspirations.

I sat down, shaken. After all these months, after all the interviews and phone calls and emails and lab tests, after all the parents who had come to us, hoping and dreading that she was their daughter, then gone away with their grief unresolved, here at last was the woman we had called G.I. Jane. She had a name and a past, she had a job and a family and friends and a life that, for reasons that might finally be traceable, had brought her to a shallow grave of leaves in a muddy ravine.

Her age was twenty-six, her hair was blonde, her eyes were blue, her nationality and passport were Swedish. Rhonda pointed a tan strong finger at the name on the faxed ID card. "But hey, congratulations to you too, buddy. Her name *is* Christine. Well, it's Kristin. Just like you called it. Looks like your saints angle gets a follow up."

Her name was Kristin Stiller. The cruise line had provided Rhonda with the family member's phone number on file for the girl. This proved to be an only sister who lived in Stockholm. Their parents were dead. When Rhonda phoned the woman, a housewife, she said in perfect English that she and Kristin had never been close and had almost never corresponded so that not hearing from her for more than six months had been no cause for alarm. She had assumed that her younger sister was still working on the cruise ship and wouldn't return to Stockholm until late summer. But in fact the girl had left the ship last December 6 in Miami, although she'd originally planned to renew her contract through the June transatlantic crossing to Marseilles.

I looked at the young woman's small smiling face on the blurry fax. "So that's why nobody missed her. And nobody reported her. And nobody in this country had any kind of record of her, no prints, no dental files. And when we checked foreign, there was no missing persons report on her."

Rhonda shrugged as she gathered the debris of her lunch into a paper bag. "Right. Zip. All she's got's this sister off in Sweden and this sister doesn't know and doesn't care. Who's gonna wonder why she's headed up the Southeast corridor of the USA?"

I compared the ID with the hair salon photo. Despite the differences, the girl with the buzz cut was clearly the same person as the longhaired blonde on the cruise line employee's card. Kristin had gotten her haircut at Shear Inspirations on Christmas Eve. She left the cruise ship on December 6 and was—for some reason—in Hillston, North Carolina, on the twenty-fourth. Dick Cohen estimated that she'd been murdered in late January or early February. All we had to do now was fill in the rest.

Rhonda suddenly lunged around the table to grab a fax coming off the machine. As she did so, her elbow snagged the side of Bunty's briefcase, spinning it off the table edge. We both knelt to pick up the spilt contents. Among all the loose papers and file folders, there were at least four different bottles of prescription drugs.

"I got it, I got it," Rhonda backed me away and I moved over to the fax machine, pretending that I hadn't seen the name "Barbara Crabtree," and the label of the chemotherapy drug, "Cytoxan" on one of bottles of pills. Bunty's weight loss, paleness, weakness, her thin hair and sudden sweats now made sense. I'd seen the worry in Rhonda's eyes as she helped her friend to sit or stand, but I wasn't sure she would want to talk about it, just as I had never wanted to talk about losing Copper, not even to Alice.

We talked about the fax instead. It was from the cruise ship's purser's office and informed us that Kristin Stiller had cashed paychecks amounting to $983 a day before leaving the ship. I said, "Think Kristin was running out of money by the time she got to Hillston? Maybe she took this photo to Shear Inspirations to apply for a job."

While Rhonda and I were talking about John Walker, son of the evasive Mrs. Doris Nutz, the phone rang. It was Zeke at the desk, saying that Cuddy wanted me down the hall in the forensics lab. "I think maybe the chief just got another one of those sick presents from Guess Who."

• • •

In the white organized clutter of Room 107, the forensics laboratory of the Cadmean Building, Etham Foster perched on a stool, his long legs folded under him like a crane, carefully dusting a baggie for prints. The delicate precision of his enormous hands was hypnotizing, and Cuddy, staring at his work, didn't notice my entrance. "Nope, nothing," Etham said.

Cuddy bent over to look at the bottom of a plastic container. "How 'bout a laser wand, Etham? Could we use a wand on them?"

Our head criminalist grumbled at him, "You're driving me crazy."

"You wanted to see me?" I called.

Cuddy made no reference to the outburst I'd witnessed yesterday between him and Mitch Bazemore in the hall. Instead, he held up a small box whose brown paper wrapping had been neatly opened. On the paper, red block letters now sickeningly familiar addressed the package to "Captain C.R. Mangum, HPD." Although hand-delivered (there were no stamps or post office markings), it had somehow found its way into the morning pouch of HPD mail that was left as always on the station sergeant's desk. When Cuddy arrived this morning, he'd checked through the mail Zeke had set aside for him. As soon as he saw the red magic marker on the box, he'd called in Bob Zolinsky, our explosives expert. But there was no bomb inside. So they'd brought the box down to Etham to dust it for prints. Inside they'd found two plastic zip-lock baggies. In the bag on the bottom was the discharged shell of a single brass-capped bullet, thirty-eight caliber. It proved to have blood of Lucy Griggs's type on it. Inside the other bag, there were two viscous filmy globules of tissue and nerves that had once been human eyes.

I said, "Eyes on a shell."

Cuddy said, "What?"

"It's a pun. Remember Paul Madison told me about the pictures of St. Lucy where she's carrying her eyes on a shell." I pointed at the bullet shell in the second baggie. "Eyes on a shell. It's another one of his puns, like headshot. Guess Who. It was in the police mail pouch? Jesus."

Cuddy took a long breath and slowly let it out. "Goddamn bastard."

There was a knock at the door, then Zeke Caleb stuck in his warrior's head with its long black ponytail, and waved an envelope at Cuddy. "Chief, sorry to bug you, but the mayor needs you to look at this and get back to him."

Cuddy took out a single sheet of paper, read it, balled it up in his fist and tossed it in the trashcan as he strode angrily out of the room. Etham swung silently back to the quiet safety of his microscope. I fished the letter out of the trash, straightened the page, and read it. It was a formal letter from the Hillston city council asking C.R. Mangum to submit his resignation as chief of police. I showed it to Etham. We both saw the important thing right away. The twelve signatures of the city council members were stacked neatly on top of one another. (Three of them were friends of Tyler Norris's parents; two others had been trying to get rid of Cuddy since the day he arrived.) But to *force* the chief of police to resign, in other words to fire him, required a formal request from Hillston's mayor as well as its city council. And Mayor Carl Yarborough had not signed the letter.

Chapter 21

Visitors Lounge

After an interrogation yesterday that had lasted more than five hours, Nancy had learned a great deal about John Everett Walker. She learned that he was a musician who hadn't caught a break because it was all about who you know. That he was living with the Mood Disorders because Lucy Griggs had been a bitch and had thrown him out of their apartment (where he'd never paid rent). That he was a small-time drug dealer because his mother, Doris Nutz, owner of Shear Inspirations, was too cheap to give him more of her money. He was a victim not of an indifferent world, but a malign one, energetically focused on doing him harm.

In short, he was an addict and whatever brains he'd once possessed had been so jangled by drugs that listening to his ping-ponging thoughts was, Nancy told me, "like walking through a shag carpet full of fleas." His anger at Lucy for leaving him had not been softened by the news of her savage death. In fact, he tearfully blamed Lucy's death on their break-up ("I wouldn't ever have let anybody hurt her like that!") and blamed their break-up on his mother. ("She was always against anything I wanted.") The other members of the Mood Disorders were also to blame: "They knew Lucy and me had something special and they couldn't rest 'til they brought us down." Everybody was to blame except John Everett Walker.

Eager for Nancy's ostensible sympathy, he had finally admitted to stalking and harassing Lucy, although he preferred to think of his phoning her a dozen times a night, chasing her down the street to shake and slap her, and smashing into her car with his mother's Thunderbird, as "just doing everything I could to get her to come back to me." As for the mysterious lover for whom Lucy had apparently discarded him, John first denied that any such person existed, then admitted that he'd tried to track the man down by following his former girlfriend. But he'd never succeeded in catching Lucy with anyone, a failure he blamed on the police, his mother, and his friends: the police for revoking his driver's license and his mother and friends for not letting him use their cars anymore.

"But get this," mumbled Nancy, eating a Wendy's burger in the squad room where we were talking. "I pull it out of him like hauling a key up from a sewer with an old wad of gum. Guess who John paid to tail Lucy?" Nancy pointed at the photo of Kristin Stiller on my desk. "G.I. Jane."

"He knew her? He admits it?"

"Yep. He's 'cooperating.' That's why he agreed to give us blood and hair samples. 'I got nothing to hide,' he says and he tells me this whole story. Jane, I mean, Kristin, hitchhikes into town a couple of weeks before Christmas—headed to New York, she told him. She just stopped here because her ride did. John says he didn't know much about her, not that she quit a cruise ship or nothing. She's out of cash so she's looking for work cutting hair like she did on her ship. John hooks up with her when she tries Shear Inspirations for a job. She gives them her photo but Doris blows her off."

I said, "Which means Doris blew us off too when she said she never saw Kristin. I guess it's mother lion protecting her cub. John's starting to look good, Nancy. He's got personal relations to two victims. He's a cokehead. History of physical harassment. Catholic? Go to a Catholic school?"

Nancy studied a small frayed spiral notepad. "Nope. Hillston High, then Roper Community. Doris was a Baptist and he's not anything."

"You ask him about saints?"

"Yeah. The best he could do was the St. Louis Cardinals."

"But John paid Kristin to tail Lucy and find out who Mr. X was, right?"

"Right." Nancy had learned that when four Frances Bush seniors sharing a rental house on Tuscadora (a few blocks from mine) had all gone home for Christmas, John had given Kristin their place to crash in for a few weeks. He'd had a key to the house. "One of the Bushers gave it to him so he could water the plants while they were gone. I talked to this girl, she was so tense I bet he was dealing her pot or worse. She says they all freaked when they got back around January 10 and it's like Goldilocks— who's been sleeping in my bed and cleaning out my fridge? But they never said anything about it to HPD." And while the coeds were gone, nobody on the block had noticed that Kristin was there. There were so many young women in and out of the place, neighbors had stopped paying attention.

Nor did Kristin ever discover on Walker's behalf who the mysterious man in Lucy's life was. Or at least she never told him if she did. What she did tell him was that she was going to spend the Christmas holidays with Bo Derek, the hairdresser she'd met at Shear Inspirations and with whom she'd struck up an apparently fast friendship. John said she told him her plans when he'd talked with her on Christmas Eve at his mother's salon. He claimed he'd never seen her again after that.

Our question now was, when Miss Derek left town so suddenly on Christmas Eve after robbing her employer, Mrs. Nutz, and stealing her landlady's car, did Kristin Stiller go with her? Had Kristin in fact been her partner in the robbery? Was it even possible that Bo Derek had killed Kristin? And if so, had she killed Cathy and Lucy as well?

It was a long shot. Serial killers are almost exclusively male, and the few female serial killers there are on record have tended to murder men. But, as Bunty admitted, there are exceptions to every rule, even at the FBI.

As for the FBI, it didn't take them very long to trace the

stolen Toyota and its thief Bo Derek, who proved to be a current inmate at the Virginia Correction Center for Women. Tracking her down (and Bo Derek actually was her legal name) proved to be a great deal easier than identifying G.I. Jane had been. Bo had been incarcerated at VCCW since January. And she'd been arrested on Christmas Day—which meant she hadn't killed Lucy Griggs.

I walked over to the medical examiner's office to check with Dick Cohen about another possibility. Was there any chance that Kristin Stiller (G.I. Jane) could have been killed as early as Christmas Eve?

Dick told me no. It would mean Jane's body had been exposed to weather for three months rather than two. If it had been much colder last winter, that might have been possible, but the January weather had been unseasonably warm with only two days when the temperature dropped below freezing. Judging from the condition of Kristin's body, Dick's best bet was that she'd lain outdoors for no more than seven or eight weeks. He felt certain that she had been murdered between the end of January and the middle of February. If Dick was right, Bo Derek was not a homicide suspect on Kristin Stiller either. But she was definitely our best lead to Kristin's last days. Nancy and I made an appointment to visit her in prison. She wasn't at all eager to hear two police officers from Hillston, North Carolina, would be coming to visit her, but then she didn't have much choice.

• • •

The task force worked until one in the morning, assembling all the information we'd gathered so far about the homicides. Cuddy had said nothing about the district attorney's ordering him to turn the Guess Who case over to Sheriff Homer Louge's department immediately. Obviously Mitch was acting on orders from A.G. Ward Trasker and Ward wanted someone running the investigation who wouldn't investigate anything awkward. Obviously Cuddy was calling his bluff.

At two, I was home on the clawfoot couch, drinking my Calvados, listening to a CD I'd just bought of Mavis Mahar's first recordings called *Light at Midnight*. No wonder it had made her a star; she offered the most intimate privacy while at the same time promising, through every gliding catch, every strange modulation of key, such large and intense feeling that the sound of her voice was like a great drum beating out not just her own heart's pulse but everyone else's too.

The doorbell suddenly rang. Because I'd been thinking about Mavis, I was not even startled that her dresser Dermott Quinn stood there, looking even paler and scrawnier in his jeans and black T-shirt. The shirt had a red drawing of the rock star's face above the words, "Mavis. *On the Devil's Horn,*" the name of her newest CD. In the dark beyond Dermott, I could see the shadowy black limousine waiting at the curb. In front of it was a BMW sedan. Both had their motors running.

He smiled when he heard the CD I was playing. "It's me, Lieutenant, Dermott Quinn. Mavis is off to the airport but she's hoping to talk to you." The Irishman spoke almost nonchalantly, as if he had fully expected to find me awake and waiting for him at two in the morning. Then he started back down my front walk as if there was no question that I would follow.

And shirtless and barefoot I did.

Dermott opened the rear door of the limousine for me. I saw her smiling in the far corner of the lush leathery seat, a glass of whiskey held out to me. There was a smoked glass barrier between her and the front seat where presumably an invisible chauffeur sat at the wheel. Music came softly from everywhere, her music, "I Want You More."

She was dressed only in a short soft linen shift the color of wheat. Slowly raising a bare leg, she wiggled her bare foot at me. Like her fingers, her toenails were painted hyacinth and on two of the toes there were silver bands with tiny bells on them. "Isn't this what you were wanting to know? Rings on my fingers, bells on my toes?"

I slipped into the seat beside her. Dermott Quinn closed the door and stepped away from the huge car as it moved smoothly mysteriously forward, taking me from the house where I knew I belonged and should stay.

"That's a fine strong chest you have," Mavis said and moved her fingers down my breastbone. "Dermott wants me to marry you. Did you know that then? So you can take care of me. It's his grand scheme. He thinks a police officer could keep me safe."

"No one can keep anyone safe," I said. I took the crystal glass from her. The amber gold of the whiskey was the color of her hair. I toasted her and drank. "So, Mavis, what have you been up to?"

"I've been up to good." She smiled. "Good Mavis mending fences, workin' hard. The likes of the little Irish scullery maid your fancy family kept in their attic."

I said, "Not many Irish maids in the South. We had other, older oppressions to call on. Are you flying off from us?"

"Aye, New York. I'm singing in the park there."

"Central Park?"

She nodded. "But then I'll be coming back in a few days. I'm giving that concert I missed at Haver Field." Her bare foot rubbed against mine and the bells on her toes chinkled. "And I'm hoping you'll cook me another fine meal at your house on the lake. Would you do that for me, Lieutenant?" Her hand moved down my chest to the belt of my pants. "I'll sing for my supper. I'll sing you all the music inside me." Her hand was warm on me.

She raised her leg so I could kiss the hyacinth toes. I moved my lips along her foot to her ankle and to the luminous flesh at the back of her knee. She took the drink from me and slipped the shift above her waist.

The deep powered engine drove us into the night.

• • •

At the airport, eerily quiet in the neon light, Dermott Quinn opened the rear door just as if he hadn't closed it on us thirty minutes earlier. He told Mavis that her plane was leaving in ten minutes and he told me that the driver would take me home and that he wished me all the best in finding my killer. On the gleaming tarmac, I could see thin young men in black quickly unloading musical instruments from a van parked in front of us onto a trolley under the direction of a tall young woman. She was also in black, with bright frizzy red hair, and I took her to be the manager Bernadette Davey. The young men I recognized from the covers of CDs as members of her band The Easter Uprising. Porters raced the luggage trolley toward a Cessna jet waiting on a runway. Very modish blue and black letters spelled the name of her recording company "MEGA" across the side of the plane.

Mavis brushed her hair with quick sure strokes. I asked her to tell me before she left if her driver had ever come across Lucy Griggs's mesh purse with the photos in it. She said no. And she'd never gone back to The Fifth Season either. All her belongings had been brought to her suite at the Sheraton. "Do you still think it was me the man wanted to murder? Because it's for certain he's not very good at killing if so. Here I am."

"There's a possibility he knew his victim was Lucy. But you should still take care."

She laughed. "I'll take care, Lieutenant. Taking care of business in a flash, that was Elvis's slogan, did you know?"

"You should meet our police chief, Cuddy Mangum, he's a big Elvis fan. And he likes your music too. Which is amazing because I thought he only liked Patsy Cline. But he wouldn't like my seeing you like this. He's a very moral man."

"Ah is he? And yourself, you're a lovely sad man."

I smiled at her. "You think so?"

"I know so. I've sold fifty million records from knowing how a heart hurts. You should listen to yours, me boyo." She put on lipstick without looking. "Oh, about that girl Lucy?"

"Yes?"

"You were asking what she was saying about loving this married man and all that?" I nodded. "It came back to me one thing she said, very dramatic like, 'His whole life's in the palm of my hand. And he knows it too.'"

The mysterious man in Lucy's life was growing more inter-esting. "Did you think Lucy meant something like, 'I'll tell his wife about us?'"

Mavis shrugged. "It was more like she was showing off how she had the power to destroy this man entirely."

The red-haired woman leaned into the door. "Lieutenant Savile, I'm Bernadette Davey. Nice to meet you. Mavis. Sorry. We're late." She stepped away from the car.

"I'm going." Mavis kissed me. "*Oíche mhaith*," she whispered. "That means good night."

"*Slán leat*," I answered her. "Someone told me that's how you say good-bye to the one who's leaving."

"Ah." She touched my face. "Tisn't much that goes by you, Detective."

"Not much at all," I agreed. "So long, Queen of the Night."

She turned in the door, leaned down, and sang to me softly, "Ah, but I'm coming home to you," the first line of the No. 1 song she'd sung to millions.

Dermott Quinn had a cigarette lighted and waiting for her. She ruffled his hair as she took it from him and then they ran together like children toward the waiting jet.

•   •   •

At dawn on Wednesday, Nancy Caleb-White and I sped up I-85, headed north through the last miles of undisturbed pine forests toward the interminable congested construction that stretches from the Petersburg-Richmond corridor all the way to Boston. Our destination was the Virginia Correction Center for Women. As I drove, Nancy munched on a Danish and talked about Guess Who. Finally I interrupted her. "Zeke said Der-mott Quinn was trying to get in touch with you. What did he want?"

She licked sugar from her fingers. "It was so nice of him. It was about, you know, Danielle being all freaked about Mavis's concert getting cancelled. Cause I'd told Dermott about it when I was interviewing him. So he gave me these two tickets for the new concert. He said they're personally from Mavis. Can you believe it? I take back anything I ever said against her. Right on the front row too. I mean, like, two hundred dollar tickets! And Dermott gave me this card so I could bring Danielle backstage afterwards and she can get Mavis's autograph. Isn't that nice?"

I said it was very nice. "Did Dermott ask you anything about me when you were talking? I mean about me personally?"

She stared at me, stricken, with beautiful green eyes that distracted you from the old acne scars on skin that she could never get to tan. (Zeke called her "Paleface" for a joke.) "Did Dermott...tell you I did? I guess I maybe...I'm sorry, Justin. I shouldn't have said anything?"

"No, it's not a problem. I just wondered because he came by my house last night and I'm not in the phone book."

"Oh shit, you mean like he's harassing you?" She squeezed my arm. "You think he's got a thing about you?"

"No, nothing like that."

"Yeah, I mentioned where you and Alice lived." Her face crumpled with regret. "Maybe he asked some personal stuff, I guess, how long you'd been married and all. He acted like he liked you so much. Zeke always says why can't I keep my mouth shut. I don't mind what people know about me, but that doesn't mean I should...I'm real sorry."

"Nancy, don't worry about it." As Interstate 85 joined 95, I moved in among the discontented morning commuters to Richmond. "But Zeke's right."

"I know he's right."

"Anybody connected to a homicide? Let *them* talk. You just listen."

Nancy nodded seriously. She wanted very much to do the right thing. "Well, Dermott talked my ear off. I'll tell you this. Mavis has a problem with drinking that's really scaring him. You know Windrush, about thirty miles south of Hillston?"

I knew it. There'd been nothing like the luxurious Windrush

Clinic back when my family took me to "the mountains" and left
me there locked in a room where the windows didn't open
because I'd had "a problem" too.

Nancy felt down in the foot well for the tie she'd thrown
there. "Well, Mavis has put herself in Windrush a couple of
times. Or somebody else put her there. She was back in there just
this past January but only for a week or so and nobody knew
about it but Dermott. He stayed with her. I guess he's really kind
of like her best friend or something."

I glanced at her. "Mavis and Dermott were in Windrush in
January?"

"Yeah?" She paused, her tie half over her head.

"So they could have been in Hillston when Kristin Stiller
was killed."

• • •

Bo, formerly Belle, Derek wasn't much interested in talking
with Nancy and me, even though we'd driven all the way to
Goochland, Virginia, to visit her. With a year to go on her sentence, Bo kept a busy schedule, what with two jobs—one in the
copy center, one in the hair salon—plus her abuse-survivors
group therapy, her AA meetings, her work-out sessions, and her
auto mechanics class. She liked the classes. If she'd known more
about auto mechanics back at Christmas, she might have solved
the ignition troubles on that stalled Toyota before the highway
patrol discovered that she'd not only stolen the car (and several
other things) in Hillston, North Carolina, but that her U-Haul
contained two motorcycles she'd stolen in the Commonwealth
of Virginia.

To my taste, Bo was overdoing the workouts. She was big to
begin with, and free weights had given her the look of an East
German Olympic swimmer just when word leaked out about the
steroids and everybody was in a terrible mood. Drawing compar-
isons between herself and Bo Derek seemed to me ill-advised, but
"Belle" didn't fit her either.

She took a philosophical approach to life, perhaps under the influence of all the self-help groups she attended in prison. The photograph of Kristin Stiller produced a contemplative silence, followed by the inquiry, "What's it matter in the long run if I knew her or not?"

I suggested a shorter-term approach to life, pointing out the pleasures of spending time in this pleasant lounge, of breaking the day's routine by talking with strangers, of feeling like a helpful citizen—all these might be made to matter. Bo didn't think so. On the other hand, the prospect of my putting in a word with the parole board had enough appeal to persuade her to accept a carton of Virginia Slims from me. Smoking, she relented enough to admit that the transitory world did still call to her. "I know it's dumb, but I wish I had a frozen dac. A frozen strawberry daiquiri. God, don't I!"

I said, "Can't help you there."

"And a long hot soak in a whirlpool. Day I get out of here, I'm headed for the Hyatt and a room with a whirlpool." Bo walked to the window, leaned out as if right through the pines she could see the beautiful hotel room from where she stood.

I brought her a cup of coffee. "If I talk to your parole board about how you've been helping the police and the FBI solve a double homicide, maybe we can get you into that hot tub a little sooner."

"Double homicide, what are you talking about?" Puzzlement spread slowly over her doughy big-featured face. But then she put it together. "Kristin's dead? That's why you're here?" She stood up. "Hey, wait a minute. You're not tying me to a murder."

"Two murders. Possibly three"

She looked from me to Nancy. "No way. Somebody killed Kristin?"

Nancy asked Bo if she'd heard of the Guess Who Killer. Yes, she had. Had she heard of his victim G.I. Jane, whose throat he'd slit and whose tongue he'd cut out? G.I. Jane was her friend Kristin.

The mystery of life and the wanton randomness of fate dropped the large woman into a seat beside us. "Whoa, you just never know. That's bad, bad luck. Wrong time, wrong place and it could have been me or you. Yeah, Guess Who was on TV all the time, like about G.I. Jane and that hooker they found back in the fall. What do you mean three?"

Nancy said, "We think Guess Who also killed someone named Lucy Griggs at The Fifth Season Resort."

"You mean the Mavis Mahar thing? How it wasn't Mavis, it was a waitress? Yeah, I saw that on the news."

"Well, that was Lucy Griggs. You probably met her. She dated John Walker and sang in his rock band called the Mood Disorders. You know John Walker, right? You worked for his mom, Doris Nutz."

Bo admitted that she knew John Walker through Shear Inspirations. And it was possible that she had seen Lucy in the salon before the two young people broke up. But she didn't know anything about his band. She didn't listen to rock'n'roll. She needed music that kept her serotonin flowing—new age and Mozart was all she could load on her system these days.

The news that she had personally met two of the victims of the Guess Who killer seemed to terrify Bo, as if Death was drawing too close for comfort. That she had been the last person to see Kristin Stiller alive shocked her into a willingness to cooperate; it spilled out like sticky syrup as she moved from "What's it matter anyhow?" to "Ask me anything."

Yes, she had befriended the young Swedish woman. She'd bought Kristin a few meals (but never at the Tucson Lounge) and a few thrift store outfits (but never a Guess T-shirt, and she didn't recall ever seeing Kristin wear one). On Christmas Eve she had given her a free buzz cut at Shear Inspirations. Yes, she'd offered her a ride to Maryland for Christmas. Kristin was trying to make her migratory way north to fulfill a childhood fantasy of visiting New York City. Bo made the Swedish girl's determination to get to New York sound as valiant as the legless Porgy taking off in his goat cart.

Their plan had been to drive together on Christmas Eve to Havre de Grace, Maryland, where Bo could spend the holiday with her ex-husband, with whom she maintained a "good relationship," and who (we subsequently learned) ran an auto paint shop where stolen cars and motorcycles were quickly given a whole new look. Riding with Bo would bring Kristin closer to her dream of seeing Manhattan. But the travel plan went awry. That same afternoon Doris Nutz, owner of Shear Inspirations, accused Bo of robbing her and fired "the best stylist who ever worked in that dump."

"But you did rob her," I pointed out.

"Just afterwards," she explained indignantly.

"And the Toyota?" Nancy asked. "What'd your landlady do, evict you, so you stole her car?"

Apparently, the Toyota was a last-minute replacement for Bo's own vehicle, whose transmission had suddenly failed, forcing her into grand theft auto. "Sometimes Life shoves you into a bad corner and you can't get out unless you do things you never dreamed you'd do."

"Tell me about it," said Nancy. "I worked three jobs in high school, starting at five A.M. cleaning office toilets and finishing up scooping the guts out of chickens 'til eleven every night. I had three little brothers and a mama in bed with pancreatic cancer and the last thing I wanted was my stepfather getting out of the hospital where I'd put him." Nancy had zero tolerance for criminal hard luck. "So you bailed on your friend?"

For Bo, there had clearly been some urgency to leave Hillston as soon as possible, not only because of the holiday traffic, but because she was sitting in a stolen Toyota full of stolen property. And so when Kristin, due at four, hadn't appeared by five (and with Bo's landlady, the car's owner, likely to return from the mall by six), Bo felt compelled to "cut a chogie" without her holiday guest. As to why Kristin hadn't shown up—well, would we like to hear Bo's theory? I held out my hand to stop Nancy from interrupting and said yes, we'd very much like to hear her theory.

Bo took a while calculating whether she was giving away something she ought to be charging us for. We waited. "Okay," she finally said, "I'm not the sort to talk ill of the dead, but with

Kristin there was a definite greed thing going. She'd been bragging about how she'd found out something juicy about some guy,
some big shot guy with money. And what I think is, this guy was
paying her to keep quiet. Because a couple of days earlier, she had
this nice new leather coat on, full length, and where's she going
to get the money for something like that?"

"So you think Kristin was blackmailing this man?" I asked.

Bo nodded. "While I was buzzing her hair Christmas Eve she
was telling me how she was going to go see this guy later that
afternoon and I said it was Christmas Eve and probably he'd be
with his family. She said ha, he'd see *her* okay. I remember 'cause
Kristin spoke pretty good English, but sometimes she got little
things mixed up and what she said was she was going to 'turn the
nails on him.' Not the screws but the nails. Get it?"

I got it. But another hour of questioning Miss Derek produced no more information than that. Not even the image of
frozen daiquiris in a Hyatt hot tub could stimulate her. She didn't
know who the man was, or what Kristin had found out about him
that was so valuable, or where he lived, or what he did for his
money, or what he looked like, or where this last meeting with
him was supposed to take place.

Nor did she know—or said she didn't—that John Walker
had been paying Kristin (possibly in drugs) to spy on Lucy Griggs
in order to find out who her lover was. Nor that Lucy's lover was
almost certainly the man that Kristin was apparently blackmailing. All Bo knew was that Kristin had gone off to meet with
someone on the afternoon of December 24 and had then failed
to show up for a free ride half way to New York, city of her
dreams.

"You never know," she mused in her philosophic way. "Every
fork in the road, you make your choice and whatever's behind
the curtain, that's your deal with Fate. Maybe they flew off to
New York together or maybe he cut her throat and dumped her
in a ditch."

"You never know," I agreed.

Driving back down I-85 in the June heat, I told Nancy that

the wealthy man Bo thought Kristin was blackmailing and the man whose "whole life" Lucy had told Mavis she held "in the palm of her hand" were likely to be the same man. We needed to find out who he was as fast as we could.

Nancy didn't see how such a man could fit the profile that Bunty and Rhonda were putting together of a serial killer. They were moving the investigation toward a psychopath, not a man trying to escape from blackmail. Given the sick things he'd done to victims, the FBI approach made more sense to her. "You know, Justin, how they say, with serial killers it's compulsions and patterns like the shaved heads and Guess shirts. And with regular killers it's like money or jealousy. I mean, if this is a guy involved with Lucy, why's he chopping everybody to pieces? It's, what's that word, redundant?"

Slowly I nodded at her. "Nancy, that's exactly right. It's redundant."

"It's confusing."

"Maybe that's why he does it."

Chapter 22

Courtroom A

The Tyler Norris trial was coming to a close. The jury had heard two stories, one from the district attorney, Mitch Bazemore, and one from the defense attorney, Isaac Rosethorn, and Judge Margy Turbot was going to tell them they'd have to choose one. But either way, the press and the city council were going to blame Cuddy. If Norris were found guilty, it would be because a conviction-crazy police department had railroaded an innocent man. If he were found innocent, a biased and bumbling police department would have *tried* to railroad an innocent man. And either way, we needed to prove right away that we knew what we were doing. We needed to arrest Guess Who.

As for the two stories about what had happened to Tyler's wife Linsley, both were supported by evidence, coherent and plausible. The big difference was that Isaac's wasn't true. It went like this:

Tyler Norris, professor of mathematics at Haver University, stayed home from a New Year's Eve party at the Hillston Club in order to complete an academic paper he was scheduled to present the following week. His wife Linsley left their house on Tartan Drive in Balmoral Heights and drove to that party shortly before eight, leaving him upstairs in his study. The Norris house is large, thirty-five-hundred square feet. The defendant's study is in the far rear on the second floor. It is soundproofed. Mrs. Norris left most of the lights on the first floor turned off and left the house unlocked and unalarmed—because her husband was in it.

It was not unusual for Mrs. Norris to attend social events alone because of the demands of Tyler's academic work. But she stayed at this party only briefly. Dr. Josie Roth testified that her sister, who was two months pregnant, told her at the Club that she felt nauseated and was returning home. Dr. Roth thought their conversation took place at nine o'clock, but she was not wearing a watch and admitted that it could have been later. In Isaac's story, Mrs. Norris did not leave the club until ten and did not arrive back home until 10:30. He pointed out that she might have told her sister she was leaving but then did not do so, or she might have made an intermediate stop on the drive home, or any number of things.

Tyler's computer records showed that he saved the document he was working on at 10:06 P.M. and emailed it to his coauthor at 10:07. He then took a shower in the bathroom next to his study. He had decided to join his wife. After dressing in his tuxedo pants and shirt, he telephoned his parents, who were hosting guests at their home, to wish them a happy New Year.

Fulke Norris, the defendant's father, testified that his son joked on the phone about how all the New Year's fireworks being shot off in the neighborhood were making it impossible for him to work, so he was going to the club to be with his wife. The older Norris claimed that during their conversation, Tyler suddenly reported hearing a loud noise coming from the first floor and said that it sounded as if someone had shot off a firecracker inside his house. He told his father to stay on the line while he checked. Fulke Norris says that it was 10:35 when his son abruptly ended their conversation. In some alarm, he stayed on the phone.

In Isaac's story, the noise had in fact been the sound of a shotgun. A burglar in the process of robbing the house (and not realizing that someone was home upstairs), was startled by Mrs. Norris's sudden return home and had fired a single shot at her head at close range, killing her instantly.

Still on the phone seven minutes later, Fulke Norris heard a second noise; he thought it might have been fireworks, but he was so troubled by Tyler's not returning to the phone that he left his guests on Catawba Drive and drove to his son's house in Balmoral Heights. He arrived there twenty minutes later and found the front door not only unlocked but also ajar. Inside on the floor of the foyer he found the body of his daughter-in-law. She had been shot in the face and was dead. Stacked in the foyer next to the front door were personal possessions of the younger Norrises—two TVs, a VCR, a CD player, two Italian racing bicycles, a leather coat, and a case of sterling silverware. Mr. Norris said he found his son lying on the carpet just inside the living room door, shot in the abdomen, unconscious but alive. He called 911.

Tyler testified that because of his soundproofed study and the noise of the shower, he was unaware that a burglar was robbing his house or that his wife had unexpectedly returned from the party and found herself confronting this armed intruder. He said he heard nothing unusual until a loud shot-like sound while he was on the phone with his father. Suspecting there was a prankster inside his house, he ran downstairs to the foyer. There he saw a man with a shotgun standing over the body of his wife. He ran toward the intruder, who raised the shotgun and shoved him back into the living room where he fired a single shot at him at pointblank range. He and his wife were each shot a single time with a twelve-gauge, over-under, double barrel Weatherby shotgun, an ornamental trap gun given to the defendant as a gift by his father. Tyler kept it (and an accompanying box of shells) on a shelf in his basement den. He had never loaded the gun and said he didn't know how one would even do so.

When Mitch Bazemore had asked, "Why would a burglar, hurrying to rob a house, even if he assumed the house to be empty, stop to load two shells into a shotgun he was stealing?", Isaac had objected that the D.A. was calling for an opinion. Margy had sustained the objection and that was that.

Tyler described the intruder as of medium height and stocky build, in his twenties or thirties, African-American, wearing a stocking mask, a Navy pea coat, and black gloves.

We never found such an intruder or any other suspect. But, as Isaac (and the judge) pointed out, the defense was under no obligation to produce an alternative. We found no one else who'd heard gunshots; no one who'd seen a burglar breaking into the house; no one who'd observed a strange car in the neighborhood. But, as Isaac pointed out, Balmoral homes are on heavily wooded lots of two or more acres, and the Norris neighbors on both sides were away for the holidays. There were no signs of forcible entry, no unexplainable fingerprints or footprints or tire prints at the Norris house. Isaac pointed out that the door had been left unlocked, the burglar wore gloves, and the trampling of the crime scene by Sheriff Louge and his deputies obscured the traces of the intruder. If Louge had been the murderer's paid accomplice he couldn't have done more to help him.

Inconsistencies that Isaac might have had trouble explaining were excluded from evidence because of the contamination of the crime scene. For example, that there were traces of Linsley's blood on the banister leading to the second floor although her body was in the front foyer. Or that her blood was splattered *beneath* two items the burglar had presumably placed in the hall, as if they'd been put there after he shot her.

For everything else, Isaac had plausible explanations: no other houses had been robbed because they all had their alarm systems activated. No subsequent burglaries happened in that area because the burglar, guilty of homicide, immediately moved elsewhere.

Tyler said that after being shot, the next thing he remembered was waking up in intensive care and being told by his mother that his beautiful, wonderful young wife was dead.

Isaac said that Tyler was, like his wonderful wife, the ill-fated victim of a random act of panicked violence.

Witnesses said that the Norris marriage was a very happy one. Other witnesses gave testimonials to Professor Norris's national standing in his field, his high position in civic and church circles, his harmonious relations with his parents and with his wife's parents, his heroic stoicism during his long ordeal. Isaac cried when he ended his story by begging the jury to let these good people mourn in peace. "Don't take the son as well as the daughter, don't add the evil of injustice to the tragedy of misfortune. Tyler had no motive to kill his poor wife. If you have no motive, you have no murder. It's that simple."

The State told a different story. There was no intruder, there was no attempted burglary. Tyler Norris ingeniously plotted to murder his wife and planned it very carefully. He chose New Year's Eve because he knew his wife would go to the Hillston Club, his neighbors would be out of town, and the noise of the fireworks (despite their illegality, common that night) would mask the sounds of his shotgun.

Whatever work he may have needed to do for the academic article that ostensibly kept him home from the party, he had done it well in advance. As soon as his wife left for the club, he began to create a burglary scene in his own home—stacking appliances, bicycles, and such in the front hall as if a burglar had put them there. His plan was to meet his wife at the party late in the evening (emailing his document just before leaving the house). He would bring her home, and as soon as she walked into the foyer, he would pick up the shotgun left ready there and shoot her. After calling 911 and claiming he'd just heard a burglar, he would then shoot himself (not critically, of course) and wait for the ambulance to arrive.

But things went wrong: his wife, feeling ill, returned home unexpectedly. Dr. Josie Roth was right that she had left the Hillston Club no later than nine. She arrived home at 9:30 and caught Tyler staging the burglary. He had to plot an elaborate new murder scheme immediately. But then this was a man who at the age of eight had defeated five adult opponents in chess games simultaneously. He had no trouble thinking fast. He picked up the gun, shot and killed her, and wiped the gunstock.

Everything else happened after the murder: he emailed the document to his colleague. He showered, dressed himself in his tuxedo pants and shirt—leaving the jacket, tie, and damp towel on his bed—and telephoned his father, suddenly claiming to hear the noise of a shot downstairs. He ran downstairs barefoot, carrying his black silk socks so that his prints would not appear on the gun when he shot himself. He did so by holding the gun out from his stomach with one hand and pressing the trigger with the thumb of the other. He had deliberately left the phone off the hook so that his father—a man of impeccable reputation— would be aural witness to the second shot and would take steps to bring aid.

But why do it? What was the motive? True, Linsley Norris came from a wealthy family and her husband was her sole bene-ficiary. True, divorce would be difficult for she was a devout Catholic, as was the defendant's mother. But did he need money? Did he want a divorce? We found two of his colleagues in the mathematics department at Haver who testified that they had seen the couple arguing in public. These two men also testified that Tyler was subject to sudden if rare outbursts of uncontrol-lable temper.

On cross-examination, Isaac brought out that both witnesses had been in direct competition with Tyler, one for a Haver Foun-dation grant, one for a promotion, and in both cases they had lost out. And that was that.

Linsley's sister, Dr. Josie Roth, was a witness for the prosecu-tion. A psychiatrist, she testified that she believed her sister to be unhappy in her marriage, neglected and even abused by her hus-band. She said that she had often encouraged Linsley to seek a divorce. But we could find no one and nothing to support Dr. Roth's view.

From his opening argument to his closing statement, Isaac had hammered at our failure to produce a compelling motive. It was his mantra. "If you have no motive, you have no murder. It's that simple." For me, there was only one problem with that. I was sure Tyler was guilty.

• • •

Judge Margy Turbot was talking when I walked into Court-room A. Her clean collegiate features and blonde pageboy hair looked even more youthful above the somber black pleated robe and neat knotted white collar that symbolized her position. On her desk was the little blue vase of fresh roses that she always brought into the court with her as if their brief fragile beauty were a necessary reminder that there is good to life that has to be cared for.

She sat behind her bench on a carpeted dais, beneath the gold-leaf seal of the State of North Carolina and the big clock with the gilded eagle that President McKinley had given Briggs Cadmean's father. She looked down to Miss Bee Turner at the clerk's desk and past the counsel tables with their plush leather chairs and out to the spectators crowded in pews. Courtroom A was a beautiful room, with sixteen brass chandeliers and sixteen tall windows painted Federalist colors. It was old Cadmean's lov-ing refurbishment of an "authentic reproduction" of the 1912 remodeling of the 1835 original.

There was a picture of Carl Yarborough the mayor on a wall next to a picture of Andrew Brookside the governor next to a picture of the president. Cuddy often points out the picture as progress: in 1835, Carl would have come into this courtroom as a piece of property. In 1912, he wouldn't have come into it at all unless charged with a crime, (certainly not as judge, lawyer, or jury). In 1947, Carl could have sat in the tiered "Colored" bal-cony but not used the restrooms or the water coolers. Now Carl was the mayor of Hillston and could sit anywhere he wanted.

It was also a change that the judge was a woman. Despite her youth and sex, Margy Turbot was as fully robed in the authority of her office as had been her predecessor, the hawk-faced octoge-narian Judge Shirley Hilliardson, a man so scathing in his con-tempt for ignorance that ill-prepared lawyers would start to stutter in his presence. Margy didn't scare people in the same way, but there was no question about who governed her courtroom.

So when Isaac Rosethorn stood up and headed over to Bee Turner's desk with an empty glass carafe in his hands and Judge

Turbot stopped in mid-sentence and said, "Mister Rosethorn!" he instantly stood still.

"Your Honor?" he said, all courtesy.

"Sit down, please, counselor. If you are in such desperate need of water that you can't wait until I finish my instructions, go get it yourself and stop bothering Miss Turner. She isn't your secretary and even if she were, she shouldn't be waiting on you."

This comment produced a gasp from some of the old-timers in the courtroom, including Bee Turner herself, who (like Cuddy) had been running errands for Rosethorn for decades.

Isaac turned his large remorseful eyes up to the bench. "Your Honor, I stand corrected. Stooped, but corrected." And he hobbled back to the defense table where his client sat looking patiently at his folded hands. Watching him was a handsome middle-aged woman seated in the first row on the prosecution side of the room, her arms tightly crossed, her eyes never leaving the defendant. She was Dr. Josie Roth, the older sister of the dead woman, the only member of her family not to side with Tyler. Her mother and father were in fact now seated right beside the elder Norrises, the four of them a formidable line of support behind the defense table.

Margy was beginning her instructions to the jury. She reminded them that a man's life was in their hands. "To prove the charge of first degree murder, the State must establish that the defendant had method, means, and motive, all three, and that he acted with premeditation and with malice. Whether the State, in the person of District Attorney Mitchell Bazemore, has done so in this case is for you alone to decide. Just because the grand jury found sufficient evidence to indict does not mean there was sufficient evidence to convict."

She studied the eight women and four men carefully listening to her. "I remind you that you are not the police, ladies and gentlemen. You are not supposed to go into that jury room and start investigating the murder of Linsley Norris. That has already been done. Tyler Norris is charged with the crime. If, given the evidence you've heard, you do not believe he is guilty, it is your duty to say so and that is the full extent of your duty. It is not your responsibility to solve the crime or even to suggest another suspect."

A female juror looked at the man beside her as if to say, "I told you so."

"Secondly, you are not the judge. It is not your responsibility to interpret the law or evaluate it or teach each other about it. That is my job."

Lisa Grecco, Mitch Bazemore's young deputy counsel, slipped into the back of the room and leaned against the wall beside me. "Back from Virginia?" she whispered. I nodded. Lisa admired Margy Turbot and wanted to hear what she had to say about a homicide case that had alienated the whole town from its police department. "I know you don't like Mitch," she told me, "but he actually did a damn good job in this trial considering what was left after the sheriff fucked everything up."

A woman on the back row turned around and hissed at Lisa to be quiet.

"So what *are* you here for?" The judge was smiling across at the jury and they were smiling back at her. It was impossible not to like Margy's frank easy openness. "Believe me, you have a big enough job. You are going into that room together, and come to a conclusion about this case, based on the facts that have been offered in evidence inside this courtroom. You are going to consider *only* those facts. Not something you heard elsewhere or read elsewhere or somebody else told you. Nor may you take into consideration any evidence that this court has excluded because of the—" Margy looked over at Sheriff Homer Louge who had just strolled in through a side door. Her face tightened angrily. "Because of the contamination of the crime scene by law enforcement officials."

She and Louge stared at each other for a moment. On one side of the courtroom, Mitch Bazemore grasped his biceps and glared angrily at the floor. At the other table, defense counsel Isaac Rosethorn bowed his head and somehow restrained himself from gleeful grinning.

Margy opened a thick yellow legal pad. "You the jury are going to decide if the State has made its case. Remember that the burden of proof is on the State. The defense did not have to prove Tyler Norris innocent. The State had to prove his guilt. The State had to make a case that even if you twelve people viewed all the evidence that you've heard, in the light most favorable to the defendant, that evidence would instead prove his guilt beyond a reasonable doubt. Not beyond *any* doubt now, but beyond a reasonable doubt. Did the State make such a case? That is what you are going to decide."

Margy turned to the next page on her yellow legal pad. She read it, then looked at the jury. "You have heard the Counsel for the State Mitchell Bazemore set before you one version of what happened last New Year's Eve in the Norris home." She pointed over at a floor plan on a bulletin board in the courtroom. "Counsel for the Defense Isaac Rosethorn has offered us a very different version of those events. Only one is true."

"The State's," whispered Lisa to me.

"Miss! Please!" hissed the woman in front of us.

The courtroom stirred as the judge paused to take a drink from a glass of water. She held up the glass and smiled at Isaac Rosethorn. "I got this myself," she said. Laughter relaxed the room. I saw Homer Louge lean over behind Mitch Bazemore and say something to him. Bazemore wheeled around and nodded. Margy startled the sheriff by suddenly addressing him. "Sheriff Louge, does your business concern this trial?" He looked up, his face flushing to a deep red. He started to speak, then stopped himself. She added, "If not, would you please allow us to continue?"

Furious, Louge stomped out of the courtroom. There was a pause until the door closed behind him. Turning the pages of her notes, Margy seemed to be struggling with a thought but may have been only distracted by her dislike of Sheriff Louge. Then she looked over at the defendant's table and Tyler Norris looked back at her. It was a strange moment, the way their eyes held. Finally her face cleared and she continued. "You must weigh these two versions of the truth, not in terms of how well they were told, but how well they are supported by the evidence."

Isaac glanced up at her sharply. He was the great storyteller in this room and everyone knew it. Was she subtly suggesting that the evidence was with the State? She looked at him a moment then moved her eyes to the jurors. "You do not have to doubt the word of all the witnesses who spoke on behalf of Tyler Norris's character to disagree with their belief in his innocence. Good and bad citizens alike have been known to commit crimes. Brilliant men, well-bred men, charitable men, rich and famous men, quiet professors all have proved themselves capable of murder."

I whispered. "She thinks he did it!"

Lisa gave a jerk downward of her bent elbow. "Yes, ma'am!"

The judge gazed along the two long rows of tall elegant windows, beautiful restorations of the nineteenth-century windows in the original courthouse. The afternoon summer's sun slanted through them, shadowing the faces in the room with a soft gold. Margy took a long breath as if her authority weighed heavily on her. "The crime of murder," she said, "is the most harshly punished of human crimes because it most denies our shared humanity. To accuse a man of murdering his own wife, of murdering his own pregnant wife, is a dreadful charge, never to be made without just cause. Ask yourselves, did the State prove that charge beyond a reasonable doubt? If so, you must find Tyler Norris guilty of murder in the first degree. If not, then you must find him not guilty. The sovereign right and the solemn responsibility of that choice is yours." And Judge Turbot sent the jury out.

Tyler Norris did not look at them as they left. Behind him, his father and mother sat waiting with the same chilling composure.

• • •

As Lisa and I were pushed along by the crowd hurrying out of the courtroom, I noticed a group gathered around Nancy and Zeke's display case of HPD homicide artifacts. It wasn't unusual to see a few people there looking over the old guns, bludgeons, straightback razors, and hangman's rope. But this was too large and too animated a crowd. I moved my way through them to the front of the case. The first thing I noticed was that the Italian Bernardelli PA .32 pistol was back in its place and the long-nosed Colt revolver returned to its normal position to make room for it.

Even if Zeke had taken the Bernardelli out of the case to lend it to the Hillston Historical Society (and he said he hadn't), I would have known that he hadn't put the weapon back. For the original tag had been removed from the gun—the tag that said, "Pistol with which Big Bob Futton killed a prostitute at the Piedmont Hotel, August 15, 1949." Now there was a new tag through the trigger guard. In the familiar red marker, it said:

PISTOL WITH WHICH THE GUESS WHO KILLER SHOT
LUCY GRIGGS IN THE MAVIS MAHAR SUITE
AT THE FIFTH SEASON HOTEL ON JUNE 25.

Lisa pushed in beside me and looked. "Hey, where'd you get that gun? What did you put it in there for? Are y'all nuts? This is an ongoing investigation. That's evidence."

I told her that HPD was not responsible for placing the pistol in the display case. The only one who could have put it there was the killer.

Chapter 23

A Clearing in Haver Forest

The miracle of modern forensic science is not only its accurate and thorough technology, but also its speed. By the next morn-ing, Etham Foster's team had matched the 1947 Bernardelli PA pistol to the spent .32 slug that Guess Who had mailed to Cuddy in the same box with Lucy Griggs's eyes. It was the murder weapon.

At some point during the past weeks, the killer had managed to pick the lock and steal the 1947 gun from the exhibit in the lobby display case. Having used it to shoot Lucy, he'd returned it to the case with a tag describing what he'd done. He'd even put a new lock on the case, a cheap, ordinary, and untraceable lock. The insolence of the joke was as embarrassing to HPD as Guess Who had meant it to be, and as public. Among the crowd who'd first spotted the tag on the weapon was a television reporter. There was no way to keep off the six o'clock news the irresistible local lead that a serial killer had borrowed his latest murder weapon from the Hillston Police Department.

Forensics collected the fingerprints of 62 individuals from the surface of the oak case and fed them into the FBI's national computer base. Only four prints produced records: mine and Nancy's from our HPD personnel files, a retired high school prin-cipal who'd been arrested at the Chicago Democratic Conven-tion in 1968, and a man who'd been found guilty three weeks ago of assault and who had been in jail ever since. On the gun there were no prints at all.

It was June 28 and there were American flags up and down Main Street to celebrate the Fourth of July. At noon, the Norris jury was still out. The task force was taking a break. I walked to Southern Depot, to the atrium where I'd sat with Isaac Rosethorn and listened to his advice to look for the pattern to find the pattern-maker. I had a bloody mary and decided one wasn't enough. Then I decided that what the drinks needed was a cigarette. Among the upscale boutiques across from me was a "Tobacconist" shop with mahogany humidors and silver cigar cutters on display in a Dickensian setting by Ralph Lauren. I told myself if I bought cigarettes I didn't like, I wouldn't enjoy smoking them and would quit after one. I bought Lucky Strikes, Mavis's brand. Just as she'd predicted, reawakening one bad habit had stirred others into life. The first breath of nicotine raced through me like ice water and, dizzy, I had to sit down. It had been a long time since I'd smoked. But by the second cigarette, tobacco and I were growing all too comfortable again.

Meanwhile, an idea about patterns was working its way along my jangled nerves. Wasn't Nancy right that all the martyred saints regalia was redundant? If Guess Who had murdered Kristin Stiller and Lucy Griggs because he knew them, hated and feared them—because they were blackmailing him, for example—then why bother to stage their deaths so elaborately, then why all the "playful" messages to Cuddy and me? And how did Cathy Oakes (the first corpse wearing the Guess T-shirt) fit in?

On the other hand, if Guess Who was murdering out of a sociopathic disorder that had nothing to do with these women individually, then wasn't it too much of a coincidence that two victims (Lucy and Kristin) were so connected? What if the murders were purposeful and personal but all the games and symbols were arbitrary, expressions of the delight he took in taunting the Hillston police with our inability to catch him?

By his messages, Guess Who was boasting that he was smart enough to get away with murder—as if he'd taken Cuddy's vaunt in the newspapers ("There are no unsolved homicides in Hillston") as a personal challenge. The Elvis tape, the cardboard star, the Mavis headshot, the gruesome detached eyes, the Bernardelli pistol returned to the display case—all of them mocked the Hillston Police Department.

The idea, tingling with nicotine, grew: if the elaborate staging of the corpses (the shaved heads and dismemberment and candles and matches) had been done for our benefit, maybe Guess Who was motivated less by psychosis about Catholic martyrs and more by competitiveness with us. He wanted us to know that he not only felt free to stroll about the Cadmean Building, despite the fact that it was the headquarters of the Hillston police, he also felt free to go on murdering women until—unless—we caught him. In general, serial killers play an end game. Like gamblers, they keep compulsively going until stopped. Some keep going in order *to be* stopped. So far, Guess Who did not give the impression that he was one of them.

I threw the pack of Luckies in a trash bin, then took it out again and slipped it in my pocket. Across the atrium I noticed one of the two small dark foreign women in black whom I'd seen around the Cadmean Building over the last few weeks. She was foraging through another trashcan in front of a gourmet grocer's called Carpe Diem. It was odd to see the woman alone without her street-corner companion. It looked to me as if she were searching in the bin for discarded bits of food. As she rummaged, some garbage fell onto the cobblestone terrace that fronted the store. A man in an apron charged angrily out of the grocery and yelled at the woman to get away from his trash. He stood behind her and, despite his closeness, she didn't seem to hear him. He shook her by the arm. Dropping the parcels she'd collected, she ran with an odd flatfooted swiftness through the mall and disappeared. After cleaning up the spilled debris, the man looked over, saw me, and shook his head as if we shared an understanding that the world had gone off its axis and chaos had come.

On my way out of Southern Depot, I passed by the shop Gifts and Goodies, whose window was filled with copies of Fulke

Norris's pretty little books of poetry with titles like *Sermons in Running Brooks*, *Fields of Heroes*, *Spring Songs*. I went inside and bought the newest one to take to my mother in the hospital. I noticed that the volume *God's Beauty* was dedicated to Tyler's murdered wife:

> *In memory of my beloved daughter-in-law*
> *Linsley Nowell Norris*

I wondered if Isaac Rosethorn had made sure the jury saw it too.

• • •

When the Task Force reconvened in Room 105, we decided to split our focus. On the chance that the killer was one of us (a city official, a police officer, someone in the prosecutor's office, someone with some legitimate reason to be in this building), the D.A.'s deputy counsel Lisa Grecco would pull personnel files on all Cadmean Building employees to look for any history of mental disturbance, particularly acts of violence against women. FBI forensic psychiatrist Bunty Crabtree would continue to work up a profile based on the three crime scenes and would develop the implications of the virgin martyrs theory. FBI criminologist Rhonda Weavis would go with Dick Cohen and Dr. Samuel Chang to Neville, N.C., the town fifty miles away where the prostitute Cathy Oakes had been found murdered, and where we'd made arrangements to have her body exhumed today. State Bureau documents analyst Wendy Freiberg would continue comparison of Guess Who's handwriting with that of John Everett Walker as well as letters from fans of Mavis Mahar's that we'd obtained through her manager, as well as with all correspondence found among the belongings of Lucy Griggs.

And Cuddy and I would focus HPD's own efforts on a search for one specific person: the married man whom Lucy had presumably been dating and whom Kristin Stiller had possibly been blackmailing. We grouped available HPD officers and gave them assignments: one pair would focus on Lucy Griggs at work, one on her music connections, one on her college days, one on her family. We wanted the name of any man other than John Walker that anyone had ever seen her with. Margy Turbot had just signed the warrants.

"We're going to get him." In his office with me, Cuddy emphasized his vow with a rap of his fist against his Elvis poster. "Not the Sheriff. Not the SBI or the FBI or the U.S. Marshals. We are."

He was still wearing a short-sleeved summer uniform. I think he'd slept in this one, here in his office, if he'd slept at all. The large office looked a mess—fast food containers on his desk, file folders and books in half-filled boxes on the floor. There were only a few pieces left on his chessboard; the rest of the Costa Rican painted woodcarvings were scattered on the coffee table in a clutter of cracker wraps and pizza crusts. I pointed around the room. "What's going on?"

"Endgame study," he said. "One of Genrikh Kasparyan's."

"I don't mean chess. Is there something I don't know? Like you're fired? You packing up, moving out?" In a large box on his desk was a jumble of all the medals he'd been awarded by HPD and by the city of Hillston over the years for a variety of heroic reasons that he normally would joke about. "You turning those back in?" I asked him.

"Hell no. Cleopatra wants them. Her husband died yesterday. He's been in the hospital for ages. It's a blessing really. She wants to bury him with some 'honors', so I'm giving her these. It's a competition thing. Nonie Upshaw's husband got buried wearing all his church attendance medals and a bunch of Shriners' pins that Cleopatra thinks Nonie got at the thrift store."

Cuddy's cleaning lady had talked so long about her husband's "sugar" (diabetes had kept him in a wheelchair for years), that it had seemed a permanent condition not susceptible to deterioration. I'd heard her just as often (as she sat on the couch with Martha Mitchell watching the shopping channel) railing against her great rival Nonie Upshaw and the woman's lifelong husband-stealing chicanery and deceit. I said, "I didn't know Cleopatra's husband was a Hillston cop."

Cuddy smiled. "He wasn't. He was a gentleman of complete leisure."

I picked up a handful of medals and let them fall into the box. "Well, if he's wearing all these, he'll look like General Patton."

Cuddy smiled. "I think Cleopatra would like that, especially when Nonie catches a look as she leans over his coffin to say good-bye."

The phone rang. "Hey, Carl, yeah, I'm right here." Cuddy frowned as he listened. While I waited, I studied the endgame laid out on his chess set. Something looked odd and it didn't take me long to see that neither of the queens was on the board, nor had they been put aside as "taken." I checked for them under the table and in the sofa seats. When Cuddy finished his call, I told him he was missing both the white and black queens from his chess set. Distracted, he said several offices in the Cadmean Building were missing small items, that since the custodial service had gone out on strike with the sanitation workers, there'd been so many different temporary cleaning women in and out of HPD it was a testament to their honesty that the whole place hadn't been stripped down to the sheet rock.

There was a knock at the door; it opened and Mayor Carl Yarborough stepped inside. Smart, easy-going, and so deeply appealing that everybody in Hillston, even Republicans, called him "Carl" and found themselves smiling when he went by, his personality was his best political asset. He was by instinct warm and friendly, a reconciler and conciliator, comfortable with the give-and-take that settled on middle ground. But Carl was now in the third week of a citywide garbage strike. Negotiations were at a standstill and a problem that he had assumed he could easily smooth over was spreading to other city agencies. The usual good cheer that animated his dark face had been replaced by a gray weariness. Still, the ever-present unlit cigar bounced between his broad square teeth as he managed a grin for me. "How you doing, Justin?"

"Doing okay, Carl. How about you?"

He rubbed at the bald top of his head. "Lousy. I want to set-tle this strike. I just don't have the money. I want to settle these homicides. You just don't have the killer."

I nodded. "I heard you wanted to be lieutenant governor."

He smiled back at me. "I do. I want us all to get what we want."

A pigeon tapped at Cuddy's window. He opened it and passed the bird part of a cheese cracker. Amazed, Carl asked if the pigeons were trained. Cuddy closed the window, leaned on it, and crossed his arms. "We have a relationship that they know they can count on."

Carl took out the cigar, pointed it at Cuddy, then put it back. Then he said, "Justin, can you excuse us for a minute?"

It was more than a minute. It was more than an hour. I strolled down the hall to make espresso in the machine I kept in the cheerful lounge that few of us used as much as Cuddy had always hoped. Off the lounge there was a small chapel, almost closet-sized, one of three "Places of Private Worship and Medi-tation" insisted upon by the old industrialist Briggs Cadmean when he'd donated the funds for the Cadmean Building. An atheist if not a devil worshipper himself, Cadmean had always insisted on public piety from everyone else. I don't think I'd ever seen a soul in this chapel, but as I waited for my espresso to brew, I heard someone inside the room. The door was cracked open, and by stepping aside, I could see into the shadowy interior. It was Mitch Bazemore in there, on his knees, with his thick neck bent to the rail of a plain wooden chair. I could see his muscular hands twisting together and hear the urgent torturous singsong of his prayer:

When I call, answer me, O God of justice.
From anguish you released me, have mercy and hear me!

I backed quickly away, embarrassed to intrude on his privacy. He looked to be in pain. I didn't know if he was praying not to lose the Tyler Norris case or praying for forgiveness for keeping quiet as his boss the Attorney General Ward Trasker ran roughshod over the Law in whose Letter Mitch so righteously believed. The muttered prayer went on.

I was leaving the lounge when Carl Yarborough almost bumped into me. "You seen Mitch?"

I answered loudly in order to give Bazemore time to collect himself. "Nope, haven't seen him. Cuddy still in his office?"

"He's making some phone calls."

At that point, his eyes bleary, Mitch marched out of the chapel with his usual bluster. He nodded at Carl and ignored me.

In the homicide squad room I had a call from Officer John Emory at the Registrar's Office of Haver University. Roid was having trouble obtaining Lucy Griggs's transcripts. Not only because of the staff's resistance (he needed a court order and a letter from a dean), but because even if he'd had those documents, their entire computer system (in which all academic records were now kept) was "down." I asked him, "What's wrong with paper?"

"Trees," he replied.

As I hung up, Cuddy stuck his head inside my glass cubicle and said, "Sorry it took so long." He checked his watch. "I need you to take me someplace and I need to go now."

"Sure. You don't want to drive yourself?"

He said, "I want you to wear a wire."

● ● ●

We didn't talk much as I drove him to Haver Forest, a beautiful two-hundred-acre preserve adjoining the university and bequeathed to it by the Haver family with the provision that it never be built on. Later trustees had cleverly sidestepped the intent of the will by using one edge of the land as a world-class golf course that abutted a luxury hotel owned by the university. Cuddy told me to park in the hotel lot. All he would say as we walked along a "nature path" to a secluded clearing near the perfect grass of the ninth hole was, "Thanks for this, Justin."

"Thanks for what? I have no idea what I'm doing."

He rubbed at his stubble of beard, looking in his slept-in uniform like a battle-fatigued soldier. "I know. That's why I'm so grateful."

Century-old walnut, sycamore, and oak trees reached high above us, dappling light on the forest floor. In that light stood Andy Brookside waiting. His white shirtsleeves and golden tie flashed in the sun as he waved us over. As we reached him, out of the shadowy trees stepped Carl Yarborough.

I stopped and pointed at them. "Is this some kind of a duel?"

"Sort of," Cuddy replied and tucked in the back of his rumpled police shirt. We kept walking until we were face to face with the governor and his new running mate.

Brookside wasn't pleased to see me there but, in his efficient way, wasted no time on the matter. "Unexpected pleasure, Justin," is all he said to me the whole time we stood under those trees. To Cuddy he said, "I'm glad Carl could arrange this."

Carl Yarborough was there to broker a deal between two men who didn't like each other for fundamental reasons. By that I don't mean only because of their relationship to Lee, although that was certainly a part of it. She was fundamental to both men. To Cuddy who had always loved her and who would go on loving her until he died, even with no hope of a life with her. And to Andy who risked his marriage to her time after time, for easy dangerous pleasures that meant nothing lasting, and yet who admired and valued her and knew he could not succeed without her.

When I say that Carl Yarborough brokered the deal, I suspect that the real broker wasn't even here in this clearing, at least not in the flesh. The real broker was Lee Haver Brookside and she had flown off to London so that she would be out of the way when the man who had always loved her did what she had come to his office in the middle of the night to ask him to do: help her save an election for the husband she would never leave.

Carl began by suggesting that everybody had now had a chance to cool down and think about what was best for North Carolina. Cuddy interrupted. "How about what's best for those old tattered banners, Truth and Justice?"

Brookside smiled with his radiant easy equanimity. "Surely, Captain, the two aren't incompatible."

Cuddy shrugged. "Well, I guess that's what we're here to find out."

Carl offered us all cigars out of an impulse similar I suppose to passing the peace pipe, but no one accepted, though it did make me want to take the Luckies out of my pocket and I would have if Cuddy hadn't been there. The mayor advised us to relax, predicting that if we did, we'd see that we were all on the same side. I say "we," but actually Carl was talking only to Cuddy and the governor. I was there in the way that soldiers, bodyguards, butlers, and drivers are there but not there. It was a curious sensation and it made me realize that no one had done a thorough interview of the driver of the limousine who'd brought Lucy Griggs and Mavis to The Fifth Season. Was there more that he had heard on that drive, seen near the bungalow before he'd left to rush Andy to the Governor's Gala?

Through the circling shade trees, shafts of sunlight crisscrossed into the clearing. Carl gestured around him. "We don't have to worry. There're no lawyers here, no media, no political opponents, just us."

Everyone was quiet a moment as if to make sure we couldn't hear a guerrilla band of lawyers and reporters creeping up on us through the forest. Then Andy motioned to Cuddy. "Go ahead."

Cuddy nodded. "Okay. First of all, I will not resign. If I am fired or the homicide commander here is fired," he pointed over at me and it was the first I'd known that the city council had planned to boot me along with him, "my last act as Hillston's police chief will be to issue arrests for the six individuals on the list I've given Carl."

Brookside said that he'd seen the list. He ran tanned fingers through his famous hair. "All right, let's start with your list since I'm on it. I'll quote you. First of all, I will not resign either. And it's pretty ludicrous even to suggest that I should."

The more easily the governor smiled—it wasn't a snide or sardonic or insincere smile, just a pleasant one—the more tightly

Cuddy squeezed his folded arms to his chest, until the sinews on his bare forearms were rigid. He tapped the insignia on his shirt. "I've taken an oath to stop people from committing crimes and arrest them if they do. No matter who they are."

"We've all taken oaths," Carl mildly interjected.

"Well hey," Cuddy threw out his arms. "Then I don't know how some of you sleep."

"Hold on—"

Cuddy interrupted Carl. "A young woman was murdered. Under the stupid assumption that she was Mavis Mahar, people who should know better altered a crime scene. They did it," he pointed at Brookside, "to conceal your presence in her hotel room the night of her death. Her body was moved and she was shot in the face postmortem by or at the behest of the attorney general of this state in an effort to convince a moron of a coroner that her death was a suicide."

Andy opened his hands as if to demonstrate he was hiding nothing. "Ward tells me that either Bubba was just mistaken about where and how he'd seen the woman's body earlier—he was certainly mistaken about whose body it was—or it was the murderer himself who moved the corpse and fired the second shot at her face."

Cuddy snorted. "Four hours after the first shot?"

Andy shrugged. "People do strange things."

"They sure do. Ward Trasker organized and carried out a conspiracy to obstruct justice, aided by Sheriff Homer Louge and others."

Andy shrugged again. "Ward denies that he did any such thing. Or that anyone with him did any such thing."

"It's not true and you know it. A young woman's dead, goddamn it."

Carl gently interjected. "Cuddy, we know that."

"Somebody killed her. What people did to protect this man," he pointed again at Andy, "has messed up that crime scene so much it's going to be harder to find out who killed her and a hell of a lot harder to convict him even if we do."

The governor turned to his running mate. "I think we need to—"

Cuddy exploded. "And you just don't care, do you, you son of a bitch!"

Andy's face flushed. He held up his hand to stop the mayor and moved himself directly in front of Cuddy. "I've told you I haven't committed a crime and I won't tolerate the continued implication that I'm lying about it. I did not participate in a cover up of anything criminal at The Fifth Season. I did not ask anyone to cover up anything criminal for me. Yes, I asked Percy to bring me my car and my raincoat. It was an awkward situation. I wanted to minimize the awkwardness. Why not? I had no idea that the raincoat had been used to cover her body and was therefore evidence."

Cuddy was fighting hard to keep his voice quiet. "You didn't know what Ward Trasker was doing in that bungalow? Bubba didn't call and tell you? *Ward* didn't tell you?"

"The first person who told me a cover-up took place in that bungalow was you."

So angry he was trembling, Cuddy snarled, "Bullshit! Ward fucking believed you'd killed Mavis Mahar yourself to shut her up and save your so-called marriage and your election!"

Livid, Brookside jabbed Cuddy in the breastbone with his stiffened fingers. "You talk to me about my marriage, you sanctimonious bastard?"

Cuddy lunged at him. I jumped between them and pushed them both backwards. "Okay, both of you step back here. Step back right now." I pushed them again.

Carl looked first confused, as if he wasn't sure what was going on, and then he focused his look elsewhere, as if he'd quickly made the decision that he didn't care to know what was going on. Then he stepped into the space I'd cleared between the opponents and urged Cuddy to face him. "Can we talk about ways to work this out, Cuddy? You're in the middle of an investigation that we've got to close fast, the press is all over us. You say you think this man's already killed maybe three women.

That's what matters."

He turned to the governor. "Andy, only a few days ago you gave Captain Mangum the highest honor for service to the state it's in your power to give. How's it going to look for you, for him, for Hillston, for North Carolina, if one week after you hand him the Raleigh Medal, all this blows up in our faces?" He moved back to Cuddy. "Andy has an election to deal with. Can we agree we need to move on now or nobody wins? Can we agree the best thing for this state is for you to catch this madman and for Andy to get back to the business of governing?"

Cuddy turned and walked away, his back to us. He stared a long silent while out at Haver Forest. The trees, the land, the university all gifts from the family of the woman he loved. Gifts to the state she wanted her husband to serve. I know that's what Cuddy was thinking because when he turned around to look at us he nodded slowly. Carl then looked questioningly at Andy, who nodded too. Carl solemnly pulled the wrapper off a long cigar. "Good. So now let's take it point by point, all right, gentleman?"

Thirty minutes later they had a deal. And I had the deal-making on tape, although the governor and the mayor didn't know it. Or who knows? Maybe they had tapes of their own.

—Ward Trasker would resign as State's Attorney General tomorrow and would plead nolo contendere to a single charge of obstruction of justice. The hearing and the verdict would be sealed.

—The former A.G. Ken Moize would be asked to step in as Acting A.G.

—Acting A.G. Ken Moize would instruct D.A. Mitchell Bazemore to remove the Haver County sheriff's department from any involvement whatsoever in the Guess Who homicide investigation.

—Mayor Yarborough would instruct the Hillston city council to inform Police Chief C.R. Mangum that he enjoyed their full and enthusiastic support.

—Police Chief C.R. Mangum would be in sole charge of the Guess Who homicide investigation.

—If on July 4 the mayor and council of Hillston were not satisfied with the progress Captain Mangum had made on the investigation, he would voluntarily resign his office. If they were satisfied, his contract would be renewed (six months early) for a period of four years.

—Osmond Bingley would retire at the end of next month as Haver County coroner.

—N.C. Bureau of Investigation agent Ted Bingley, Osmond's nephew, would be reassigned to a field office in the western part of the state.

—The governor would immediately ask the Haver County Commissioners to appoint an external review to investigate the competence and the character of Sheriff Homer Louge. Until its findings were concluded, Sheriff Louge would take an involuntary leave of absence.

—Other than the misdemeanor to which Ward Trasker would plead nolo contendere, the Hillston police would file no charges against anyone for what happened at The Fifth Season on June 25 in connection with the murder of Lucy Griggs. Any HPD files containing evidence of possible illegal acts committed at that time (such as evidence tampering, felonious assault on the victim's body, and so forth) would be closed and sealed.

—All parties to this agreement today pledged themselves never to discuss its terms with anyone, nor ever to make public any of the events surrounding the alleged "cover up" at The Fifth Season, nor to comment on any alleged relationship between the governor and Mavis Mahar.

—Oh, and discretionary funds in the state budget would be transferred Monday into an undisclosed supplement to the Hillston town budget. These funds would enable the city council to agree to the pay raise that the striking sanitation workers demanded, and frankly, admitted the mayor, had long deserved.

Although Carl cheerfully suggested at the end of the bargaining that we all stroll back together to the hotel bar for a friendly cocktail, I was the only one interested. Andy and Cuddy shook hands as we stood there in that clearing, but it was chillingly clear that they would be just as glad if they never laid eyes on each other again.

Andy then shook hands affably with me. "Good to see you, Justin."

"You too, Andy."

"Tell Alice to come see me. I'd love to get her back in the campaign. She still in the mountains?"

"Still in the mountains."

He was good at that personal touch. Then with a last smile he turned and briskly strode through the crossed shafts of sunlight toward the shadowed forest where I supposed there was a limousine waiting. Like always, the light shimmered around him until he took on a glow—like one of the old pagan gods come down to earth to find a mortal girl and convince her that one moment of love with a swan or a bull or a shower of gold was worth a lifetime of regret.

After the governor left, Carl gave Cuddy a quick hard but heartfelt hug. "Thank the Lord," he said.

Cuddy tilted his head in that bluejay wink. "Well, I think it's Dina we probably need to thank. She always was the best thing that ever happened to you, Carl."

Carl smiled at us as he held a match to the long cigar. "That is for damn sure, my friend."

Cuddy waved away the smoke. "So you ever going to tell me how close you came to trading me in before she stopped you?"

Carl shook his head affectionately. "Cuddy, you're one of the smartest men I know, you're a great administrator, you're a great cop, you may even be a great man, but you're a lousy politician. You don't ask questions like that."

I said, "That's a lesson you better teach Dina then."

"Don't I know it," smiled the mayor. "She's worse than Cuddy." He puffed away on the cigar, sending blue swirls of smoke into the slanted light. "Now let's get clear. You got your investigation back and you got Homer and Mitch off your back. Listen to me, *everything* stays as squeaky clean as my daddy's Cadillac on a Saturday night. Cuddy, you go by the book like it was the Holy Bible. I spent a *lot* of capital holding this thing together. I got three guys on that council bent out of shape over the Tyler Norris arrest because they are pals of his daddy. This Guess Who mess has got Homer bending their ear and them bending my ear how you don't know what the hell you're doing. They are drooling to chew your ass. And you know who they are."

Cuddy nodded yes. "I know who they are."

"Well, don't pull your pants down and stick your fanny in their teeth. I'll see you back downtown. Take it easy, Justin." Then Carl followed the path Brookside had taken into the forest.

Cuddy stood staring after him until finally I said, "Like a beer?"

"No." He started back across the golf course toward the hotel parking lot, his long legs stretching in fast strides over the grass. "I'd like Guess Who locked up before he kills somebody else."

I caught up with him. "By July 4. That's six days." For it had been Cuddy who'd volunteered to resign if he hadn't arrested Guess Who by the Fourth. "What is it with you?"

He turned toward me, his bony face earnest, his thick nut-brown hair twisted oddly by the afternoon breeze. "I don't think people ought to get away with doing wrong. That's all." We walked out of the beautiful pines of Haver Forest.

• • •

As I was driving him back to the Cadmean Building, Cuddy handed me the little spiral notepad he'd carried when we'd walked in on Ward Trasker and friends at The Fifth Season. "Take this, take the tape you're wearing, take any notes you have on the bungalow scene. Lock them up and leave them alone. And, Justin, you don't talk about this to anybody. Not anybody."

"Except Alice. I tell her everything."

He swiveled toward me on the car seat. "Oh really?"

I looked over at him and felt such a flush of heat move up my neck that I quickly turned away.

"I'm real glad to hear it," he said.

• • •

Waiting at my door was a Federal Express deliveryman with large boxes sent from a gourmet store in Manhattan. Inside one box was a case of Dom Perignon champagne. Inside the other, packed in ice, was a fourteen-ounce tin of Beluga caviar. The note said, "Champagne and caviar. Sorry it's not apples and whiskey." It was signed "The Queen of the Night." A quick calculation suggested that Dermott Quinn or Bernadette Davey or whoever had been sent to buy my presents had paid around three thousand dollars for them. But then, as Mavis had said, she had much more money than time. When I turned on my television, ironically enough there she was on the screen, singing joyfully about imported ale that she'd no doubt been paid millions to kiss the can of.

I put the case down beside the untouched pile of mostly junk mail lying on the hall floor and noticed a postcard of scarlet rhododendrons blazing over a slope of Carolina mountains. The card said, "Please remember my plants. I love you always, Alice."

I put one bottle of the champagne in the freezer. It was cold when I finished watering all the palms and ferns and fig trees and jasmine and azaleas that Alice had kept alive year after year. Their pots were dry, the leaves wilting. I was just in time.

Chapter 24
Main Street

The Norris jury was out all that night. Cuddy began to hope we'd get a conviction after all. Friday morning he and I met with Dr. Isabel Sonora, an assistant dean of Haver Medical School. She took us past a dissecting arena where two young men in white coats, presumably students, were cheerfully laughing about something as they fiddled with a long human leg on a table. The dean was tall and thin with a bony look to her rather like the row of skeletons hanging around the walls. A large fan blew through the room and the skeletons trembled as if they were hearing a musical cue to start a medieval dance of death.

As Dr. Sonora pushed open the door to a huge freezer room labeled Cadaver Storage, she sternly repeated the lecture she'd already given us in her office. "Next time, if you people think you're going to need your cadavers back, don't donate them. You're lucky we found as much of her as we did."

The dean pointed at a long counter surface where neatly arranged in a row were the dismembered skeletal remains of one full human arm, one forearm, one detached hand and a footless lower leg.

"That's it?" Cuddy asked, upset. "Some arms and legs?"

Dr. Sonora opened a cadaver drawer. "I said you were lucky. This was going into a classroom next week." The dean showed us a female torso with no arms or legs. But the flesh was still on it and the head was still attached. I knew who it was. Having been embalmed, stored in freezers, first at the city morgue, then here at Haver Medical School, Kristin Stiller had decomposed not all that much more since I'd first seen her lying in a ditch of rotted leaves and raw red earth where her murderer had left her. But eerily enough, her eyes were now missing (having been used in a class), giving her a macabre resemblance to her fellow victim Lucy Griggs.

We presented Dr. Sonora with the court order to release what was left of Kristin Stiller's body to Dr. Samuel Chang, the forensic pathologist, when he arrived here this afternoon. She accepted the legal papers rather grumpily and on the way out of the building couldn't stop herself from scolding us again not to expect to be able to show up two months after donating an anonymous cadaver and find it waiting for us. "These things are expensive. You're very lucky."

"Luckier than Kristin Stiller," I agreed.

She looked at me then at an oil painting on the paneled wall of the reception room. "What did you say your name was?"

"Justin Savile."

She gestured at the oil painting. "Dr. Justin Savile was head of this medical school." I nodded. "Your father?" I nodded again. "Good man, people around here say." I kept nodding. "Died in a car crash?"

I said no, he'd had a heart attack in the car crash and died from it later. She said she was sorry. I didn't say that it was snowing that night on Catawba Drive, that I was driving him home, that I was drinking. I was surprised she didn't already know. Years ago it was the talk of the town.

Walking back to the car, Cuddy examined his drivers' license. "I'm donating my organs. I like the notion of my eyes seeing Hillston and my heart feeling good about a nice spring day. But don't give them the rest of me, okay? I swear I'm not sure I want med students yucking it up over my femur after I'm gone."

Just as we reached Haver Hospital parking lot, a woman came running through a line of cars toward ours. I heard the beeping of a nearby Land Rover as she clicked her remote key. It was Dr. Josie Roth, Linsley Norris's older sister, still in a white lab coat. She didn't stop or even slow down as she raced to open her door. But she recognized and called to us, "The jury's in. Court's reconvening in fifteen minutes." Her tires screeched as she backed out of her parking spot.

We watched her speed off. Finally Cuddy said almost wistfully, "They were out sixteen hours. But that may not be long enough."

Headed back to town, he leaned his head out the car window as if he needed clean air. "Well, comrade, so much for my new improved justice system in the South. Looks like your old grandpa judge—what was his name? You know, the judge that averaged sentencing twenty black men a year to the electric chair and kept it up 'til they made him Chief Justice of the State Supreme Court?"

"His name was Benjamin Virgil Dollard." I took out the old gold pocket watch my mother had given me with those initials on one side and the female figure of Justice on the other and gave it to him.

He looked at the watch, spun it on its chain. "Right, BVD. How could I forget? Well, BVD would feel right at home in Hillston today, 'cause it's looking like if you're white, rich, come from a good family, and talk nice, you can still get away with murder in the South."

I took back my watch. "It's no different in the North."

"You got me there."

"Cuddy, you keep expecting America to keep its promises. Maybe that's why the Fourth of July is so damn important to you."

"Jesus, Justin. Don't start analyzing. I don't expect anything to keep its promise.... Except me."

"Sounds lonesome."

"It is." He looked out at the town he'd policed his whole adult life as we drove down a block of Main Street. The lampposts were decorated with clusters of small American flags. Wryly he saluted them as we passed.

• • •

Courtroom A was so jammed with sightseers and journalists that Judge Turbot made the bailiff move the crowd back from the side aisles and away from the jury box. Cuddy and I stood against the back wall watching as Bee Turner took the folded verdict from the foreperson of the jury—a nervous middle-aged woman whose hand shook as she passed it to her. Miss Turner stood on tiptoe in her oddly youthful bright blue high heels to hand it up to the judge on the bench. Margy read the verdict, folded it, crossed her hands over it, and asked Tyler Norris to stand.

In his blue blazer, striped tie, and gray slacks, Norris looked more as if he were waiting for a dinner table at the Hillston Club than news about whether he was going to live or die. Beside him, Isaac Rosethorn painfully pushed himself up against the defense table. Tyler watched the judge. Isaac watched the jury. Cuddy watched Isaac.

Margy asked the foreman, "On the charge of murder in the first degree, how do you find the defendant Tyler Gilbert Norris?"

"Not guilty," whispered Cuddy to me.

"Not guilty," said the foreman to the judge.

"The jury finds the defendant not guilty." Margy raised her gavel, expecting the commotion that usually follows a verdict in a homicide case, shrieks of joy, shouts of anger. But Courtroom A was strangely subdued, maybe because no one was surprised. There was a short rumbled murmur from the crowd. Scattered applause. People started leaving before Margy finished her final remarks, dismissed the jury, and set Tyler Norris free.

The senior Norrises and Linsley's parents politely embraced each other and moved together to the defense table where Tyler coolly received a round of hugs. Then they shook hands with Isaac Rosethorn who messily shoved papers into his tattered, taped-up briefcase and hurried away, almost forgetting to limp. The Norris group was soon joined by a dozen other well-dressed WASPs, all shaking hands and looking like a reception line at a society wedding.

The clumped mass of the crowd pressed through the doors and clotted together in the lobby. Cuddy was trying to push aside a cluster of reporters to reach Dr. Josie Roth, the one member of Linsley's family who'd testified against Tyler. Still in the white medical coat in which she'd run through the university parking lot earlier, she stood alone against the wall, trying hard not to lose control before she could make her way through the crowd to get out of the lobby.

Suddenly one of the small dark foreign women, the one I'd seen at Southern Depot, the one I'd decided was deaf, hurried up and stepped in front of Cuddy. She shoved a long thin parcel wrapped in old newspaper into his arms and then scurried away through the crowd.

"Drop it," I said to Cuddy as I took off after her. But when I reached the broad stone portico outside, she was already running down the sidewalk in her odd flat-footed way, beneath the rows of clustered American flags. I saw Nancy and Zeke starting up the steps and yelled at them, "Stop her! Woman in black! The Ninety-fiver!" Nancy and Zeke raced dodging back through the puzzled crowd. Zeke was remarkably fast; he swept down upon the small woman, lifting her off her feet. She began to scream.

I hurried back through the revolving door into the lobby where Cuddy had naturally not listened to me but had unwrapped the newspaper. He was staring down at a dead fish. Sticking out of the fish's mouth was the white queen from his office chess set.

Upset, he gingerly slid out the painted wood figure of the Indian queen with a Kleenex. Because the set had been given to him by children in the Costa Rica village where he'd taught as a volunteer twenty years earlier, it was one of his beloved possessions.

"You think Guess Who did this?" I asked him.

"Yes." He wrapped the chess piece in the tissue.

"What's his point? Queen? White Queen?"

"First Lady," said Cuddy.

part three

The Tooth of Time

Sunday, July 1–Wednesday, July 4

Chapter 25

Gambit

Unlike Odysseus, I had not chained myself to any strong mast of character or will so that I could hear the siren's song yet still sail past the fatal rock on which she sat singing me toward her. Unlike his sailors, I had not stopped my ears.

"You want everybody to share your sins?" I had asked her.

"Oh, not everybody," Mavis had smiled.

I was smoking—not in the house where the smoke would linger and be detected by Alice, if she ever came home—but on my porch and on my walks to work and in a bar in East Hillston called Smoke's, where no one I knew was likely to see me drinking. I was drinking alone in my house late at night, alone in restaurants at lunch, and alone in my car. I was waiting for Mavis Mahar to return to Hillston.

Meanwhile, I was still in the early stages, early enough for drinking not to get in the way of my work on the Guess Who investigation. In fact, I was more focused than I'd been since before Copper died. Or at least I told myself so.

By now, Cuddy, once so skeptically dismissive of my intuitions about the Elvis tape and the cardboard star, had begun reading everything as a coded message from Guess Who. For example, he assumed the fish (a flounder) handed to him in the lobby was supposed to make us think of the adage, "Guests and Fish Stink in Three Days." That meant we had only three days to locate whoever had given the wrapped newspaper to the Amerindian migrant woman and told her to take it to Cuddy.

Because of the earlier puns (like "headshot"), Cuddy took flounder to be a pun as well; an insulting one. He, Cuddy, was floundering, unable to solve the riddle of Guess Who. If another woman died, Cuddy's stupidity would be to blame.

Over the weekend, we had checked out and warned all women in the area who were named Chess or Queen or White (including Nancy) or who lived on Queen or White Street. We called in a delighted Carol Cathy Cane and had her interrupt Channel Seven broadcasts through the day with repeated warnings that *all* women in the Piedmont should be cautious, avoid strangers, never travel alone. We took every precaution we could think of. But deep down Cuddy feared that the white chess queen symbolized one woman only, Lee Haver Brookside, because she was always talked about in the press and on television as the First Lady of North Carolina.

Finally he made a phone call to a man he hated. He advised Governor Brookside to give his wife immediate twenty-four-hour protection. When Andy told him that Lee was on her way home from a trip to London, Cuddy insisted that there be state troopers waiting at the airport to escort her to the Governor's Mansion and that they should stay with her at all times.

We knew Guess Who was somewhere in the area. He had gotten close enough to replace the gun in the display and to have the wrapped fish delivered to Cuddy. The migrant woman could tell us only that a man had approached her on the steps of the building just as the trial let out. He led her into the lobby crowd, pointed at Cuddy and pushed her in his direction, gesturing that she should take him the folded newspaper.

We wouldn't have known even this much if it hadn't been for Cuddy himself, who'd come into the homicide squad room that afternoon while we were futilely attempting to question the terrified woman after Zeke and Nancy caught her. By then she'd quit fighting—she'd spit at Zeke as he carried her into the Cadmean Building—and had turned her back and was quietly whimpering to the wall, twisting her peculiar rosary of beads and feathers in her short thick hands. We told Cuddy that she wouldn't answer our questions, although she did appear to be able to hear them. We'd brought in Eddie Vega, a detective in robbery, to talk to her in Spanish, but she hadn't responded to that language either. Eddie figured she spoke some mestizo dialect, but we had no idea from where. She carried no identifying papers and might not even be legally in this country.

Cuddy asked to see what Brenda Moore had found on the woman: we showed him a tiny leather pouch with herbs and bones in it, two photographs of what looked like a family gathering in front of a tin shack in a dense tangle of green vegetation, a fast food coupon, a five dollar bill, and some odd looking coins. Cuddy looked for a while at the woman, at her broad torso and strong wide face, her braided bun of thick raven black hair. Feeling his gaze, she pressed closer to the wall. Finally he leaned down and said to her, "*Garinagu?*"

Startled, she jerked around to look at him.

He repeated, "*Garinagu? Garifuna?*" and then added a few sentences in a strange language.

The woman nodded at him in grateful relief; she stood, grabbed at his shirt, and started talking quickly in the unknown language. Cuddy waved his hands to show that she'd lost him. Then he began speaking with her in Spanish. After a pause, she responded in Spanish, which it was now obvious she did understand. Occasionally asking a brief question, he listened as she explained who she was. I brought him a glass of water to give her and finally she drank some. After a while, he asked Brenda Moore to take her to the lounge and find her something to eat.

While they were gone, Cuddy told us that the woman's name was Lupe Guevarra and that a "tall, fat, black-haired" man had given her the five dollars for handing Cuddy the newspaper. It seemed unlikely that this man—if someone of that description even existed—was Guess Who himself. He had doubtless been an intermediary—someone who paid Lupe to hand over the package. Still, we had to find him. The small coins she carried were quetzal, the currency of Guatemala. Lupe was an Amerindian, more specifically a Garifuna. They were, Cuddy explained, Black Caribs descended from Arawak and Kalipuna Indians (the ones who'd greeted Columbus when he "discovered" the New World). Over time, they'd mixed with Mayans and shipwrecked Nigerian slaves and their Spanish masters, and now lived mostly along the coasts of Central America. While teaching in Costa Rica, Cuddy had spent time in Garifuna villages, one of them in Guatemala, not far from this woman's home. She appeared to be migrating north from Florida along I-95, but for the past month she had been working here in Hillston (doing cleaning jobs during the strike). Homeless, she had apparently been sleeping in Haver Gardens at the university.

With great intensity, Lupe claimed to possess papers (a passport and a green card), but insisted that her sister Maria had them. Now she couldn't find this sister, who she said had not only their papers but all their money and clothes as well. Cuddy was skeptical of this "sister's" existence.

I wasn't. I said to ask Lupe if her sister was the woman I always saw her with, standing on the street corner in front of the Cadmean Building. When Cuddy did so, she eagerly told me yes, the one I'd seen her with was her sister, Maria. Holding up her rosary in her folded hands, she begged me in Spanish to tell her where her sister was. I didn't know.

The legal ramifications of holding Lupe were complicated (if we notified Immigration, they'd take her into custody and we'd lose a possible lead to Guess Who). On the other hand, she had rights and needs we had to address. Finally we sent her off with Brenda Moore and Eddie Vega to look for her sister. Afterwards they were to take her to Trinity Church where Paul Madison ran a homeless shelter. Meanwhile Eddie was to find her a Spanish-speaking pro bono lawyer to help sort out her legal status in the country.

The rest of us went back downstairs to Room 105 where the task force worked once again through the night. Those of us who cared fought against being sick at heart about the not-guilty verdict for Tyler Norris, although—as those who didn't much care pointed out—it was hard to see how we could have expected anything else. And everyone fought against the suspicion that Guess Who was going to kill another woman sooner rather than later.

Of course we tried coming up with different explanations for what looked like his warning: that the fish wrapped in newspapers hadn't even been meant for Cuddy. Or that a sanitation worker had sent it to him as a hostile jab about the stench of the strike. Or that Lupe Guevarra had found the chess queen while cleaning Cuddy's office and had stuffed it in the fish for some obscure reason of her own (odd mixtures of voodoo and Catholicism were practiced by the Garifuna). Or that a political enemy had sent it (the fish was wrapped in the old edition of the *Star* which had the editorial calling for Cuddy's dismissal).

But none of us believed any of that. We believed Guess Who had stolen the chess queen and sent it to Cuddy like the slap of a glove in his face to taunt him with a death he wouldn't be smart enough to stop.

• • •

On Sunday after the Tyler Norris verdict, Cuddy and I met in the evening with the six original members of the task force. Over the past week, our investigation team had tripled in size— with State Bureau agents, detectives from neighboring homicide divisions, and the Neville County sheriff joining us. Paper was everywhere, whirring out of fax machines and computer printers, grinding into shredders, swelling files. Even with us working around the clock, information piled up faster than we could sort it out. Room 105 was looking like a disaster shelter, crowded with tired bodies in ripe clothing. Plastic liters of soda and containers for junk food filled trash cans. People had made small areas personal by setting out a photo, an NPR mug, a pot of miniature daffodils, a tiny TV. In one corner, beside a computer bank, the forensic psychiatrist Bunty Crabtree pretty much lived in a rocking chair with a heating pad and spongy pillows propped against its back. Her partner Rhonda would quietly walk by to straighten the pillows or bring her a drink or ask her if she didn't want to go home to rest; sometimes she would bring the cancer medication I'd seen falling out of Bunty's briefcase when Rhonda and I had both pretended I hadn't noticed what it was.

When I walked in, Rhonda, Wendy Freiberg, and Lisa Grecco sat together near Bunty's rocking chair. Etham Foster stood by the fax machine sending data to Dr. Samuel Chang, the forensic pathologist who had gone to examine the exhumed body of Cathy Oakes. Dick Cohen was still with Chang in Neville County. With coffee in a Tarheels go-cup, Cuddy stepped in the front of the room. He was back to his jeans and T-shirt style—this shirt with an American flag on it. He told us, "I got y'all here early to tell you a couple of things. Last night, Ward Trasker announced he was going to step down today as A.G. The governor's appointing Ken Moize Acting A.G." He stopped the eruption of questions with both hands. "Hang on, hang on, let me finish. Yesterday, I met with Mitch Bazemore and Homer Louge. They both have decided that since HPD has been on top of this Guess Who case, plus now we've got good federal help," he pointed at Rhonda and Bunty, "they agree we oughta leave things the way they are. So the D.A.'s office and the sheriff's department are withdrawing from this investigation."

Another outburst, this time punctuated first by cheers then with puzzled questions: was this fallout from the cover-up?

Cuddy sidestepped their conjectures (as he'd agreed in Haver Forest to do), and said only, "This is Mitch's decision and Homer's decision. I think it's a good one."

"A great one," agreed Rhonda with a skeptical stare.

"Last thing. Over breakfast, I met with the Hillston city council and they want us to know that our task force has their full support."

Ironic applause.

Cuddy smiled. "Now, one little rub. I've told the council and the mayor that if they aren't completely satisfied with our progress on this case, then on July 4, I'll resign as police chief."

Silence deadened the room, quickly followed by groans. "Honch," Rhonda shook her head at him melodramatically, "doesn't your mouth ever get worn out with you sticking your big feet in it?"

Cuddy winked at her, a flash of Carolina blue. "Rho, when those boys on that council fire up the grills in their yards on Independence Day, they're going to have satisfied minds. And a killer in custody. Am I right?" He grinned. "It's simple. You guys come through. I don't have to resign."

Wendy Freiberg threw her arms to the ceiling, jingling bracelets on both wrists. "It's July 1. We don't come through by July 4, you lose your job. That's low, Cuddy, that's really low."

He made a kissing noise at her, then handed out what he called the "update"—every day we got a handout of all new information collected the day before. He said, passing the pages around, "Still nothing on the guy that gave Lupe Gueverra the fish. And no sign of her sister. But we've had a few slam-dunks these last couple of days. We're getting there. And Justin's got a couple of interviews to report."

He read out the data in today's sheet:

—The gray car carpet fibers taken both from G.I. Jane's corpse and off the floor of Bungalow Eight came from the floor mats of a Ford Explorer, 1996 to 1999 model.

Etham growled, "These days even serial killers are driving SUVs."

—The straw hat with the candles had belonged to Lucy Griggs; her mother had identified it. She'd also identified Lucy's mesh bag, which we'd found in the woods off the access road to The Fifth Season Resort, as if the killer had tossed it out the car window as he drove away. A gray carpet fiber was found on the bag.

Lucy's camera was missing from the bag, but the audio tape was still in there. Cuddy stuck the tape into a small player and we listened to it. The thoroughly untalented Lucy Griggs and the Mood Disorders singing the Mavis Mahar hit "I Want You More" produced a rare communal moment of comic relief from the task force, evoking such groans that Chuck Grant came from his dark room to ask us what was going on.

—The partial shoe print taken from the floor of the bunga-low shower was a Nike running shoe, man's size nine, of a model that matched the shoe found at the construction site and the shoelaces on G.I. Jane's "necklace." The shoe did not appear to belong to any law officials, mortuary per-sonnel, or hotel staff who'd been in the bungalow after the shooting. It was likely that it belonged to the killer.

—The headshot of Mavis slipped under Cuddy's door had been an insert in a program sold at the Haver Field con-certs. Possibly Guess Who had bought one there the night of the first concert, which meant he had gone to see Mavis. (Of course, so had forty-seven thousand other people.)

—We still had no printout of Lucy Griggs's Haver University transcript. Although their computer system was back up and running, now apparently Lucy's name wasn't listed in registration files because of some glitch. John Emory was pursuing the matter.

—The kitchen matches left in the earth around Kristin's head, the white candles in Lucy's hat, the baggies in which her eyes had been mailed—all were brands sold at a Kroger's in North Mall.

—Also in North Mall, a Walmart's sold cardboard glitter stars of the brand attached to Cuddy's slider.

—A search was in progress at Lucy's lodging (a shabby one-room furnished with items from the dump). Unfortu-nately, at least so far she didn't seem to be very sentimental (no cards, no tickets stubs, or pressed flowers from a lover), nor very introspective (no old-fashioned diary, no letters, no inscribed books). She had collected clothes, makeup, and rock'n'roll. There must have been five hundred CDs in her bedroom where a huge poster of Mavis hung over a lumpy mattress on the floor.

"Now folks, drum roll!" Cuddy did a tattoo on an imaginary snare drum. "This is the big one." He told us that while there were no gray car fibers in the Frances Bush coeds' Tuscadora rental where John Walker had arranged for Kristin Stiller to stay, the relevant fibers *had* been found in Lucy Griggs's apartment. Forensics had pulled them, for example, from the bottom of a pair of her heavy-tred walking shoes.

"There it is," I said. "Guess Who knew Lucy. He was around her prior to the night he killed her."

Cuddy nodded. "We are on Terra Firma, friends. The Eagle has landed. If he knew her before, there's a thread between them—a place, an occupation, mutual acquaintance, something." He turned to the blackboard. "Let's talk suspects." His chalk flew squeaking along as he wrote:

—Guess Who—Unknown local or transient? Or Cadmean Building job-related?
—Lucy's lover, Kristin's blackmail victim?
—John Walker

"Okay, let's look at the full list, see if we can clear things out." He drew a line and then added the following names:

—Andrew Brookside
—Randolph Percy
—Dermott Quinn
—Ward Trasker

He paused, the chalk moving in air, and then added another name:
—Lee Haver Brookside.

"Okay." He gestured at his list. "We're not discussing *why* these names might be up here. Let's just talk alibis for the Lucy Griggs homicide. Because of the shared car carpet fibers, we're saying whoever did Lucy did Kristin too. And maybe Cathy Oakes. So who can we definitely clear on Lucy? Bunty, ready?"

Bunty twisted around uncomfortably in her rocking chair and found a file folder. "Okay. We can drop the first lady. I guess she's there with a jealousy motive, thinking it's Mavis she's shooting?" Bunty looked around. Nobody said anything. She nodded. "Well, doesn't matter. Phil Golden at SBI interviewed six of Mrs. Brookside's staff. She's not viable. From three to seven, she's alibied: speech to the NAACP, tea with the state library association. Never out of view of at least two staff members 'til she went to her rooms at the Governor's Mansion at 7:15. From then 'til midnight, couldn't have left that place without being seen by a dozen people."

I wondered if any of them had noticed her leaving at three in the morning to drive herself to Cuddy's office in downtown Hillston. But that nocturnal visit was outside our time frame and why bring it up?

Cuddy held the eraser over Lee's name. Everyone nodded and, expressionless, he wiped her off the blackboard. "Okay, then, how about Dermott Quinn? He was wandering around The Fifth Season grounds the night of the Griggs's murder. He was in the area again back in January when Mavis went to Windrush. Maybe Cathy and Kristin were crazed Mavis fans like Lucy and this was his sicko way of protecting her."

"Can we just go one time on my instincts?" I asked.

Everyone laughed as Etham grunted, "That's how you go *all* the time."

I argued that Dermott Quinn was by nature incapable of stepping on a roach, much less cutting women's throats or shooting them in the face. He hated guns, he was scared of knives. "I'd stake my life on it."

Wendy quipped, "What about Cuddy's job?"

Rhonda took Cuddy's eraser and removed Dermott's name.

"Quinn's a white-out. His taxi driver got lost bringing him from the Sheraton to The Fifth Season. He was stuck in that cab from nine-thirty 'til ten-thirty and Lucy was already long dead by then."

Ward Trasker's name was erased because Ward's children had sent him and his wife on a world cruise that had begun last New Year's Eve; he'd been playing putt-putt aboard a ship off Bali when Kristin Stiller was killed. That brought us to Randolph Percy.

"No way," I said. "Come on, Cuddy. He did it to save the election for Andy? I doubt it."

"And his job." Cuddy shrugged. "By the book, okay? He's covered 'til the banquet starts, but after that we lose him. He could have bopped off to The Fifth Season, shot somebody he thought was Mavis, zipped back, and told the governor she'd killed herself."

A hoot from Lisa Grecco. "Sure right! Bubba Percy stood six inches from a woman's face, mistook her for Mavis, and blew her away with a gun he stole out of this lobby. Trust me, Bubba gets that close to a woman, he knows who she is. And he's not there to stick a *gun* in her face."

We all looked curiously at the young voluptuous deputy counsel, wondering if she meant what it sounded like she meant. She saw our stares and shook her head at us. "I'm not even going there," she said.

"Sounds like you already went," muttered Rhonda.

Wendy said she'd bet her job as SBI's chief documents examiner that Bubba's handwriting couldn't be made to match Guess Who's.

Rhonda adjusted Bunty's heating pad for her. "Guys, he's cleared by the gun in the display case. The Bernardelli got put back in that case yesterday and let's face it, the killer's not about to ask a pal to do something like that for him." She made a vertical line in the air. "We know it happened after ten A.M. because an eighth-grade class was looking at the case on a field trip at ten sharp and they would have noticed that Guess Who tag." She made a second line. "And it was put there before six-thirty P.M. because that's when Justin and Nancy spotted the switch."

Bunty read from her notepad. "At 9:40 that morning, Percy was in the governor's jet on his way to JFK to meet Mrs. Brookside. They landed back in North Carolina at 7:53 P.M."

Rhonda comically stuck her leg out in the air and wiggled her foot. "Not to mention the Nike shoe print in the shower was size nine and Percy's got some serious Longfellows. They must be like size fifteen."

Wendy leaned over to Lisa and whispered something.

"Oh yeah," Lisa nodded. She and Wendy laughed together. "Definitely." Bubba would have been thrilled.

Cuddy held up his eraser. We all nodded yes and Randolph Percy's name was erased. Above it was the name, "Andrew Brookside."

"Hey, I voted for him," said Wendy. "You're kidding?"

Cuddy looked over at me. "Everyone in this room already knows the governor was in Bungalow Eight the night of the murder. The question is, can we legitimately eliminate him?" I nodded. "Then do it," Cuddy said.

I told the group, "Last night I had a second interview with the driver of Mavis Mahar's limo. It's taken me a long time to persuade him to admit that the governor had ever been in that car on the 20th, but finally he opened up. He drove Mavis and Lucy to The Fifth Season. Forty minutes later, he drove the governor out of there. He says when they left, Lucy Griggs was standing, very much alive, on the porch of the main house and she was talking on a cell phone. If we believe him, then the governor's covered. After that, he's at the mansion and then the Capitol for the gala."

Bunty said, "Well, they could have gotten to the driver."

"I don't think they did. Brookside may have a few of JFK's bad habits but nothing in the 'let's have Bobby take out Marilyn' league."

"Yeah," said Rhonda, "Brookside doesn't have a brother." Apparently she wasn't a fan of the governor's. Jumping from the table, she erased Brookside's name. "JayJay, wait a second. Where's Lucy's cell phone? We could pull the last number off it, whoever she was calling."

I explained that we had been able to find neither the phone nor any record of Lucy's ever having cellular phone service. It was possible that the killer had taken the phone after the murder; it might even have been his.

"You try John Walker or his mother on the phone registration?" Walker was Rhonda's pick for our killer. While Cuddy didn't think the surly "musician" was bright enough to be Guess Who, he was certainly a strong candidate. He had claimed to have an alibi for the time of the Lucy Griggs homicide: for the six hours after I'd seen him in the Tucson staring sullenly at Mavis Mahar and his ex-girlfriend Lucy, he'd been "rehearsing" with Griffin Pope, the other guitarist for the Mood Disorders. He and Griffin had been alone in their apartment "practicing" all that time.

Etham growled, "Not even white people could practice six whole hours and still sound as bad as that band on that tape you just played."

Even if they could, they hadn't. Griffin Pope had spent that evening in a holding cell right upstairs, a probability that Walker should have looked into before he offered up Pope as his alibi. Walker also had a large collection of S&M porno sites bookmarked on his web browser. And he'd flunked a lie detector test. He'd been hauled into the Cadmean Building often enough on petty charges to draw its blueprints and to nourish a grudge against the Hillston police. He knew two of the victims and had been rejected by one of them. He even had a cousin in Neville where Cathy Oakes had been killed. I said, "No, it wasn't his phone. And listen, we've got to charge him or let him go."

Lisa Grecco, the assistant D.A., didn't think so. "You brought him in on possession, right?" I nodded. "Didn't you say he pulled a gun on Nancy Caleb-White?" I nodded. "New charge. Attempted assault, deadly weapon."

When I told her it was just an air pistol, Lisa shrugged. "You can shoot your eye out with an air pistol," she said. "Didn't you see *Christmas Story*?"

We worked 'til midnight and started again early Monday morning. It was almost six P.M. when the fax machine finally began to beep with the report that Etham had been impatiently waiting for all day: the fax from the pathologist Dr. Chang. Eagerly he watched the paper curving slowly out of the feed. The rest of us waited while he read the first two pages. With a puzzled headshake, he rubbed hard at his grizzled hair. I noticed for the first time that there was gray in his sideburns.

Cuddy joined him. "That from Chang?"

Etham pulled his wide expanse of shoulders to his neck. "Hang on." More pages fell from the machine. Etham finally looked up from them and said, "Guess Who didn't kill Cathy Oakes."

Bunty made a sharp gentle noise. "Didn't think so."

Etham skimmed the pages as he spoke. "Knife blade's different on the first victim, stroke's different too. Killer came up from behind Oakes, tall guy, no hesitation. Then he ran over her twice pre-mortem with a pickup truck. Broke nine bones." He looked at us.

Cuddy said, "That doesn't mean he's not Guess Who." Etham silently handed him the fax sheets. He raced through them and then whistled. "Chang's amazing. He pulled a partial off the petal of one of the roses the guy tossed on her stomach. He pulled a latent off the skin on her ankle, where the guy had dragged her. He has Neville homicide feed them in the computer and out pops a ten-print card right there in their own county. The killer's an ex-con, did three years in Dollard State Prison for attempted rape."

I asked, "How do we know he isn't Guess Who?"

Cuddy handed me the first page of Chang's report. "Because he's dead. His brother killed him the Saturday after Thanksgiving. They got in a fight about a football game." He looked up from the pages he was speed-reading. "Stick to basketball, right, Etham?"

"I don't like either one," mumbled the famous Doctor Dunk-It.

"Well, there goes our St. Catherine on the wheel idea," I said.

Rhonda rubbed my back. "There goes the Guess T-shirt too, buddy."

Bunty sipped at hot tea from a thermos. Quietly she said, "Kristin Stiller's a copycat of Cathy Oakes. But not for the fun of it."

I asked, "You mean, he tied it together after the fact?"

She nodded. "Exactly what I mean. He mimicked Cathy Oakes's Guess shirt to connect his homicide to hers and start the press on a stampede to screaming serial killer."

Bunty had to be right. Perhaps he'd even thought of St. Catherine's wheel when he read about Cathy's broken bones, and then set up corresponding mutilations in his victims to represent other female saints.

Etham's long forefinger pointed out something on a fax page to Cuddy, who gave a long whistle when he saw it. "Boys and girls," he told us, "when you go to bed, thank Elvis in heaven for Dr. Chang. Listen to this."

The pathologist thought we should know a few things, based on his preliminary examination of Kristin Stiller before he returned to Hillston for a second look at her torso: the knife used on Kristin was similar to but was not identical with the one used on Cathy Oakes. Slashes on Kristin's throat had been tentative at first and then deep and extensive. The excess seemed to Chang designed to mask bruises from a choking. Kristin had been *strangled* before her throat was cut, and that strangulation was the cause of death. The tongue might have been cut out to hide that evidence. There had been a probably postmortem act of sexual perversion: deeply embedded at the base of her gum-line, the pathologist had found (and managed to extract) a miniscule piece of male Caucasian pubic hair. Preliminary analysis showed it to be compatible with a pubic hair found on a pair of thong panties on the floor of Lucy Griggs's closet.

The killer was someone who knew Lucy well enough for his pubic hair to be on her underwear. He was someone shrewd enough to throw us off track by seizing upon the accident of a murdered prostitute's Guess T-shirt and broken limbs and

326 • michael malone

mimicking their significance when he killed Kristin Stiller. He was someone sick enough to cut out a dead woman's tongue and insert his penis into her mouth cavity. He was someone arrogant enough to boast to the Hillston police about his past murders and to threaten us with murders to come. Further analysis would give us details of this man's blood and hair, eventually give us his DNA. Meanwhile, we would let John Walker know that we'd broken his alibi and see what he had to say.

At that point, Carl Yarborough called to remind Cuddy he'd agreed to go out to dinner in half an hour. Dina Yarborough had asked me to come along with them because she'd invited Margy Turbot whose birthday it was, and she wanted my help in initiating a romance between Cuddy and the judge. I went, but I didn't want to. I didn't want to leave my house. I'd had a message from Mavis that she was back in town.

Chapter 26

Exchange

The Pine Hills Inn is a nineteenth-century barn on the outskirts of Hillston in the hills above the lake. It has a bronze placard boasting that when Sherman's troops stabled their horses here, three teenaged rebels sneaked inside and shooed half the animals away. One of the teenagers was caught and shot to death, thus entering immortality as a martyr to the Cause. (A local high school is still named after him.) The invading Yankees spent the next few days catching the runaway horses while a group of elderly Confederates waited on the banks of the Shocco River to surrender to them. Finally the surrender party gave up and went home, and the Yankees left for Bentonville. The War was over anyhow; General Lee had already surrendered up in Appomattox. But the horse raid incident had turned the barn into a place of pilgrimage, preserving it until seventy years later when the Yankees came back and turned it into a French restaurant.

It was July 2 but more like a summer night in the mountains than in the humid Piedmont—a big moon, a cool crisp sky full of stars. Everyone was out to revel in the respite from the exhausting heat. Our party—the Yarboroughs, Cuddy, Margy Turbot, and myself—might not have succeeded in getting a good table at the busy Pine Hills Inn if one of us hadn't been the mayor, another the police chief, and a third the district's chief judge. "I guess you and I are just along for our looks," I told Dina as the maitre d' fell all over Cuddy, Carl, and Margy.

"Well, we are mighty good looking," she agreed.

Now the truth is, what Dina and I also had in common should have assured us of a table at the Pine Hills Inn: Dollards had had a good table saved for them there since the place opened in 1933, and Dina and I were both Dollards. She and I had the same great-great grandfather, Eustache Dollard—although (of course) Dina's great-great grandmother didn't call herself Mrs. Dollard and mine did. My grandmother had told me this bit of history when I was a teenager. My mother's mother, the widow of Chief Justice BVD, was in her nineties when she confided in me. Grandmama called me into her bedroom and showed me old photos of people called Kipleys. She said the Kipleys were my "tarbaby cousins from the wrong side of the blanket." Kipley was Dina's maiden name, as it was my uncle Senator Kip Dollard's first name.

Grandmama claimed that the reason that the Kipleys owned half of Canaan, the African-American section of Hillston formerly known as Darktown, was because their Dollard relatives had lent them the money to buy it. When my mother heard Grandmama telling me these stories about "tarbaby cousins," she hurried me away from the old woman and told me that my grandmother had lost her mind and was capable of any silly thing. She had a point. A week later, the newspaper heiress Edwina Sunderland pretended not to notice that my Grandmama Dollard was standing in the Hillston Club wearing hat, gloves, pearls, heels, and a girdle and a bra, having forgotten her slip and dress (as well as her name). Mrs. Sunderland came to get me on the tennis courts and said, "Justin honey, I believe your grandmama is feeling a little tired out and would like you to escort her home." The South rests on a foundation of such pretences.

After Grandmama's mind "wandered" and took her discretion with it, she told me all sorts of wonderful scandalous secrets and mysteries about the Dollards and everyone else in Hillston that I suspect were absolutely true. I also suspect she was the genesis of my desire to be a detective.

It may be that Dina and I were the first two people from our respective sides of the very separate and not very equal branches of our family to sit down together to dinner at the Pine Hills Inn, although lying down together in beds had apparently been going on for over a hundred years. I'd always assumed she knew she was Dollard, but it wasn't the sort of question one traditionally asked in the South.

Until a few years ago, the Pine Hills Inn was thought to offer the oldest and fanciest public dining in town. Now it is just the oldest. Now the place to be seen is The Fifth Season. The Hillston Club is still the "nicest" place, but it isn't public and Carl and Dina haven't been asked to join even though they're the mayor and first lady. At the Hillston Club, members never see their bills until the end of the year and then they don't care what the bill is or they pretend they don't.

In the same Southern way, this evening at Pine Hills, our party pretended not to notice that Dr. and Mrs. Fulke Norris were seated with their son Tyler and a member of the city council near the big yellow stone fireplace. And the Norrises pretended not to see us walk past them into the quietly bustling high vaulted room. They were presumably there to celebrate the not-guilty verdict that three days ago had set Tyler free.

Our own group didn't talk about this verdict, although after we were seated I did ask Margy why she'd agreed even to a million-dollar bail that allowed Tyler as much comfort and liberty during his trial as if he'd been charged with a far lesser crime. Margy said, first of all, that Tyler hadn't been allowed to leave the Hillston city limits and he had been required to report to the sheriff's department every eight hours. "Sure, it was a judgment call," she told me, looking with her platinum pageboy and pearl gray linen suit more like someone in Town and Country than a judge. "But I knew he'd stay put. It wasn't just that bail was a lot of money, and not just his strong ties to the community. Isaac Rosethorn was betting on a not-guilty verdict and any bail violation would risk that."

Cuddy refilled his beer glass. "Well, too bad you were right and Isaac was right. Because the sad fact is that Justin was right. Tyler killed his wife. Not that it appears to amount to a hill of beans in this crazy world. See, Justin, I can quote the movies too."

"You can quote *Casablanca, Jailhouse Rock,* and *Coal Miner's Daughter.* I believe that's it." I poured the Dom Perignon champagne I'd brought from home and had the restaurant uncork for us.

Carl squeezed Dina's hand in his darker pudgy one. "I don't ever want to hear either of you mention the words Tyler Norris again. We are here to celebrate. And Justin's helped us do it in style. I better check into your salary, Justin." He lifted his glass of champagne. "So Happy Birthday to Margy. And may she join our ticket someday as attorney general." We toasted her.

She laughed. "I like being a judge." Then she pleaded with us not to let the waiters come out singing, carrying tiramisu with a candle in it.

I toasted Carl's running for lieutenant governor and Dina's letting him. Then Cuddy toasted the end of the garbage strike at midnight tonight. "To no more trash on the streets."

I said, "You sound like my grandmother Dollard."

He winked. "She was talking about *my* grandmother."

Carl laughed. "My grandmother thought *everybody* was trash except her, Jesus, and Mr. and Mrs. Franklin D. Roosevelt. And that includes her husband and her children both."

I heard a pleasant laugh I recognized. Sure enough, at a table behind us the President of Frances Bush College was saying good-bye to a well-dressed group of the elderly affluent, including the philanthropic Inez Boodle. The president stopped at our table and greeted us, wishing the Yarboroughs well in the coming campaign. There was a disappointment in her eyes as she joked with Cuddy. I suspect it came from the fact that he was sitting beside her good friend Margy Turbot. Both women were single. Cuddy was like one of the last lifeboats on the *Titanic.*

Inez Boodle stopped by the table as well and said she recognized me. "Kip Dollard's boy, right?" I told her Senator Kip Dollard was my uncle and confessed that I had been wondering how such an intelligent woman had ever been a close friend of the silver-haired senator. Close to what? She grinned, showing teeth as yellowed as her hair, and informed me that brains weren't the only thing a man had to offer a woman.

"Ahhhh," I nodded. "True, Uncle Kip was a really good dancer."

"That too," she cackled. On her way out, she headed over to hug Mrs. Fulke Norris, who then must have reminded her that I'd arrested her son Tyler, for Inez wheeled around and gave me a look of outraged indignation.

It was one of the best evenings Cuddy and I had had together in a long time, except for the unspoken absence of Alice. I could tell from their tiptoeing around the subject that the Yarboroughs and Margy weren't sure whether Alice had left me, I'd left her, or if she really had simply gone on a long visit to her family in the mountains. But apart from that, and Cuddy's surveillance of my refilling my champagne glass, and my own private urge to smoke at the table (the Pine Hills Inn is one of the few places left where you *can* smoke), it was an easy friendly time for us. Cuddy and I could talk freely to Margy again now that the trial was over. We could talk freely with the Yarboroughs again now that the Haver Forest Accord (as I called it) had been sealed. We even joked that starting at midnight we could breathe freely again because the sanitation workers would then start removing the trash from the streets. True, we had only a few days to catch Guess Who before the Fourth of July, but the task force was moving so quickly that an arrest seemed, if not imminent, imminently possible.

And then, when our cheerful party was leaving Pine Hills Inn, several small things happened that were to make a great difference. As Cuddy and Margy walked arm in arm past the huge stone fireplace, Fulke Norris stood up to block their path, his trademark white hair flopping perfectly over an eyebrow. He breathed like a man who thought he might be having a heart attack. "It's not surprising to see you two together, but I wonder that even you don't have the decency to leave us alone."

Cuddy said mildly, "I believe this is a public restaurant, Mr. Norris."

"Dr. Norris," he announced loudly. Heads at nearby tables turned.

His wife plucked with annoyance at his sleeve. "Fulke, sit down."

The poet of the people ignored her. "Your criminal collusion to destroy my family failed, didn't it?" He pointed backwards without looking at Tyler, whose face, reddened by the flames of the fire behind him, swelled with anger he was trembling to control. Oddly enough, the emotion appeared to be directed as much against his father as the police chief and the judge who'd arrested and tried him.

"You want to be careful about making such allegations," Margy said.

Cuddy added, "Dr. Norris, we weren't trying to destroy your family. We were trying to convict a man who murdered his pregnant wife."

Mrs. Norris's voice was glacial. "Fulke, please, this serves no purpose."

"Mary, be quiet."

Tyler did a mock salute. "You heard him, Mother, be quiet."

Margy took Cuddy's arm. "Let's go."

We kept walking.

At the bar by the door, a crowd was distracted from their long wait for tables by drinks and a pianist at a baby grand. This slender seventy-year-old with an almost pinkish toupee had been playing from a fake book there nightly for at least thirty years. Once every few weeks he'd have a second martini and suddenly launch into a terrifying rendition of Chopin's "Revolutionary Etude" but otherwise kept to quiet pleasant pop tunes. He affably described himself at least once a night as the "oldest gay man in Hillston," which may or may not have been true. Margy now tried futilely to stop him from playing "Happy Birthday" to her as we paused at the keyboard to slip money in his little cut-glass vase.

Dina pulled me aside and pointed at Cuddy and Margy who were close together laughing by the coatroom. "What do you think?"

Frankly I didn't think anything romantic would happen for Cuddy as long as Lee Brookside was alive. After his breakup with old Briggs Cadmean's daughter, there'd been an attractive lawyer, Nora Howard, who had lived in the apartment across from his. For a year, we had hoped his camaraderie with Nora would turn to romance. When she moved out of River Rise to take a job with a firm across the state, she told me, "Cuddy wishes he could fall in love with me but he can't. He didn't say why." But we both knew why. The why was Lee Haver Brookside.

I said to Dina, "We'll do our best."

My cell phone rang. It was Rhonda, still working in Room 105. She told me there was bad news. The male pubic hairs found on Kristin Stiller's corpse and on Lucy Griggs's underwear were not compatible with samples voluntarily given us by John Walker. "Guess Johnny Walker's walking," Rhonda sighed. "And he looked soooo damn good."

Margy was offering Cuddy a ride home when I gave him Rhonda's news. He wasn't surprised. He'd never thought Walker had the brains. "Bunty says we need to look for pride in intellect. And, JB Five, you're not going to find it in John E. Walker."

"Pride in intellect? Bunty ever wonder if you were Guess Who?"

Margy looked dejected when he told her he'd have to take a rain check on her ride. He was heading back to the Cadmean Building. Carl was headed there too, for a late-night meeting about the traffic problems of removing all the garbage before tomorrow's rush hour. Dina sighed. "Oh well, I guess life can't be all bouillabaisse and champagne for politicians."

"Sure it can," I told her. "It was for Senator Kip Dollard." And then under the influence of all the champagne I'd drunk, I decided to add something. I said, "Your relative and mine."

"Excuse me?"

I opened my hands. "Well, we're Dollard cousins, aren't we, Dina?"

She blinked the odd emerald eyes in the coffee-colored face. She stared at me a moment. "Cousins?"

"That's what I've heard." I smiled. "Isn't that what you've heard?"

Slowly she smiled back at me. "Yep, that's what I've heard." We shook hands solemnly.

Dina took the ride with Margy that Cuddy had declined. Carl wanted to smoke a cigar before he and Cuddy left, so the three of us walked around to the long side porch. There we bumped into Bubba Percy and Shelly Bloom sitting closely together in green rockers under the big full moon. They were drinking brandy from huge snifters and looking for all the world like a couple—albeit a couple who might (in their Dolce e Gabbana blues and blacks) suit a Soho sushi bar better than a Hillston barn. Embarrassed to be found together, they instantly rushed to deny or at least camouflage any suggestion that they were together by choice.

Unasked, Shelly explained that she was paying off a bet by taking Bubba to dinner. Checking her watch, she added that she was glad it was almost over. She rocked to her feet, set her drink on a wicker table, and briskly hurried inside. After she left, Bubba rushed to let us know that he'd felt so sorry for Shelly, and was so worried she really would bring a lawsuit against him, that he'd hoped to bribe her with a nice meal and a new job. He'd called in some chits and they'd taken her on permanently at his old paper the *Star*. "Praise Jesus it's over," he added and drank down the rest of Shelly's brandy, which I'd been eyeing myself.

"Bubba," smiled Cuddy, "how long is this Billy Graham bit going on?"

"Through all eternity, isn't it?" grinned the big redhead as he accepted the large cigar the mayor offered him. "Carl, we'll be puffing these babies in the White House before it's over. You have just been signed by a World Champion Yankee. Andy's going all the way. "

Carl puffed peaceably. "I'll be happy if I get to Raleigh."

Cuddy said, "That's what Napoleon said about Moscow."

Bubba stuck the cigar in his pretty mouth, then slapped Cuddy on the arm. "So you did it, Porcus Rex. I hear Ward

Trasker resigned yesterday. Go figure, huh?" He grinned around the cigar.

"Yeah, go figure," said Cuddy. "How was New York?" Bubba had flown up there to meet Lee and they'd come home together.

"It's there, Boonie Boy, it's alive and well, which is more than we can say for hillbilly Hillston."

Thinking about Bunty's "pride in intellect" phrase, I excused myself and went looking for Shelly. I found her at the bar, maybe waiting there for Bubba. "Shelly, you want an exclusive with the head of HPD homicide?"

The big black eyes sparked with interest that contradicted her reply. "I've had about all the exclusives I can take."

I told her we were close to an arrest on Guess Who. The killer had made too many mistakes and we'd broken the case. As I'd predicted, she couldn't resist.

Back on the porch, Carl, Bubba, and Cuddy were telling political jokes. I was mostly wishing they'd leave so I could take out the cigarettes in my pocket, but instead Bubba asked to borrow my cell phone because he had left his in his car. While he was using it, a long white limousine suddenly thundered onto the gravel drive. Young thin people jumped out of it, hyped and laughing, like an ad for hip casual clothing. They looked high on looks and fame and other exhilarating substances easier to buy.

It was the Mavis Mahar entourage and her band the Easter Uprising, back from their concert in Central Park where two nights ago a hundred thousand people had sat under the stars to listen to her sing. The news had said she'd started on time and sung for three hours, she'd been "electric," "extraordinary," she had crowned herself "the undisputed empress of rock and roll" by giving "the best performance of her brilliant career." I was just glad to be looking at her again as I watched her moving around the car and toward the steps. She wore black pants and T-shirt and over them a beautiful loose-weave Irish shawl, like the cloak of an ancient queen, pinned by a large silver circle with a huge stone in it that looked like a real ruby and probably was.

Suddenly she saw me watching her. Her smile squeezed at my heart then released it with a sharp pain.

"Hello, Lieutenant Boyo," she called merrily. "Come have a drink with Mavis and her mates." She skipped up the steps and as her musicians bunched around us, she ran the back of her hand slowly across the zipper of my pants. She got the response I'm sure she wanted. She turned her head and grinned at me as she was swept through the door. A few seconds later the pianist struck up her big hit "Comin' Home to You," and the restaurant burst into applause.

"Bitch," said Bubba Percy, whom she'd completely ignored.

"I don't know, she seemed pretty friendly." Cuddy glanced pointedly at me with an expression I didn't want to interpret.

"Bitch." Bubba took off down the steps, pausing to comb his hair. "Oh, I hear you caught some leads on Guess Who."

"Well, we finally crossed you off the prime suspect list," Cuddy said.

Bubba was so conceited he was pleased. "I was a prime suspect?"

Cuddy sighed. "Yeah, but Lisa Grecco told us you were more into sticking your dick in women's faces than guns."

Unfazed, Bubba nodded. "Nine times out of ten."

"So you and Lisa, that's a confirmation, huh?" Cuddy nodded.

"Me and Lisa and your mama in a three-way." And he was gone, bouncing down the wide stone steps into the night. Cuddy asked me if I was ready to leave. He gave me a suspicious look when I told him I was going to hang around awhile. "My advice is, don't do it in the bar," he said, then left with Carl. My focus was so centered on what Mavis might be doing inside the restaurant that I didn't realize 'til hours later that Bubba had taken my cell phone with him. As a result, when John Emory tried to phone me to say he'd finally gotten hold of the transcript of Lucy Griggs's Haver University record and that there was something on it I needed to see, I didn't get the call.

I might not have taken it anyhow. It was after midnight and I was in bed with Mavis Mahar.

Chapter 27
Foolsmate

The poor part of Hillston was always East Hillston, where Cuddy Mangum grew up in a dark little duplex on Mill Street, where the workers at Cadmean Textiles kept their broken-down cars in dirt yards and kept their broken-down dreams to themselves except when they took them out on black people. The poorest part of East Hillston was always Canaan where the black people lived. It was to Canaan that I took Mavis Mahar at one in the morning to listen to the woman they called Blind Eva sing the blues in a bar called Smoke's. I'd been sneaking into Smoke's since my adolescence when a girl called Jenna Cobb first took me there to hear the music that played all night.

I grew up as far from Canaan as the town could stretch, on Catawba Drive in North Hillston where everyone in our circle lived near the country club and close to each other. My home, a stone house built in the twenties, was called a Tudor manor and was designed to resemble an entire block of a village in the Cotswolds. My mother, a Dollard, had been born in this house. It was next door to the house in which her grandmother had been born.

In the ninth grade I was sent away to a prep school in New England. I didn't want to go because I was desperately in love with Jenna Cobb, the young woman who'd introduced me to Smoke's. I wanted to be around her all the time and couldn't bear to think of a life where that wouldn't be possible. Jenna lived in East Hill-ston, near Cuddy Mangum. I only met her because she earned money by playing the organ in the church that my family attended. We were both thirteen.

The first time I saw Jenna, she was perched high on the oak stool at the organ in the choir stall, surrounded by all the musical stops and pipes. I remember the moment when her foot, in its black flat with a small pink silk rose at the toe, reached out, stretching for the far pedal on the organ floor, and her leg—slen-der, pale, tense with the effort—appeared from beneath the black choir robe, exposed to above the knee in a startling intimacy that the girl was unaware of, so intent was she on her music.

I had seen nothing so beautiful since the ballerina Margot Fonteyn had arrived in Hillston when I was six years old to dance *Romeo and Juliet* at Haver Auditorium. My mother, her-self a pianist, loved to tell the story of how enraptured I'd been watching the ballet and how I'd had "a fit" when they wouldn't take me backstage to meet Miss Fonteyn. "I could tell even way back then how Jay loved the fine arts and I had every hope he would be more serious about his piano lessons, but you know how boys are."

But it hadn't been so much the dance that I was in love with, but the dancer. It was Margot Fonteyn doing the dance. It was Jenna Cobb playing the organ, raising herself on the seat to pound down on the keys, pulling out all the organ stops on the hymn's last verse with an energetic abandon that never failed to give me an erection. It was Mavis Mahar singing in Smoke's, where so long ago Jenna had brought me in secret (slipping me through in the back kitchen door) to hear Eva Wilcox singing my first live blues music in a place where whites were no more welcome than blacks in the Hillston Club.

Despite the claims of the Pine Hills Inn, Smoke's was in fact the oldest public eatery in Hillston and certainly the most authentic, for it looked very little changed from its 1927 photo-graphs. It still had its nickel-plated cash register, its twenty-foot cast iron bar rail, its black fans and hanging globe lights in the shiny tin ceiling, its cloudy mirrors and tile floor. Built by a man from Chicago, "Smoke's Colored Bar & Restaurant" hadn't closed even during Prohibition except when tipped off that Police Chief Pork Doad was on his way over. According to the Historical Society's "Official Guide to Old Hillston," it was apocryphal that the original owner's name was "Smoke" because he was a gangster and smoke was what was always coming out of his gun after he shot people. On the other hand, another old legend about the place was true. Bessie Smith had dropped into Smoke's one night when driving through North Carolina. In exchange for some barbecue and a water glass full of gin, she had sung there while the crowd grew until it was spilling out of windows and doors and into the street.

A very different crowd (a third of them white college students) was crowded tonight in Smoke's as Mavis sat at the battered upright and played four-hand stride piano along with Blind Eva Wilcox, the woman I'd brought her to hear. They were singing "St. Louis Woman," and a young Haver musicologist who'd followed Mavis here was filming the impromptu performance with a small camcorder that he seemed to hope no one was noticing. Eva Wilcox was in her eighties now; she lived with her grandson Fattie McCramer, the current "Smoke" (all owners of the place were renamed "Smoke," like all heirs to the Roman Empire were called Caesar), but she preferred the company in the bar to an empty house in a nice suburb and so she spent her days and nights at Smoke's, talking with old friends, criticizing new cooks, and playing the piano when she felt like it. She was now stooped, blind, bony, her big long crooked hands almost gray.

After I went away to prep school, Jenna Cobb and I never saw each other again. Her family moved from Hillston and our letters couldn't keep us together. But for that first year, we were so in love, every song we heard was about us. Afterwards, what remained was my lifelong passion for women like her, and my love of jazz and blues. By introducing me to Eva Wilcox, Jenna had changed my life.

Mrs. Wilcox had taught me who was worth listening to and who wasn't. She'd been there listening when Bessie Smith had sung that night in Smoke's; she'd performed with Fats Waller and Lester Young; she'd made five recordings in the forties, toured the "Negro club circuit," was an amazing singer and a great jazz piano player and very few people had ever heard of her outside Hillston, North Carolina. But one of those people was Mavis Mahar, and so when (sitting with the raucous young drunks at the Pine Hills Inn bar) I'd asked Mavis if she'd like to meet Blind Eva Wilcox, she'd drawn me out onto the porch and kissed me and told me that now I was the perfect man.

Only Dermott knew where we were going, and he of course thought I was her salvation, whereas I'd quit trying even to save myself.

Take all my money. Black out both of my eyes.
Give it all to another woman. Come home and tell me lies.

The two women laughed together as they played, leaning arm to arm on the rickety bench, one so young and astonishingly beautiful; the other blind, so old and bent that only undefeatable character seemed to keep tightening the muscles in her skinny arms and jumping her long flat black fingers over the keys. She'd put her hand down over Mavis's, a split second ahead, leading her to the notes. "Naw, honey, naw honey, that ain't right. Here you go. Now you cookin' in Smoke's!"

He got to get it, bring it and put it right here,
Or else he goin' to keep it out there.
That's right. Or else you gonna keep it out there!

Their hands crossed, crossed back, faster and faster, black on white, white on black, until with a run in the treble and a rumble in the bass they were done and the place shook with shouted cheers and stomping feet.

The Haver musicologist kept taping as Mavis took Blind Eva's hands in her own, kissed them, raised them to her face so the woman could feel who she was. "Thank you," she said. "*Bail ó Dhia is ó Mhuire duit.*"

Mrs. Wilcox said, "What the fuck kind of talk is that?"

Mavis laughed and kissed her cheek. "It's my language. Gaelic. I'm from Ireland. It means the blessing of God and Mary be on you."

"Well, you a pretty little thing," said Mrs. Wilcox, feeling the shape of Mavis's head with both large tensile hands. "And you a foreigner and love our blues like you do? That something. Well, honey, I wish you all kinds of luck with your music." (She didn't seem to know that Mavis was already one of the most famous rock stars in the world.) "But you 'member this. The friends you got befo, they gone stay yo friends. All the rest...." She played a run and sang, "Nobody knows you when you down and out."

"I'll remember that," Mavis promised, but you could tell it wasn't a lesson she expected to learn. No one does before they have to.

A group of Haver students crowded around the piano thrusting out books and napkins and even their shirts for Mavis to autograph. She held them off as she said to the old woman still crooked over the piano. "*Muillean muilte Dé go mall, ach muillean siad go mion.* That means God's mill grinds slowly, but it grinds fine. Now here's what I'm telling you, people know about you, Mrs. Wilcox. People will remember you and what you taught us."

Blind Eva said with a kind weary tolerance, "That's sweet, honey. I didn't figure on living to hear that said." She grinned widely. "Oh now, I figure it'd *be* said. Just I wasn't gonna live to hear it." She punctuated her own joke with an astonishing riff of a triple-timed "Danny Boy."

"So long, Irish girl," said the old blues woman. "You damn good."

"Ah darlin', you haven't seen the last of me." Mavis took off the beautiful Irish shawl and re-pinned it with the ancient silver circle around the old woman's shoulders. Then she kissed her again and walked away to sign the autographs. I leaned over to say good night to Mrs. Wilcox, but she jerked me down to her with fingers whose strength always shocked me. "What you doing, Justin, you fucker?"

I pulled away. "I brought her to hear you sing."

"Don't lie to me. Where yo wife?"

I said, "In the mountains."

The withered blind face turned in disgust from side to side. "Well, she better get her ass home fore her man gone off with that Irish girl over the damn ocean and start talkin' like a cat coughin' up a fur ball."

As I pushed the crowd back to lead Mavis out of Smoke's, I could hear the old woman singing from the shabby upright:

You low down alligator, watch me sooner or later.
Gonna catch you with your britches down.

• • •

In bed with Mavis in my family's summer place on the lake, we made love listening to old records that Eva Wilcox had taught me to seek out.

"You're good at this," Mavis said, lying on the woven rug by the fire.

"Thank you." I kissed the back of her neck. "You're bad for me." A cigarette in one hand, a glass of Jameson's in the other, I looked up at the clock on the mantel, ignored what it told me.

"Ah don' be blamin' me for your sins, you feckin' tosser." She leaned her head back against my kiss. "You're good because you pay attention. Like thinking I'd like to meet Eva Wilcox. None of the shites I pay a bloody fortune to told me about Smoke's."

"Probably didn't know." I turned her over, kissed the small of her back.

"I pay them to know. Pay them to do my living. Buy me food and houses and feckin' tampons. I don't have to pull up my own sheets and still I'm tireder than when me and my ma had our heads down scrubbing in other people's toilets. Now that's what Andy understood."

"What's that?"

"How it wears you out racin' round the fast track with the bright lights on you. He used to say, 'Mavis, we do more in a day, we're asked to do more, than most people in a lifetime. We're in the diamond lane, going a thousand times faster than everybody else and they're sprawled out on their couches in the dark yelling, "Faster!" at us. Because it's us makes them feel alive.'"

So what she had enjoyed about Brookside was that he was, like her, a star, and had felt, like her, "the terrible heat of all that light shining on you every blessed minute. If you've not felt it, you don't know. We had that between us." She smiled at me. "Truth to tell, he wasn't much good at sex."

"Do I have to hear about this?"

She walked across the room, unself-conscious without her clothes and poured us both more whiskey. "He likes a romp through the wild kingdom, Andy does. Now some folks really like the way fish taste and some just like to land the big ones."

I said again, "Do I have to hear about this?"

She laughed. "Sure you love to hear you're better. Andy liked the hooking the fish, but he wasn't much for the frying them if you know what I mean. But now you don't still think he killed that girl, what was her name?"

"Lucy Griggs. No, we don't think he killed her. Murder would be a serious stumbling block to getting reelected. And that's what Andy wants."

She lay back down beside me. "If you're a comet, you keep shooting through the sky. Because, isn't it so, if you stop, you explode?"

"I don't know. I'm not a comet."

She bent above me. "Ah, Mr. Savile, you are for certain."

• • •

We were startled out of a dead sleep at nearly two in the morning, chilled, hung-over, by a loud sudden pounding at the door.

Before I could pull anything over us, I heard the lock snap like a gunshot and the door bang open.

I managed to cover Mavis with my jacket before Cuddy had made it to where we lay in front of the fire. Furious, he kicked over the whiskey bottle and then kicked once at my leg. "Get up, you stupid shit, and get over to Southern Depot. They just pulled another woman's body out of a garbage bag." He was gone again by the time I'd staggered to my feet.

Mavis yawned. "Who the bloody hell was that?"

"Cuddy Mangum. My boss. The police chief." I reached for my pants. "I gotta go. Can you get Dermott to come get you?"

"Sure. Didn't I see him with you at Pine Hills tonight?" She ran her hand over whiskey pooling on the floor and put her fingers to her mouth.

I said, "Yeah, he's my best friend."

She shook her tangled hair. "Is that so now? Well, I don't suppose he wants to be mine."

Chapter 28
Blunder

Except for the crack-up that sent me to the mountains, I'd always been able to sober myself quickly if I had to. I was sober as I passed Cuddy's cruiser on the bypass just before the turnoff to downtown and I'm sure he recognized my Jaguar as I flew around him. The thudding in my heart came more from dread than shame: they'd found another woman's body. Whose? If it had been the first lady's, if it had been Lee's, wouldn't Cuddy have told me so?

While driving, I tried to use my cell phone, usually in the well, realized it was missing, and remembered that Bubba had it. I'd disconnected the phone at Nachtmusik. Maybe Cuddy had called there, maybe he had gone by my house on Tuscadora before coming out to the lake house where he'd guessed I would be. Maybe even guessed with whom I'd be.

From blocks away I could see the brick checkerboard cupolas of the huge Victorian train station that was now boutiques and markets and known as Southern Depot Mall. Its parking lot was cordoned off by yellow plastic tape reading "HILLSTON POLICE DEPARTMENT. DO NOT CROSS." Four HPD patrol cars, their blue barlights whirring, nosed to the edge of the pedestrian walk, while white spinning lights atop a waiting ambulance gave the scene an eerie silent film look.

Nancy Caleb-White stood on the hood of her cruiser, looking I think for me, because as soon as she saw me, she began wildly gesturing for me to hurry. The equipment on her uniform belt flew about as she led me in a sprint to the side of the building. There a rear passageway was sign-posted "LOADING UNLOADING ONLY."

"Jesus, where you been?" She yelled over her shoulder. "The chief went ballistic when he couldn't find you!" Jerking her head around in a double take, she noticed that I had on trousers with suspenders, a sleeveless undershirt and loafers without socks. I didn't answer. We skidded around a corner into a small group of curious late-nighters, held back by the tape from the loading ramp of the International Fish Market. High intensity portable standing lights shone down on a hill of gleaming black garbage bags and on the opened pneumatic jaws of a city garbage truck. Looking into its cavity was a cluster of HPD officers—among them Augie Summers from forensics and the crime scene photographer Chuck Grant.

Suddenly Shelly Bloom shoved her way between two patrolmen. "Justin, hi! So what's going on?"

Nancy and I quickly slipped under the tape where she couldn't follow and made our way over to where Dick Cohen, his pants on over his pajamas, leaned beside his assistant medical examiner, looking at a body that hung in the truck opening, half out of a black plastic garbage bag.

I recognized the thick short arm, the raven black hair. Pushing forward, I leaned in next to Dick.

"About time," he said grumpily.

"What happened?"

Nancy squeezed in beside me and Chuck, who was taking photos as fast as he could. She said, "The garbage guys started at midnight loading all the stuff piled up from the strike. So this guy here—" She pointed over at a stocky African-American in his forties, wearing a Hillston Sanitation uniform, who sat anxiously on the edge of the ramp, waiting. "—Name's Walter Webb. Walter here is tossing bags in the rear. The bottom on one of the bags rips and half of her falls out."

"Rats," mumbled the medical examiner. "Rats chewed holes

in the bag trying to get at her."

"What time?" I asked Nancy. "When Webb found her?" She said the sanitation worker had called 911 at 1:05 A.M. It was now 2:28.

Dick gently turned the battered face toward me. "This the woman that handed Cuddy the fish in the newspaper, right?"

I said, "No, it's not. That was Lupe Guevarra. This woman is her sister Maria. Lupe was upset, remember, because she couldn't find her."

"So here's why," Dick grumbled.

I told Nancy to drive over to Trinity Church as fast as possible and see if she could find Lupe Guevarra. She was supposed to be staying in the homeless shelter there. Twenty seconds later, I heard Nancy's siren shriek as she peeled out of the parking lot.

Dick estimated that the Garifuna woman had been dead as long as seventy-two hours. Someone had savagely crushed in her skull with a blunt force instrument. He showed me the multiple fractures, any one of which could have killed her. I asked him, "Gun butt, car jack, crowbar?"

He scratched at his narrow face. "Nah. Smoother. Round. Like a pipe. They're saying she picked up some work cleaning fish at the market here. Cuddy hauled the owner in—why should he sleep when I can't?—so you want to talk to the guy?" He jabbed a long hairy thumb at the back of the building. Then he motioned for the ambulance attendants. "Okay, Justin, we're going to lift her out now, head back with her. You agree with Cuddy? You think this is Guess Who–related or what?"

I said, "I think it's Guess Who–related."

Dick looked at me with an odd sort of awkwardness. "I feel bad I missed that stuff on G.I. Jane, you know? I mean this psycho had practically sawed her head off, but Chang caught the asphyxiation—guy's amazing."

"Don't worry about it, Dick. We all missed things. Well, if it hadn't been for the rats, by now this bag would be compacted under tons of garbage in the town landfill. We'd have never found her."

"Isn't that a problem? Doesn't Guess Who want you to find things?"

I said, "He's not proud of this one. He's just tidying up."

The medical examiner shrugged. "He's got a real hard-on about us, doesn't he? I mean HPD. What'd we do to him?" He yawned. "So why don't you people ever find bodies at three in the afternoon? See you later."

"You doing the autopsy tonight?"

"Why not? I'm up."

"I'll drop in. Thanks." I was watching Cuddy duck under the yellow tape. John Emory ran over to him with a computer printout.

I called to Augie Summers. Guess Who would want to discard the murder weapon as quickly as possible. He wouldn't want blood on his clothes or in his car. If he'd killed her here, he had most likely left both her body and the weapon for the garbage men to pick up. Augie and the two uniformed officers with him weren't happy when I told them that if they weren't able to find anything that resembled a blunt force weapon in the bag containing the body, they'd have to check all the garbage bags already loaded from this area into the truck or still piled in the passageway. I told them to look for something resembling a length of round metal pipe.

A light chilly drizzle had started to fall. As I walked over to Cuddy I pulled on the jacket I'd tossed in the Jaguar. Without looking at each other, we talked efficiently and impersonally about the victim's identity, the murder weapon, the likelihood that Guess Who had killed Maria Guevarra because she could identify him. The question was, could her sister Lupe identify the killer? And, if so, was there much chance that she was still alive? We did not talk about where and how he'd found me.

John Emory had just handed Cuddy a list of all Ford Explorers registered in the county that were blue, gray, or black, 1994–1999 models (the models that would match the gray fibers we'd collected as trace evidence on Kristin Stiller and Lucy Griggs). As soon as we'd learned the make of the vehicle, we'd started checking DMV records. There'd been 893 SUVs of that description on the original list. John had narrowed it down to 264. Back at the task force room, Rhonda was checking for any owners with criminal records. I called her, told her also to check whether any of the owners lived near or worked at Southern Depot. In the morning, HPD detectives would start interviewing the staff of all the stores in Southern Depot Mall to see if anyone had noticed a Ford Explorer in the area three days ago, if anyone had noticed a man talking to Maria Guevarra, or if anyone had noticed Maria Guevarra at all.

John Emory's cell phone rang. It was Nancy. She asked Roid to put me on. She was with Father Paul Madison in the parish hall of Trinity Church. Lupe Guevarra wasn't at the shelter and hadn't been there last night either. Two days ago, Paul had found her a Spanish-speaking lawyer to help her with her papers, she'd never shown up at the lawyer's office. Nancy was going to question other residents at the shelter. She'd get back to us. I asked Roid to call Detective Eddie Vega to see if the migrant woman had told him anything that might help. But my fear was that Lupe Guevarra was as dead as her sister, and for the same reason.

Then Roid handed me a folded manila envelope. "I meant to get this to you earlier, Justin, and I tried calling you, but it was weird. Bubba Percy answered your phone."

"Yeah, sorry, he ran off with my cellular. What's this?"

"Haver transcript. Lucy Griggs. They finally pulled a hard copy out of her department." He started to say something else about it, but just then a brown van with yellow stars on the doors and red lights on the roof pulled into the passageway, forcing us to jump out of its way. Sheriff Homer Louge hauled himself out of the van and pulled on his brown Stetson.

"Hey, Mangum, looks like you need some help," he called to Cuddy.

We waited as the sheriff loped toward us. "Having trouble sleeping, Homer?" Cuddy smiled. "Must be that investigation the county commissioners are putting you through. Least you can take it easy now. What'd they call it—leave of absence? I heard about that."

"You heard about it? You fixed it." Louge actually spit on the asphalt.

Cuddy pointed at the spittle. "I'm going to let this go with a warning. But spitting in public's against the law in the city of Hillston."

"You're not as smart as you think you are, Mangum." The sheriff stepped right up to Cuddy, almost chest-butting him.

Cuddy nodded. "Probably true," he said. Then he stepped back and walking around Louge made his way through reporters to the mall entrance.

I followed him. "I know I'm not supposed to mention Haver Forest, but I thought the deal was, the sheriff would stay out of this case completely."

Cuddy pulled me aside, staring strangely at a thought he was having. "I want you to put somebody on Louge right now and keep them on him."

"Tail Louge? Why?" I looked behind me. The sheriff leaned against the side of the patrol van, unwrapping a piece of gum, dropping the paper to the ground, watching the body loaded into the ambulance.

"What about him for Guess Who?" Cuddy looked at me for the first time.

"For Guess Who?" I was taken aback.

"Who knows more about us, who hates us more? Who's in and out of the Cadmean Building? Who was messing up the evidence at The Fifth Season as fast as he could? Who had two wives divorce him and a hushed up record of domestic violence?"

I looked around again as Louge walked over to where Augie Summers was dumping the contents of a trash bag onto a sheet of plastic. "Okay," I said. I called over John Emory and told him to follow Sheriff Louge until further notice. Roid asked no questions.

Like the small pretty bird of prey she resembled, Shelly abruptly darted at us again. "Come on, guys, this is a homeless woman somebody found in a garbage bag." She tugged at Cuddy.

"What's the big deal, why're you here?"

Cuddy shook his head. "Dignity of human life, Shelly. Don't they teach civics anymore?"

He walked ahead, leaving me to handle the determined reporter. I asked her if she'd gone to press yet with the quote about breaking the Guess Who case that I'd given her earlier at Pine Hills Inn: how Guess Who had made such stupid mistakes that we were close to an arrest. If Bunty Crabtree was right, being called stupid would agitate this man so much that maybe he *would* make a mistake. Despite the truth of everything Cuddy had just said about Louge, he just didn't feel like the man Bunty had described. And I trusted her description. She might have the wrong facts, but she was going to have the right personality.

Shelly said she still had an hour to file. I told her I was about to remake her career by telling her, and only her, that Maria Guevarra was a Guess Who killing. She was already on the phone as she ran off through the rain.

• • •

International Fish Market, known as IFM, was a very upscale shop selling fresh seafood and exotic luxury items like Japanese sashimi, Russian caviar, and New Zealand clams. The owner was a Vietnamese man in his sixties named Harry Minh. He had nothing much to tell us about Maria Guevarra or her sister Lupe, who had worked for him briefly but whose names he had never known. After he'd caught them food-foraging in back of the store, he had hired both for a few days at the end of last week because he was shorthanded. One of his cleaners had cut his hand open with a gutting knife, and Mr. Minh had fired another one for poor work habits.

"Too sloppy, too slow, I tell him, 'You history, you out of here.'"

I said, "So the Guevarra sisters were gutting fish for you?"

Yes, and they had apparently met Minh's high standards. "Work good, very fast." He'd paid them a total of forty dollars (which averaged a bit more than a dollar an hour each) three days ago and had seen neither since. Had they left together? He thought so. Had they bought or had he given them a whole flounder before they left? The question puzzled him. No, but it was quite possible that they'd stolen any number of fish from IFM. His workers robbed him all the time. Could he check in his records to see if anyone had bought a flounder, specifically a flounder, the last afternoon the Guevarras had worked here? It would take too much of his time, Mr. Minh told us. Finally he agreed to go through his receipts in the morning.

"C´am Ön anh," Cuddy told him in what I assumed was the Vietnamese he'd learned while over in that country in his teens.

"No problem," Mr. Minh replied, then turned away, uninterested in a dialogue about the bad old days.

I was looking around the store at the beautiful counters of all the varieties of fish, arranged like artworks on the ice, each species labeled by an exquisite handwritten card on a pin. My eyes moved along the rows—yellowfin tuna, halibut, coho salmon, pompano…. And then suddenly I saw a card that stopped my breath.

"Cuddy!" My urgency brought him to the counter. "It was a flounder, right? We're sure it was a flounder? The fish the chess piece was in?"

He still looked angry. "Yeah, flounder, fluke, it was a flatfish."

"A right-eye flounder or a left-eye?"

"Jesus, Justin, I don't know."

I pointed down at the neatly layered row of wide thin gray fish with both their filmy eyes on the right side of their flattened heads. Cuddy saw the sign and knew instantly what I meant. It read, "CURL FIN TURBOT."

"Turbot. Goddamn it, we missed it!"

We were both running, ignoring HPD staff shouting was there a problem? Cuddy yanked a young uniform right out of the cruiser where he sat behind the wheel eating a burrito.

The siren howled as we shot through the mall gates and raced past downtown stoplights at eighty miles an hour.

I asked him, "You know where Margy lives?"

"Yes!" He was calling her phone. No one answered. He called the dispatcher. Any car in the vicinity was to go to her address. Criminal assault in progress.

Judge Margy Turbot's home, a white frame Italian gothic with a mansard roof, was on one of the gentrified blocks of downtown Hillston, ten blocks from my own home. We made it there in five minutes from the time we left Southern Depot. Her BMW was in the driveway, which was hidden from the house by a tall border of boxwood shrubs. No one answered the bell. Through the windows we saw that lights were on and so was the television. Together we snapped the lock on the front door.

The large living room was wrecked, furniture knocked over, rugs awry, a phone on the floor, a broken glass. Cuddy kept calling, "Margy! Margy!" as we ran down the hall into a country kitchen. A great deal of work had gone into the renovated glass cabinets, the black granite counters and the brushed steel appliances. They were now splattered and smeared with so much blood the room looked like a butchery. "Oh Jesus God, no," Cuddy groaned.

In the middle of the terracotta floor was the woman who'd invested all the care and taste and cost in the room. The woman whose blood now covered the floor and cabinets. Still in the pearl gray suit she'd worn to dinner with us, Margy Turbot lay sprawled and twisted beneath a large oak cutting block. There was no question this time about how the victim had died. The bloody implements had been placed neatly back on the cutting board. She'd been struck repeatedly and savagely on the head with a large serrated wooden mallet. Her throat had been hacked open to the vertebrae with a Chinese chopping cleaver. A tin biscuit or cookie cutter had been jammed into her mouth to hold it ajar. Her chest had been hacked apart, the ribs broken back, the heart sawed out with a fillet knife.

"Fuck. Fuck. Fuck." Cuddy smashed his head so hard against the door frame that he cut open his forehead. "Stupid! How could I be so stupid?!"

The mallet, cleaver, knife, and cutter, slick with blood, lay side by side on the oak block. Beside them was a small white scale of the sort weight watchers use to count calories. A bloody human heart lay on this scale. Next to the heart stood the other queen from Cuddy's chess set.

A long-haired white Persian cat was rubbing back and forth against the dead woman's side until it saw us. It came over, rubbed against my legs and then ran away.

Chapter 29

Blitz

There were three cars at the Turbot house within minutes of our arrival. One of them was Shelly Bloom's. She'd followed Cuddy and me from Southern Depot. I'd spotted Shelly crawling around behind the high hedge of boxwood that formed a barrier between Margy's house and her driveway. The young reporter was trying to take a photograph through the living room windows. I grabbed her and pulled her back.

She looked torn between excitement and distress. "Come on, Justin. You told me you were this close to an arrest. How did he get her? I saw through the window. Judge Turbot was one of the best things in this good ole boy state. If you were so damn close, how did this happen?" I let go of her. I didn't have an answer.

I called John Emory. Where was Homer Louge? He said he had followed Homer to the ByWays Massage Parlor. The sheriff had gone into a trailer twenty-five minutes earlier and still hadn't come out. I told him to see if he could get any alibi out of Louge for the hours—I glanced up at the clock on Margy's kitchen wall—from ten P.M. 'til we saw him at the Southern Depot crime scene. A silence followed, then Roid said slowly, "An alibi for what, Lieutenant?"

"Judge Turbot's dead. Just see what you can pull out of him without making it formal. But don't let him get away from you."

An hour later, Margy Turbot, with her hands and head bagged, in a black plastic body pouch on a mortuary gurney, was wheeled from her house past a crowd of reporters and TV cameras. Carol Cathy Cane herself was there. Two bodies in one night and one of them a judge? It brought out the big guns. When Cathy (her hair and make-up perfect even at five A.M.) trotted toward us with her mike thrust out like an Olympic torch, Cuddy said in a dead voice, "Keep her away from me. I mean it."

I blocked the cameraman's path while Ralph Fisher led Cuddy past the police to a patrol car and drove him away from the scene. Cathy made the best of things by asking me if I was ready to admit that we had a serial killer running amok in Hillston. Was I ready to admit Hillston was in an absolute crisis, a disaster zone, that the whole town would soon panic and riot?

I said the town wouldn't panic unless people like her talked it into it.

"Three women, that's three, have now been murdered in one week!"

"I know that, Cathy."

By dawn, the bloody weapons, the chess queen, and the scale had been secured and booked into HPD property.

By dawn, every inch of the living room, hall, and kitchen had been videoed, dusted, and vacuumed by the Identification Section detectives, and the house sealed. Margy had been transferred to a stainless steel table where her body was photographed with an MP-4 Polaroid and scanned with a laser for prints. Trace evidence was being collected in small metal evidence boxes. Serological evidence was sought. Dick Cohen's external exam was being recorded on tape. Endocrine, urinary, hemic, biliary— the tests went on and on in the morgue while down the hall our task force supervised a county-wide dragnet for a Ford Explorer with gray carpet.

By dawn, we'd talked to Margy's ex-husband, a local tax lawyer, who seemed to me both very decent and very pained. He'd done what he could to help—including giving us his alibi (he'd been home with his new wife and two children all night).

He'd volunteered to call Margy's parents and they were now on their way to Hillston by plane from Florida.

By dawn, John Emory had called in with Sheriff Homer Louge's alibi. It was as solid as his third wife, his grown son, and his son's fiancée—all hefty people. With the three of them he'd been driving back from an emergency visit to his wife's sick mother in Cummings, Georgia. They'd all been inside the Haver County Sheriff's cruiser on I-85 from seven P.M. 'til nearly two A.M. Despite the late hour, Louge had then dropped off his family and headed out for a "massage" to relieve the stress of the trip, but had stopped along the way to check out the crime scene under the lights at Southern Depot.

So Homer Louge wasn't Guess Who. It was a blow to Cuddy. But at least, thank God, Roid had managed to elicit the alibi without having to confront the sheriff, who would have run straight to the city council, howling against HPD. Roid found out by calling Louge's family and pretending to be Mayor Carl Yarborough. I was proud of him.

As the sun came up, six of us—Bunty, Rhonda, Etham, Lisa Grecco, Cuddy, and myself—were still in Room 105 going over the scenario we'd pieced together. Lisa, for whom the young judge had been an admired role model, couldn't stop crying. Cuddy was still so beside himself, so maddened by his failure to stop the murder of his friend, that he periodically burst out in a rage of self-hatred. Why hadn't he taken Margy home? Why hadn't he picked up on the flatfish/turbot connection? Why hadn't he thought about the fact that his name was publicly linked with Margy's because of his support for her candidacy as state's attorney general—so that if Guess Who's purpose had been some deadly game of wits with Cuddy, he would naturally choose a woman Cuddy was known to like?

Privately Cuddy must have been cursing his myopic focus on Lee as the killer's inevitable next victim, for he'd done so out of emotions that Guess Who couldn't possibly be aware of, and the energy spent worrying about protecting Lee should have gone elsewhere. He asked himself endless questions. Why hadn't it dawned on him that the chess queen could symbolize Judge Turbot of Superior Court, the first lady of the judicial system in our county? "The queen of her court," a newspaper had actually called her only a month earlier. Clearly Guess Who was very aware of Margy's high position. He had weighed her heart on the scales of justice and placed the queen he'd taken from Cuddy beside it.

Cuddy was furious that he hadn't paid more attention to Paul Madison's books on early church saints. If he had, he would have noticed the book illustration that Bunty Crabtree was now showing him of St. Margaret. It hadn't registered on him that Margy's full name was Margaret (she never used it) and that Margaret was another of the martyrs whose head had been cut off. Bunty held up a picture of St. Margaret leading by a chain the dragon who'd swallowed her (as the chess queen had been swallowed by the fish) and then been forced to spit her out.

It was no consolation to Cuddy that none of the rest of us had been any smarter that he. Guess Who had challenged him personally. And won. Finally Bunty offered to call him in a prescription for a tranquilizer. Offended, he refused. It was Etham Foster who ultimately calmed him down by grabbing him from behind when he started kicking a dent in the wall. We'd just heard that Guess Who might have killed Margy as early as ten P.M., so that if Cuddy had driven home with her from the Pine Hills Inn, the assault might never have happened. Or if he hadn't told her he might drop by later, she might not have opened her door to the killer.

Etham told his police chief flatly, "You want to blame yourself, go home and do it. You're wasting our time." Then he unlocked his arms—long enough to reach the full length of the table that he pressed Cuddy against—and he let him go. When he did, Cuddy took a very slow deep breath, then turned around toward the task force. Everybody in the room looked as if they were playing a game of "Freeze."

Then Cuddy said, "Doctor D is right. I apologize. Excuse me." He left the room. When he returned, his hair and face were damp and he was calm.

Soon afterwards, Nancy came back from Trinity Church. An old woman living at the homeless shelter there had told her that two nights ago she'd watched from her bed as Lupe Guevarra had gotten up at three A.M., put together a bag full of clothes and food, and sneaked off. It had been her impression that Lupe was frightened. Immediately we sent out a description of the Garifuna migrant and wired the photo we'd taken of her to precincts up and down the East Coast.

Nancy brought us in the early edition of the July 3 *Hillston Star* with its "Exclusive! Guess Who Strikes Twice In One Night!" article by Shelly Bloom. In her scoop, she quoted the head of Hillston homicide (in other words, me) as saying, "We are extremely close to an arrest. Guess Who has made some serious and very stupid mistakes—sociopaths always do—and these errors have given us invaluable leads. I can't say anything more specific, but we have a prime suspect and his arrest is imminent."

"JayJay, what the hell does that mean?" Rhonda asked.

"It means flushing your pheasant," Bunty said, nodding at me.

Cuddy said, "It means the lieutenant's got twenty-four hours to make Shelly an honest woman."

I understood him completely. We didn't have a prime suspect. We needed to arrest one by July 4. It was July 3.

Nancy also brought news from Augie Summers at Southern Depot. As I'd suspected, the killer had thrust the murder weapon deep inside another of the hundreds of large garbage bags that lay piled in the loading area. The weapon was a short steel-handled grapple hook used for slinging fish around by the gills. The grip was caked in blood. There were no prints on it.

Nancy had already heard on the radio dispatch in her car that Judge Margy Turbot had been murdered that night. She sat down miserable. "Guess Who's killed three women in one week."

We were all very much aware of that.

An hour later, a message came from the morgue. By means of a chemical thermometer (the body loses one to two degrees of heat every hour after death), Dick Cohen now placed Margy's murder somewhere close to eleven. Rigor had just been setting in when we'd discovered her. So the killer now had more than a six-hour lead.

Tracing Margy's steps wasn't that difficult. She'd left the Pine Hills Inn at 9:30, dropped Dina Yarborough off at 9:50, declining an invitation to come in for a nightcap. There was no sign of a break-in at Margy's house; it seemed probable that Guess Who had arrived just after she returned home. She hadn't changed her clothes yet, but she had listened to her messages, poured herself a drink of single malt, turned on and muted a news channel, and fed her cat. Our best guess was that she'd incautiously answered her doorbell (perhaps assuming it was Cuddy).

Guess Who must have pushed his way in and struck her immediately, knocking the glass out of her hand. It looked from the disarray of furniture and rugs as if he'd knocked her uncon-scious right there at the door. Neighbors had heard no scream or sounds of a struggle. There were no defensive wounds or skin and hair traces under her nails to suggest that she'd fought her assailant. But what had he hit her with? With her skull so bat-tered and fractured by the wood mallet, would it be possible to distinguish a blow from a different blunt force instrument? It looked as if he'd then dragged her back into the kitchen (one of her shoes had caught in the phone line on the floor) and there found the means to finish the murder.

Bleary with lack of sleep, our stomachs in cramps from too much coffee, we went over the sequence again and again. I acted it out. "He drags her down the hall, drops her in the kitchen by the cutting board, beats in her head with the mallet. Then what? He uses the tin cutter to pry open her mouth? He does his thing before he hacks open her throat?"

Rhonda said yes. "The way her lips bled, looks like she was still alive when he jammed that cutter in her mouth. And you know why the son of a bitch did it too."

Cuddy called the morgue for the tenth time. Had Dick Cohen found any evidence of semen or pubic hair in the mouth cavity? No, Dick had not; he promised we'd know ASAP if he did.

Bunty was looking out the window at the slow purple lightening of the sky. She said quietly. "G.W.'s lost it. Lost control. And he hates that."

Cuddy studied her eyes. "It looked more like Jeffrey Dahmer in that kitchen. Blood splatter everywhere. At least ten blows to her throat, another dozen to her chest."

Bunty nodded. "He had to use his hands to break those ribs, pull that heart out. He wouldn't like that. Not at all. Our boy's always been into neat and tidy. Everything under control. Matches just so, candles just so. Everything's disintegrating on him now."

I pointed out, "There's no way, with that cleaver flying around, that he didn't get her blood all over him. I don't understand why there's *nothing* on the floor, walls, somewhere, on his exit route."

Rhonda studied the photos of Margy's cloth Roman shades pulled down over the three kitchen windows. "He dragged her back here unconscious, took off his clothes, cut her up, washed off in the sink—look at the water here on the counter—put his clothes back on and walked out."

I said, "Doesn't sound disintegrated. Sounds careful."

Lisa said, "But those clothes are blood soaked. Wherever they are."

"They're someplace we aren't going to find them, like the bottom of the Shocco River." Cuddy looked directly at me, almost the first time since he'd found me with Mavis. "Okay, that's it? Is Guess Who done? If he killed her just to show me he could do it, is that checkmate?"

It was hard for me to believe that the man who'd hacked the heart out of the breast of Margy Turbot would be able to stop now, even if he wanted to.

• • •

At seven in the morning on July 3, Bunty and Rhonda were asleep on air mattresses they'd inflated and set up in a corner. Lisa had gone home. Etham was back in his lab. Cuddy was down the hall in the morgue with Dick Cohen looking at autopsy results on Margy. I was studying a DMV list of Ford Explorer registrations that he had left on top of his briefcase. I noticed that among the five vehicles he'd circled was a black '97 model registered to a Dr. Roger Ferraro at 5171 Dumfries Court. Dumfries Court sounded familiar, but I couldn't place it. When I reached over into my jacket for my pen and note pad, the manila envelope that Roid had given me at Southern Depot fell out of the pocket. It was the information he'd obtained finally from the Registrar's Office at Haver University. I'd forgotten all about it.

Idly I read down the sheet cataloging Lucy Griggs's college courses for the four semesters she'd attended Haver:

> Eng. 21a. Brownlee B-
> Span. 125 Martinez A-

Then all of a sudden I saw something. I hadn't been looking for it, much less expecting it, and yet the instant my eyes fell on the name, I felt a sickening turn in my chest. In the spring term of Lucy's freshman year:

> Econ. 115 Kasdan A-
> Eng. 21b. de Grazia B+
> Intro Wm. Studies Auerbach A-
> Math. 201 Norris A
> Music Hist. 350 Korshin B+

And in the fall term of Lucy's sophomore year:

> Calculus 503 Norris A

And in the spring term of that year:

> Algebraic Topology Norris A

"Norris." She'd taken three courses with Tyler Norris. Professor Tyler Norris of the Haver University Mathematics Department. Tyler Norris who'd just been found not guilty of murdering his wife, who'd been set free by Judge Margy Turbot. Over two years, Lucy Griggs had repeatedly taken courses with Norris, the only courses in which she'd received straight As.

The key turned and all the doors blew open onto a vista of hell. I couldn't stop myself from seeing flashes of Norris's face. The way he'd turned and smiled so chillingly at me in the courtroom after Margy Turbot sent the jury out. The terrible rage suffusing his face as his father unctuously signed the autograph on his book of poems at Southern Depot. Last night, the way he was looking at Margy as we walked out of the Pine Hills Inn. Other images rushing back through the months since I'd arrested him. The chess pieces. Norris was a chess whiz; as a small child he could play five games simultaneously. Norris and Rosethorn outside the Tucson. Norris. Norris.

I made myself close my eyes and concentrate on deliberate deep breaths. Lucy Griggs had also taken more than one course with someone named Martinez and had done very well in them. It didn't mean she was having an affair with that teacher, it didn't mean Martinez had killed her.

The image of Tyler's smile would not go away.

I looked at the Hillston map that we'd pinned to the corkboard. Dumfries Court had sounded familiar because it was in Balmoral Heights, only three blocks from the Norris house on the Tartan Drive cul de sac. I went back to the DMV list and found three more Explorers registered in the same neighborhood. I circled the owners' names.

Nancy came quietly to the door with a bag of breakfast biscuits. I motioned her back into the hall. She said, "Are they asleep?" I nodded. "What's wrong with you, you look like total shit."

It was true that I was unshaven, wearing last night's clothes, and probably smelling of the alcohol Mavis and I had consumed. I sidestepped the question. "Nancy, I need something fast. What kind of car does Tyler Norris drive? And I want the car color on these registrations!" I thrust the circled DMV list at her. "Don't ask. Just go!"

She stared at me, spun around, and took off. I hurried back into the room, looked up the Norris home phone number and called it. The phone seemed to ring forever, but finally he picked up and groggily said, "Hello?" It was Tyler himself, I was sure of that. I hung up the phone without speaking, went back out into the hall, and paced its length. I lit a cigarette although there were NO SMOKING signs at both ends of the hall.

Was I crazy? My brain felt tangled like a packet of firecrackers. Each "pop!" set off another. Dick Cohen had groused, "He's got a real hard-on about us, doesn't he? I mean HPD. What'd we do to him?" But if it was Norris, how easy to answer. What had we done to him? We'd charged him with murder and put him on trial for his life. We: the Hillston Police Department and the judge who'd made it almost apparent that in her heart she believed him guilty. The tag on G.I. Jane had said,

> LT. JUSTIN SAVILE V,
> PLEASE DELIVER YOUR FRIEND TO:
> CAPTAIN C.R. MANGUM
> HILLSTON POLICE DEPARTMENT

The tape in my car, the star in Cuddy's apartment, the gun returned to the display case, it was all overkill to pay us back, to prove that he was going to win. Tyler and Linsley Norris lived in Balmoral Heights. Kristin Stiller had been found near the new construction area there. What if Kristin had discovered that Tyler was Lucy's married lover and she was blackmailing him? What if Lucy had decided to force her lover's hand? According to Mavis, Lucy had bragged that the married man's life was under her control. "And he knows it too." She must have had proof then. Letters? Photos?

Nancy came running back into the hall. "I don't believe it, Justin! You're smoking? You quit years ago."

"What about Norris's car?"

She handed me a slip of paper. "Volvo station wagon. 1995. White. His wife had a Lexus, but he sold it after she died. Why do you want to know? Crap, I can't believe you're smoking!"

Of the four Ford Explorers in Balmoral Heights, the only one of a color that coordinated with gray carpeting belonged to

Roger Ferraro on Dumfries Court. He was a professor of the history of science at Haver, with a specialty in eighteenth-century navigational instruments. According to the secretary of the department whom Nancy had called, Professor Ferraro and his family were spending the entire academic year in Greenwich, England, and had left their house in the care of neighbors. I said, "Come on, Nancy. Let's go."

"Go where?"

"Why do you keep asking me questions?"

"Because that's what you taught me to do."

• • •

At the door of the large gray-stained fake French chalet where so many months ago I'd watched another woman, Linsley Norris, carried out on a gurney in a plastic pouch and wheeled down a brick walk to an ambulance, Nancy and I waited for someone to answer the bell.

"This is crazy, Justin. We're gonna get our butts fried," Nancy whispered as we heard locks click and the door open.

In black Lyrca biking pants and a Haver sweatshirt, Tyler Norris stood there with a mug of coffee. The mug demonstrated that he'd donated to public radio. I could see a razor-thin Italian twenty-speed bicycle leaned against the wall beside him. I looked down at his feet. Nike running shoes.

"What do you want?" he said coldly.

"This is Officer Caleb-White. Could we come in and talk to you, Professor Norris?"

"No, you can't. What's this about?"

I explained that we were looking for a black Ford Explorer that might have been used in the commission of a local homicide. Such a car was registered to a neighbor of his, a Dr. Roger Ferraro. Dr. Ferraro was out of the country and another neighbor had just told us that she had the impression that Professor Norris was checking on his house for him. She thought she'd seen Norris driving the Ferraro car.

Norris's flat blue eyes glanced from me to Nancy and back to me. And it was then that I saw it in his eyes. Deep down in the iris, yet unmistakable. A scared but smug evil. He'd killed them. He'd enjoyed it. I knew it.

We stared at each other, all the truth going on in our eyes. My bland question: had he driven his fellow faculty member's Ford Explorer?

"No, I haven't," he said curtly. "Which neighbor supposedly said this?" I didn't answer him. He swung the door. "I'm calling your superiors."

I quickly shoved my shoe in the opening. "You didn't use the Explorer last night?" He shook his head. I kept my voice low-key, nonchalant. "Where did you go last night after you and your parents left Pine Hills?"

His lips moved but nothing came out. He stretched his mouth as if his jaw hurt. "You're trespassing." he finally said.

"Just tell me where you were last night between ten and midnight."

"All I'll tell you is if you ever appear on my property again, I'll file a suit against this city that will bankrupt it." The door closed. It didn't slam. He was in control. But the coffee in his mug trembled.

Five minutes later, I was shoving Nancy through a small window in the rear of the locked Ferraro garage a few blocks away but easily reachable by a wooded path from the Norris backyard. I heard her footsteps moving inside the garage, then silence, then she stepped back to the window. "Yeah. It's in there. Locked and alarmed. I can't get the carpet fiber. But it's black. Gray cloth carpet. Somebody's drove it. Still damp from last night's rain. And some wet oil on the tarmac under the engine."

I helped pull her back through the small window. She hopped down effortlessly. "There's something stuck under the wheel frame. It's wet too." She said it was a tiny twig of leafy boxwood. I remembered there was boxwood bordering Margy Turbot's house.

Chapter 30
Stalemate

Half an hour later, two HPD officers sat in a line-repair truck in Haver Power Company outfits a block away from Tyler Norris's home. If Tyler drove out of his house, John Emory (looking like an investment banker in a BMW) would pick him up at the single gated entrance to Balmoral Heights and follow him wherever he went. Nancy headed back to Lucy Griggs's apartment to look for anything that would tie Norris personally to his dead student—best of all any letters or photos. Other detectives were talking again with Lucy's mother, friends, and classmates for clues to the relationship between the dead girl and her math professor.

On my way to the Cadmean Building, I kept reconfiguring the variables that dozens of us had already worked on hard and long. Over and over Tyler Norris made sense of them. Tyler Norris was Guess Who. He'd killed his wife Linsley Norris and gotten away with it. Now there'd been four more murders, maybe even five. Kristin Stiller. Lucy Griggs. Maria Guevarra and, I feared, her sister Lupe. Margy Turbot. Presumably he'd killed Kristin and Lucy because they'd threatened him with blackmail. Presumably he'd killed the Guevarra sisters because, after he'd used them to pass messages to us, they could identify him. And he'd killed Margy for no cause but to take revenge on her and us—because we'd sat in judgment on him and believed him guilty. I had no doubt that he'd murdered those women. I'd seen it in his eyes. But a chilling look was far from proof. Without proof, we couldn't stop him. If we didn't stop him, he would kill someone else. And how could we stop him when we'd already been warned by the mayor and the city council, by the district attorney and by the attorney general of the state, not ever to go near him again?

As I parked the old Jaguar, I saw Isaac Rosethorn in his rumpled black suit and Miss Bee Turner in her crisp bright blue suit heading together into Pogo's, a favorite restaurant of local lawyers because of its proximity to the county jail. Everyone knew that Isaac and Bee had been "dating" for a good three or four decades but that she refused to socialize with him during any trial in which she was clerk and he was defense attorney. One local lawyer quipped that he never had to wait for the news to know when the jury had given its verdict in a big case; he could tell by whether Isaac was eating lunch alone or with Miss Turner.

Following the two inside, I ordered a bloody mary at the bar. The next morning's bloody mary for the headache from the night before; the old bad habits were quickly coming back. It was just after eleven, so the place was quiet. Shortly after the courtrooms emptied at noon, it would be impossible even to reach the bar. In the long mirror, I could see Isaac gallantly holding out a chair for Miss Turner at "his" table. Drawn directly on the walls of Pogo's were cartoon drawings of Hillston's civic and legal luminaries. There was one of Cuddy. There was one of Judge Margy Turbot that already had a funeral wreath of white carnations on a stand beneath it. Isaac always sat at a table beside a large color caricature of himself wiping tears from his eyes with a huge white handkerchief as he addressed a jury. Waiting for my drink, I walked back to their table where we talked quietly for a moment about Margy's murder. They speculated about whether she would have been tempted by Cuddy's "plan" to get her nominated as state's attorney general.

Isaac didn't think so. "One of my Slim's problems has always been his abysmal inability to understand women." This remark evoked a suppressed ironic cough from Bee Turner who'd been misunderstood by Rosethorn for forty years. "The Supreme Court," he explained. "That was Margy's dream. The Supreme Court." Isaac sighed. "Ah dear dear dear. She was really a very good young judge. Neither a bleeding nor a hard heart. A wise heart."

I said, "The killer cut out her heart and left it on a kitchen scale."

So they had heard. We sat in silence for a while.

"Judge Turbot was very knowledgeable about the law." Miss Turner patted the blue silk peony on her lapel. "And she trusted the law."

I looked hard at Isaac. "Maybe if she'd been a little more skeptical about trusting her last jury, she wouldn't be dead now." The old man's head came up sharply to meet my glare and read it.

Sometime later, I watched in the mirror as Isaac said goodbye to Miss Turner, then shuffled over to the bar. Unlike most people in my life (and therefore a relief), he didn't appear to care (or notice) that I was an unshaven wreck, both smoking and drinking; in fact, he took one of my Luckies and lit it. For a while he stared at me from behind the smoke, like a woeful Saint Bernard in a snowstorm, until finally I said, "Is there something the matter?"

"You tell me, my boy." Blue smoke swirled from the fleshy lips up into the tangled white eyebrows. "Tell me why you just suggested that you think Tyler Norris murdered Margy Turbot."

I finished my drink, held it up for another. "I think he not only killed her—and his wife, of course—he killed his mistress Lucy Griggs and three other women. I think Tyler Norris is Guess Who."

Isaac studied me carefully. "On what basis have you arrived at this very alarming conclusion? What evidence is there for this?"

"I'm not sure I should tell you what evidence. Look what you did with our evidence last time. It never got into the trial."

He sighed. "I did nothing with your evidence; I did much with Homer Louge's contamination of your evidence." Hostile stares greeted our return to the table that a quartet of waiting public defenders had been eyeing. The old attorney sat down. "Tyler's trial is over. And he can't be retried for what happened to his wife."

"I'm talking about the five other women he killed."

Issac's mournful eyes widened skeptically. "What five?"

"The one he was sleeping with, the one who was blackmailing him, the two who were planting false clues for him, and his judge."

He frowned. "His mistress Lucy Griggs. Is that theory or fact?"

"She took three classes from Tyler at Haver. She got As in all three."

Isaac looked at me thoughtfully. "That makes her his student Lucy Griggs. It's theory then."

"Her ex-boyfriend John Walker paid a woman named Kristin Stiller to find out who the man was that Lucy had left him for. Kristin found out. The man killed her. She's G.I. Jane. The man's Tyler."

We stared at each other. Pogo's was crowded and noisy, with groups of impatient lawyers glaring at other lawyers who were lingering over their checks too long. Then, without a comment, Isaac pushed himself up from the table, leaning on his cane. "I have an appointment," he said.

I was surprised. "You're not even going to tell me I'm crazy?"

He looked sadly at the wall where a funny caricature of Margy Turbot dressed as a little girl, playing with a doll of Justice, was half hidden by the bouquets of fresh flowers. "Tell Slim to come see his old friend. I'm always home." He pointed at a caricature of the district attorney Mitchell Bazemore on the wall. "Mitch has a pure heart." He shrugged. "But without understanding. Linsley's sister, Dr. Roth, for example. Mitch had her as a witness and didn't seem to know what he had there...."

I looked at him sharply. "What are you telling me?"

"I'm not telling you anything. I'm only suggesting Dr. Roth might have something to tell you."

• • •

By the time I made it back to Cuddy's office, a furious Carl Yarborough was in there with Mitch Bazemore, yelling about HPD's renewed harassment of Tyler Norris. "For God's sakes, Cuddy," Carl spluttered. "You knew how thin this ice was with the council. We just had this conversation! And right after it, what happens? Not only do we get a night in hell—a murdered woman in a garbage truck and a popular judge butchered in her own kitchen—because you can't catch this maniac—"

"Carl, you want to watch what you say—" Cuddy spoke quietly but dangerously.

"You got the press crawling right back up your you-know-whats, and all your people can think of to do is run over and hassle an innocent man you just got your asses reamed for dragging through a murder trial! I told you, go by the book. I told you, leave Norris alone."

Cuddy sat behind his desk. The wooden Costa Rican chess set was back in place except for the two queens, sealed with other evidence in the property room. He quietly jumped a knight across the board. "You through?"

Mitch Bazemore, rhythmically squeezing his biceps, stood next to the mayor, nodding like a choral refrain. "You knew you had to go by the book."

Cuddy glanced up, saw me, said, "What isn't by the book here, Mitch?"

"Listen, Mangum, Ken Moize is your buddy not mine. He's acting A.G. and he's the one just chewed my ear off that the Norris book is closed, finished, finito, over with, the end."

"I think I get your drift."

"Don't you get sarcastic with me."

Cuddy motioned me over. "Justin, did you just visit Tyler Norris at his home?" I nodded yes. "Did you just accuse him—for some reason I'm not privy to—of murdering Judge Turbot?"

"No, I did not. I asked him some questions." I explained about the DMV list directing us to the neighbor's black Ford Explorer.

Cuddy nodded toward Carl. "Well, I'm afraid the mayor here just had a phone call from Tyler Norris's lawyer—"

"You mean Isaac Rosethorn?" I asked.

"No, he doesn't mean Rosethorn. He means Amory Waller." Carl named the most successful civil litigation lawyer in the state, the man who'd taken on tobacco companies and won. "Mr. Waller told me that the commander of the Hillston homicide division—"

"You," explained the D.A., jabbing his forefinger at me.

"Thanks, Mitch," I told him.

Mitch read from notes. "—Tried to force his way into Norris's private residence this morning in order to continue making the same type of libelous accusations that led to Norris's false arrest for homicide last March."

"I asked Norris where he'd been last night between ten and midnight. That's all. I think it's interesting he interpreted it the way he did."

Cuddy tilted his head, studied me curiously. "Why'd you go over there and ask him anything?"

I took a breath. "He killed Margy."

"What?" In his surprise, Mitch Bazemore shouted the word.

"I think he killed Kristin Stiller too. And Lucy Griggs and both the Guevarra sisters. I think it very probable that Lupe Guevarra is dead. God knows if we'll ever find her. I think Tyler Norris is Guess Who."

The three men stared at me. Carl took the unlit cigar out of his mouth, put it back, took it out again. Then he shook his head. "I don't know if you're crazy or drunk or both, and I realize you've been under a lot of personal stress, Justin. But that kind of wild accusation never leaves this room. I'm not having this city bankrupted by litigation from the Norris family. A jury found him innocent. Drop it. The district attorney here—"

Mitch actually stepped forward as if summoned.

"—instructs you to drop it. The acting attorney general instructs him to instruct you. Is that clear enough? Drop it."

I said, "What if he did it?"

Carl furiously lit his cigar until smoke puffed around him like a steam engine leaving the station. "Sure, a Haver math professor ran around killing women for fun while he was in the middle of a trial for killing his wife which he didn't even do!"

Mitch forgot himself and muttered, "Well, he did do it."

"Don't you start." Carl pointed the cigar at him. "The jury found him not guilty. He went through a nightmare and it's over. He's innocent in the eyes of the law." The mayor turned the cigar on Cuddy and shook it at him. "This is what comes of that bullshit of yours! All that 'I'll resign if we haven't caught him by the Fourth of July!' Obviously your staff is determined to bring you a suspect if they have to handcuff the goddamn Pope. Jesus H. Christ!" The mayor strode heavily out of the room, slamming the door so that the circular dartboard on the back fell off. There was a campaign poster of Sheriff Homer Louge taped to the board with darts stuck all over his grinning face.

Mitch stepped over the circular board. "Mangum, I'm instructing you to put Savile here on unpaid leave as of right now, pronto, this minute." He kicked at the black wood board with Louge's picture. "And this is puerile."

Cuddy hung the board back on the door after Mitch left. "What did he say? Homer Louge is puerile?"

I sat down. "Yeah and then something about me and Tonto."

His face gray with exhaustion, Cuddy went behind his desk. "No, I believe the last bit was about me tossing you out of here pronto. Got an argument why I shouldn't?" He pulled off his hushpuppy loafers, crossed his long white-socked feet on the corner of the desk, leaned back, and opened his arms. "How many days have you been drinking now?"

"I'm not drunk."

"You're not sober. You're back to smoking. You're back to drinking. You're back to the guy I first met a long time ago and didn't much like. Fucking up and fucking off and fucking on the job. Oh, one difference. Now you're married to a very nice woman who deserves better."

Stung, I pulled out a pack of cigarettes and waved them at him. "I least I'm just *smoking* tobacco." I gestured across at the window where a billboard atop a huge complex of brick buildings said HAVER TOBACCO COMPANY. "So if I were you, I wouldn't be talking about—" I stopped myself.

Cuddy lowered his long bony legs from the table, leaned forward and said with a quiet deadly seriousness. "If I were you, Justin, I wouldn't compare my feelings for Lee Brookside, my long unhappy hope of marrying Lee Brookside, with your," he came around the desk toward me, "with your diving back into the bottle so you could punish Alice by screwing a rock star you met two weeks ago." He walked rapidly around the perimeter of his office, and out the door.

After a while, he came back. I made myself look at him. I was surprised, not by the accusations—they were true—but by his sense of my motive. "Punish Alice?"

He'd thought about what he was going to say. "Way down deep, you've been blaming Alice for Copper's death. That's what I think. I don't mean consciously. But you shut that baby out of your life—you won't even have any pictures of him anywhere around. And you shut Alice out. And it's not her fault."

• • •

After a time, he found me sitting on the stone steps of the Cadmean Building. City workers and policemen looked at me curiously as they sidestepped around me. I must have looked like a derelict—dirty clothes, tangled hair, unshaven, sitting on the steps, smoking. Cuddy sat down on the step below mine. He said, "I apologize. It's none of my business."

I nodded, ground the cigarette under my shoe.

"Okay?"

"Okay."

He let the silence fade, then he said, "You think Tyler Norris is Guess Who. Convince me."

For the next half hour I talked through my theory. When I finished, Cuddy started asking questions. For most but not all I had good answers. He listened to them. Then I said, "It's got to be your call. You've had direct orders not to investigate Norris.

I've got Roid tailing him in a BMW rental."

"What's Norris up to?"

"Just driving around town for hours. He hasn't gotten out of his car. You want me to pull Roid off him?"

He thought about it then he shook his head. "You didn't ask me that question so I didn't tell you so you left Roid on the case."

I nodded. "I didn't hear anything you just said."

We went back inside and walked downstairs to Room 105. Bunty Crabtree and Rhonda Weavis were the only ones there just then. Cuddy told them, "Justin's got an idea. I want to know what you two think about it."

We sat down together. This is the theory I told them:

Tyler Norris was having an affair with Lucy Griggs, a student who'd signed up three times for courses with him at Haver University. When his wife found out about the affair, he killed her—now we had the motive—and disguised the murder as a botched burglary. Meanwhile, Kristin Stiller was tailing Lucy on John Walker's behalf. Kristin found out about Lucy's affair with Tyler (maybe even suspected the killing) and she tried to blackmail him. By that time, Cuddy and I were already investigating Norris for the murder of his wife. He couldn't afford to have his affair exposed; it would provide the prosecution with the ammunition it needed. So he met with Kristin on Christmas Eve, just before she was to leave for Maryland with Bo (Belle) Derek. At their meeting, they made some kind of arrangement—no doubt he began paying her off. She decided to stay in Hillston to collect.

But by mid-January their deal had fallen apart. To remove the threat, Tyler murdered her by choking her to death. And then, remembering a homicide that had taken place in Neville a few months earlier—a prostitute with her throat cut, wearing only a Guess T-shirt—he cleverly disguised Kristin to look like the second victim of a publicity-hungry serial killer. "Addressing" Kristin's body to the head of homicide and the chief of police was something such a killer might do. Tyler was even luckier than he'd hoped. Carol Cathy Cane announced that a Guess Who Killer was loose in the Piedmont. The press not only bought the double murders, they promoted them. They started screaming that a serial killer was on the loose.

Tyler's scene-setting also was a way of taunting the police who had forced him to stand trial for his life. But he couldn't resist all those extra touches, what Nancy had called the redundancies, touches created out of his own particular sick and sickening psyche. The idea of virgin martyrs meant something specific to him. Perhaps it had to do with the fact that his mother and his wife were both Catholic. At any rate, when he'd read about the murder of Cathy Oakes, how all her bones were broken, he must have thought of the Catholic St. Catherine broken on the wheel. He knew his own victim's name was Kristin, Christine. So he cut out her tongue and decapitated her. He added the halo of matches, the stone around her neck with the ring of the bride of Christ, and he covered her with leaves, on the edge of the subdivision where he lived, Balmoral Heights. If she wasn't found, fine. If she was found, everything was in place to mislead us.

As it happened, not only did months go by before Kristin's body was found, but we couldn't identify her when we did find it. Cuddy was probably right: the bridge where the Shocco River fed into Pine Hills Lake was little more than a mile from the Balmoral Heights subdivision. By now the young Swedish woman's duffel bag (with all the belongings she'd planned to take on her car trip to Maryland with Bo Derek) probably lay rotted in the deep weedy mud of the lake bottom. They'd probably been joined last night by the bloody clothes Tyler had worn out of Margy Turbot's house.

In March, we had arrested Norris for the murder of his wife. In June, the state put him on trial. He was actually shocked that we'd had the guts to do it. The press was behind him, public opinion was behind him, the university and powerful family and friends were behind him, and only Lucy Griggs threatened him, a last loose end to tie up. And yet he had to stand trial for his life. It enraged him. The Hillston police, Cuddy and I in particular, must have come to represent to Tyler the one enemy between him and freedom. His hatred and contempt (and fear) grew as he faced first an indictment, then a judge who suspected his guilt.

At some point Tyler decided he would take his revenge by making fools of all of us while, at the same time, solving the growing problem of Lucy Griggs by murdering her. Perhaps Lucy had discovered (or deduced) that he'd killed Kristin Stiller and/or his wife. Perhaps she had threatened to reveal their affair midway through his murder trial. (Hadn't she told Mavis, "I hold his life in the palm of my hand"?) Maybe she had wanted him to marry her or maybe all she wanted was help with her musical career. Whatever she wanted, it was more than he was willing to give.

What a coup—to commit a third murder while on trial for a first! And then to pass the Lucy Griggs homicide off as another Guess Who killing. More delicious still, to pass it off as the intended murder of Mavis Mahar.

And again, it all worked beautifully. Tyler was free to carry out the murder of Lucy because Judge Turbot had granted him a million-dollar bail (paid for by his father whom he apparently hated). Having spotted Lucy at the Tucson Lounge, he was free to follow her and Mavis Mahar to The Fifth Season. He shot her there while she indulged in the trespass of showering in her idol's suite after Mavis wandered off drunk and passed out.

Bunty and Rhonda looked at me, at each other, back at me. Rhonda asked me how did the Guevarras fit in.

I told them Tyler had hired the migrant workers to take things and leave things in the Cadmean Building as he bid them. Migrant workers were scabbing during the strike for most of the city government offices there. No one ever pays much attention to cleaning ladies. Among his six languages, Tyler spoke fluent Spanish. He had cajoled or threatened and paid the Guevarra sisters to slip the envelope with the Mavis head shot under Cuddy's door, to slip the package with Lucy's eyes and the .38 shell into the HPD mail pouch. Maybe he had used them to steal and then to replace the Italian pistol in the lobby display. Tyler himself would evoke no surprise if seen in the Cadmean Building. He was, after all, there every day for his trial.

Rhonda and Bunty heard me out. Afterwards they looked at each other some more as if they could talk without speaking. I had no idea what they were saying. Finally Bunty said to leave her alone to think. That was fine with me. I had to go to Haver Hospital. I said I'd be back in an hour or so. Meanwhile, Isaac Rosethorn wanted to see Cuddy as soon as possible.

"You told him this theory of yours about Tyler Norris?" Cuddy asked. I nodded. "And he said he wants to see me?" I nodded.

"Old windbag," snorted Rhonda. "He defend anybody wasn't guilty?"

"He defended me all my life," Cuddy told her.

Rhonda patted me on the arm. "Well, if JayJay here hasn't gone psycho on us, maybe your friend Isaac shouldn't have done such a good job defending Tyler Norris. Maybe if he hadn't, your friend Margy Turbot's life wouldn't have been so short."

Bunty was studying the huge folders of notes I'd brought her—all the records I'd kept on the Linsley Norris homicide, including all interviews, depositions, and a transcript of the trial. She looked up. "Are you saying Tyler was having this affair at the same time he got his wife pregnant?"

"It can happen."

"Let's find out if it did," she said and started to read.

Rhonda stretched her strong wide hand over the map of Hillston to touch both Tartan Drive and the wooded area where Kristin Stiller's body had been found. Then she pulled herself up onto the table. "Bunty, psychology's not going to do it for us, baby, no time. We gotta get a direct physical connection between him and a victim fast. What about the pubic hair on Kristin? Don't we have blood of his booked on the Linsley Norris homicide?"

I said, "Yeah, but no DNA breakdown. His blood was all over because of his own injury, so there was no argument. We can send it off, but that kind of lab work takes weeks and Chang wasn't sure about the integrity anyhow."

Rhonda looked at me. "You know what we need?"

I nodded. "What we need's that Ford Explorer of his neighbor's with Margy's boxwood under its wheel hood."

"JayJay, you're reading my mind."

Cuddy said, "I've got direct orders for HPD not to go near that car."

I had an idea. I said, "You won't have to."

On my way out, I stopped at the desk where Sergeant Brenda Moore was re-glueing a long pink nail to her baby finger. She said, "I hear you're smoking again, Justin. Bad bad bad."

"Yeah, well, I hear you were parked in front of Dairy Queen again last night." Brenda was overweight and blamed it on the seductions of Dairy Queen banana splits.

She came around the booking desk, her hands comically posed on her wide hips, and leaning over did a short shimmy, shaking her large-breasted figure. "I guess you rather hear a skinny little white girl singing the blues, is that it? I saw you at Smoke's last night falling all over Mavis Mahar. Here, take these." She handed me an opened pack of cigarettes. "Ralph asked me to hide them from him. 'Least he's *trying* to quit. Oh and, listen, that big redhead works for the governor—"

"Bubba Percy?"

"He left this for Cuddy." It was a postcard with a huge hog that read, "Greetings Pig King. Only two more shopping days 'til the Fourth of July!"

"Don't give that to Cuddy."

"Like I would." She flipped it into the trash. "Plus he said give you this." She handed me my cellular phone. "Call him at eight o'clock tonight. Tell him it's a big emergency and he's got to get somewhere right away."

"Why?"

She rolled her eyes. "Man, I don't know. I don't why he felt like he could ask me if I'd had silicone implants either."

I said, "You look like a natural woman to me."

She laughed. "Take it on faith, baby."

I asked Brenda what had happened to the young Pope she'd booked a few nights ago for joyriding. "I think he's Graham Pope's son. He plays with a group called the Mood Disorders."

She rolled her eyes. "Griffin Torii with two *I*s?" I nodded.

"You call what he was doing joyriding? Joyriding is when me and my man shoot down to Charlotte for the NASCAR races in our own Buick LeSabre that we're making our own payments on. You call what Griffin does 'stealin.'" She went back to her desk where she checked a sheaf of papers. "We already booked his ass again. Failure to appear on grand theft auto."

"He's in the holding cell now?"

"Honey, that cell is Griffin Pope's *pied a terre*. He picks up cars like some folks pick up loose grapes at the Food Lion. You could put your car in a vault in the basement of Fort Knox and he'd steal it. He'd steal the Pope-mobile with the Pope still waving from the back seat and say because of the name he thought it belonged to his family. Now I got to call his poor Mama to come back down here and bail him out again."

I told her I would call Paula Pope about her son's bail. I wanted to talk with the young man anyhow.

Brenda applied glue to another long square nail tip and stuck it to her finger. "Well I hope you take that harmonica away from him. You white people should stick to the accordion."

I slid the cigarettes into my pocket. "Brenda, is it fair not to let us white people play music just because we don't happen to be as good at it as you are?"

She cheerfully gave me the finger with a freshly applied nail. "Well, sweetheart, no fairer than how y'all wouldn't let us read, vote, marry, move, or fart just because we happened to be slaves."

• • •

Since I'd seen him last, Griffin Pope had dyed his red hair a greenish-yellow that cast an unfortunate jaundiced hue on his pimpled face. His harmonica playing was as misguided as Brenda had claimed; it might even be called tragic—evoking as it did both pity and fear. Griffin was glad to see me, particularly when I told him I'd arranged for his release until his next court date. As for the small favor I needed him to do for me as soon as he left here, "No problem." His mother and father had always both spoken well to him of Captain Mangum and myself. He added with contempt, "And that's about all my Conehead parents got in common, except I'm shit-for-brains. Now they're mad 'cause I didn't ask them to my wedding at the beach. My dad tells Brittany she's dumber than road kill. Then he's mad 'cause she don't want them there on the happiest day of her life."

Apparently this marriage ceremony, in the surf at Wrightsville Beach (he carried a photograph from it in his wallet—the groom shirtless in white baggy shorts, the bride in a white halter and a wrap-around skirt, both carrying big sunflowers, the minister straddling a surf board), was the reason he had failed to attend his recent hearing on a charge of auto theft. "Give me a break," he said indignantly. "How many times does a man get married?"

"Well, Griffin, I hope not as often as he steals a car."

"Hey, exactly." He nodded eagerly, vindicated. "So what's this favor?"

I asked him if he knew where Balmoral Heights was. He told me he did indeed. Sometimes he and Brittany drove around in the new subdivision looking at the houses. They wanted to move there. "We've had it with East Hillston, it's nothing but trailer trash."

A half-hour later the young Pope pointed out to me his favorite Dutch Colonial with its two-car garage option as I drove him twice past the empty Ferraro house on Dumfries Court. Since standard model houses on sixty-foot lots began at three-hundred forty-nine thousand dollars in Balmoral Heights, I suggested to Griffin that he needed to think about a different career path. Music and larceny weren't going to do it for him. He admitted that Brittany couldn't agree with me more. Far from the bimbo his meathead dad thought her, Brittany was in accounting at The Fifth Season and had already talked to the manager about maybe Griffin's starting a limo service there to take guests to the airport and golf courses and such. I said I thought that was an excellent idea, particularly since Griffin was so obviously fond of driving.

When Griffin hopped out of my car at the corner of Dumfries Court, I wished him luck. He said, "I don't need luck, I got talent. Brittany thinks I got talent. And I do." Another Pope male had found the right woman. He headed blithely to the Ferraro house to steal their car.

Chapter 31
Sacrifice

Despite Cuddy's lectures to me about not visiting my mother, I actually dropped in to see her in Haver Hospital every day. Usually, as now, I came around five in the evening, the moment she had once called "sherry time"—when she'd sat with us at home hearing about our school days as she sipped a tiny amount of that amber liquid from a tiny crystal glass engraved with her family *D* for Dollard. Mother was in the hospital with pneumonia. She'd contracted it while recovering from a broken hip. But there was a problem from which it seemed unlikely she would ever recover. My mother, who once in her life could play by heart the Goldberg Variations, the Chopin Etudes, the Beethoven piano sonatas, now at times could not remember her address or her phone number or the names of her sons.

When my father resigned as Dean of Haver Medical School, he was supposed to retire, as he'd promised my mother he would. Instead, he took on the directorship of Haver Hospital in order to oversee the construction of a new wing that had been donated by old Briggs Cadmean. After the wing was finished, there was another reason why he couldn't leave. And then another. He died in Haver Hospital while still its director. Mother so disliked the place that it was some comfort to think that although she'd been here for over a month, she often had no idea where she was.

The present was receding from her, pulling her down the

rabbit hole back to childhood where the red queen in *Alice in Wonderland* was right: you do have to move twice as fast to stay in the same place, and when you're old, you're too slow to do it and so you lose ground. The future vanishes. You can't remember what you should do tomorrow and then you can't remember what you did today. And in the end all you have is long ago.

But Mother hadn't yet left for good. There were days when she was so much like her old vivacious, talkative self that I grew hopeful that she might return completely, might even be able to go back home to Catawba Drive and call her friends to come over for bridge. But those hopes inevitably crashed into senseless confusions that broke my heart.

I fed her another spoonful of the lemon sorbet she loved for me to bring her. "Mom, I want to ask you something."

"You go right ahead, honey, ask away." She smiled, an imitation of her old bright smile. The pneumonia had so weakened her that for weeks she could barely keep her head from the white pillows fluffed behind her, although she very much disliked how the pillows flattened her hair. My mother, Peggy Dollard Savile, had been blonde, petite, and pretty when it was the fashion to be so. As a result, she had never doubted her attractiveness and felt a responsibility to maintain it for the enjoyment of others. Today she wore a pink lace bed jacket and had a thin pink band in her hair. As soon as I saw her, I knew she was having what she called one of her "Hello, Earth, I'm back" days and that this would be a good time to ask her something.

I had brought one of her gold-leaf bowls and a Georgian silver spoon to serve her the sorbet in. I think she liked the memory of elegance even on "bad days." Then I asked, "Do you remember Fulke and Mary Norris?"

"Of course I do. They only lived two blocks down from us." And she pointed shakily at her bedside table where there was a small stack of poetry books by Fulke Norris.

"You remember what happened to their daughter-in-law Linsley?"

"Oh that was so tragic. Linsley finally pregnant after trying so long and then gone in a second. She was the sweetest thing, and Fulke and Mary both loved her like an angel on earth. I remember Inez told me—"

"Inez Boodle?"

"You remember, she had that dreadful husband Pete that you just couldn't tolerate. Or *wouldn't*, even though I said, 'These are our neighbors and you can't *say* if he comes in the front door I go out the back—'"

She'd confused me with my father, as she often did. "I think you mean Dad didn't like Pete Boodle."

"He *hated* him!"

I fed her more sorbet. "Inez said something about...?"

Mother had once loved to gossip, spending hours on the white and gold phone in her "sitting room" off their bedroom, swapping scandals with her friends, often while I pleaded with her to hang up and drive me somewhere. She said, "Inez told me in the beginning of their marriage Tyler and Linsley were having troubles and Fulke had to step in. He told Tyler if he didn't keep his marriage together he'd be cut right out of the family. I don't think that's right. Family's family, that's what I was taught and that's what I tried to teach my sons. Is Vaughn home yet? Was I supposed to go get him today?" Agitated, she pulled herself up into the pillows.

"No, Vaughn and Jennifer live in Richmond. Vaughn's a doctor like Dad. He'll be here soon.... Tell me what Tyler Norris was like as a child."

She was happy to be able to help. "Oh, very, very smart. He was so smart they never knew what to do with him. I mean it wasn't even funny sometimes, like Fulke had this big aquarium with some rare fish in it and Tyler wasn't much more than four or five and he let out all the water to see what would happen. Well, of course those fish just died. They called it 'scientific curiosity,' but I could tell Fulke was mad as a hornet. Well, I said to Mary, I have two boys myself and why the Lord didn't give me a girl...with all the Dollard china and silver. Of course, Jay, you do have an appreciation—"

I distracted her with the last of the frozen lemon. "Did you like Tyler?"

She patted her lips slowly on a thin scalloped handkerchief embroidered *EAD*, her maiden name Elizabeth Ann Dollard, the handkerchief older than her long marriage. "Did I like who?"

"Tyler Norris. Mary's son."

She looked past me, back in time. "He could play the piano." She frowned, listening to old music. "But he didn't have your nice touch, Jay. I hate to say it and don't tell Mary but, well, there wasn't any…feeling in it. And that was funny because he was a very…intense little boy. One time I remember, oh, he was maybe six or so, he vomited right in front of everybody at a little publishing party for Fulke—because Fulke had brought him out and stood him on a table to show off how he could do any math problem in his head and Fulke would do them on a calculator and Tyler got one wrong and just vomited all over everywhere. Mary was mortified, mortified."

"You ever hear of his doing anything…strange when he was young?"

"Strange? Well, it's not fair, but I thought the way you'd turn around and he'd be smiling at you for no reason, that was strange."

"Creepy?"

"Well, yes, but isn't that terrible of me, he was just a little boy."

"What about any trouble in school?"

"Oh, Tyler didn't go to school, Jay. He was much too smart for our schools. Mary got permission to teach him at home. And she was his tutor 'til the accident, I believe, and then he went off to boarding school. I think it was someplace in Georgia."

"The accident?"

"Yes, poor Mary said she fell asleep with a cigarette and just about burned herself to death because somehow her bedroom door got locked and she couldn't get out. Little Tyler was only eight and I guess he got scared and ran off. It was just lucky the maid forgot her house keys and had to get off the bus and walk back. They couldn't find Tyler for hours and hours and finally they found him hiding in this little tree house he had on their lake property. He'd gotten himself all the way out there on his bicycle."

"Where's this lake property?"

"Oh honey, you know. They still have it. A nice little place. Not as nice as Nachtmusik. You know Vaughn thinks we ought to sell Nachtmusik, but it's been in the family so long...."

"Where's the Norris place?"

"You know. Right next to that new resort, what's it called? Something about Vivaldi."

"The Fifth Season?"

She asked for her little satin make-up case and looked at the mirror in its lid. "Yes, Fulke and Mary sold some of their land to that new hotel. I don't believe people ought to sell off their land to all these Yankees that honk their horns if you don't shoot out like a wild horse when the light changes. But after the fire, you'd never see Mary at the club in a swimsuit or even a short sleeve dress. Luckily it didn't get her face. I am so damn old." Mother touched her own face, still the "peaches and cream" my dad had called her. "Peggy Peaches will now play for us," he'd announce at the lake house as he pulled back the bedspread curtain, revealing my mother—tan in the beautiful starched white shorts and shirts that other women ironed for her—seated smiling at the small white spinet.

We talked awhile about those old summer days at Nachtmusik on the lake. And then slowly she slipped away into that long past time. Finally she sank down into the pillows. "I'm feeling a little tired, honey."

I sat by her bed and took her hand and moved each finger to play along with the CD I'd put on her small player by the bed. Together we struck the imaginary notes of the first Bach variation she'd taught me. Back then, my hand had fit inside hers, had held onto hers to climb a stair, to cross a street. Now her hand was very small, the tan faded, the strength to make music gone. When I raised her fingers to kiss her good-bye, she tugged my hand toward her lips. Her face collapsed into a painful frown.

"Oh, Jay. You've been drinking again." I pulled my hand away. "I could always tell because your skin smells funny. Where's Alice? Tell Alice I want to talk to her."

"I'll tell her, Mom. You go on to sleep now."

"Is Vaughn home? I want you to be nice to your little brother."

"I will, Mom."

"You're the most beautiful little boy in the whole wide world. And smart and sweet and everything nice."

"I love you too, Mom. Go to sleep now."

When I left, I took with me from her bedside table one of the volumes of Fulke Norris's inspirational verse that people were always bringing her on their visits. This one was titled "Saints" and had on its cover a portrait of St. Margaret leading a very domesticated dragon by a golden chain.

● ● ●

Dr. Josie Roth's lab was across the handsome Haver quad from the hospital. A graduate student pointed her out working at a bank of microscopes. She was attractive, but not as pretty as her younger sister Linsley had been. Her features were stronger, slightly asymmetrical; her frame too large for her weight. She'd grown thinner since the murder of her sister. She was surprised I'd wanted to see her. We talked a while about her work in psychiatric pharmacology. When I told her I didn't think of psychiatrists as working in labs, she said, "I'm not interested in listening to middle-aged businessmen whine about having affairs with twenty-year-olds because their wives don't appreciate them." She gestured around the long chrome counter of microscopes and centrifuges. "I'm interested in figuring out which chemicals can help readjust a brain that's out of kilter."

I leaned against the wall. "Like your brother-in-law Tyler's brain?"

She finished jotting tiny meticulous numbers on a piece of graph paper. "I don't want to talk about Tyler anymore. Linsley's dead. He got away with it. You tried, I tried, it's over."

I shook my head. "It's not over. He killed Judge Turbot last night."

Stricken, she stared at me. It was a struggle to speak. "What are you talking about?"

"He butchered her, cut out her heart."

She sank into one of the lab stools. Her hands were shaking. "The news thought it was this serial killer Guess Who."

"Tyler is Guess Who."

Dr. Roth burst into tears. I waited while she fought her way back to control then I said, "I'm here because I need you to help me stop him."

She shook her head confused.

"Were you aware that Tyler was sleeping with a college student of his named Lucy Griggs, the young woman killed at The Fifth Season?"

She said she'd be very surprised to hear that Tyler was sleeping with anyone. But she did recall seeing him once in the library food court having an intense conversation with a young woman who seemed to be furious about something. She had assumed that the girl was upset about a poor grade. I showed her a photograph of Lucy Griggs. Slowly she nodded. Yes, that was the girl. She'd seen them just before the fall term had ended, so in December, less than a month before Linsley died.

Roth excused herself to repair her tear-stained face. When she finally returned from the ladies room, she asked me, "You really think Tyler is Guess Who? You think he killed the other women?"

I said yes, I did think so, and warned her that she herself might be in danger and should take every precaution.

"Why don't you arrest him if that's what you think?"

I said I was very afraid we weren't going to be allowed to arrest him. I explained that we'd been forbidden by the district attorney's office to investigate Tyler Norris, who was threatening the city with a suit for harassment. "Nobody thinks he killed your sister, including his jury."

Pain seemed to shrink her until she looked not thin but frail. "I could testify that I saw him arguing with Lucy Griggs, but I have no proof that there was an affair. It's the last thing Linsley thought, believe me."

I used the suggestion Isaac Rosethorn had given me. "Dr. Roth, I wonder, is there something in that marriage that maybe you didn't testify about at the trial? Maybe something about Linsley, something you didn't want your folks to know or the world to know? Maybe you still don't."

Josie Roth walked to the end of lab, watched for a moment as a white mouse scratched at the side of its cage. I followed her there and said, "The man's a sociopath. You know it. He's killed five, maybe six, women." She didn't answer me. We stood there in the silent lab for a few minutes. Then I wrote my cell phone number on her note pad and told her that if she should think of anything useful, to call me.

I was in the parking lot opening the car door when my phone rang. Josie Roth said, "The baby my sister was carrying. It wasn't Tyler's."

• • •

An hour later, Dr. Roth sat in Cuddy's office repeating to him and to Bunty and Rhonda what she'd told me in the lab.

A few months before she died, Linsley Norris had confided to her sister that while Tyler was capable of penetration, her husband had never had an orgasm in her presence during their seven-year marriage. He had refused to discuss his inability or unwillingness to ejaculate and he had refused to seek help—either physical or psychological. Linsley was a college convert to Catholicism; in fact, it was at a local Catholic church that she'd met Tyler's mother Mary, and through her had met the son. It was Mrs. Norris who'd pushed the two together. Because of her faith, Linsley would not consider divorce, despite her unhappiness in her marriage. But her deep longing to have a child finally led her into an affair for just that purpose.

Cuddy asked, "Did Tyler know?"

She shook her head. "She never told me so, but I think he did. I watched the way he treated her that last month. He hated her."

Bunty asked softly, "Do you know who Linsley had this affair with?"

Josie Roth didn't answer. She was struggling against tears and finally lost the fight and began crying.

I stepped beside her and offered her a handkerchief. I said, "Dr. Roth went with her sister when she had amniocentesis because she was worried about the baby's status. It was at that point that she told Dr. Roth about her affair. The baby's father was Fulke Norris."

Chapter 32
Endgame

At seven in the evening, Cuddy called the task force together. Or what was left of it. The sheriff from Neville County had gone home once the Cathy Oakes homicide case was cleared. The volunteer cops from neighboring towns had been told that the FBI had taken charge of the Guess Who investigation, and thanks anyhow. Cuddy said he wanted the rest of us to know that we could withdraw from the case right now if we wanted to, but as chief he had made a decision. We were going to focus on a prime suspect whom we could not—could not, he repeated—officially investigate. We were going after Tyler Norris. Cuddy waited until the shock in the room settled. Then he said that if he were wrong about Tyler, he would be resigning as police chief tomorrow, July 4, Independence Day, at five P.M., and the rest of us at HPD might not even have the choice of resigning, since his successor would most likely fire us all immediately. So if anybody felt like they were trapped in the Alamo and didn't want to be there, it was time to polish up their Spanish and head for the door.

Nobody moved.

Cuddy advised us to warn any woman vulnerable to Norris that she should avoid being at home alone and should go nowhere unescorted.

Nancy came by to report that a search both of Lucy Griggs's

apartment and of her old room at home had turned up nothing to tie her to Tyler. Nancy had shown his picture to John Walker and his mother Doris Nutz. John had identified Tyler only as Lucy's "teacher." He'd never suspected an affair between them. Doris wanted HPD to know we ought to be sued.

Roid came by to report that Tyler Norris had continued for three hours on his strange rambling drive through town without ever leaving his vehicle, but had finally returned to his house, in front of which we had stationed another officer in another unmarked car.

Cuddy had to go to a meeting of the city council with the mayor. Carl Yarborough and he had the task of assuring the town managers that they shouldn't worry about the fact that Hillston had just been dubbed on Channel Seven, "the Southern Capitol of Sex, Death, and Rock'n'Roll." They shouldn't worry that the streets had been gridlocked all day by a hundred television news vans on the lookout for serial killers and by a thousand motor-cycles in town to hear Mavis Mahar sing. They weren't to worry that the meadow behind Haver Stadium looked like Woodstock, a squatters' village of tents and trailers that had christened itself "Mavistown," where the faithful waited for a chance at the ten thousand free tickets the rock star was giving away to her upcoming concerts—the one tonight and the one tomorrow night. That they shouldn't worry that vendors were hawking both Guess Who T-shirts and Mavis go-cups right here on the steps of the Cadmean Building.

We made jokes that Cuddy and Carl could point out to the council that they should look on the bright side—store shelves were empty and hotels were full, the media was fighting over the few taxis, restaurants had reprinted menus to double the prices. The circus was in town, the sky was Carolina blue, and Hillston looked good on television all over the country—well, except for the fact that a serial killer was on a rampage.

• • •

In Room 105, Rhonda, Bunty, Lisa Grecco, and I were trying to put together what we'd learned about Tyler Norris from his sister-in-law Dr. Roth. The summer night was cool enough for Bunty to wear a faded handmade quilt wrapped around her thin shoulders. "Oh I buy it," she said in her slow mountain twang. "From what I've read so far—and Justin, your book on this homicide is good, real good—" From the FBI psychiatrist, this was high praise. She shifted in her rocking chair. "—I buy it from Fulke Norris. Weak man, vain man—teenage war hero like that, goes to your head. Women all over you. Then you write greeting card poetry, read it on the radio, beautiful voice. Women all over you again.

"But after a while, you're getting up there in years, your son's the smart one, you're jealous, he's jealous. You send him off to a damn military academy, make a man of him, but he'll never be the man you are. Son's pretty wife comes on to you, instant Viagra."

"Why would she?" asked Rhonda, disgusted.

"Oh I buy it from Linsley too. Husband won't sleep with her. Even discount her religion, family pressure from both sides not to divorce is heavy duty. She wants the gene pool, she cons herself how it's all in the family. Fact is, it's payback. It's her lethal weapon. So maybe she does tell him about it. Maybe it's her Christmas present. 'Guess what, Tyler, we're having your dad's baby.' Now we've got that big stressor that kicks it all off for our killer."

Rhonda's tanned open face, so different from her friend's pallor, shuddered. "I've got relatives calling me a pervert and this nice normal girl gets her father-in-law to knock her up?!"

Bunty sipped the mug of tea Rhonda had brought her. "Faster we can pull him, the better. We're getting way out in deep water now. Tyler's in the equivalent of a feeding frenzy. It's gone beyond fixing things—getting rid of a blackmailer, getting rid of a witness. He's like a binge drinker. He's gotten to where self-protection's not his first impulse anymore. And when these guys get to kamikaze time, all bets are off. That's when your death toll takes you into double-digits."

I agreed that there was a big difference between the fastidious, ritualized burial of Kristin Stiller and the slaughterhouse in which we'd found Margy Turbot, but I wasn't sure what Bunty was predicting. "You mean like mass murder, like shooting up a McDonalds?"

Bunty said, "No, no, nothing like that. We're headed for suicide, but it could be he wants to take a few with him."

"Suicide's better than losing another innocent woman," I told her.

"Can we avoid both please? I'd rather study him than bury him." Bunty tapped the thick book of files.

Rhonda moved back and forth along the large map of Hillston and the surrounding county. There were colored pushpins in the murder sites as well as in Tyler's Balmoral Heights home and his family's lake house. The groups made clusters. She frowned. "I want to get in that house on Tartan Drive. He's keeping souvenirs in there. They always do."

"Forget it, guys," Lisa Grecco reminded us. "We can't touch him. We can't go near him. You do it, and even if this weirdo's got a whole drawer full of human eyeballs, he'll walk. That's the game, okay? This is all a game." Lisa, the youngest deputy counsel in the D.A.'s office, was only two years out of law school. Like many of her generation who naïvely believed they could trust more in cynicism than sentiment, she always took a hardball approach to the law.

Rhonda groaned sarcastically. "Well, what do you think we oughta do, Lisa, follow him around and videotape him hacking another woman's heart out of her chest? Oh, sorry, we can't film him without his permission!"

I said, "If we had letters or photos, we could move on him. Lucy Griggs told Mavis Mahar in the limo. 'I've got proof and he knows it too.' Couple of hours later, she's dead."

Lisa took a drink of water from her plastic bottle. "What do you people think, you're going to come across a stack of creamy envelopes with a satin ribbon around them? I haven't written a letter on a piece of paper since my mom used to make me send thank you notes to my aunt who was still giving me video tapes of *Cinderella* when I was a junior at Princeton."

I said, "You mean email? Just because I use wax and a goose feather, doesn't mean I haven't heard of computers. Lucy had a little cheap laptop in her apartment. She had web access through Haver, but believe me we checked that thing. No incoming saved mail. No sent mail on file offline. Nothing. Either she cleaned it out or somebody else did."

"Maybe Norris?" suggested Bunty. "He'd think of a detail like that."

The young deputy counsel was twisting hard at her hair as if she hoped the pinch would make her think more clearly. Then she clapped her hands together. "Justin, what did you just say? She used the Haver Internet?"

"Yes," I told her. "Students get it. But if she printed those emails out, we can't find them. Maybe she actually carried them around in that mesh bag and he got them, along with the camera."

Lisa nodded eagerly. "Listen to me. Faculty use that web too." She checked her watch. "I'll give you two cases, okay. Wendy Freiberg got involved with one a year ago. She got called in because this was at State so NCBI caught the case. Some professor in the—I kid you not—religion department is checking out some skuzzy child porn on the web. So the university gets wind of it because—get this—they monitor their server. Hey, I mean, they're not as bad as the FBI Carnivore." She waved her arm at the two female Bureau agents.

"Chomp chomp chomp," Rhonda grinned: it was a comic reference to the FBI's extremely invasive national email surveillance technique that had come under attack from civil libertarians. "Hey, you kill six women, I say you lose some rights."

Lisa nodded. "So State fires this professor, even though this is like some old geezer with tenure. He files a grievance, screaming invasion of privacy, yada yada yada, and the university goes, 'Sorry, Sleazo, you log on through us, it's not private. It's State business and the State is not happy being in the child pornography business. So bye-bye.'"

"I see where you're going," murmured Bunty. "There was a Haver civil suit back in the spring, right?"

Lisa nodded. "Couple of Haver biochemists were emailing each other all these genome schemes—patentable biotech-type stuff. So Haver seizes the correspondence. It goes to civil court. Haver claims they own the patents because they say anything on the Haver web is Haver intellectual property. Guess what, they win. Guess why this relates to our friend Professor Tyler Norris?"

Bunty said, "Because all email sent through the Haver server is stored in a back-up system for 365 days. If Norris and Lucy Griggs corresponded by email, there'll be copies in the Haver mainframe."

Lisa grinned at her. "You got it."

I said, "How do we get it without the mayor, the D.A., etc., etc., etc.?"

"I know a judge'll give me a warrant right now in the middle of the night to subpoena those files." Lisa started looking up a phone number in her cell phone. "She's appeals court, lives nowhere near here. She'll do it for Margy Turbot."

Dick Cohen, entering, passed Lisa as she hurried out the door of 105. "Sorry guys, I got nothing for you. No hairs, no prints, no semen, no help."

"Nothing in Margy's mouth?" I asked.

"Sorry. I'm headed home," he yawned. "I wanna see if my two kids, the ones I left off in sixth and seventh grade, are now attending the colleges of their choice. Anybody for strudel?" He set a large tin box on the conference table. "All the way from Brooklyn. My mother made it."

Rhonda affably opened the box, broke off a piece of pastry but had difficulty chewing it.

Dick shrugged. "My mom should spring for priority, I keep telling her, Parcel Post won't cut it with strudel."

"She could freeze it," I suggested.

"Oh crap, that reminds me." Dick turned around in the door. "Sam Chang faxed me this. Amazing guy, here he is testifying in Seattle and his brain's still spinning on our problem."

I said, "A star is a star is a star."

Dick found the paper. "We were muddling over some tissue discoloration extending from those match burns on G.I. Jane—"

"Kristin Stiller," Rhonda reminded him.

"Right. Well, Sam was going along with the idea it all came from the sulfur matches, but now he's thinking you know maybe it's actually freezer burn. Maybe G.W. tried to cover the freeze spots with the match burns—"

I interrupted. "I thought you told me you checked weather reports. The ground out there never really froze."

Dick waved off my question. "No, Sam's talking a real freezer, like she was kept in a fridge before the guy dumped her. Okay, see you guys tomorrow."

R&B and I looked at each other. We all three knew what Dick's news meant. If Sam Chang was right, Dick's original certainty that Kristin had died no earlier than mid-January did not hold. In fact, she could have died Christmas Eve, the last day anyone actually saw her in Hillston. If so, and if Tyler Norris killed her because she was blackmailing him, he killed her *before* he murdered his wife. She was his first victim; Linsley, his second.

Rhonda tossed a hardball from hand to hand; it was like worry beads to her. "JayJay, we need to get in Tyler's house, see if he's got a deep freeze."

It's a legend in the department that I can remember the location of almost any object I've ever seen; it's why I've always been the detective first to walk the scene of a homicide. I closed my eyes now and walked into the front hallway of Tyler Norris's house on Tartan Drive back on New Year's Eve, six months ago. Tyler had just been rushed to the hospital. His dead wife still lay on the floor, now covered by a plastic sheet. In memory, I kept walking—down three steps into the living room, through a double pocket-door opening into a dining room, through a swinging door into a kitchen, then into a rear hallway. On one side, the interior door to the garage. On the other, the door into the utilities room. In that room, appliances, shelves, a sink. A washer and dryer. Against the far wall, a large white object with a heavy lidded top. I told Rhonda, "He does have a deep freeze. I saw it."

Was it possible that Kristin Stiller had been in that freezer from Christmas Eve until he dumped her off the access road? Was it possible that Linsley Norris had somehow discovered her in the freezer? Had we been wrong about his motives? Had Tyler killed his wife not because she was pregnant with his father's child and he hated her, but because she knew he was a murderer?

I said, "Big problem. I try getting a warrant in this county, Mitch Bazemore'll shut us down fast."

Bunty thought as she dutifully swallowed the pills Rhonda held out to her. "Kristin Stiller was a Swedish national. We go to a *federal* judge. If she was a crime victim, the FBI, maybe INS, are involved. Rhonda and I don't even talk to local judges, we don't bother with local police."

I smiled. "You hot shots don't even know we exist."

There was a sharp knock at the door to 105. Zeke Caleb stepped inside, or rather was pulled inside by a large, dark short-haired dog.

"Hey there, Geronimo," Rhonda called to Zeke. "See you finally got your dog. You going K-9 then?" He nodded happily. "What is that, a Malomois Shepherd? I heard about them."

"That's right," he said, pulling the big animal back beside him by the short thick leash. "This is what they call an aggressive indicator."

"He looks it," Bunty agreed.

"She. Name's Heidi. Speaks Dutch, this dog. Trained in Holland. She knows seventeen commands—I'm starting to learn them." Zeke yanked the dog back toward him, patted her head. He said something that was presumably "Sit" in Dutch. At any rate, the dog did so. "Justin, you wanted me to tell you if a match came over the dispatch. They just picked up a black Ford Explorer abandoned with its lights on. Registered to a..." He looked at the pad he carried. "Guy named Ferraro. No answer at the residence. Dumfries Court."

"Where'd they find the SUV?"

"Parking lot of the Rib House Bar on the byways. Kids, huh? What's wrong with them?"

The SUV had been dutifully impounded by the Hillston police and was now in the HPD garage. I phoned the forensics lab down the hall and spoke with Etham Foster. "Doctor D, you can thank young Griffin Pope. I've got your car for you. Place Tyler in it and I'll never call you Doctor Dunkit again."

"Hang on," he growled.

Chapter 33

Check

It was nearly nine. I was watching Etham Foster's teamwork on the Ford Explorer under the high-intensity lights. They'd already cut out a small square of the gray carpet fibers from under the seat. They'd already photographed the car interior and filmed the removal of the small piece of boxwood that Nancy had seen caught in the wheel frame when she'd looked at the car in the Ferraro garage. Now Etham was removing the evidence that—the minute we saw it—showed us not only that we were right about Tyler Norris but that we'd be able to prove that we were right. We saw cat hairs. Four separate white cat hairs. In their translucent latex gloves, Etham's large hands patiently tweezered each of the short straight hairs from the gray velour seat fabric. He placed them in small round metal evidence boxes.

"You're sure?" Etham asked me again. "You saw a white cat in Margy Turbot's kitchen?"

"I'm sure. It was a big white Persian. It was staying close to the body. It rubbed against my legs just the way it must have done to Tyler's. I bet I got the same hairs on the cuffs of my pants as he did."

"Bring me your pants tomorrow."

I said I would.

"And find that cat. What happened, a neighbor took it?"

I admitted I didn't know.

"So find it." Etham unhooked the accelerator footpad in order to study it under a magnifier. Embedded in one of the treads he found a miniscule speck of blood that might belong to Margy Turbot. I left him with it. He looked as happy as anyone was likely ever to see our dour criminologist.

• • •

It was karaoke night at the Tinwhistle Pub that everybody still called the Tucson Lounge. A skinny man with long yellow sideburns was trying to hold onto a Mavis song ("The Tooth of Time") that was galloping away from him. A dozen young motor-cyclists (complaining loudly about being turned away from the sold-out, standing-room-only Mavis concert tonight) were not only booing the hapless singer for defiling their idol by his poor imitation, but were also throwing onion rings and plastic cups at him. The air-conditioning couldn't compete with the crowd and the place smelled like sweat, beer, and urine. I'd gone to the bar for a quick dinner and, admittedly, for a drink. Now I lit a ciga-rette, one from the opened pack Brenda Moore had given me. A young woman drinking next to me screamed as the cigarette exploded in my mouth with a loud pop when I lit it. The bar-tender actually ducked under the edge of the bar, and I had a jolt of adrenaline that may have aged me. "A friend of mine," I explained. "She's a practical joker. Very anti-smoking."

"She could get somebody killed, somebody could have a heart attack," the bartender protested.

"Don't talk about killing," the young woman beside me said. "I'm waiting for my girlfriend because I'm scared to go out in the streets with Guess Who loose. I think they ought to fire that whole police department, what good are they?"

I decided I didn't like this young woman, finished my scotch (it was at least the right color for scotch), and walked out to the alley to answer my ringing cell phone. It was Lisa Grecco, who wanted me to know she'd be at the Computer Services Office of Haver University at eight in the morning with the subpoena she'd managed to acquire. She'd impound any emails they had on file to or from Tyler Norris. By the way, could Lisa ask me something personal? I said of course and she asked if I knew whether Bubba Percy was seeing anybody seriously? I told her my impression was that Bubba did nothing in his life seriously except comb his hair. Lisa just wondered because she was going out with him later tonight, and she hated to start back up with him if in fact she was just something on the side. Again, I suggested that everything in Bubba's life was on the side.

Lisa's question made me remember that Bubba had, for some reason, wanted me to phone him at eight. It was now after nine and the long lazy summer dusk was finally darkening to night. He answered the phone on the first ring. "Bubba, you wanted me to call?"

"Justin?" Instead of blasting me for being late as I expected, he sounded suddenly shocked and distressed. "Yeah?... Yeah... Oh Jesus, Justin, that's unbelievable."

"What are you talking about?"

"Oh, Justin, man, I'm so sorry....It's a big shock." He appeared to be carrying on an intense conversation with me that I was no part of. He said, "Okay, I'll get right over there..."

"What are you up to, Bubba?" As I asked, I heard someone else, someone very close to his phone, asking the same question, "What's going on?" It was Shelly Bloom. And Bubba was, I suspected, in her bed and trying to avoid hanging around for the afterglow so he could make his date with Lisa Grecco.

Ironically, I'd been thinking of calling Shelly Bloom myself; she'd impressed me with her reportage this morning in the *Star*. She could not only get the story (which few reporters bothered to do anymore), she could write it. I wanted to tell her, and this time it would even be true, that we had a prime suspect—although claiming we were close to an arrest might be problematic. But if we did find a way to collar Tyler Norris, why not let Shelly hand a big coup to her new paper the *Star*? If she was falling in love with Bubba, she was going to need some other ego boost to rely on.

The press secretary was still commiserating with me about whatever he was talking about. "Thanks for letting me know, Justin.... This is real bad news. You hang on. I'll be there as fast as I can."

I said, "Tell Shelly to call me right away."

"What? Who?"

But I hung up. I tried to imagine what this fictional "unbelievable bad news" was that I had ostensibly just told him. Maybe that my mother had died. I wouldn't put it past him.

My phone rang again. This time it was Brenda at the dispatch desk. Before I could chastise her for the exploding cigarette joke, she said Dermott Quinn was trying to reach me about something "important." The Irishman was on one of her lines right now. She transferred me.

I could scarcely hear him. "Where are you, Dermott?"

"Feckin' zoo," Mavis's dresser said. "Backstage. Haver Field. The eejits let a few thousand too many in and they're hangin' off the bloody lights. Ah, shite! Okay, okay, she's on now."

Just then I heard the loud long roar of forty thousand human throats, cheering together on a summer's night in an open stadium. Then a wild Celtic burst of drums, fiddles, and flutes.

"Lieutenant," he shouted, "we can't talk on the phone." That was certainly unarguable. "Can you come to the stadium then? Ask in security for Bernadette Davey, she'll bring you backstage."

"What about?" I asked. "Shout. Tell me now." I didn't have time to hear any more about how I was the type of man he wanted Mavis to marry.

But it wasn't that, or only that by inference. He said, "Somebody got in her feckin' room at the Sheraton. Paul and I came up to her suite after dinner. He's a bodyguard. Since the murder, we make her stay at the bar 'til we check everything out and call her. So we're walking into her sitting room and all of sudden we hear these noises in the bedroom. We run in, door slams, we run to the hall, a feckin' man's running down it."

"What did he look like?"

"Middle-size. Thirty or so. White man. Had on a cap. Tight black running-like outfit. Her bedroom's a bloody mess. Tore up her covers and left this feckin' chess piece on her pillow. You know, the game chess?"

"Is it the queen? Is the chess piece the queen?" Nothing about the two Costa Rican chess queens had been released to the press.

"Yeah, that's right, the queen. Black queen, from one of those cheap wood sets. Mavis thinks it's a fan goo-gooing about this song she did a while back called 'Midnight Queen,' but I don't know, I don't mind saying it, I nearly soiled meself."

I asked if they'd called the police or notified hotel security. But they'd done neither. Mavis had told them not to. "She had a bloody fit. And Mavis in a temper's something you don't feckin' argue with." She'd said they had a performance to do tomorrow night that was being filmed for a documentary. As soon as it was over, they were flying to Tokyo for another concert. She'd said they didn't have time to get mixed up with the police.

I told Dermott I'd get over to Haver Field before the end of the concert. "If she comes off the stage, stay with her."

"I'm never not, Lieutenant." I heard a screaming rumble of cheers and applause, presumably as a song ended. "Oh Jaasuz, got to go." He hung up.

• • •

Moving through the alley back toward the Cadmean Building garage, I used my cell phone to call John Emory. Roid swore that Norris had never once gotten out of his car the whole time he was tailing him but had just driven aimlessly around Hillston and then returned to his house at four P.M. He checked with the officer who replaced him and called back to say Norris hadn't left the house. His car was still in the garage. As soon as Roid said it, I had an image of Tyler in his doorway in his professional-looking black Lycra sports pants with the thin Italian racing bike leaning against his foyer hall.

"Roid, get over there. Norris went out through the back

woods. He's not driving, he's on a bike. A couple of hours ago he broke into Mavis Mahar's suite in the Sheraton."

Emory paused awkwardly. "Justin, listen. We got a problem. We all just got phone calls from the A.G.'s office telling us the investigation had been shut down and we can't touch Tyler Norris."

"Roid, he's the killer. Believe me. Call Nancy, tell her what I just told you." I disconnected, phoned Room 105. When Bunty answered, I told her to get some FBI out to Tartan Drive as fast as she could. She said Rhonda and another agent were already on their way out there with a warrant to search the Norris house. I asked her, "You already got a warrant?"

"We're Feds," she told me in her soft wry twang. "We don't care about mayors and D.A.s and city councils."

• • •

I found Cuddy standing under the gaudy yellow awning, looking worried. He wore his khaki suit and Carolina blue tie— his uniform for city council meetings. His new white Taurus was parked beside him at the curb. I yelled at him to drive me to Balmoral Heights, that Norris had tried something else, that the FBI had a federal warrant to search and seize.

As he wheeled us onto Main Street, Cuddy slapped the flasher light from under the seat onto the roof of his car by its suction cup. Quickly as I could, I explained that Norris had broken into Mavis Mahar's hotel suite.

"Why the hell would he mess around with her now?" Cuddy looked at me. "Unless he saw you two together and it's just to get at you. In which case, thank you, Elvis, for keeping Alice in the mountains. And that's all I'm saying on that subject."

I had another idea as to why Tyler Norris would wish to extinguish Mavis Mahar, but I didn't want to discuss it, or even believe it was true. But it had occurred to me that Mavis had actually seen Norris on the grounds of The Fifth Season at some point in that drunken night when she'd brought Lucy Griggs back to the bungalow, that there'd been if not a brief encounter with Norris at the resort, then at least a glimpse of him. That would make Mavis a witness that Tyler was in the area at the time of a homicide. He may have just realized that she was a witness—perhaps because of Shelly's reporting yesterday in the *Star* that the police had a prime suspect and an arrest was imminent. Mavis had returned to Hillston just before the article's appearance, and maybe he assumed that she'd talked to the police.

If I was right, Mavis had lied to me when I'd first questioned her, and she'd done so in order to protect herself from any involvement in the case. Being a witness in a homicide meant depositions and court appearances and other tiresome responsibilities for which the fast-moving star had no time. I didn't want to think there was a ruthlessness in her as cold and dark as space. A careless self-interest that had helped to cost Margy Turbot her life.

I said none of this aloud, but explained to Cuddy what we'd now set in motion: a search of Norris's house to check for evidence that he'd kept Kristin Stiller's body in a deep freeze. A search to learn whether he and Lucy Griggs had used the Haver email system to correspond. A search to prove that cat hairs found on the seat of the Explorer that he had driven matched hairs of the Persian cat we'd seen in Margy Turbot's kitchen.

Cuddy told me he had gone to see Isaac. Reaching in his jacket he pulled out a rectangular box. "He said Tyler came over to his place the night after they won and smiled the scariest smile he'd ever seen and handed him this box as a thank-you present. He said he now thinks Tyler just couldn't resist boasting about how he'd gotten away with murder and had used Isaac to do it. I'm telling you, the old man was pretty shaken up. Could be he suspected Tyler killed Linsley, but he was totally blindsided by this Guess Who stuff."

I opened the box. It was full of ribboned marksmanship medals from a place called Stillhurst Academy, most of them first prize medals. Rifle, pistol, trap shooting—there must have been a dozen of them.

Cuddy said, "Right. Tyler Norris testified he never shot a gun in his life. That he had no idea how to load a shotgun. And we didn't catch it."

I said, "There was no record of his being at Stillhurst Academy. The family must have buried it. Like I told you yesterday, my mom just happened to mention how they sent him somewhere after the fire (which I bet you anything little Tyler started), but she thought it was a Georgia boarding school, not all the way to—this place is in Mississippi! There was no way we could have known."

Cuddy frowned. "There's always a way if you work hard enough." We sped off the bypass at the North Hillston exit. "Learned Hand," he said sadly.

"What?"

"Margy's cat, Learned Hand, she named him after the Chief Justice of the Supreme Court. Nice cat."

"Nancy's got him," I explained. "He'd gotten up into an attic crawl space and was hiding from all the chaos."

Cuddy shook his head, fretful. "I wish Nancy would go over to River Rise and find Martha Mitchell for me."

I was surprised. "Where'd Martha go? She never goes anywhere."

"I know. Just steps out through her doggy door and uses the facilities and then back in she comes. Tell you the honest truth, sometimes, every now and then, Martha doesn't even step out."

"You think this is news to anybody?" Cuddy's blind adoration of his old dirty white poodle was an HPD joke.

"She does her best. Give her a break. When you're her age, you'll be in diapers. But I'm worried, okay, Martha's wandered off and it's dark. I know she can get in on her own, but her eyesight's sort of bad."

"She's blind!"

"Okay, real bad. Cleopatra called me before she left, said she couldn't find her anywhere in the apartment."

"Cuddy, I'm sorry to say it, but Cleopatra Skelton can't seem to find your vacuum cleaner or your washing machine either. I know, I know, give her a break. Hey, see the lights up there, turn, turn."

We swung in through the Balmoral Heights entrance. It wasn't a gated community in the sense that admittance was controlled by locks and guards, but on either side of the access road there was a distinctive stone wall with a huge bronze sign embedded in it announcing "BALMORAL HEIGHTS." A van that I recognized as an unmarked HPD vehicle sat parked beside the wall under the floodlights. Hopping out, I learned from the driver that a car with government plates and a young tan woman in the shotgun seat had just driven through the gate.

"Goddamn it!" I ran back to Cuddy's car. "It's Rhonda. They're going to get there before we can secure the rear! If he's home and they push him, he'll take off for the woods! He's got a racing bike. Gun it!"

But as we skidded around the corner of the intersection, still half a block away, I saw Rhonda in her gray pants suit already at the opened door of the big fake chalet. The entry light shone down on her and a huge young man who looked as if he'd left a career in pro-football to join the FBI. Rhonda was holding up her agent's badge to someone inside the house. Then I saw Norris step forward into view to look around, drawn by the screech of Cuddy's tires. He saw us, jumped back, and slammed the door shut in Rhonda's face. Rhonda kept knocking, then stepped aside for her fellow agent. He raised a gigantic leg and kicked open the door.

There was no way to maneuver Cuddy's car in the dark through the thickly landscaped lot to the rear of the house. I jumped out running, but by the time I reached the back door it was wide open and Norris had already disappeared—on his racing bike I was sure—into the heavy black wall of pines that sloped away from me. I ran all the way down into the woods. Dark dead silence in all directions.

Returning up the slope toward the open back door of the house, I heard Rhonda yelling at Cuddy, "Christ almighty, Honch, get in here! Good god!"

I could see the two FBI agents through the window of the utility room where they'd turned on bright lights. Rhonda had the large white lid of the deep freezer raised over her head and she was looking inside.

Chapter 34

Mate

The huge white metal box looked grotesquely like an ancient sarcophagus. But that was because of the dead body frozen inside it, the human being hidden beneath an international variety of frozen vegetarian dishes. The dead woman was bent at the legs, just as Tyler must have lowered her into the freezer, although she was short enough to have lain straight in her curious tomb. Her dark skin and jet black hair made a startling contrast with the white ice around her. It was Lupe Guevarra, the Garifuna woman. Her skull was crushed, much as we'd found her sister Maria's in the garbage bag at Southern Depot.

Rhonda moved aside for us. "She's been in here a couple of days. Probably since the night she left Trinity."

Cuddy said, "Norris probably told her he was bringing her here to her sister. Goddamn it, how many more?"

"No more," I promised him. I left Rhonda and him on phones calling for an HPD SWAT team to help search the woods. The other agent was already out there with a big flashlight following the bicycle tracks. The ID people, forensics, photographers, the medical examiner, they'd all be here soon. No one—not even Norris family friends on the city council—was going to tell us to leave Tyler alone anymore.

But around the subdivision there were at least five hundred acres of undeveloped woodland bordered by only partially

cleared land where new houses were under construction. If G.I.
Jane could lie undiscovered for two months a mile from the
access road, how likely was it that in this dense forest we would
find a man in black riding a black bicycle, even in full moonlight?

Unless we knew exactly where he was going.

I closed my eyes, listened to the conversation with my
mother in the hospital:

*Finally they found him hiding in this little tree house he had on
their lake property. He'd gotten himself all the way out there on his
bicycle."*

"Where's this lake property?"

*"Oh honey, you know. Right next to that new resort, what's it
called? Something about Vivaldi."*

Sprinting to the frontyard, I was already opening the door to
Cuddy's car (where I knew he'd left the keys in the ignition),
when I saw a red Jeep slam to a stop right behind it. Nancy was
driving, Zeke beside her in the front seat; behind them I could
see the huge dark head of Zeke's shepherd Heidi. Nancy was
yelling at me out the window, "Roid called. You get Norris?"

"No! Turn around!" I ran back through the house to the utility room where I'd seen a wicker basket of dirty clothes; I grabbed
a Haver sweatshirt off the top and raced outside again. Zeke
pulled the dog over when I jumped in beside him. The jeep took
off with me shouting directions at Nancy as she skidded out of
Balmoral Heights on two wheels.

We were on our way to North Cove on Pine Hills Lake. If I
was right, Tyler Norris was headed for his family's lake property.
He was still doing what he'd done as a child, escaping to his "safe
place" when threatened with danger. And once we'd looked
inside his freezer, he was in fatal danger and had to know it. If I
was wrong about where he'd gone, the HPD team would be walking the Balmoral woods all night and maybe they'd find him
there.

As we drove, I phoned the stables where I boarded Manassas. The teenage girl whose parents owned the place sounded as

if I'd interrupted her favorite television show. (It was eleven at night.) But finally I talked her into saddling Manassas and waiting with him by the croquet lawn of The Fifth Season. The resort shared a boundary with the stables on one side and the Norris property on the other. By crossing the terrain that hid the luxury bungalows, we could reach the bridle path beside the lakefront and approach the Norris house from its blind side without the sound of a car engine.

Speeding north, I briefed Nancy and Zeke. We agreed that we'd have a better chance if we came at Norris from more than one direction. Zeke and I would come in through the woods. He hadn't wanted me to borrow a horse for him, claiming he could move faster on foot. Nancy would block the driveway into Norris's family's home in case he tried to flee by car or bike, but I told her not to get out of her Jeep and not to attempt to approach Norris if she saw him. "Listen to me, Nancy, what he said in his trial about never using a gun. Not true. He's got a fistful of marksmanship medals."

"You're kidding?"

"No, I'm not. So forget being Annie Oakley."

"Who?"

"Jesus, okay, forget about being Mel Gibson. Just block the road."

"You hear him?" Zeke asked his wife.

"Yeah yeah yeah."

Nancy dropped us off on The Fifth Season's circular drive. We found the teenage girl beside the lush clipped green of the croquet lawn with an unsettled Manassas dancing on the lead she held. I took him and gave her two twenties which cheered her more than she acknowledged as she left.

Up on Manassas, I had to calm him from twisting in a circle to keep his wary eye on the large Malomois shepherd Zeke had on its leash. Zeke shook out Norris's dirty sweatshirt and let the dog Heidi smell it. Then he set out with her at an easy loping run into The Fifth Season's woods. I followed them. Zeke was remarkably fast, and he proved right about the terrain. Manassas and I, picking our way through the uneven and branch-cluttered forest floor, could do little more than keep Zeke in sight as the big man and his dog threaded their speeding way through the trees. He made no more noise in this familiar land than his Cherokee ancestors might have hundreds of years ago, before my ancestors harried them westward.

Suddenly ahead of me, Heidi began lunging and growling. Zeke must have then unsnapped the leash, for I saw the dog streak away into the night with Zeke racing effortlessly along the path after her.

I kicked Manassas into a canter as the path took its curve past the clearing in the pines and opened onto the small pebbled beach owned by The Fifth Season. In the moonlight I could make out the shadowy gray outline of the wooden dock where I'd seen Mavis Mahar diving into the lake on a summer dawn that now felt very long ago.

We'd gone over two miles now, and neither Zeke nor Heidi showed any sign of strain as they ran along the moonlit gravel. All at once, they turned off the path into thick woods. Deep in the pines I could see a strange flickering light. I followed the back of Zeke's broad white polo shirt into the dark. Suddenly he stopped, grabbed Heidi's collar and, leaning down, spoke to her. I pulled Manassas over beside him and looked where he was pointing.

Forty feet away from us, the woods ended in an unkempt lawn leading to a large gingerbread Victorian house whose pale yellow paint was cracked and peeling. Lights illuminated a screened-in back porch. The lights were bright enough to show blood splattered against the siding.

At the lawn's far edge, an immense old sycamore tree, its white bark glowing in the light of the full moon, shadowed two cars. Tyler Norris was throwing kerosene from a large red can onto the tree base where small branches had been stacked. About twenty feet above his head, I saw the weathered flooring of a tree house that had been built in the fork of two huge boughs. On this platform, an American flag draped over his body, and kindling wood stacked neatly beneath and around him, lay Fulke Norris, the killer's father. I could tell who it was because of the beautiful white hair haloed in the moonlight. I could even see the red of the blood in his hair.

I calmed Manassas. "Jesus, he shot his dad and hauled him up there," I whispered to Zeke, who was straining to hold back the lunging dog.

About to dismount, I checked for my gun in the back of my belt. Suddenly I heard a woman's voice. "Tyler Norris! Halt! Police!"

"Goddamn it," I whispered.

"You're under arrest," Nancy shouted. "Put your hands behind your head! Do it! Now! Do it!"

But Tyler dropped to the ground and started rolling. My eyes shot ahead of his motion and spotted the double-barrel shotgun against the sycamore. Next to me, Zeke saw it too. His hand flew up from Heidi's lead and the dog surged forward. With a long low growl, she was on Norris, her jaw clamped on the hand inches from the stock of the shotgun. The two of them twisted kicking in an indistinguishable blur of noise and motion. Zeke was running onto the lawn, yelling at Nancy, "Don't shoot! Don't shoot!"

Norris had remarkable strength, the force that madness gives to rage. He kicked free of Heidi and scrambled up to the closest tree branch, swung onto it with a scream of pain. One of his hands was bloody and the dog had probably broken bones. With Heidi leaping and snapping at his feet, Tyler pulled himself by pure will up onto the branch and then climbed quickly higher, from bough to bough, following a path through the tree that he'd climbed since childhood.

He reached the platform and squatted beside the improvised funeral pyre on which his dead father lay.

Kicking Manassas forward, I gestured for Nancy and Zeke to keep back out of range as I shouted up into the tree. "Tyler, you got any weapons up there, throw them down! Game's over!"

In the still night air, I could hear his rasping open-mouthed gasps for breath. Finally he called down to me, "Think so?"

"You're under arrest. You have a right to remain silent, you have a right—"

"Savile, you people have been so stupid, it almost wasn't fun."

"You think murdering six women and now your father is fun?"

He laughed in an eerie childish way. "You think that's all there is?"

All at once, a whoosh of fire leapt in a red arc beside him as if lightning had struck the tree bough. He shouted, "Checkmate!"

The kindling on the platform must have been soaked in kerosene too. In seconds, a ring of fire circled the body of Fulke Norris. Smoke quickly engulfed the platform.

I kicked Manassas to the tree trunk as he fought me to keep away from the fire. Reaching up, I grabbed the bough and swung onto it. Pulling my shirt up as a mask against the smoke, I started climbing the tree. If Norris had another gun, he was going to use it on himself or on me or on both of us. It was impossible to see where he was. All I could do was keep climbing, hoping that if I couldn't see him, he couldn't see me either.

Coughing and blinded, I flung myself onto the platform and crawled forward. I found Tyler about five feet from his father's burning body. He was seated like a Buddhist monk, cross-legged, his hands neatly folded in his lap, his insane eyes watching the flames dance around him, smiling at the fire.

I pulled him away from the flames, back toward the tree trunk. "You are under arrest. You have the right to remain silent. Anything you say can and will be used against you in a court of law…" He ignored me.

• • •

"Nancy," I told her as the medic finished wrapping my arm in gauze. "You want to tell me why you don't listen to my orders?"

In Zeke's large embrace, she shrugged, unrepentant. "You never listened to Cuddy's."

"She's got you there," said the police chief stepping forward to join us. Cuddy looked at his cheap watch that always worked. "Well, Justin, it's the Fourth of July. Looks like I'm still your boss and as I recall, you're supposed to be on two week's suspension. So I don't want to see you 'til after Bastille Day."

By now there were at least twenty law officials and firemen walking around the lake house yard. The first ambulance had just left with Fulke Norris's body—what could be recovered after the fire. The silver of one of his World War II medals had melted all the way into his charred flesh.

The second ambulance was waiting for the gurney on which two attendants were wheeling Tyler Norris, conscious but badly burnt, strapped down to the stretcher with a splint on his leg. Even with Zeke's help, I'd only been able to lower his unresisting weight half way down the tree before he fell, shattering his leg bone. Cuddy stared at him as the stretcher went by.

Norris turned his bandaged head and looked at Cuddy with that monstrous cold smile of his. He coughed. "Should have castled, Captain. Protect the home front."

"Get him out of here," Cuddy said.

Norris twisted his face around as he was lifted into the ambulance and said, "Seen your dog lately? Try your trunk."

Cuddy stared as the ambulance doors closed. Then suddenly he turned to run for his white Taurus parked among the cruisers on the lake house lawn. I could see him reaching into his pocket for his keys. He clicked the trunk door with his remote and then moved to lift it

"*Don't!*" I yelled and flung myself through the air at him. My hands stretched out, I was just able to catch his ankle as I landed, tackling him and then knocking him away from the car.

But it took Zeke's help to hold Cuddy down and stop him from trying to open the trunk.

It took the bomb squad over two hours with the white Taurus up on the rack at the HPD garage before they managed with meticulous precision to cut their way into the trunk without raising the lid. Raising the lid more than six inches would have set off the dynamite that was taped around the still-living body of the old poodle Martha Mitchell, for all these years the faithful first lady in Cuddy's life.

I handed him his dog, cradled in my bandaged arms. "Cuddy, when I tell you there's a bomb in a car, you've got to believe me. Sooner or later, I'm going to be right."

Epilogue

The Hillston Fire Department was able to save the shell of the sixteen-room Greek Revival Norris house on Catawba Drive, but not the second-floor wing where the floor collapsed before they could free the charred body of Mary Norris. She was chained with a bike lock to a radiator in her bedroom.

The Haver University Registrar's Office was able to provide the Hillston County District Attorney's office (rather begrudgingly as it was the Fourth of July) with 272 emails from Tyler Norris to his student Lucy Griggs. The fourteen reply emails from Ms. Griggs to Professor Norris made it clear that the young woman had grown increasingly disturbed by the peculiar sexual needs of her partner, and toward the end, increasingly suspicious about what had really happened to his wife. The professor's boastful, solipsistic, unctuous, compulsive, self-serving, and self-hating "love letters" to Lucy were, as Bunty Crabtree said, "a Rosetta Stone" of research for profiling the sociopathic personality.

The capture of the Guess Who Killer—the news that he was the same brilliant math professor and local social scion who had only this week been found innocent of murdering his wife, who *had* murdered his wife, and his famous father, the people's poet, not to mention burning his mother alive, not to mention killing those other women while his own murder trial was in progress, not to mention that one of the young women had been mistaken for Mavis Mahar—was irresistible to press and public.

The fact that Norris had told the family lawyer (not that he had any family left) that he planned to act as his own attorney and to plead not guilty (which was either very foolish or, as Isaac Rosethorn said, the best case he could make for an insanity plea) made it all even more irresistible.

Even the fans who had invaded Hillston to hear Mavis Mahar sing were more interested in the capture of Guess Who than in the rock star. At the Mavis press conference that afternoon, when she distributed the first of the free tickets to her final concert, the photo opportunity was sidetracked by shouted questions about what Mavis had known about the affair between Tyler Norris and her look-alike Lucy Griggs. Mavis said with intriguing elusiveness that everything she knew she was telling to the police.

Guess Who made the news on all three networks and in fact took up much of the Fourth of July coverage on CNN, where Shelly Bloom (who'd broken the story in the *Hillston Star*) was interviewed every few hours—in between her interviews with MSNBC and Fox.

Despite the holiday, the Hillston city council invited Captain Mangum to a special breakfast meeting that was covered by CeeCee Cane live on Channel Seven. Cuddy brought me along. As he walked into the meeting, back in his jeans, his blue cotton shirt, and Tarheels tie, the whole council greeted him with a standing round of applause for his timely capture of the Guess Who Killer. Councilman Penley, who only a few nights earlier had been eating dinner with Tyler Norris at the Pine Hills Inn, praised Cuddy for taking Guess Who off the streets. Here was a madman who'd slaughtered a fine young lady judge with her whole life ahead of her, not to mention his own parents (leaders of Hillston's social elite), and also had given a fine university and a great Southern town a black eye.

Cuddy thanked Councilman Penley and noted that parenthetically Norris had butchered four other women that maybe Penley hadn't known as well. Their names were Kristin Stiller, Lucy Griggs, and Maria and Lupe Guevarra. We should remember them too. He then pulled me to my feet beside him and said that the town owed a great deal to members of the Hillston Police Department: to its medical examiner Dick Cohen, its forensics chief Etham Foster, and most of all to the homicide division and its commander Justin Savile. The council clapped for me as well. How could they not, with my bandaged arms and lacerated face? Cuddy also generously commended Mitch Bazemore and the district attorney's office, especially Lisa Grecco, as well as the Raleigh field office of the FBI—in particular agents Rhonda Weavis and Barbara Crabtree—as well as state bureau documents examiner Wendy Freiberg.

He said it all just went to show how much we needed to work together. Beside him, Sheriff Homer Louge, eating a ham biscuit, swallowed it too fast and started to choke. Cuddy nonchalantly handed him a glass of water. The mayor raised his coffee mug and toasted the Hillston Chief of Police and we all said "Hear hear!" It was terrible coffee.

Later in Cuddy's large office looking out over the town he loved, I gave him a present. It was an eighteenth-century silver Spanish chess set that my Dollard relative had liberated in 1898 from a general's home in Havana. (It was not considered theft at the time since we were taking all of Cuba too.) I gave it to Cuddy because his Costa Rican chess set had been impounded as evidence in Tyler Norris's upcoming trial and his office didn't look right without a chess game going on in it.

Cuddy said that two power brokers on the council had followed him into the men's room after the breakfast and asked him if he'd like to run for mayor. Polls suggested that the Brookside-Yarborough gubernatorial ticket was headed for a big victory in the fall and Hillston would need a new mayor. Cuddy had told the councilmen that he'd think about it.

I said, "Are you crazy?"

"As my old mentor Fatso the Bald, AKA Mr. Briggs Cadmean, always advised me, 'Son, never say no even when you know it's no. Because *maybe* leaves open many doors to the brothel of fame and the outhouse of fortune. And son, fame and fortune are the only two places where this trashy world says a man ought to risk sticking his dick.'"

"I swear, Cuddy, I don't believe Briggs Cadmean ever said any of these things to you. I think you just make them up."

"Verbatim, I swear," he told me grinning.

"But tell me there is no maybe. I know you don't want to be mayor of Hillston."

He didn't want to be Governor Brookside's Secretary of Criminal Justice and Public Safety either. And this time he said so when Carl Yarborough brought him the offer on the governor's creamy stationery. "Carl, I'm all for justice and safety and that's why I want to go on being police chief of Hillston. I don't want us to have the best crime prevention record in the Southeast. I want us to have the best crime prevention record in the whole country because I don't want there to be *any* crime in Hillston. I want everybody living in tranquillity, I want peace in the valley as the good Elvis tells us." He pointed at the big poster of the dead star.

Carl chewed on his cigar. "Cuddy, you've got the talent and brains to move up in the world. Dina and I were having lunch a few days ago with the first lady. Know what Lee said? She said, no one ever deserved the Raleigh medal for service to this state more than you. She said you were the most decent man she'd ever known."

"I'm glad of her good word," he said quietly.

"You could work on that sort of crime prevention in Andy's cabinet."

Cuddy fed the waiting pigeons far too much of his Big Whopper, then closed the window behind him. He gave a tug at his thick shock of nut-brown hair. "Carl, I'm not a cabinet type guy. I'm more a modern wall-to-wall entertainment system. Right, Justin?"

I smiled. "Right."

After the mayor left, Cuddy balled up Brookside's invitation and banked it off Elvis's jeweled belt into the trashcan.

"That's your only good shot," I told him. "Happy Independence Day. Well, I guess you can go on saying you're never wrong. You told them Guess Who would be in custody by the Fourth of July. And that's what I was thinking as I shimmied down that burning tree hanging onto Norris. He'll be in custody by the Fourth of July."

He tilted his head at me. "You know what Janis says about freedom? It's just another word for nothing left to lose." He sat back at his big desk, began setting out his new chess pieces on the silver and onyx board. "And you know what Patsy says about love?" Patsy Cline was his favorite singer, "Sweet Dreams" his favorite song. "Patsy says, 'Why can't I forget the past and love somebody new?'"

"It's a good question, Cuddy."

He set the silver queen down beside the silver king. "Well, Justin, some folks can't. If I were you, I'd go bring Alice home."

• • •

I wasn't sure which was more astonishing. That in a crowd of fifty thousand people at Haver Stadium I should find myself next to Father Paul Madison or that he should be at a Mavis Mahar concert. But the small Episcopal priest told me he had bought his ticket to the original (canceled) concert six months ago. I'd had mine hand-delivered by Dermott Quinn at HPD this afternoon, where he'd come to tell me that he'd been mistaken and that the man who'd run out of Mavis's hotel suite had actually been (as Mavis thought) just a fan.

"You're lying, Dermott," I told him. "But lying's the least of what you'd do for her, isn't it?"

The scrawny pock-faced Irishman gave me the ticket in his hand. On the back of it Mavis had sent an invitation for me to come to her dressing room after the concert. "I'd die for Mavis," he finally said. He looked up at me with an intense solemnity. "I'm not a fool now. There're gifts worth dying for. She's one of God's great ones."

She was certainly one of the world's great ones. While the warm-up act performed before her entrance, Paul Madison and I walked to the stadium arcade where hawkers were selling Mavis CDs, T-shirts, videos, polyester scarves, and cheap rings. With his polo shirt and docksiders and blond curls, Paul looked more like a Haver University undergraduate than the rector of Trinity Church. The vendor selling him a Guinness was quite taken aback when a young parishioner stepped into the line behind us and said to him, "Hi, Father Madison. Mavis rules, right?"

Across the arcade I saw Nancy Caleb-White buying a black satin jacket with "MAVIS" in red glitter on the back. She slipped it happily onto her smiling little niece Danielle. We said hello. Nancy asked if I'd seen the local papers. "Finally saying good stuff about us. Nice, isn't it?" she grinned.

"Very nice," I agreed.

As Paul and I hurried back to our seats, I looked around at the crowd waiting for Mavis, and I asked him what he thought made a star. The priest thought about it a while, and then he said, "Light, I think. They draw all the light to them."

"Yes," I nodded. "But they throw it off too. Like real stars." I pointed up at the shimmer in the black sky above us. "A star's light can dazzle this whole stadium full of people," I waved my arm around the vast dark space, lit only by the flickering candles a few fans already held, "into believing, every one of them, that they are seen. Seen and loved."

Paul sipped his Guinness. "It's different with saints. I've been thinking about the saints since you were asking me about them."

"Thinking what?"

"What makes a saint. If stars are the light, then I'd say saints are people the light shines through." He smiled at me. "Not just the famous saints, because the famous ones are stars too. But the everyday saints around us in the world. Light shines through them and illuminates what they see. The light just goes right through them to what they love so that we can see its beauty. They don't get in the way because they're looking too."

When Paul said this, images of my wife Alice suddenly started to pour into me so quickly I caught my breath. I saw Alice bent over the green shoot of a narcissus, brushing off its weight of unexpected snow.

I saw Alice handing a check to the tall blushing cheaply dressed leader of the East Hillston High School Band, promising them more help from the state next year.

I saw Alice kissing our son Copper good-bye.

I saw Alice.

Because for the first time in a long time, I let myself look at her. For the first time in a long time, I let myself feel for her. And when I did, suddenly I was crying.

Paul looked over at me, then asked, "Are you all right?"

I said I was fine, but then I had to bend away from him with tears I couldn't stop. "Good Lord," said Paul.

"I don't know," I told him.

"Probably you do."

"I think my heart broke."

He patted my bandaged arm. "Don't worry about it," the priest said. "It's a good sign. And I don't think your heart broke. I think it broke open."

• • •

Above our heads giant spotlights shooting beams of white light through the sky crossed and recrossed faster and faster. And then together great rays of light blazed down on the stage in the middle of the huge stadium as the Easter Uprising struck the opening chords of "Coming Home to You." The crowd roared to its feet. The music was primitive and strong and as seductive as the beautiful golden singer who now danced out into the middle of the light, into the middle of thousands of people, into the guitars and mandolins, piano, cello and bass, drums and fiddles and pipes and whistles and hurdy-gurdy, all making music together for her.

Mavis Mahar danced into the center of the light swirling on the stage. And, by her gift and her will and her arduous unseen labor, she made of us all who were a part of the night—the music, the lights, the stadium of strangers side by side—she made of us all for one instant the perfect cosmic harmony that we long for without knowing it. She gave us for a little moment that grace that the saints in heaven enjoy together without effort and forever.

• • •

"To tell God's truth, I'll miss you, Lieutenant." In her small disorderly dressing room after the concert, Mavis poured herself a glass of Jameson's. She was exhausted, her hair and body wet with perspiration, still wearing the gold sleeveless T-shirt and the tight gold lamé trousers in which she'd ended her show—as she always did (at least in America) with an encore tribute to American rock singers that (according to magazines) personified her appeal to both males and females, at least in America.

This last medley was a pulsing carnal tour de force, showing off her skill and vocal range. She stood at the piano and pounded out Little Richard's "Good Golly Miss Molly," then Jerry Lee Lewis's "Breathless," then Aretha Franklin's "Respect," and then from there ran forward to the footlights to join Janis Joplin's "Try" to her own erotic anthem "I Want You More" and to keep both songs going until waves of fans broke loose and began climbing onto the stage to touch her. Tonight someone ran up to her and draped her in an American flag. The Haver police locked arms with the sheriff's department to hold back the fans while Mavis leaned over their bodies to touch the crowd's outstretched hands. Finally she fell to her knees and flung her arms out wide. I don't know if it was staged. The movie cameras set up around the stage filmed it all.

In her cramped, messy dressing room, Mavis leaned back in the shabby rehearsal chair, stretched out the sore distended tendons in her forearms. "I have to be on a stage doing this again tomorrow tonight in Toyko." She gave me a toast. "*Níl aon tinteán mar do thinteán féin.*"

I raised an eyebrow in inquiry.

She said, "There's no place like home."

"There's the truth," I smiled. "Now from one drunken beetle

to another, would you tell me another truth, Mavis? Would you tell me if you saw Tyler Norris at The Fifth Season that night?"

"Is he the fellow that killed the waitress?"

"Yes. After you went to the beach, he slipped into your bungalow and shot her. Did you hear the shot? Did you run back and see him?"

"You caught him, didn't you?" she asked.

I nodded. "After he killed five more people, we caught him. It's a high price to pay to avoid some inconvenience if you did see him."

Slowly she shook her head. She said, "The sad problem with drinkin' the way I do, you black out from it. And well, Lieutenant, you don't remember a thing."

I looked at her. She was too good an actress. I really didn't know if she was telling me the truth or repeating what lawyers had told her to say to avoid having to testify at the Norris trial.

She held up the bottle. "Come on now. A glass will do us no harm."

But I shook my head. "It did me no good. *Slán agat, Mavis.* That's right, isn't it, when I'm the one leaving?"

She smiled that amazing seductive smile that made the world want to love her. "Right as a hard rain fallin', love of my heart. *A rún mo chroí.*"

"If I hadn't just heard you say those same words to fifty thousand people, I'd be a little more touched." She laughed. "Take care of yourself, Mavis. And take some advice. You don't have to die young to be one of the greats. I know you think you do." I pointed at the whiskey bottle.

She poured another glass. "So tell me one who didn't?"

"Eva Wilcox. Blind Eva's in her eighties. You played piano with her in Smoke's. She's there every Saturday night."

"Ah, boyo, you are something, true enough. As for smokes, have you got one on your gorgeous self, bruised and bandaged as you are?"

I threw her the new pack of cigarettes I'd bought before the concert and the old lighter I'd carried around for years.

"Thanks." She caught them perfectly, incapable of a grace-less movement. The little flame leapt in her hand as she lit the lighter.

"Keep it," I said. "A memento. Otherwise, I guess you won't remember a thing."

She didn't argue with me. "And what can I give you to remember me by? Because I don't want you to forget."

I smiled at her. "Your music."

She held up the lighter. "Don't let your fire go out, Justin," she said.

"I won't." I turned in the doorway, waved, and left.

If I drove all night I could be in the mountains by morning. I could be in the mountains in time to kiss my wife Alice awake.

ABOUT THE AUTHOR

Michael Malone is the author of nine novels and two works of non-fiction. Educated at Carolina and at Harvard, he has taught at Yale, at the University of Pennsylvania and at Swarthmore. Among his prizes are the Edgar, the O.Henry, the Writers Guild Award, and the Emmy. He lives in Hillsborough, North Carolina, with his wife, Maureen Quilligan, chair of the English department at Duke University.

A Note on the Type

This book is set in Goudy Old Style. The type was designed by Frederic W. Goudy in 1915 for American Type Founders. Notable for the diamond-shaped dots on i, j, and on punctuation marks; the upturned ear of the g; and the base of E and L, Goudy Old Style is one of the most popular typefaces ever produced.